ENIGMA

ISAAC'S STORY

SHANDI BOYES

Edited by MOUNTAINS WANTED PUBLISHING
Edited by SWISH DESIGN AND EDITING
Illustrated by SSB DESIGN

WANT TO STAY IN TOUCH?

Facebook: facebook.com/authorshandi

Instagram: instagram.com/authorshandi

Email: authorshandi@gmail.com

Reader's Group: bit.ly/ShandiBookBabes

Website: authorshandi.com

Newsletter: https://www.subscribepage.com/AuthorShandi

ALSO BY SHANDI BOYES

Couple on Hold(Regan & Alex #3)

Enigma: The Wedding (Isaac and Isabelle)

Silent Vigilante (Brandon and Melody #1)

Hushed Guardian (Brandon & Melody #2)

Quiet Protector (Brandon & Melody #3)

Bound Series

Chains (Marcus & Cleo #1)

Links(Marcus & Cleo #2)

Bound(Marcus & Cleo #3)

Restrain(Marcus & Cleo #4)

Psycho (Dexter & ??)

Russian Mob Chronicles

Nikolai: A Mafia Prince Romance (Nikolai & Justine #1)

Nikolai: Taking Back What's Mine (Nikolai & Justine #2)

Nikolai: What's Left of Me(Nikolai & Justine #3)

Nikolai: Mine to Protect(Nikolai & Justine #4)

Asher: My Russian Revenge (Asher & Zariah)

Nikolai: Through the Devil's Eyes(Nikolai & Justine #5)

Trey (Trey & K)

K: A Trey Sequel

The Italian Cartel

Dimitri

Roxanne

Reign

Mafia Ties (Novella)

Maddox

Demi

Rocco

Clover

Smith

RomCom Standalones

Just Playin' (Elvis & Willow)

Ain't Happenin' (Lorenzo & Skylar)

The Drop Zone (Colby & Jamie)

Very Unlikely (Brand New Couple)

Short Stories

Christmas Trio (Wesley, Andrew & Mallory -- short story)

Falling For A Stranger (Short Story)

Coming Soon

Skitzo

COPYRIGHT

DEDICATION

My dedicated fans who inspire me to continue writing.
I hope you enjoy Isaac's story.
Our enigma.

CHAPTER 1

A frigid breeze causes the hairs on my arms to bristle and goosebumps to form on my nape. It isn't just the plummeting evening temperatures causing this reaction to my body. It's fear.

When I press my hands against the railing, I relish the coolness of the stainless steel on my sweat-drenched palms.

Snapping my eyes shut, I take in a lung-filling gulp of air. "You can do this, Isabelle," I chant to myself.

Millions of people do it every day.

I've spent the majority of my time today at airports. To say I'm fearful of flying would be an understatement. I'm petrified. My flight this morning was on a Boeing 777 from San Francisco to New York. I gripped the armchair so tight for the entire eight-hour trip, my French-tipped nail nearly snapped off.

There's no logical reason for my fear of flying. I've never been on a plane that plunged from the sky or lost loved ones during a disastrous flight. My fear is just something embedded deep inside me. I want to say I'm generally fearless, an adventurous person who regularly takes calculated risks, but when it comes to flying, I'm a quivering bundle of nerves.

Gritting my teeth, I push off the railing before I lose my nerve and collide straight into a wall of hardness that sends me sprawling onto my ass. I wince in pain when my right wrist jars hard on the rigid gray marble-tiled floor.

"I'm used to people falling at my feet, but not quite as undignified as that," says a deep, thick voice from above. Although his tone is stern, it also has a hint of amusement behind it.

Mortified, I raise my eyes, drinking in black polished dress shoes, a well-filled, impeccably tailored three-piece suit, and one pair of the most exquisite eyes I've ever seen in my life. The pain zinging my wrist no longer exists as my eyes roam over the magnificent creature in front of me.

More features come into focus—plump lips, powerful jawline, thick, luxurious hair long enough to run your fingers through, but not too long to be unkempt, and an ideally placed dimple in a chiseled chin. The very definition of a man is standing in front of me, and the visual is riveting.

Shifting his head to the side, he arches a brow. He assesses me as vigorously as I perused him. His penetrating glare has my heart rate quickening. Now I wished I had taken my roommate's advice and dressed more professionally instead of for comfort, but when your backside is going to be planted in a seat for a minimum of sixteen hours, you want it encased in comfort, and there's nothing more comfortable than my black Juicy Couture sweatsuit.

No, I didn't pay two hundred dollars for a pair of sweatpants. I found these beauties at the thrift shop in San Francisco nearly two years ago. They have faded a little, now more a charcoal gray than their original black, but they still get the job done. I've removed my jacket and am wearing a white, fitted cotton shirt that has risen to my stomach during my tumble.

After yanking down my shirt to a more respectable level, I return my eyes to the mysterious stranger. Once he has finished his perusal of my body, his mouth etches into a firm line, and his eyes narrow.

Clearly, he's a man who prefers class over comfort. His apparel does scream wealth and superiority, not to mention his composure, which exudes importance and authority. Grimacing with embarrassment, I scamper from the floor. My heart leaps when he grips my elbow to assist me with steadying my footing.

"Thank you."

I glance down at the contents of my satchel strewn on the floor from our collision. My bag is full of the necessities a girl needs for traveling—lip gloss, a Snickers chocolate bar, loose change for snacks, a Kindle loaded with my favorite books, and tampons. *Oh God.*

In a scurry to grab my possessions, I bob, he dips, and we headbutt.

"Fuck," he curses.

I manage to keep my curse word inside my head, even though it feels like I've suffered a grueling left swing from Oscar De La Hoya to my right eye.

My hand shoots up to rub the sting as I move toward the hard, plastic chairs lining the hallway of the airport. My vision blurs, and my footing becomes unsteady as the first signs of a headache form.

Plopping down on the chair, my eyes lift to discover the suit-clad gentleman gathering my satchel contents from the floor. Tampons included. *Great!*

Once he has collected my items, he places my bag on the chair next to me. His masculine scent engulfs the air when he crouches down in front of me. Seeing him displayed directly in front of me has the depths of his eyes hitting me full force. It's not just their unique gray coloring that has my brows scrunching, it's their intensity.

"Are you okay?" The rasp of his voice sends an exciting thrill through my body and causes butterflies to flutter in my stomach.

Unable to establish words through my dry, gaped mouth, I nod. He removes my hand covering my eye to run his index finger along the area pulsing with pain. Now, instead of feeling the sting of pain, I'm feeling the zap of his touch.

He raises two fingers in the air. "How many fingers am I holding up?"

"Two."

A mouth-watering smirk forms on his face. "What's your name?"

I smile. "Isabelle."

His handsome face is contorted with strictness, but his remorseful eyes give away his genuine concern. "I don't think you have a concussion, but you need to ice it as a bump is already forming." His minty breath fans my hungry mouth.

I lick my dry lips before replying, "I'm fine, really." *Totally embarrassed, but fine, nonetheless.*

A gold cufflink becomes exposed on the crisp white sleeve of his business shirt when he stands, then holds out his hand. His brow cocks, wordlessly requesting me to accept his gesture. I swallow a lump in my throat before accepting his well-manicured, yet manly hand.

After curling his hand around mine, his other snatches my satchel from the chair. He grips my hand firm enough to indicate his superiority, but not tight enough to cause pain to my wrist still throbbing from my tumble.

When he arrives at the frosted door of the first-class business lounge, I dig my heels into the carpet, lessening his quick pace. When he stops and turns, the air sucks from my lungs from the sheer closeness of his striking face. Most people would feel threatened by his complex gaze, but my body heightens with anticipation.

He tilts his head, his brow cocking again. If I hadn't heard him talk earlier, I'd assume he's a mute.

I gesture my free hand to the luxurious business lounge. "I can't go in there."

My voice sounds so weak, and I almost roll my eyes at my naïveté. Yes, this guy standing before me is entrancing, but I've had plenty of eye-catching men in my life, and my composure is usually more composed. However, this mysterious stranger has me flabbergasted like a teenage girl meeting a member of One Direction.

"I'm underdressed."

My eyes dart down to my Juicy Couture-covered thighs. This time, I sound how I usually do—friendly, but not a total pushover.

I suck in my stomach when he scans my body. When his eyes return to my face, he smirks. "You look perfectly fine."

Unsure of a reply, I return his smile. His eyes snap to my lips for the quickest second before he again quickly strides to the business class lounge.

"Mr. Holt," the doorman greets him without so much of a sideways glance in my direction.

My mysterious companion's surname is Holt. I like it. It's direct and stern but edgy—just like its owner.

When we arrive at a countertop bar that's so well polished I can see my reflection in it, Mr. Holt lifts me to sit on a high-backed barstool. His effortless lift makes it seem as if I'm as light as a feather. After snagging a midnight-black napkin from the countertop, he leans over the bar. His suit strains against his back, allowing me a glimpse of a spectacularly firm backside.

Flipping open a cooler flap nestled in the bar, he removes a handful of ice. My eyes shoot to the bartender, who isn't batting an eyelid at Mr. Holt assisting himself to their supplies. He wraps the cubes of ice in the napkin, then raises it to my throbbing eye. "Hold that."

Arching back over the counter, he snags two crystal glasses from a wired rack before signaling for the bartender. He must be a regular at this establishment because the bartender doesn't ask what drink he'd like. He just grabs a bottle of whiskey from the glass shelves behind the bar and sets it in front of him without a word escaping his lips.

Mr. Holt dips his chin in thanks before pouring two generous nips of whiskey into the glasses. He then hands one to me. "It will help with your headache," he explains to my shocked expression.

When he downs the shot without a shred of hesitation, my mouth becomes parched from the sensual way he swallows the flaming liquid so effortlessly. Desire surges through my body when his tongue darts out to remove the remnants of liquor from his lips. Needing something to soothe the dryness in my mouth, I grab my glass off the countertop to drink the generous helping in one hit.

I grimace, hating the burn that sets my throat on fire. I slam the glass onto the countertop as my watering eyes lift to Mr. Holt.

"Another?"

Not giving me the chance of a reply, he fills my glass again before sliding it across the ebony counter. Due to the overgenerous serving, whiskey splashes over the rim to puddle the glistening countertop.

I lift my eyes to his, which are glaring into mine, but his expression is neutral, even with his lips curved. "Are you trying to get me drunk, Mr. Holt?"

"Would it make it easier to get into your panties?"

The veins in my neck strum as my pulse quickens.

He winks, cockiness oozing out of him. "I'm joking."

I sigh a disappointed sigh. Hearing my shameless response, Mr. Holt's eyes lock with mine. His gaze is primal, commanding, and strong. It freezes me in place and heats my face. My brazenness surprises even me. I'm not usually so bold, but with his self-assuredness and grace, I have no doubt he'd be extraordinary in bed—sheet-clenching, multi-orgasms, can't-walk-straight-for-days sex.

My hand holding the ice trembles as I turn my gaze to anything but Mr. Holt's sinfully handsome face. Even without looking at him, my pulse still quickens. I can feel him studying my profile.

We sit in silence for several minutes, but my awareness of his closeness is still paramount.

Once the ice has melted, I dump the napkin onto the countertop, then drag my hand down my thigh to remove the inky stains smeared on my fingers. I gulp when, in the corner of my eye, I spot Mr. Holt's tongue delving out to lick his thumb. I stop breathing when he lifts the same spit-covered thumb to my right eye.

Suddenly, he stiffens as his nostrils flare. His eyes are darker now, even more demanding. It appears as if he's unearthed my body's response to his briefest touch. I'm about to assure him everything isn't as it seems when the shrill of a cell phone saves me from making a fool out of myself for the third time this evening.

With his eyes darting between mine, Mr. Holt slides a sleek phone out of his trousers pocket. "Yes."

His tone alludes to his authority, but I'm too busy taking in the time on his Rolex to work out who he's bossing around. I only have twenty minutes before the check-in for my flight closes.

"Thank you for your assistance, but I must go, or I'll miss my flight."

I snag my satchel off the countertop, then push off my barstool. Mr. Holt seizes my wrist before I can dash for the exit. He advises his caller to wait before he lowers his phone from his ear.

"Are you sure you're okay?"

"Yes, I'm fine, thank you," I reply graciously.

With reluctance, he relinquishes me from his grip. After exhaling a long, tedious breath, I hot-foot it to the exit doors of the business class lounge, not once glancing back at the mysteriously captivating Mr. Holt.

CHAPTER 2

As I splash water on my face to calm the heat spread across my cheeks, I take in my disheveled appearance. My eyes are wide and bright, my dilated pupils making them appear darker than usual. Sunbathing for hours has given my beige skin a vivid glow, meaning the hue of my cheeks is less illuminating, and my lips are plump from the sting of whiskey.

I want to say my rouged appearance isn't entirely based on the enthralling Mr. Holt, but that would be a lie. At least my clumsy display in front of the most self-assured man I've ever met warranted a moment of reprieve from my panicked state. I've barely thought about my fear of flying the past thirty minutes.

After exhaling a big breath, I hook my satchel over my shoulder, then pull open the heavily-weighted door of the ladies' restroom. I rush toward my departure gate, hustling to avoid being late since my run-in with Mr. Holt has left my time stretched thin. I swerve, dart, and weave between thousands of commuters who appear just as frantic as me.

By the time I make it to my departure gate, my neck is drenched with sweat, and my cheeks are blemished. I blow an unruly hair out of my face before handing my ticket to the immaculately dressed airport staff member behind the counter. Her top lip snarls as her eyes roam my flustered appearance.

"It's not as it seems."

A *tsk* escapes her lips as her slitted gaze lowers to the computer monitor on her desk. With my bright-eyed expression and flushed cheeks, my appearance could be mistaken for someone who just tumbled out of bed after a night of rigorous activities. I wouldn't mind being reprimanded if that were the cause of my late arrival. After all, it's been a while since I've seen my sexually satisfied face in the vanity mirror, but that's not the reason I'm arriving at the departure gate without a minute to spare. It was my disastrous run-in with the most strikingly handsome man I've ever met that has me scampering.

Once my ticket is thrust back into my hand, I head down the gangway. My knocking knees become more apparent with every step I take. I focus my attention on the male flight attendant standing at the end of the corridor, hoping his light blue eyes that pop right off his face will distract me enough to board without incident.

They do—*somewhat.*

My hand tremors when I give him my ticket. "Good afternoon, Ms. Brahn."

I fleetingly smile. I've lost the ability to speak now that fear has once again emerged from deep within.

"Today you're seated in 1A. Upon entering, take a left at the second corridor." He hands me back half of my ticket.

Nodding, I take a hesitant step forward. Loud pounding rings in my ears with every shaky step I take. After walking through the galley, I turn toward the coach section of the plane.

A flight attendant clipping back a pair of dark blue curtains moves to stand next to me. "Can I help you?"

"Umm, I'm looking for seat 1A."

She glances down at my ticket before returning her eyes to my face. "Seat 1A is this way, Ms. Brahn."

Gesturing behind me, she skirts by before walking through another set of curtains. I apprehensively shadow her. After ruffling through the thick curtain, I discover her standing near the front of the plane. My brows furl as my eyes bounce around the elegant-looking space—luxurious, well-spaced black leather reclining chairs, elegantly dressed men and women sipping on glass flutes of champagne, and the piquant aroma of wealth filtering through the air.

There must be a mistake. I don't belong in business class.

I scamper down the wide corridor, not missing the numerous gasps of disdain when my rhinestone-embedded Juicy backside sashays by. "There must be a mistake," I inform the flight attendant.

Her manicured brow shoots into her auburn hair before her eyes turn down to my ticket. "1A." She points her French-tipped nail to the 1A marked on my ticket. "1A." She extends her long, skinny finger to the 1A displayed on the overhead compartment two seats down from where I'm standing.

After rubbing my arm soothingly, she saunters back down the aisle, snubbing my shocked expression. I stand mute, frozen in both fear and shock until the 'Fasten Seat Belt' sign illuminates a few seconds later.

I shove my jacket and satchel into an overhead compartment, then skedaddle to my assigned seat. I may be scared, but I'm not flying without a seat belt. When I move my eyes from the fluorescent lights lining the aisle, I'm confronted by an intense gaze that has me clumsily tripping over my feet.

You've got to be kidding me!

"A beautiful woman falling at my feet twice in one day. This has to be a new record," Mr. Holt banters when I crash into his thigh.

I greet him with a grin before scampering past him to take my seat, which is next to his. When I plop into my chair, my hands lurch out for my seat belt. My nerves have me jittering so much, I have trouble fastening the silver clips together.

Sensing my struggle, Mr. Holt stills my shaking hands before he clasps my belt. He tugs on the light gray strap, securing my belt firmly around my waist.

"Thank you."

He smirks before dropping his gaze to my white-knuckled hold of the armrests. "Scared of flying?"

"Is it that obvious?"

"You do know recent studies have shown—"

"Traveling in a car or a truck is one hundred times deadlier than flying. Yes, I'm aware of that. It still doesn't help."

"Actually, I was going to say recent studies have shown the endorphins released during sexual activities can overtake cortisol and other fear-induced chemicals." He glances at me with entrancing, wicked eyes. "You should consider testing the theory out."

My pulse quickens. *Is he propositioning me?*

Before I can form a response, our intense stare-down is interrupted by a radiant voice above. "Can I help you with anything, Mr. Holt?" When I raise my eyes, I'm met with a beautiful blonde flight attendant who is appreciatively glancing at Mr. Holt. "Perhaps I can take your jacket?"

Mr. Holt's gaze remains on mine as he stands to remove his suit jacket. I lick my dry lips when his suit-covered crotch that's straining to hold in the enormity of his, umm, manhood is shoved into my peripheral vision.

When my perverted gaze returns to his face, the situation becomes ten times more heated. He has a mouth-watering smirk formed on his sculptured lips, revealing he spotted my ogling glance. Mortified at being busted staring at his crotch, I divert my eyes, catching the mad glare of the flight attendant in the process. She plays the part of a scorned woman well.

"Would you care for a drink, Mr. Holt?" Although her eyes are narrowed into slits, her tone doesn't allude to her anger. Her performance is remarkable—a genuine ten out of ten.

Mr. Holt hands her his suit jacket. "Teeling 30-Year-Old Single Malt Irish Whiskey."

"Excellent selection, Mr. Holt."

When Mr. Holt retakes his seat, the flight attendant walks away. She barely gets two feet away before Mr. Holt's hand shoots out to snatch her wrist. "Are you going to ask Isabelle if she'd like something to drink?"

I'm unable to see his face, but if the flight attendant's pupils are anything to go by, he's infuriatingly angry.

The flight attendant's feared eyes drift to me. "W-would you like something to drink?"

I shake my head. "No, thank you."

With the somersaults my stomach is doing, I can't trust it to hold down anything.

"Are you sure?" Mr. Holt cranks his neck to face me. His intense eyes have me swallowing harshly, but unlike the flight attendant, I'm not scared by his angry glare. I'm turned on.

Unable to speak through the lump in my throat, I nod. Spotting my agreeing gesture, Mr. Holt relinquishes the flight attendant's wrist. She scurries down the aisle, her steps as wobbly as my heart rate.

After offering Mr. Holt a grateful smile, I lean my head on the leather headrest. When I take a breath to settle my nerves, a strong aroma overwhelms my senses. Expensive cologne, body wash, and a smell I can't quite identify make an enticing, mouth-watering scent I'd happily spend hours smelling.

My eyes snap shut when the plane jerks toward the runway. *Here it comes, the one part of flying I fear the most.* After tightening my grip on the armrests, my teeth gnaw on my bottom lip.

The closer the plane gets to the end of the runway, the more my heart palpitates. I'm on the verge of a debilitating panic attack.

My heart jumps out of my chest when a jolting buzz electrifies my clenched hand. Glancing down, I spot a long, elegant finger tracing the veins protruding in my hand. My breathing lengthens as my eyes lift to Mr. Holt. He's staring at me, his gaze penetrating and utterly consuming.

"How about we test the theory?"

Too terrified to form words, I fleetingly nod.

The hairs on my body bristle when his finger leisurely runs up my arm until it stops at the throb in my neck. When his big, manly hand grips my throat, my pupils widen. His hold isn't tight enough to cause discomfort. It's a domineering clutch that has me releasing a husky moan.

After loosening his grip on my neck, he saves my bottom lip from my menacing teeth. "I'm going to bite that lip." His words are more a confirmation than a suggestion.

When his thumb slides over my lips, wetness pools between my legs. Brazenly, I nibble on the tip. I've never been bold, but his demanding eyes are making me reckless.

My body temperature turns excruciating when his hand curls around the nape of my neck. The sting of his fingers adds to the tingling in my core, and they turn my breathing ragged. His eyes skim my face before darting down to my famished mouth. His stares at me for several long seconds, his head tilting like he's preparing to kiss me.

I snap my eyes shut and lick my lips, preparing to taste his perfectly structured mouth.

When a whoosh of air hits my cheeks, my eyes pop back again. Mr. Holt isn't advancing toward me. He's retreating. Once he's again sitting on his side of the plush leather seat, he takes a hefty gulp of whiskey. Even being disappointed, my core can't help but spasm when his Adam's apple bobs up and down. When his glass is void of liquid, he places it down before shifting his eyes to me. His heavy-lidded gaze still shows his hunger, but something in them has altered.

Slanting his head, he gestures to the window behind me. I gasp when I follow the direction of his gaze. Nothing but puffy white clouds in a brilliant blue sky reflect back at me.

"I'd say the theory has been proven," Mr. Holt mutters aloofly.

Although he distracted me long enough I survived the take-off without a meltdown, a ping of disappointment hits my chest. The touching, the rush of excitement, the desire, it was all a game? A ploy to lessen my panic?

CHAPTER 3

I press my palms on the black marble vanity of the business class bathroom. Although this washroom is larger than the economy bathrooms I've become accustomed to, I still can't extend my arms without hitting a partition wall.

After taking a big breath, I lift my eyes to the gold-encrusted vanity mirror. My face is flushed, my lips are swollen and red from Mr. Holt's thumb rubbing along them, and the unbridled look of lust is in my eyes. That's what reflects back at me—a look that doesn't belong on my face. This isn't me. That woman nibbling on a stranger's thumb isn't me. I have rules. I have morals—morals I'd forgo just for one taste of his sinfully delicious-looking mouth.

What? Jesus, Isabelle, get a grip!

I've been hiding in the washroom for the past twenty minutes, trying in vain to reel back the dignity that eluded me when I sucked on Mr. Holt's thumb. Thankfully, the flight has another hour and twenty-three minutes until we land.

Yes, I'm counting.

Unfortunately, that means I still have an hour and twenty-three minutes of being seated next to a man who makes me disregard all my ethics. I swear I'm not generally like this. At the very least, I expect to be wined and dined before allowing any man to get close to my panties, but one look from Mr. Holt's piercing gray eyes makes me want to tear off my panties and hand them to him on a shiny silver platter.

An urgent knock on the door startles me. "Just a minute."

I shouldn't be surprised by the interruption. I've been hogging the only bathroom in business class since the 'Fasten Seat Belt' sign was switched off.

I exhale the nerves fluttering in my stomach before swinging open the door. My breath hitches when I discover who's knocking. Mr. Holt's six-foot-plus, well-formed physique fills the doorway. As his eyes roam my body, he boldly steps into the washroom. My thighs touch when his enticing scent permeates the air, ridding the space of its offensive sanitizer smell.

His gaze is unyielding like a man who knows what he wants and has no intention of backing down until he gets it. And from his gaze alone, I can tell he wants me. Pleased by my inner monologue, a pleading moan vibrates my lips. Don't judge. I may be in a washroom thirty thousand feet in the air, but I haven't had sexual contact with a man in months, let alone with one as devastatingly gorgeous as Mr. Holt.

"Why are you hiding in the bathroom?"

"I'm not hiding." My tone hints at my deceit.

Seconds feel like minutes when we stand across from each other in an intense gray-eyes-versus- brown-eyes, lust-driven stare-down. We're close enough for the hum of intimacy to be felt, but far enough apart I still hold a shred of composure.

A victorious smile tugs my lips when he turns his gaze away first. Scrubbing one hand over his head, he shoves his other into his pocket. "I don't have time for relationships."

Brazenly, I reply, "That's okay, neither do I."

In my industry, I can't have a pet much less a relationship.

His eyes lock with mine, shocked by my blasé response. "If we do this, you need to be aware it's a one-time-only deal. There won't be any calls in the morning, no dates next week. One time only."

I nod. Even with my shrewdness blinded by lust, I can appreciate his frankness. I hate the false promises men give to get in your panties. Don't get me wrong, I'm an old romantic at heart, and one day, I hope to have my fairy-tale ending, but for now, I'll happily unleash my inner vixen to participate in what I'm sure will be mind-blowing sex with another consenting adult.

Mr. Holt smirks at my agreeing gesture before stepping closer to me. His movements are effortless, yet still demand my attention. My brows furrow when he places a business card for a nightclub called The Dungeon into my palm. "Meet me here Saturday night at ten o'clock." A moan spills from my parched lips when he adds on, "Make sure you wear a dress. Panties are optional."

I gasp in frustration when he pivots on his heels to make his way back to the door. Upon hearing my groan, he spins back around. His heavy-lidded gaze is ruthless, pinning me in place with desire.

"Believe me, there's nothing more I'd like to do right now than find out what you look like under *all* those clothes, but if I start, I won't stop."

Who said I wanted you to stop?

Mr. Holt arches his brow, making me realize I said my last statement out loud instead of in my head.

"Are you on your period, Isabelle?"

"What?"

Although his disrespectful question has credit, I'm too embarrassed to articulate a better response. His captivating allure has entranced me so much, I forgot I'm smack-bang in the middle of red week.

Seeing the forlorn look on my face, Mr. Holt mutters, "That's what I thought. There's no way I'll only be able to sample half of you, Isabelle. I want to taste *all* of you."

Oh God.

My pulse intensifies when his eyes rigorously assess my body. Once his appraisal is finished, he makes his way out of the restroom even hastier than he arrived.

After gathering the minute smidge of dignity I have left, I exit the bathroom and head back to my seat. The flight attendant's eyes narrow as I walk by. I don't refute her accusation. My flushed face alone warrants her allegation.

Mr. Holt's gaze strays from his crystal glass when he notices me approaching. His gorgeous lips curve into a seductive smirk that has my insides purring like a kitten.

"Isabelle." His one word is a ravishing roar.

"Mr. Holt."

I hurry past him to take my seat where I strive to keep my focus on the brilliant blue sky outside my window, but my quintessential need to know everything gnaws at my insides until I eventually blurt out, "How did you know I was on my period?"

His lips brace the rim of his whiskey glass before his eyes turn to mine. "Other than the fact your Kindle was open on a sappy Mills and Boons romance book and the two empty chocolate wrappers in your satchel, the tampons were the biggest indication."

I smile at his unease from saying 'tampons' out loud.

"They could have been my emergency stash."

He shakes his head. "Like guys who carry condoms in their wallet?"

When I nod, he alters his position to lean closer to me. "Any guy who tells you he's carrying a condom in his wallet in case of an emergency is full of shit. We only put a condom in our wallet with the full intention of using it the night we put it in there."

"So, let me guess, the first thing you do when you wake up is place a condom in your wallet?"

He chuckles an intensely scrumptious laugh that awakens my core. "Not every morning." He saucily winks. "Just every second morning."

Ignoring the bitter taste in my throat, I continue my interrogation. "Did you put a condom in your wallet this morning?"

Before he can answer me, a cough sounds from above. Raising my gaze, I'm confronted with the slitted eyes of the flight attendant.

Ignoring her, Mr. Holt's entrancing eyes never once leave mine. "No, I didn't. Why do you think it took me so long to join you in the bathroom?" His reply is loud enough for the flight attendant to hear.

Once she finishes serving him his glass of whiskey, I whisper, "So even if I weren't on my period, we wouldn't have done anything?"

Excitement melds through me when he leans in close to my side. His whiskey-laced breath flutters my lips when he motions his head to an overweight gentleman seated in 3A. The formally dressed man has a white napkin tucked in the front of his ivory business shirt. Oblivious to Mr. Holt's and my intense appraisal, he continues munching on a marinated chicken drumstick.

"He'll need to replenish his wallet before he goes on the prowl tonight."

My jaw drops as my blemished cheeks darken. "You didn't... you wouldn't... you can't ask someone to borrow a condom, can you?"

I'm rambling, but I'd never have the audacity to ask someone to borrow a condom. Although Mr. Holt doesn't lack confidence, I'm still astounded he was bold enough to do that.

"I'm joking, Isabelle," he admits a short time later.

My breathing shallows when he leans in intimately close to my neck. "You would have just had to ride me bareback."

Oh God, I think I just had a mini-orgasm.

He snickers at my reaction before turning his attention back to the glass of whiskey in his hand. I set my focus on the blue sky outside of my window, hoping to calm the heat in my veins. Even after inhaling numerous lung-filling gulps of air, an intense pulse of desire still rages through my body.

For the rest of my life, I'll be eternally grateful to Mr. Holt. He once again used his irrefutable sex appeal to divert my panic that usually surfaces during landing, proving sexual endorphins can overrule fear-induced chemicals. If every flight ends up like this one, my fear of flying will soon be nonexistent.

Mr. Holt remains quiet as we walk down the gangway side by side, but I feel him glancing my way on numerous occasions. When we reach the end of the departure gate, I pivot to face him. "It was a pleasure to meet you, Mr. Holt."

I thrust my hand toward him in greeting. He clasps my hand in his, but instead of shaking it, he presses a kiss on the side of my palm. "Until Saturday, Isabelle."

Seriously, his voice alone is sufficient to bring my climax to fruition.

Brazenly, I nod while struggling not to scream in excitement. With a smile, I remove my hand from his grasp and head for the departure lounge. Every step I take amplifies the pang in my chest. That notion alone is terrifying, considering only four hours ago he was a stranger.

Stranger or not, I feel a bizarre kinship flourishing for the charismatic Mr. Holt.

I freeze just outside the double frosted glass door of the departure lounge. "Don't turn around, Isabelle, just keep walking," I chant to myself, not wanting to be disappointed if he isn't standing at the gangway watching me.

After rolling my shoulders, I lift them high before walking through the double doors, only glancing back for the tiniest glimpse. A broad grin spreads across my face when my eyes lock with Mr. Holt, who's still lingering at the end of the gangway, tracking my every move.

Yes!

I wave before dashing into the seating area, not missing his flirtatious wink on the way.

CHAPTER 4

*M*y sluggish eyes scan the crowd at Ravenshoe Airport in an attempt to locate Regina. After an intense two-hour flight, I'm beyond exhausted, both physically and mentally. After inhaling a breath of fresh air, I jerk her photo out of my satchel and run my eyes over her profile, wanting to ensure I'm seeking the right person. While holding the faded Polaroid picture out in front of me, I walk through a jubilant gathering of people greeting each other, happy their loved ones have returned home or have arrived for a visit.

Several minutes later, my eyes flick between the photo clutched in my hand and the lady standing in front of me. Scrutinizing every detail of her face, I compare it to the picture. I'm reasonably sure the person standing before me is a match for the woman in the photo. She has the same black afro hair, high, illustrious cheekbones, freckles along her nose, big brown eyes, and a broad smile. Although I'm now wondering how many decades have passed since this photo was taken?

When the lady I'm appraising notices my curious glance, she cautiously strolls toward me. She's shorter than I'd expected and a little rounder, but she has a magnetizing aura.

Her dark brown eyes peer inquisitively into mine. "Isabelle Brahn?"

"Regina?"

When she nods, I squeal and curl my arms around her neck. Regina is a very dear friend of my Uncle Tobias. By dear friend, I mean *close* friend, although Uncle Tobias would have never admitted that in public.

Regina is uneased by my friendliness. I don't mean to startle her, but I don't often get the opportunity to meet any friends of my Uncle Tobias. I'm also known for being a little over-friendly. When she pulls away from my embrace, her eyes drift around our surroundings, making sure no one witnessed our exchange.

Satisfied no one is watching, her eyes lift to scan my features. "I don't see the family resemblance."

Smiling, I slap her forearm. Grinning as if she's pleased with herself, she scoops down to collect my suitcase from the ground before making a beeline for the exit. I promptly shadow her. I smile when I spot her car parked in a tow-away section at the front of the departure gate doors, the red and blue lights beaming out of the rear window ensuring it would never be towed.

"There have to be some perks to the job." She shoves my over-stuffed suitcase into the back of her unmarked police car before gesturing for me to enter.

By the time we're two miles away from the airport, I'm grateful I didn't forgo my seat belt because Regina drives like she's in pursuit. When the afternoon commuter traffic becomes dense, she turns on her lights and sirens, making the backed-up traffic part like the red sea.

Once we emerge from the densely populated roads, she rummages through a bag of donuts sitting in the console. I giggle over the cliché that a well-decorated and respected police officer appreciates a good donut.

"Don't laugh, once you try these bad boys, you won't be able to stop."

After digging her hand back into the greasy paper bag, she thrusts a gigantic cinnamon donut toward me. My stomach grumbles when its pleasant aroma invades my nasal cavities, and my mouth salivates just from looking at its deliciously rounded perfection, but I hesitantly shake my head. I'd have to run ten miles just to work that baby off.

Regina huffs before taking a big bite out of the donut she was offering me. A growl erupts from her lips as she attacks the donut with unbridled fury. Her pleasurable moans echo through the interior of her car, forcing my bottom lip to droop. Once she has devoured every last smidgen of the donut, she teasingly pops her thumb into her mouth, ensuring not one speck of cinnamon remains on her finger.

"Can you grab me a napkin?"

Prying my hungry eyes away from the donut-filled bag, I open the worn and battered glove compartment she's pointing to. Numerous manila folders and a handful of napkins plummet into my lap when the old hinges crank open.

I grab a handful of napkins for Regina before collecting the folders so I can return them to the glove compartment. "Keep the gray one out," Regina instructs. "I color-coordinated that one just for him."

After shoving the non-required folders back into the overflowing glove compartment, I flick open the gray folder to eagerly scan the extensively noted documents inside.

"Page two." Eagerness is clear in Regina's voice.

My heart lurches in my throat when I turn the page. Piercing gray eyes, high and defined cheekbones, soft and plump lips, and a dimple in his chin, the very definition of a man is displayed in front of me.

Oh God.

"Can anyone say gorgeous?" Regina squeals, scaring the living daylights out of me.

She pulls on the steering wheel to correct her car from veering off the road since her eyes were too busy inspecting the photo in my hand. Confident we won't have a fender bender, she says, "That unbelievably handsome man is Isaac Holt, a twenty-seven-year-old businessman who is unmarried, has no kids, has lived in Ravenshoe the past six years, and has one sibling named Nicholas Holt. He owns a handful of highly successful nightclubs within the state. His current estimated worth is forty-three million dollars." Her brows waggle when she mentions his wealth.

My stomach rolls when I peer at the man who had me mesmerized mere minutes ago. There has to be a mistake. That incredibly captivating man can't be the same person Regina is investigating.

"Why is law enforcement interested in him?"

"He's twenty-seven years old and already a multi-millionaire. That alone warrants an investigation," she replies coolly.

My eyes dart back down to the documents in front of me. The more I read about the elusive Mr. Isaac Holt, the more my interest is piqued. Although today he wasn't evasive, he indisputably exudes mystery and intrigue.

"He made his first million before his twentieth birthday and before he even left college."

Regina glances at me before nodding. "We had nothing on him the past four years, but an undercover agent has spotted him numerous times this past year entering an illegal underground fight ring. Normally, those types of functions don't gain the attention of law enforcement, but this particular fight ring has some very notorious members."

I continue to peruse the documents. Isaac is in several photos with two extremely large gentlemen. One looks like he's been recruited from the military. His hair still has the same military-issued crew cut. He's ruggedly handsome but lacks the mysteriousness that makes Isaac so intriguing. The other guy has blond hair clipped close at the sides but longer on the top. His eyes are ocean blue, and he's smiling in nearly every photo. He's also handsome but in a humble, boy-next-door way.

"The brunette remains anonymous, but the blond is Jacob Walters," Regina informs me when she notices the photos in my hand. "We believe the brunette is either an associate of Isaac's or his bodyguard. Jacob is his fighter. Isaac owns him."

My eyes rocket to Regina's. When she frowns and nods, my

stomach churns. *How can you own someone in the twenty-first century? I thought slavery ended years ago?*

In silence, I flick through the extensive collection of Polaroid photos displayed in the gray manila folder.

"Col Petretti and Vladimir—"

"Popov," I interrupt.

"You've done your research." Regina seems impressed by my extensive knowledge.

Vladimir Popov and Col Petretti are two names frequently exploited during FBI training. My superiors used their names during numerous exercises and case studies while I was in training.

"What does Isaac Holt have to do with the mob?"

My heart erratically pounds my ribs as I wait for Regina to answer. She doesn't keep me waiting long. "He's one of them."

"Who am I here for?"

My eyes return to the profile picture of Isaac, silently praying she doesn't say his name. My prayers are left unanswered when she says, "The Bureau's primary focus is Isaac. If we get anyone else, it's a bonus."

Nerves tap dance in my stomach. Who would've known the very first case thrust into my hands upon leaving FBI Headquarters would be to hunt down some of the country's most notorious mob bosses, let alone a man who can ignite my senses with the simplest touch of his fingertip?

I was barely swimming above water during my training at FBI Headquarters. Now, I have no doubt I'm in way over my head.

A rookie FBI agent versus the mob—I don't see how this will end well.

CHAPTER 5

"*Y*ou do realize that during surveillance you're supposed to be incognito with the rest of the population?"

When Regina cocks a brow, I glance down at my black linen pants, white short-sleeve shirt, and black cropped boots. "What's wrong with what I'm wearing?"

Regina's eyes dart to the top of my head. Shooting my hand up, a smile forms on my face when I discover I've instinctively put on my black FBI cap. It's become a habit the past two years to brush my thick brown hair into a low ponytail and place my FBI cap over the top. The pants are the standard government-issue black trousers, and my shirt is now plain instead of having 'Trainee' emblazoned on the front in thick black ink.

"Much better." She nods when I remove the cap and put it on the mantelpiece. "Your Uncle Tobias would've been very proud of you, Isabelle."

Her words compel tears to well in my eyes. My Uncle Tobias raised me from a small child. He passed away six months before I sent in my application to join the FBI. He had initially been a police officer, and that was how he met Regina. He took her under his wing and taught her everything he knew about the local beat, even though he was ten years her senior. A few years later, he became a detective, and then he was recruited by the FBI.

My Uncle Tobias is the sole reason I decided to join the Bureau. I want to make him proud, and I want to help people the way he helped me. I can still accomplish that, even if I have to go against a man who can make my heart beat faster with only a sideways glance.

I aim to keep my focus on the task at hand and not on the man who has invaded my dreams every night this week. "Have you ever worked with Alex Rogers before?"

Alex is my superior officer. He's four years older than me and was the talk of the town at FBI Academy. He was the golden boy, the beloved son of the trainers. He started his illustrious career like the rest of us rookies do—at the bottom of the rankings—but he soon climbed his way to a very lucrative position. He's now the head of his department and has a handful of staff underneath him. It's inspiring considering he's only twenty-eight years old.

"No, but he's a pretty little thing."

My lips tug higher on my face. I saw a photo of Alex on the wall at FBI Headquarters in San Francisco. My first thought was also that he is a pretty boy. He looks like he would spend more time in front of the mirror than I do each morning. I'm not saying he isn't good looking—he most certainly is—but he has that plastic Ken-doll type of look.

The flash of a camera blinds me. "Smile."

Once the bright light clears from my vision, I spot the source of my sudden blindness. Regina is holding an ancient-looking Polaroid camera. She smiles a full-tooth grin while placing my half-exposed picture alongside two similar-looking photos on her refrigerator. The only difference between the images is that I'm in plain clothes, and she and Uncle Tobias are wearing police officer uniforms.

"It's tradition."

After wiping under her eyes to ensure her tears haven't fallen, Regina flurries around her eat-in kitchen, gathering her purse and keys. The year before my Uncle Tobias died, he shared many stories about Regina and him. He loved Regina, but their work kept them apart. Their interracial relationship already raised eyebrows, but a rookie officer dating her superior was also frowned upon.

He thought once he became a detective, he'd no longer have to hide his relationship with Regina, but he did. Not because it was frowned upon anymore, but because he had gone undercover. He had to keep his whole life a secret, not just his relationship status.

"How come you never married and had your own family?"

Regina freezes with her coffee mug halfway to her mouth. Her dark eyes shift to the Polaroid picture of Tobias on her refrigerator before they stray to face me. She doesn't need to say anything. Everything is relayed in her pained eyes. They reflect not only pain but love as well. Just like Tobias, there was nobody else for her, either. I often asked Tobias the same question, and he merely replied, "Why do I need anyone else but you, kiddo?" But I could see his heartache in his blue eyes. He was a good man who sacrificed his own happiness for the sake of others. He passed that trait on to both Regina and me.

"Are you ready?"

After exhaling my nerves with a big breath, I nod.

"Excuse me," I interrupt.

I've just walked into an office on the third floor of a brick and mortar building located across the street from Isaac's eighteen-plus dance club, The Dungeon. Considering there's only a handful of people, the atmosphere is surprisingly bustling.

The middle-aged lady I addressed walks right by me, rudely ignoring my introduction. "Hello," I greet again, this time to a young blond gentleman sitting at a desk urgently ruffling through a stack of papers.

His eyes leisurely glide over my body before they settle on my face. Just as he's about to speak, we're interrupted by a profound voice across the room. "I need that document now, Brandon."

Brandon smiles a lopsided grin before his eyes shoot down to the documents he was tousling through before I disturbed him. Enthusiasm beams out of him when he locates the item he's searching for. My eyes track him as he bolts to the other side of the room where I spot a face I recognize. It's Ken from the Bureau wall. *Oh, shit, I meant to say Alex.* At least I didn't call him Ken to his face. Imagine how embarrassing that would've been?

The room plunges into silence, amplifying my quiet giggles. I mask my laughter with an impromptu cough. My gesture doesn't fool Alex. His eyes narrow, and his lips set in a hard line.

Great first impression, Isabelle, I chastise myself while making my way to the man glaring at me in disdain.

Alex studies my body just like Brandon did, except when his eyes return to my face, he fails to smile, making me falter in my step. He's just as pretty in person as his photo shows. His blond hair has every strand faultlessly placed, though it does look like he drags his fingers through it several times a day, giving it that sexed-up look. His eyes are light blue, his nose flawlessly straight. His cheeks are well-defined, and his jawline is razor-sharp. He's preppy and pretty at the same time. I might have even said he was deliriously handsome if his eyes weren't narrowed into thin slits and planted on me. An angry scowl never looks good, no matter how gorgeous your face might be.

"Hi, I'm Isabelle Brahn, your new agent."

"Michelle," he screeches, making me jump in fright. "I thought I ordered a blonde?"

My bewildered eyes bounce between Alex and a middle-aged lady who has just joined our group. Apprehensively, I pull my hand away since my gesture of a handshake wasn't acknowledged. Michelle is also pretty, mid-forties, and has sandy blonde hair cut to sit just above her shoulders. She's wearing a pleated black pencil skirt and a pastel pink blouse.

"Does she look brunette to you?"

When Alex's blue eyes snap to mine, I square my shoulders, remembering what my Uncle Tobias would always quote, "Don't let them scare you. Never show your fear."

"Umm, yes, she does appear to be a brunette."

"In the past two months, have you ever seen him with a brunette?" Alex seeks Michelle's gaze, which has darted down to the floor.

"What does my hair color have to do with my placement?"

Alex's slitted gaze rockets to mine. "Isaac Holt fucks blondes, and you're a brunette."

"Excuse me," I hiss, my tone harsh.

Although I have unequivocal knowledge what he's saying is untrue, irritation outweighs my desire to dispute his allegation.

"I wasn't brought here to sleep with Isaac Holt. I was brought here to help with your investigation."

"You were brought here as eye candy," Alex interjects rudely.

The room no longer bustles with activity. Instead, they keenly watch the altercation between Alex and me. I'm so astonished at his disrespect, I can't form any words to express my outrage. I didn't train at the academy for months to become a piece of eye candy. I trained to become an agent, a good agent, just like my Uncle Tobias.

"We could bleach her hair," suggests Brandon.

"Not happening," I disrupt sternly.

When I cross my arms in front of my chest, Brandon and Alex's eyes dart down to my breasts. A snarl forms on my top lip. Alex's scowl remains stagnant as he once again appraises my body. This time, when his eyes lift, I don't miss the flicker of lust he fails to conceal with his gaze.

"Once you're in a dress and a pair of stilettos, Isaac won't care you're a brunette," he utters, snarling.

"Once you have a personality transplant and a plastic groin inserted, nobody will care you're a Ken doll."

When chuckles erupt around the room, it dawns on me that I said my last statement louder than I'd initially planned.

Alex's lowered gaze darts around the space, forcing the diminutive office to once again bustle with activity. Once everyone's focus is no longer on us, Alex walks over to me. He's a few inches taller than my five-foot-seven-inch height and looks down on me since my boots have no heels.

"I know who your uncle was. I know his reputation, but you need to learn your place. You were only brought here as a distraction for Isaac. He never lets anyone in, and you're supposed to be our way in."

I swallow harshly but maintain a strong stance, not once backing down or showing my fear. I plan to make my Uncle Tobias proud, but I can't do that and lose my morals at the same time.

"I'm an agent for the Federal Bureau of Investigation. I'm not a prostitute."

CHAPTER 6

One month later...

"*S*tupid, arrogant, pompous prick. He probably already has a plastic groin, and that's why he's always so cranky. You can't have sex if you don't have a dick."

The gentleman at the front of the line pivots around to eye me curiously. *I really need to learn to mumble more quietly.* I smile at him before returning my eyes to scrutinize the menu boards above his head. I'm once again doing the team's early morning coffee run. It's been the primary focus of my position the past month—that and filing.

The instant I refused to put on a skimpy dress and sashay myself in front of Isaac, Alex put me on desk duty. I spend my days twiddling my thumbs, filing useless reports, and doing coffee runs. Who would have thought months of grueling training would land me a job as a glorified coffee girl?

I place my order with the coffee barista before collecting the mountain load of sugar packets the agents requested.

"Do you have any Splenda?" I ask a staff member named Harlow, who's been preparing my coffee order every morning this past month.

Harlow is a ball of mischief bundled into a bakery uniform. Her humor is a little crude and dry, but she has kept me on my toes with her wittiness.

Harlow hands me a handful of Splenda. "Sugar wouldn't kill you."

I try to think of a sharp comeback, but I'm left a little speechless. I have a slender build, but I wouldn't say I'm skinny. I have a runner's body, although I have more boobs than Olympic athletes have. I work hard to maintain my body shape. By skipping the sugar in my coffee, I won't feel guilty devouring the blueberry and chocolate chip muffin I ordered with it. It's all about getting the balance right.

Instead of giving an appropriate comeback to Harlow's taunt, I stick my tongue out.

"Earlier this morning, I licked the muffins."

She sticks out her tongue before moving away from the coffee machine to hand some customers their orders. I tug open the white paper bag holding my muffin to inspect it for lick marks. It doesn't appear to have been licked, and with how hungry I am, I'd still eat it even if she did lick it.

Harlow's rowdy chuckle echoes around the bakery when she notices me inspecting my muffin. "I was joking about licking the muffins." She hands me the two crates of coffee I ordered. "Same time tomorrow?"

Rolling my eyes, I nod. Although I have no doubt I'll be revisiting this bakery this afternoon.

Upon exiting the bakery, a black Mercedes-Benz town car halts my hasty departure. I don't need to see the occupant to know who's inside. The license plate is all the indication I need. *Isaac.*

Stepping back into the nook, I stalk the car that has come to a stop at the corner of First Avenue and Welsh Boulevard. My chest thrusts up and down when Isaac glides out of the back passenger door of his shiny black car. Just the authoritative way he walks adds an exciting visual to my nightly routine. It's been over a month since our flight, yet he still invades my dreams every night.

My eyes dart up and down the street, anticipating to see the blue surveillance van that tails Isaac's every move. I'm surprised when I fail to locate it in the street.

This is it—the opportunity I've been waiting for to prove my worth to Alex.

Dumping the coffees into a waste bin, I creep closer to Isaac. My years of training activate in an instant. I maintain a safe distance and stay on the opposite side of the road to ensure my pursuit goes unnoticed.

Today, Isaac is wearing a tailored, fitted dark blue business suit with a light blue dress shirt underneath. He's minus the tie he usually wears in most surveillance photos. His black dress shoes are so polished, they gleam in the sunlight, and his gray eyes are covered with a pair of expensive-looking aviator sunglasses.

When he enters a flamboyant-looking restaurant, I cross the street. As I dart between a steady line of cars, my eyes once again scan my surroundings. There's still no blue surveillance van in sight.

I stroll up to the restaurant expecting the doorman to welcome me with open arms. He doesn't. He snubs me, and the door remains closed. I eye him peculiarly, wordlessly demanding an explanation for his rudeness. With quirked lips, his eyes roam my trousers, fitted ribbed shirt, and black ballet flats. Grinning, he nudges his head to the patrons seated inside the restaurant. They're dressed more elegantly than me.

"There's a public restroom one block over," he announces, his tone snobbish.

Masking the urge to stick my tongue out at the pretentious man, I smile sweetly before heading to the far corner of the restaurant. *Peering through the paned glass windows won't cost me a cent.*

I spot Isaac in the restaurant, kissing the cheek of a lady with shiny black hair. He removes his suit jacket and hooks it on the back of the chair before sitting across from her. She smiles an evil grin when he hands her a sealed white envelope.

Come on, where the hell are you? I silently question when my third scan of the street still fails to locate the surveillance team that's been tailing Isaac for months.

More times than not, Isaac's meetings are with reputable business associates or his fighter, Jacob. This morning, they're missing a prime opportunity. This lady has never popped up in the numerous surveillance photos I've scanned into the FBI database every day since I have been here.

Realizing I need to match brains with brawn, I yank my cell out of my pocket. My hands grow clammy when I snap a sneaky picture of Isaac's companion while the doorman is distracted by clientele entering the premises.

Hiding behind a potted hedge, I drop my eyes to the screen of my cell. A grunted sigh puffs from my nostrils when the early morning sun reflecting on the window covers half of Isaac's companion's face.

Scarcely breathing, I snap another pic. It turns out just as bad as the first.

"Think, Isabelle, think."

I know, I'll call Alex.

It takes me scanning my short list of contacts twice before I realize Alex never gave me his cell phone number. *He'd hate to make me feel like I'm a part of his team.*

After taking a few seconds to settle the nerves fluttering in my stomach, I dial a number known by heart.

"Federal Bureau of Investigation, how may I direct your call?" questions the switchboard operator.

"My name is Isabelle Brahn. I'm a Federal Agent. My number is 5586718. I need you to patch me through to Alex Rogers, head of the Ravenshoe Division," I inform her as my eyes flick between the doorman and Isaac.

"Patching you through now."

Alex's phone rings several times, making me worried he won't answer. Just as I'm about to disconnect the call and try again, he finally answers.

"Alex Rogers," he snaps down the line.

"Alex, it's Isabelle—"

"Did you mess up my coffee order again? Black with two sugars. It isn't that hard, Isabelle."

Anger lines my face. "No, I didn't mess up your order."

Although his coffee is now sitting at the bottom of the garbage bin. If he keeps speaking to me so rudely, I may fish it out and serve it to him from the trash.

"Why isn't the surveillance team following Isaac?" I question gruffly, trying my hardest to simmer my anger.

Alex grunts. "He's still in bed."

My brows furrow as my gaze drifts to Isaac sitting in the over-priced restaurant sipping on a cup of coffee. Even without seeing his distinctive eyes, I can't mistake him. He is too attractive not to notice.

"He's not in bed, he's right in front of me having breakfast with a lady at a restaurant on the corner of Welsh and First Avenue."

While Alex summarizes a reply, I glance back into the restaurant. Time stands still when Isaac's head suddenly lifts to the window. He appears to be staring straight at me.

With my heart in my throat, I dash around the corner, praying he didn't spot me spying on him.

"Are you sure it's him, Isabelle?"

"Yes," I assure, my pitch as high as my heart rate. "I'm one hundred percent certain it's him."

Alex barks orders at everyone surrounding him, sending the flurry of activity I've witnessed every day the past month barreling down the phone.

"We'll be there in five minutes," he informs me before disconnecting our call.

I lean against the outer wall of the restaurant to take in some big breaths. I'm clutching my phone so tight, my knuckles are white. I never knew surveillance was so thrilling. I always envisioned it as spending hours eating donuts and busting to use the bathroom, but it's much more exciting than that.

Or maybe it isn't surveillance that has my heart palpitating so fast it feels like it's going to escape my chest cavity. Perhaps it's seeing Isaac again?

"Bring the car back around," says a ruggedly handsome voice I immediately recognize.

Plastering my back to the brick wall, I peer around the corner. A sizable potted hedge aids in keeping me concealed. Standing just mere feet from me is Isaac. Even from this distance, his commanding aura is highly notable.

As if he has spotted my gawk, he yanks his cell phone away from his ear so his narrowed gaze can scan the street. He stops seeking me when the lady he greeted in the restaurant stands beside him. When she lifts a cigarette to her mouth, Isaac lights it for her with a gold lighter.

Isaac's date is attractive, mid-thirties, with shiny black hair cut into a fierce bob. Her body is fit, well-groomed, and covered in a feminine, black designer pantsuit. Ignoring the pang of jealousy forming in my chest, I raise my phone to snap a picture of her. This may be the FBI's only opportunity of capturing her face.

In the silence of the morning, my camera click is easily audible.

Shit!

I splay my back on the wall, the roughness of the brickwork scratching my delicate skin. Softly, I curse over my stupidity. *How could I have forgotten to turn the sound off on my phone during surveillance?* My heart flips as my panic surges, confident they heard the clicking noise.

After many calming breaths—and a few more expletives—I peer back around the corner. Isaac's black Mercedes-Benz is parked in front of the restaurant. His acquaintance is already seated in the back passenger-side seat. Isaac places one foot into the car before turning his eyes in my direction. I'm confident he has spotted me spying on him through the green hedge, but I can't tear my gaze away. I'm trapped, captivated by his entrancing eyes.

Several tension-riddled seconds pass before he shakes his head and slides into the back of his car. The instant his shiny black vehicle glides down the street, I crumble onto the concrete sidewalk, knowing without a doubt that I'm in way over my head.

That wasn't just thrilling, it was highly addictive.

CHAPTER 7

A loud gasp parts my lips as I dive for the computer mouse. I click anywhere and everywhere on the monitor, praying my manic clicks will stop my personal photos being uploaded to the FBI database. Realizing my excessive clicking isn't alleviating the situation, I use my hands to cover the flurry of images flicking across the monitor, meaning only tiny portions of my bare skin are on display for the world to see.

"I'm so sorry!" I apologize, mortified.

Except for a rare grin tugging his full lips high, Alex's expression remains neutral. Brandon's response isn't as reserved. I kick him in his shins when he attempts to pry my fingers away from the screen, hoping for a more in-depth preview of my raunchy vacation snaps.

"I had a two-week vacation at Del Mar before I arrived here," I inform them, giving them any excuse I can as to why there are several photos of me in a very skimpy bikini being uploaded into the FBI's database.

Darn selfie sticks have made it too easy to get full body-shots when vacationing alone. Although, I do love that bikini. I shouldn't, though. It took months of grueling workouts for me to feel confident enough to wear a bikini like that.

After a few margaritas and a stern lecture on body image, I slipped into the scraps of material society classes as a bikini. Knowing I'd probably never wear it again, I got a little excited about taking several photos from multiple, and what I was hoping at the time, appealing angles.

"It was hot in Del Mar," I murmur when neither Brandon nor Alex reply to my admission.

A genuine smile morphs onto Alex's face. Although I despise him and call him several crude and entirely accurate names under my breath multiple times a day, my heart still skips a beat when he smiles.

"That wasn't the only *hot* thing there." Brandon playfully tugs on the collar of his shirt.

I try to hide my gratitude at his compliment. Only the smallest smile creeps on my face, but it's enough of a reaction for Brandon to notice.

"No," I inform him delicately, stealing his chance to ask me on a date for the tenth time the past two weeks.

"Who said I was going to ask you out?"

Arching my brow, I glare into his hazel eyes that are a little greener today than usual. His composure remains calm for all of two seconds before the biggest smile stretches across his face.

"One date won't kill you." He once again tries to pry my fingers from the computer monitor.

Brandon is cute, but our personalities are too similar for us to become a couple. I don't agree with the whole opposites-attract notion, but I do believe your partner should bring qualities to a relationship you don't already have. If you like sweet foods, they should like sour. If you're a live-your-life-on-the-edge-of-your-pants type of person, they should be more reserved and prefer taking their time to consider their options. That way, over time, you eventually get a perfectly balanced relationship.

Well, that has been my logic. I could be wrong since my theory has yet to be proven, considering I'm single and living with an old flame of my uncle and her two cats. *Oh God. I'm going to become one of those crazy, dressing-gown-wearing, chain-smoking, hair-a-ratted-mess cat ladies.*

"Our next weekend off, we should go out," I suggest to Brandon.

Brandon's glowing eyes dart to mine.

"Only as friends, though. And just drinks... no dinner or movies, just drinks."

When he nods, a stern cough demands the attention of my eyes. Alex has his brows furrowed, and his lips have thinned. His whole stance is projecting uncontrolled anger, and I could be mistaken, but a smidge of jealousy.

"If you have time to organize dates, I need to increase your work-load." His blue eyes shoot daggers at Brandon.

Yep, he is definitely jealous. His unexpected jealousy makes me wonder if he is a treat-them-mean- to-keep-them-keen type of guy.

"Sorry," Brandon mumbles under his breath.

Hesitantly, I remove my hands from the computer monitor. Relief washes over me when I notice my bikini photos are no longer flicking across the screen. Barely breathing, I scroll down to the photo of Isaac's companion I captured this morning. An impressive groan vibrates Alex's lips at the same time a pang of remorse stabs my chest.

"Run facial recognition," requests Alex, slapping Brandon on the shoulder three times.

Brandon nudges me with his elbow. When I move away from my desk, he pulls a black swivel chair in close and runs his fingers over the keyboard. I turn my reluctant gaze to Alex, hoping some commendation will lessen the guilt I'm feeling for spying on Isaac.

Alex's eyes scan my face, but not a word seeps from his lips. My shoulders slump and a sigh spills from my mouth.

You're just doing your job, Isabelle, I silently justify, hoping to ease my remorse.

Dropping my gaze back to the computer monitor, I watch as the facial recognition software scans potential matches for Isaac's companion. Alex shifts in close to me. He's so near I can smell what he had for breakfast. I never picked Alex as a blueberry-pancake-with-maple-syrup type of guy, but there's no denying that aroma—sweet and sickly at the same time.

My stomach grumbles. Unfortunately, not only did I dump the coffees into the bin this morning, my blueberry muffin went right along with them.

"I bet you wish you didn't ditch your muffin in the bin now," Alex whispers into my ear.

My confused eyes dart up to his. I'm confident I kept my mumblings to a bare minimum this time. When he notices my perplexed expression, he smiles—not a genuine, heart-fluttering smile, but a sly grin that makes me wonder what he's concealing underneath his pretty-boy exterior. It's dangerous and conniving.

"Bingo," shouts Brandon, interrupting the uncomfortable stare-down between Alex and me. "Facial recognition has a match."

I scan the information displayed on the monitor in front of me. Delilah Anne Winterbottom, thirty-six years old, publicist and divorcee, spouse of Henry Theodore Gottle, the third, before their divorce settlement was finalized eight months ago. She lives in New York City, has no siblings, no children, and no criminal history.

"Looks like another dead end."

I thought I was discreet until Alex's firm eyes lift to mine. "A dead end?" His eyes bore into mine as if he's a parent reprimanding a child for failing an exam.

"She's a publicist…" I attempt to reply before catching a glimpse of Brandon shaking his head.

With a pivot, he points to something on the screen. The overhead lighting reflects on the monitor, making me unable to see what he is referencing.

"Please continue, Isabelle." Alex spits out my name as if it's venom. "I'd love to hear your reasoning as to why this is a dead end."

My eyes shoot to Brandon. When Alex follows the direction of my gaze, anger reddens his face. Recognizing that our ruse has been busted, Brandon's finger slips off the computer monitor as he swallows several times in a row.

"Henry Theodore Gottle, the third," Alex informs sternly. "Son of Henry Gottle, suspected mob boss of New York City."

"Just because he's the son of a mob boss doesn't automatically make him part of the mob."

Alex laughs, seemingly amused by my reply. His chuckle doesn't match his charmingly handsome looks. It's a scary, witch-like laugh that has everyone in the room stopping what they're doing to glance at him peculiarly.

It takes several long and tedious minutes for his laughter to die down. When it does, he says, "You surely can't be that stupid, Isabelle."

When I fail to respond to his taunt, he stops grinning and steps toward me.

"And here I was thinking you made it through the academy solely by using your brain. I guess today proves what I'd originally suspected." He keeps his voice loud enough that the agents watching his charade can hear him. "You weren't brought here for your academic abilities."

My arms fold in front of my chest when Alex's squinted gaze leisurely assesses my body.

"Since you're so determined to utilize your brain instead of your other more *desirable* assets..." his eyes drop to my breasts, "... be a good girl and fetch my coffee you failed to produce this morning."

With a flick of his wrist, I'm dismissed from the room, once again degraded from a respectable FBI field agent to a glorified coffee girl.

CHAPTER 8

Two weeks later...

"You have a stalker." Harlow's face is animated. "A total drool-in-the-corner of-your-mouth tall drink of water, but a stalker nonetheless."

When my baffled gaze floats from the floor, she gestures her head to the corner of the room. I bleakly swallow when I catch the intense gaze of Isaac Holt peering at me from behind the morning newspaper. *Shit!*

When he realizes he has captured my attention, he smirks while folding his newspaper in half to place it on the table. His eyes never once detour from mine. Although my initial reaction is to run, it would look mighty suspicious if I fled now.

For the past two months, I successfully avoided any impromptu run-ins with him. The establishments he dines at are a lot fancier than this humble bakery, but I knew this run-in would eventually happen. Ravenshoe is large, but it isn't large enough to get permanently lost in the crowd.

"He's been here over half an hour, and he's never paid anyone any attention, until now." Harlow hands me the whole grain and rye toasted cheese sandwich I ordered for lunch.

Once I have a mug of coffee in my hand, Isaac motions for me to join him. My eyes dash around the bakery, seeking a spare table. A throaty groan escapes my lips when I discover there are no empty tables in the entire shop.

My panicked eyes shoot back to Harlow, who mouths, "Go on, he's hot."

Rolling my eyes, I gingerly pace to Isaac. Harlow can look at him for his irrefutable sex appeal, whereas I must look at him through the eyes of an agent. Ruthless, cunning, heartless, and unlawful are the first thoughts that pop into my head when I read his FBI file, but when I look into his gray eyes, they disclose an entirely different story.

The closer I get to Isaac, the more my eyes absorb every impressive feature of his face—sculpted cheekbones, plump and full lips on a mouth that could have me toppling into ecstasy just from hearing him speak, and one pair of the most exquisite eyes I've ever seen.

No photo will ever do his eyes justice because they'll never fully capture how alluring and intense they are in person.

"Hello, Isabelle." Even with his angry tone, my name still rolls off his tongue seductively.

"Hi," I reply as my heart violently flips.

A smile sneaks onto my face when he pulls out a chair for me, then air snags in my throat when he sits next to me instead of the chair opposite me. Trying my hardest to ignore his masculine scent, I dump my satchel on the ground under our table, then pull my toasted sandwich out of the white paper bag. He remains quiet, but his entrancing eyes track me. The air is suffocating, riddled by the thick stench of awkwardness.

Snubbing the nervous tension between us, I take a sizable bite of my sandwich since I'm famished from not eating since breakfast. An appreciative moan rumbles up my throat as the gooey, cheesy goodness infiltrates my taste buds. When a string of cheese snaps off my sandwich and lands on my chin, my tongue instinctively darts out to lick the residue off my face.

Isaac groans a low and menacing growl that forces my eyes to his. My cheeks heat when I'm confronted by his intense gaze staring ravishingly at my lips. I dart my eyes away before I become trapped by their allure.

My nervous eyes shift to the window at the front of the bakery. If anyone in the surveillance team witnesses our exchange, Alex will force me into a skimpy dress and parade me in front of Isaac by this evening. I refuse to be treated as a commodity. I'd rather spend my years in the Bureau gathering coffees for narcissistic, self-centered assholes than be forced into prostitution.

"I have to go." I shove my half-eaten sandwich back into its paper bag, then snatch my satchel from the ground. My coffee is in a ceramic mug, so much to my dismay, it will remain untouched. "I forgot an important deadline."

I dart for the entrance of the bakery as quick as my shaking legs can take me. Harlow's anxious eyes follow my hasty retreat. "Do you want me to pour your coffee into a takeaway cup?"

I shake my head and continue for the door. Cold air blasts my face when I emerge through the single glass door. After a few brisk strides, someone clutches my elbow, and I'm dragged to the corner of First Avenue. My angry eyes lift and are met with the stern profile of Isaac. His lips have thinned, and his jaw is twitching. My panicked eyes dart up and down the street. I sigh when I discover the blue surveillance van is nowhere in sight.

He pulls me into the dark alcove of a run-down old pub that looks like it hasn't opened its doors in the past century. After releasing his tight grip on my elbow, he takes a step closer to me. I back away, intimidated by his stern, livid eyes. With a smirk, he moves closer, trapping me between him and the black door of the pub. My pussy tingles from his closeness. *Stupid, traitorous body.* He's the enemy, yet, my body still gets excited from his attention.

"I assumed you must have left town when you failed to arrive for our date, but lo and behold, here you are, months later."

I remain silent as his eyes—full of turmoil and uncertainty—dart between mine.

"Are you going to at least attempt a pathetic excuse?"

Remorse claws at my chest as I shake my head. Trying to fool a man who has eyes that can see through to my soul would be stupid and ineffective.

Teeth grinding together fills the eerie silence between us when Isaac clenches his jaw tight.

"That person you met on the plane isn't me. I'm not usually like that," I reply, deciding honesty is the best policy. "I don't do random hookups with strangers."

"And you think I do?"

"Yes," I answer without a smidge of hesitation.

His eyes snap to mine before the most wicked grin creeps onto his face. I try not to return his smile, but I'm defenseless. Someone as gorgeous as Isaac would have an extensive list of women vying for his attention, so I'm somewhat surprised—and a little excited—that my failure to arrive for our date ruffled his feathers.

The air shifts from tense to teasing, the crackling of attraction heightening my senses. His commanding eyes glance at my lips when he mutters, "I still want to bite that lip."

My pupils widen when he caresses my cheek. I should be pulling away from his embrace, but I can't. I'm frozen with desire.

My knees meet when he runs his thumb along my top lip before his head tilts closer to mine. Just before his lips brush mine, a deep voice interrupts, "Sorry, boss, but we've gotta go."

I sigh when Isaac steps back from our embrace, leaving only the linger of expensive cologne in his wake. Upon hearing my pathetic response, his lips furl as his lust-filled eyes rake the street. Following his gaze, I spot a gentleman I've seen in numerous surveillance photos sitting in the driver's seat of his town car. Just a few blocks down from Isaac's black Mercedes is the blue surveillance van that tails his every move.

Shit!

When Isaac's eyes return to mine, I gulp. If I thought his eyes were intimidating before, now they're downright dangerous.

"Meet me at the bakery tomorrow," he requests, his tone stern.

I shake my head. "I can't."

Seeing the surveillance van is the only reminder I need that I can't associate with him, no matter how loud my inner vixen is screaming at me to ignore my rational-thinking head.

"It wasn't a request, Isabelle."

He runs his index finger over the cupid's bow of my lip before striding to his awaiting town car. Just as he is about to step into his car, his head swivels back to me.

"Tomorrow," he instructs before he glides into the back of his car.

The instant his car dashes down Welsh Boulevard, the surveillance van pulls away from the curb and commences its pursuit. I lean into the darkness of the alcove to ensure the surveillance team doesn't detect me as they zoom by.

While leaning on the peeled-paint door, I calm the erratic beat of my heart. I can't believe I was so senseless. I nearly kissed Isaac Holt. *Isaac Holt!* A man currently under investigation by the FBI. A man who has half of the county following his every movement. A man so deliriously handsome and good-smelling, I want to run my cheek along his jaw just to capture his scent.

What? Jesus, Isabelle!

After reprimanding my lack of judgment, I emerge from the niche of the pub and walk back to my workplace.

Approximately halfway there, my phone dings with a text message. When I yank it out of my dark denim jeans, I notice it's a message from an unknown number. My excitement intensifies, wondering who the message could be from.

It vanishes when I read the message.

Alex: *You're late.*

Sighing, I jog down the bustling street, weaving in and out of the heavy foot traffic. My quick strides halt when another message dings on my phone.

Alex: *Pick up coffee on your way back.*

Dammit! I don't think I could ever despise someone as much as I do Alex Rogers.

CHAPTER 9

"*Y*ou can stop hiding, you know," jests Harlow. "He hasn't returned here since he left you that card on Monday."

I've been eating lunch at a local burger place every day this week just to avoid any more run-ins with Isaac. I can't trust myself to be in the same room with him. Just one look at his deliriously handsome face, and my inhibitions fly out the window. When I returned to the bakery bright and early Tuesday morning for the agents' morning coffee fix, Harlow handed me Isaac's business card. On the back of the card, he simply wrote, 'When you stop denying what your body wants,' with his cell phone number at the bottom.

I crumpled the card up and tossed it to the ground, but no matter how hard I acted as if it weren't there, I couldn't tear my gaze away from it. By the time Harlow finished preparing my order, I'd gathered the business card off the ground and shoved it into my jeans pocket where it has remained the past four days.

Harlow hands me two crates of coffee. "Do you work seven days a week?"

I freeze as I struggle to think of a legitimate reason why my cover as a secretary would be collecting so many coffees on a Saturday morning. "Umm, no. It was a big night for a few friends and me last night. I was the designated driver, which also means I'm responsible for the morning caffeine fix."

I cringe at my pathetic excuse, but when Harlow smiles, I realize she's accepting my explanation.

"Do you work seven days a week?" I ask since I've just realized she's here every morning right alongside me.

"It's a requirement when you're the owner," she answers, staring into space. "I miss late nights and long sleep-ins."

I gawk at her in surprise. Harlow seems around my age, which is young to own a business already.

Noticing my expression, she smiles. "I've always loved to bake. This was a dream of mine since I was a young girl." She gestures her hand around the bakery. "But I'm slowly realizing dreams don't always turn out how you envision them."

I nod. I was so excited when I was accepted into the FBI Academy. I thought I would live a life of suspense and intrigue, but I'm learning what I visualized as an FBI agent varies a great deal from what I do every day. I have nine months, two weeks, and one day left on my contract to work with Alex's department, then hopefully, I'll be reassigned to a better unit, and the dreams I envisioned might transpire.

I offer Harlow a sincere smile before I head for the exit. Just as I'm about to walk out into the street, she calls my name. "If you have any more exciting nights planned, can you throw a dog a bone?"

Smiling, I once again nod.

It's only when I'm in the alcove do I remember I'm going out with Brandon tonight. I invited Brandon out with me under the strict understanding it's a friends-going-out-for-drinks-night-only invitation. No assumptions, no false promises, just friends. He readily agreed.

When I dart back inside the bakery, Harlow's head lifts from the cash register.

"Do you have any plans tonight?"

She smiles and shakes her head, excitement is beaming out of her.

"It isn't a raging party, just a friend and me having some drinks. You're more than welcome to tag along," I inform her, smiling.

Since I don't have a car, Harlow offers to pick me up from Regina's house at nine tonight. By the time I walk back into the office building located across from Isaac's nightclub, the coffees I purchased are stone cold.

Alex grumbles under his breath as he reheats his coffee in the microwave in the galley kitchen, but his angry mood can't sour my excitement. I haven't been out dancing in months, but even more thrilling than that's the fact I've made a friend.

I miss having the close connection of a girlfriend. As much as I love Regina, she mothers me too much for me to consider her a confidante. I need a female companion to discuss the conflicting emotions I'm currently feeling for Isaac Holt.

Hold on, what?

I'm an FBI agent. Any feelings I'm considering need to be squashed. I can't consider befriending someone like Isaac Holt, let alone develop feelings for him. I need to crush the idea of any relationship and treat him like the blood-sucking leech his FBI file leads me to believe he is.

But, my Uncle Tobias always said you should never judge anyone by other people's opinions. He'd often quote, "Until you have a legitimate reason not to like someone, you should treat them how you wish to be treated." Isaac certainly hasn't done anything to me that warrants me disliking him.

He may be crude and cocky, but I'd be lying if I said his vulgarity didn't turn me on. I haven't stopped thinking about the way he smelled when he cornered me in the run-down pub's alcove, let alone the scenes from the plane playing on repeat in my dreams every night.

When a hand slams down on my desk, I jump in fright. I'm so startled, I spill my now iced coffee down the front of my shirt. After grabbing a handful of tissues out of my desk drawer, my furious eyes lift to the unamused face of Alex staring down at me.

"I've been calling your name the past five minutes," he rudely informs me. "What has you so intrigued you can't follow a simple command?"

"Umm, I was just thinking…" I scan the photos on my desk, trying to think of a legitimate reason why I failed to respond without mentioning I was once again fantasizing about Isaac. "... that I don't believe this gentleman is an associate of Isaac's." I lift a photo of the man I saw driving Isaac's car earlier this week. "I think he's his bodyguard."

Alex removes the photo from my hand to appraise it more thoroughly.

"What makes you think he's a bodyguard and not an associate?" For the first time in the past two months, his tone sounds neutral.

"Anytime he's been photographed with Isaac, he's either driving his car, or he completes surveillance of the area." I rise from my desk to gather several other images of Isaac's bodyguard I have printed the past few days. "An associate wouldn't drive the car while Isaac sat in the backseat, he'd sit in the back right along with him," I continue, impressing myself with my ability to think on the spot.

An impromptu grunt rolls up Alex's chest as he flicks through the photos. "So, I guess we can cross him off our list and focus our attention solely back onto Isaac."

"No," I shout, probably a little too loud as Michelle lets out a squeal. "There's something about this guy that has me intrigued." I snatch the photos out of Alex's grasp to find the picture I was researching yesterday. "I can't for the life of me work out why he hasn't come up in any of the facial recognition searches I've completed on him the past two days."

Alex's brows squeeze, apparently unimpressed I've been undertaking searches without seeking his permission.

"He has worked in a government department before, which means he should be in our database," I advise, pacifying the angry scowl on Alex's face. "This tattoo is a symbol of an Air Force squadron. That squad only returned from Afghanistan two years ago. Only squad members can get that tattoo." I hand Alex two photos. One is the original picture of Isaac and his bodyguard jogging, and the other is zoomed in on the tattoo I'm referring to.

My fingers run over the keyboard on my desk to bring up the information I found on the tattoo yesterday afternoon. I enlarge the squadron member tattoo on the screen and turn my monitor toward Alex. He holds the photo against the computer screen mere seconds before a heart-fluttering smile tugs his lips high.

"Brandon, I need you to get me someone high in the U.S. Air Force, now!" Alex strides toward Brandon. His hasty retreat stops before he turns around to face me. "You did a good job, Isabelle."

A mammoth smile spreads across my face.

"See if you can find any other members of his squadron. Maybe they can help us identify him."

Eagerly nodding, I sit at my desk. My heart is galloping with excitement at being assigned my first official task as an FBI field agent.

CHAPTER 10

*W*hen Harlow picks me up at nine, excitement is beaming from me. I've spent the majority of my day searching for ex-squadron members. I secured a reliable source that may assist me in discovering the identity of the man who works with Isaac. I scanned his photo to my contact earlier tonight. He's going to show it to a tattoo parlor owner who has tattooed the squadron symbol previously. He may be able to assist me in tracking down an ex-squadron member who's willing to talk to me. Most hang up the instant I advise them I'm from the FBI. Obviously, there's no comradery amongst colleagues.

"Wow, you scrub up nice," praises Harlow when I slip into the passenger seat of her car.

Smiling, I roam my eyes over her tight black dress. "As do you." A wolf whistle sounds from my lips.

Other than her big, beaming smile, she looks completely different out of her work clothes. Her hair is no longer pulled back in a low ponytail, instead, hanging loosely down her back. This is the first time I've realized her auburn brown hair is curly. Her lips are glossed with bright red lipstick, and her eyes are done in a dramatic Cleopatra way.

She's gorgeous, and she will give all the young girls on the dance floor a run for their money tonight.

"Here." Harlow offers me a tube of lipstick as she pulls her car away from the curb. "It will match the color of your dress perfectly."

Yanking down the visor in her car, I put on the bold red lipstick she handed me. The color does pair well with my tight, strapless red dress. I hand her lipstick back and pucker my lips. The three cocktails I'd downed getting ready are already enhancing my playful mood.

"Wow, we won't buy a drink all night," she predicts.

She wasn't joking. The instant we enter the nightclub, we're inundated with requests to buy us drinks. We wrangle our way through a mass of sweat-drenched, heated bodies to locate Brandon in a private booth at the side of the dance floor.

Brandon must have arrived super early to secure such a prime spot in the bustling nightclub. The brown button-pressed leather booth has a sense of intimacy with thick, luxurious red velvet curtains hanging off black metal A-frames. The stream of purple LED strip lights running along the roof reflect on the sheer curtain draping down each booth, giving the illusion of privacy.

Leaning over, I press a quick peck on Brandon's cheek before introducing him to Harlow. The bustling nightclub is packed to the brim. Most of its patrons appear to be of college age. The interior is lavish but outdated. It isn't usually the type of club I'd hang out at, but it was the closest nightclub in our area that didn't have an association with Isaac Holt.

I spend the next two hours sampling a range of fruity cocktails and accepting invitations to dance. After one dance partner gets a little handsy, I saunter to the bar for a bottle of water. I've been downing cocktails like they're soda water, and they are rushing to my head in quick succession, making me woozy and my footing unsteady.

Brandon curls his arm around my waist to lessen my stumbles. "Are you okay?"

"Yeah." I slightly slur. "I've just had too many cocktails too quickly."

He chuckles before requesting a double scotch on the rocks from the bartender. "Lucky for us, we have the day off tomorrow." He winks cheekily.

Alex is a slave driver, and tomorrow is my first day off in two months. It's probably been even longer for poor Brandon. Grabbing the bottle of water off the countertop, I spin around to face the dance floor, slipping out of Brandon's grip in the process. I smile when I spot Harlow sitting in our booth. She also has a bottle of water in her hands. I giggle to myself. I haven't even been out for two hours, and I already want to go home. *Can anyone say grandma?*

Brandon snatches the bottle of water from my hand to replace it with a colossal size cocktail glass full of a frothy pink liquid. "Who knows when we might get another day off?"

He downs his double scotch on the rocks in one hit, his face scrunching up as he slams the now empty glass onto the countertop. He looks like he's about to puke at any moment.

I giggle when he groans, "I forgot how much that burns."

"Oh, do you think you can do better?" His loud voice gains us the attention of a handful of college students gathered around us. "Chug, chug, chug."

The college kids surrounding us soon catch on to Brandon's chant. Never one to back down from a challenge, I scrunch up my nose before chugging down the pink concoction as dared. Luckily for me, the drink is deliciously fruity, so it goes smoothly into my empty stomach.

The crowd erupts into a roaring chant when I consume every drop of liquid in the large cocktail glass. I attempt a curtsy but end up stumbling and bumping into Brandon when I trip over my own feet.

Brandon waggles his brows. "Another?"

Cringing, I shake my head. I'm already stumbling, so once my latest drink makes its way into my bloodstream, I'll be well over an acceptable limit to be drinking in public. It's time for me to call it a night.

When Brandon turns back to the bar, I head toward the private booth to check if Harlow is ready to go home. Halfway there, my elbow is seized in a tight grip. I don't need to look up to know who is grasping my arm. The jolt bolting up my arm the instant he touches me is all the indication I need.

Isaac drags me into a paint-peeling hallway that houses the outdated bathrooms. His slitted eyes dart up and down the bustling hall before he walks us toward the manager's office located at the end. I should be pulling away from his hold, but with the alcohol in my system and my pulse tripling from his closeness, my inhibitions evaporated the instant he touched me.

A middle-aged gentleman wearing a cheap knock-off Ralph polo shirt with greasy, slicked black hair lifts his head the instant we enter his office.

"Get out." Isaac's tone is threatening.

The manager's bewildered eyes bounce between Isaac and me before he scurries out of the office as Isaac demanded. Once he leaves the room, Isaac releases his firm grip on my arm and turns to lock the door. When he pivots back around to face me, I stiffen, and my pulse intensifies. Even though his eyes are furious, it's what he's trying to mask with his unyielding gaze that has me pinned in place. His eyes expose his pure, unbridled jealousy and lust.

"Did you get my card?" he questions in his sexy-as-hell voice.

Crossing my arms in front of my chest, I strengthen my stance, striving to portray that my body has no desire for him. "I'm not sleeping with you—"

"I never said you would get any sleep." Butterflies flutter in my stomach when he steps close to me. "Well, not for at least a few days."

My eyes bounce between his as my throat works hard to swallow. I attempt a rebuttal, but I'm rendered speechless, my mouth only capable of gaping open before closing.

"Still trying to deny what your body wants?"

When he takes another step closer, my senses are engulfed by his intoxicating scent. Remaining quiet, he brushes his thumb over my top lip. A croaky moan vibrates in my chest when he dips his thumb into my moist and hungry mouth.

Brazenly, I suck off the smears of pink cocktail from his thumb like I haven't been fed in months. When his eyes darken from my frisky tease, I sway toward him, craving his body closer to me. When I lose my footing in the process, his carved brows stitch. "How many drinks have you had tonight, Isabelle?"

Chomping on my bottom lip, I shrug. *I stopped counting over an hour ago.*

"How many drinks have you had?" he questions again, his voice sterner this time.

"A few," I huff. "Who are you, my dad?"

"Are you drunk?"

My eyes shoot back to his as my lips curve into a playful grin. "Maybe a little."

A husky groan tears from his throat when I hold my thumb and index finger an inch apart, indicating how drunk I think I am. I'll be honest, an angry Isaac is as sexy as fuck.

He ignores my playful taunt. "How are you getting home?"

"I wasn't planning to go home alone." My intoxication is making me more daring than normal. "But you just ruined my chances of finding a suitable companion for the night."

I'm lying. I have a minimum three-date rule to get into my panties. Well, I usually do. My strict rules are just null and void when it comes to Isaac Holt.

"I don't play games, Isabelle, so if you're attempting to make me jealous, you're wasting your time."

Ouch! That was a harsh sting to my ego.

I huff and skirt past him, eager to return to my friends so I can continue enjoying my weekend off. I chose this nightclub because I knew Isaac didn't own it, but here I am, having my confidence slapped by the very man I was trying to avoid.

As I dart toward the door, a rush of dizziness causes me to lose my footing in my pretentiously high stiletto heels. Isaac grabs my arms and steadies me before I stumble to the floor in my drunken state.

Shamelessly, I lean into his firm body to take in a deep whiff of his manly scent.

"You smell so good," I slur. Obviously, the cocktail is hitting my bloodstream a lot quicker than I'd anticipated.

When he leans in close to my ear, the hairs on my neck prickle to attention. *Oh God, I hope he's finally going to kiss me.*

"Go tell your friends you're leaving. I'll wait for you out front."

My eyes snap to his, triggering a rush of queasiness to form in my stomach. "I can't leave with you."

I may be extremely tipsy, maybe very close to drunk, but I still know I can't risk my career by leaving the club with him.

"It wasn't a suggestion, Isabelle. Go and tell your friends you're leaving and meet me out front."

Frozen in place, I watch him move toward the office door, his strides long and effortless. He unlocks it before turning around to face me. His beautiful features are constricted with anger. "If you aren't outside in five minutes, I'll come and find you," he advises me before strolling out into the hallway, not once glancing back in my direction.

CHAPTER 11

An appreciative groan erupts from my throat as I snuggle into a smooth and soft texture. I don't know what thread count these sheets are, but they're the softest I've ever laid on. I'll have to thank Regina for replacing my bedding as these sheets make me feel as if I'm sleeping on a cloud.

After pulling my arms out of the quilt, I have a long and leisurely stretch. My muscles feel exerted, but that's expected when you spend hours dancing in four-inch heels. When I sluggishly open my eyes, I come face to face with my disheveled reflection.

Oh, shit, where the hell am I?

I quickly sit up, causing a rush of dizziness to cluster in my head. My hands dart up to rub my temples, easing the furious pounding that makes it feel like my brain is escaping my skull. Once the urge to vomit passes, I glance around the starkly decorated bedroom. The space is vast, but it's cold and sterile. I'm on the right side of a king-size four-poster bed. Other than the bed and two mahogany nightstands, the room is empty. There are no photos or knick-knacks on the bedside tables that would indicate whose bedroom I'm in, and no paintings adorn the walls. Other than the mirror on the ceiling, the room is as basic as they come.

When I peel the dark sheets away from my body, I discover I'm wearing nothing but a small, white V-neck cotton shirt. I don't need to run my hands down my body to know I'm braless. Not just because I can feel the heaviness of my breasts, but because I didn't have a strapless bra to wear with my strapless dress last night, but even more concerning than the fact I don't have a bra on, is the fact I'm also not wearing any panties.

Oh God, Isabelle, what did you do?

I dive out of bed and yank open the top drawer on the bedside table, hoping it may give me some indication as to whose bedroom I am in. Other than a large, open box of condoms and a bottle of lubricant, the drawer is empty. I pull on the hem of my shirt, vainly trying to cover my buttocks as I rush to the other drawer. Inside this drawer is an extensive collection of ladies' panties. On close inspection, I realize they don't look recently washed.

Bile rises from my stomach to my throat as I slam the drawer shut. The chance of me being sick doubles when a door creaking open echoes through the room. I jump back into the bed to cover my naked derriere with the super-soft comforter and sheets.

My heart pounds louder than my head when Isaac strolls into the room wearing nothing but a small white towel. My eyes open wide as memories of last night come filtering back in. Him pulling me into the manager's office. Me sucking on his thumb like it was my last meal. My eyes pleading with him to take me on the very desk we were standing next to. Just one look into his entrancing gray eyes had me throwing caution to the wind.

I remember Brandon's disappointment when I said I had to go. I made a pathetic excuse about being sick in the bathroom stall and that I was too embarrassed to stay. Harlow offered to drive me home, but she had been drinking just as much as me, so I asked Brandon to call her a taxi.

My stomach swirled as I walked toward the exit of the club, but it wasn't from nerves—it was in excitement. Isaac was standing at the entrance door. His lips crimped when he spotted me sauntering toward him. It was raining, so his bodyguard sheltered us with an umbrella as we hopped into the back of a waiting BMW 4WD.

"Hugo."

That was what Isaac called his driver when he instructed him to lose the tail. *Lose the tail. Does Isaac know we are following him? Oh shit, did the surveillance team capture me with him last night?*

My panicked eyes dart to Isaac, who is watching me curiously. I try to keep my eyes secured on his, but the urge to run them over his body is too strong. In nearly every photo I've scanned of him in the FBI database, he's wearing a suit. Although there's been the occasional photo of him in gym shorts and a shirt from when he goes jogging, I've never seen him like this, so up close and personal. His body is perfect.

When my eyes return to his face, I realize I'm not the only one assessing desirable assets. Isaac's heavy-hooded gaze has lowered to my chest, his gaze so molten it activates every one of my hot buttons. Spurred on by confusion, I yank up the comforter to cover my thrusting chest. Amused by my attempt at modesty, Isaac chuckles a deep, throaty laugh.

"Don't you think it's a little late to be shy, Isabelle?"

He paces to the corner of the room. Although I'm petrified I've thrown my career down the toilet from sleeping with this man, my body still shudders from my name rolling off his tongue. Once he reaches the side of the room, he presses his palm on the white wall. My interest piques when a secret door pops out two seconds later. I'm so intrigued. If I weren't half-naked, I'd love to discover what's hiding in that secret room.

Plastic ruffling filters into the room when Isaac walks out with a dry-cleaning bag in one hand and a pair of polished black shoes in the other. I sigh. I was anticipating something more extravagant than a hidden wardrobe.

An improper gasp escapes my lips when he commences dressing in front of me. Against the screamed demands on my inner vixen, I dart my eyes away, only glancing back for the occasional peek.

Holy fuck.

I don't usually swear, but there are no other words to describe Isaac's, umm, *well-endowed* package. When he catches me staring at his junk, he winks. Slapping my hand over my mortified face, I turn my eyes to the wall, embarrassed he busted me ogling him like a virgin who's never seen a penis before. I've seen them before—plenty of them.

Well, not plenty, but I'm definitely not a virgin. I just haven't seen any penises quite as handsome as his.

Can you call a penis handsome?

"No, you can't," Isaac says with a hint of amusement in his tone.

My mortified eyes dart back to his. I really need to learn to stop babbling out loud. He finalizes doing up the last button on his light blue business shirt before he strides over and sits on the bed near me.

"I have a meeting I must attend this morning. Your dress was sent to the dry cleaners, but there are spare clothes your size in the wardrobe." He gestures his hand to the hidden robe.

I cringe. *I hope the clothes are cleaner than the panties I found in the drawer earlier.*

"They've never been worn. Catherine purchased them specifically for you this morning."

I freeze. *Can he read my thoughts?*

When he tilts closer to me, my sex tingles. I really wish I hadn't drunk so much yesterday. Not just so I could remember what happened, but so I could recall what his kisses taste like. Then I wouldn't need to spend hours every day fantasizing about them.

"Stop looking so worried, Isabelle." His minty breath settles the swirling in my stomach. "You wouldn't have any doubts if I'd fucked you, no matter how many drinks you had."

My eyebrows scrunch as my eyes bounce between his. "We didn't have..." My words trail off, unable to articulate the word 'sex.'

"No, we didn't."

"Why?"

Does he not find me attractive? Am I not his type? My eyes turn up to the mirror above the bed. Even though my hair is a mess, and I have mascara smeared under my eyes, I'm still half-presentable. I'm not a complete wreck.

"I like my women... not comatose," he responds with a growl.

I gulp when he licks the tip of his thumb before he rubs it under my eyes, removing the smears of mascara plastered there. Once the mess is cleared away, his gray eyes lift to mine. "You passed out within ten minutes of sitting in the back of my car." He seems angry at my lack of control while drinking.

"I generally handle my liquor a lot better than I did last night, but I was drinking on an empty stomach."

I grimace. Most people would happily use that as a reason for their inebriated state, but it's a weak excuse.

"And what would have happened if I didn't arrive at that club when I did, Isabelle? What if it were another man who carried you into his apartment and undressed you?" His livid eyes wander over my face. "Do you think he'd have slept next to you all night long, smelling your sexually enticing scent without touching an inch of your seductive curves and skin?"

The pulse in my neck strums when he leans in close to me and inhales an unashamed whiff. The fine hairs on my body prickle with attention as slickness forms between my legs. "I could smell you all night long, but I couldn't do a darn thing about it. A lesser man wouldn't have resisted."

A moan vibrates in my chest just thinking about him sleeping in the same bed as me. When he pulls away from my neck, my eyes dart up to his. My breathing shallows as my body tingles.

Two years of training, Isabelle. Are you willing to throw everything away for one night in bed with this man?

Even though I should be screaming 'no,' the word 'yes' is the first thing that pops into my brain.

"Ruthless, cunning, lawless," I chant over and over again in my head, willing myself out of a seriously dangerous situation.

Isaac removes himself from the bed to gather his suit jacket. "Hugo will return after dropping me off. He will take you home." His voice is gruff, making me wonder if I said my silent chant out loud.

"I can take myself home."

After all, I'm a grown woman, although I may have acted like a child last night.

He nods before striding toward the double white wooden doors. Upon exiting, his head turns to face me. His eyes study my covered body before returning to my face.

"If you go out drinking with your friends again, only go to my clubs."

With my shrewdness blinded by rampant horniness, I nod. His lips curl, seemingly pleased by my agreeing gesture before he exits the room. Groaning in frustration, I flop down onto the bed. I swear I'm not usually this senseless. There's just something about Isaac that makes me throw my levelheadedness out the window, and it's more than just my sexual attraction to him. I've known plenty of eye-catching men, but none of them have made my body react the way it does when he's near, which is scary considering he hasn't even touched me sexually yet.

Imagine how explosive it will be once he does?

Oh God, I need to get out of here before I make any more stupid decisions. Quickly diving out of bed, I scamper toward the hidden door. My mouth drops open when I walk into the massive room. There are several dozen dry-cleaning bags housing expensive suits lining one whole wall. At least two dozen dress shoes line the floor underneath them, and an extensive collection of ties are hanging on a display rack.

I run my hand across the dry-cleaning bags as I head to the far corner of the room which houses a selection of women's clothing. A smile breaks across my face when I notice a pair of white running shoes sitting next to my black pumps I was wearing last night. I've never seen the sense in wearing high heels during the day. I've always preferred comfort over appearance. I grab the sneakers and yank down a pair of jeans and a short-sleeve shirt before walking back into the room.

My eyes dart to the bedside table that contains the women's underwear. *Did Isaac place the underwear I was wearing last night in there?* Although the temptation is healthy, I can't stomach the idea of having my panties collected like some sort of trophy, so I put the jeans on without any undergarments. I'd rather go without panties than open that drawer again.

After pulling the short-sleeve shirt over my head, I pull my unruly hair out of the neckline and run my fingers through it to get the frazzled pieces under control. Once the laces on the white Converse sneakers are tied, I exit the room. The living area is just as sparse as the bedroom. There are two white leather sofas and a coffee table in the middle of the room. The white marble kitchen sparkles with cleanliness, and the appliances look like they have never been used.

Pulling open the stainless-steel fridge, I help myself to a bottle of cold water. I need something in my stomach to absorb the alcohol sloshing around in there. As I mosey to the front door, I spot my cell phone and purse sitting on the entry table. My phone is sitting on top of several open envelopes. From this distance, they look like personal correspondence as the addresses are handwritten. My pulse increases as I scan the envelopes that could hold something invaluable in them for our investigation. Even something that seems so minute in detail can be important in an investigation like ours on Isaac, but I can't break his trust, can I?

Isaac hasn't done anything that would justify me snooping into his private life. I'm here at my own choice. I didn't go home with him last night because of my job. I left with him because I wanted to. Looking past the details in his criminal file, Isaac has me intrigued, intrigued enough I risked my job by leaving with him last night. So, no matter how hard I try to justify that I should snoop in his personal life, I can't bring myself to do it.

Snatching my purse and phone off the table, I exit the apartment. The first thing I spot when leaving the foyer of the apartment building is Isaac's Mercedes-Benz town car parked across the street. The back window is rolled down, and his stern gray eyes are staring at me. I hesitantly wave. He doesn't wave back.

Rejection overwhelms me when the black-tinted window glides back into place before his car pulls into the Sunday morning traffic.

CHAPTER 12

"*I* thought I gave you the day off," Alex remarks from the corner of the room.

He's lurking near the window looking down on The Dungeon nightclub. From the padded box seat, there's an uninterrupted view of the entire nightclub and the parking lot below. Alex sluggishly turns to face me. His unshaven face appears guarded, and dark circles are plaguing his eyes. *Does he ever leave this office?*

"You did, but I have a lead I can follow, so I thought I should get a head start on that."

I shuffle to my desk. After dropping my satchel into my bottom desk drawer, I fire up my computer. My mood is dreary and clouded with confusion. To be honest, my ego is scarred by Isaac's dismissal this morning. Half of me is here to pursue answers as to why he's so mysterious. He's an enigma. He only allows people to know what he wants them to know. I don't believe anyone truly knows the real Isaac Holt, not even those privileged to be included in his close-knit team.

"What's your lead?" Alex listlessly strolls to my spotless, well-organized desk.

I'm tempted to tell him I've unearthed Hugo's first name, but my intuition strongly advises me to keep that snippet of information to myself, at least until I get more concrete evidence on who Hugo is. For all I know, he could be using an alias. Furthermore, how could I justify stumbling upon his name without disclosing I went home with Isaac last night?

"The tattoo parlor owner emailed me back this morning. He said he might have a squadron member willing to talk to me," I reply, half-deceitful. I do have a contact, but they haven't agreed to talk to me yet.

Alex's reticent eyes gaze into mine for several awkward seconds before he nods.

"Did you have any luck with the Defense Department?" I question, prying him for any information that may contribute to my investigation of Isaac.

He groans in frustration before vigorously shaking his head. "I'm filing them under a dead end."

My lips curve higher. This is the first time we've had a normal conversation in the past two months.

"I'm impressed with your dedication, Isabelle," he commends me. "Keep this up, and you may get off coffee duty sometime within the next year."

His boisterous chuckle echoes in the desolate space as he strides to his private office. I clutch my wireless mouse, trying my hardest to keep it planted on my desk and not pegged at the back of his arrogant head.

After squandering the last four hours at my desk, I'm no closer to finding out if Hugo is indeed his real name. Although Hugo was part of the American Hornets Squadron, there are no pictures of him in any of the squad photos, and no records of him exist in the Air Force database. The only information I've located on any Hugo in the county is a death certificate for a Hugo Marshall who died two years ago.

Frustrated with my lack of progress, I scan Hugo's surveillance photo into the facial recognition database and expand my search to include every possible angle, including social media sites. If his face is on something, I'll ultimately find it. Well, I will in a few hours as the expanded searches take hours to run through the FBI database.

When my stomach grumbles declaring its hunger, I decide to go and grab something to eat instead of glaring at my computer monitor, yearning for it to come up with some resourceful information.

"I'm going to grab a bite to eat," I notify Alex.

His gaze doesn't falter from the photos he's scrutinizing, but he does nod his head, acknowledging he heard me.

"Did you want anything?"

When he grins a full-tooth smile and arches his manicured brow, I sigh and roll my eyes.

"I'll bring you back a coffee," I grumble before snatching my satchel out of my bottom desk drawer and rushing out of the building.

A giggle vibrates my lips when I spot a rumpled Harlow leaning against the counter at the bakery. Hearing my laughter, she shakes her head and groans. "This is all your fault," she whispers like her voice is too piercing for her hungover head.

"Same time next week?"

Her bloodshot eyes dart up to mine. When she notices my smile, a cheeky grin sneaks onto her pale face.

"I guess that will depend on whether you're going to ditch me again."

"Sorry," I apologize.

When I move to the bakery counter she's leaning on, my stomach grumbles furiously. The smell of scrumptious fresh-baked goodies filters through my nose. Harlow's eyes roam my face before her mouth breaks into her famous mischievous grin.

"That's okay, I would've ditched you, too, if I were going home with who you left with."

Oh shit. She saw me leaving with Isaac last night? Does that mean Brandon also saw me leaving with him?

"Please don't tell me he was bad in bed," she probes when she spots the forlorn expression on my face. "He can't have devilishly handsome looks and an aura like his and not deliver the goods. It's a disgrace to mankind."

A grin stretches across my face. This is the reason I need a girl-friend who lives close by. I need someone to help me wade through the confusion muddling my head.

"I couldn't tell you what his sexual prowess is like."

"Huh," huffs Harlow, appearing noticeably confused. "I saw the way he was looking at you, Izzy. He was more than ready to take you to his bed."

"I didn't say I didn't sleep in his bed, I just didn't sleep with him last night."

She remains quiet as a mask of shock slips over her face. "Go and sit, I'll make us a strong brew of coffee, then you can give me all the juicy details."

Once she joins me at one of the tables in the half-empty bakery, I occupy the next twenty minutes of her time giving her a rundown of everything that happened with Isaac this morning. I also extend my story to include the first time we met.

By the time I've finished relaying every lucid detail, my confusion has intensified.

"First, I must say I knew he'd be hung like a donkey."

A giggle escapes my lips when she uses her hands to fan her over-heated, flushed cheeks.

"Second, I can understand him not sleeping with you last night. Having sex with someone who's intoxicated is too rapey in my eyes, but having sex with someone who is hungover is a different story altogether. There's no reason you shouldn't have been screaming his name at the top of your lungs this morning."

I have to agree with her. No self-respecting person would sleep with someone who's intoxicated since they can't give consent, but the fact Isaac didn't attempt *anything* with me this morning when I was capable of making rational decisions, makes me feel rejected.

"Maybe he did have a meeting he had to attend, and he knew he wouldn't have enough time to thoroughly knock your socks off?" she suggests, running her hand down my arm in a supportive manner.

"Yeah, maybe," I reply, although my gut is telling me that isn't the case.

After talking to Harlow for another thirty minutes, drinking enough coffee to keep me awake for a week, and eating a club sandwich, I walk back into my workplace with my mind less jumbled than before. Upon entering, I spot Alex sitting at my desk. His dour eyes lift to mine as I apprehensively stroll toward him.

"What are you doing?"

He gestures his head to the computer monitor on my desk. "You found Isaac's mysterious companion."

Once Alex accepts the black coffee I brought back for him, my eyes dart to the computer screen. My extensive search has located a match for Hugo. It's a Facebook profile opened seven years ago, but it has been inactive for the past two years.

I skim the information in front of me. Hugo Marshall would now be twenty-eight years old. At the time his account was opened, he was unmarried and had three siblings—Helen, Chase, and Marjorie. He lived in Rochdale, New York, and his employment status shows he was working in security.

"It appears he's just a bodyguard," he exclaims, rising from my chair and moving around my desk. "I don't think we need to focus our investigation on Hugo any further. It's time to return our attention to our original target."

I nod in understanding, even though my instincts are telling me not to drop this. The death certificate I found earlier was for a Hugo Marshall who died two years ago. At the time of his death, he was twenty-six years old. That's too much of a coincidence for me to disregard.

Now I'm no longer planning just to unearth the mystery of Isaac Holt, but I'm also planning on finding out every sordid bit of information I can on the elusive Hugo Marshall.

CHAPTER 13

Six weeks later...

"*I*sabelle."

"You've got to be kidding me," I babble under my breath.

My eyes shift down as I suck in air. My heart clenches when I'm met with the piercing gray eyes of Isaac Holt.

Shit!

This wasn't the plan when Harlow and I decided to go out and celebrate. I had no inkling Isaac would be here. We merely chose this restaurant from the rave reviews it received on Yelp. We were unaware this type of establishment books up months in advance. When a handsome blond gentleman eavesdropped on our conversation with the restaurant hostess, he graciously offered for us to be seated with him.

Harlow's excitement shone out of her when she accepted his invitation with no pause for consideration. To say I was surprised when I followed him to his booth and heard my name roll off Isaac's tongue would be a major understatement.

"Hi," I greet him anxiously.

My eyes leisurely glance over Isaac's dark gray dress shirt and black dress pants. Tonight, unlike every other time I've seen him, he's minus his suit jacket and tie. He sports a dark gray business shirt rolled up at the sleeves. The top two buttons are undone, revealing inches of his smooth, muscular chest. He looks ravishingly drool-worthy.

He gives me a casual smirk as he stands from the booth to offer me his hand to shake. "Hi."

When I accept his gesture, he doesn't shake my hand—he places a kiss on the edge of my palm. Air sucks from my lungs when his electrifying touch scorches my skin. I yank my hand out of his grasp, skittish from my body's reaction to his humblest touch.

He smiles at my wary reaction before accepting Harlow's greeting. He gawks at Harlow peculiarly, seemingly dumbfounded. His lips purse as his eyes wander over Harlow's body. A rush of nausea churns in my stomach, riddled with panic that they may already be familiar with one another.

"I'm from the bakery," Harlow informs him when she notices the confused expression on his striking face. Her statement doesn't ease Isaac's uncertainty. "The bakery you left your card at for Izzy."

"Ah. The card that has yet to be utilized."

When Isaac shakes Harlow's hand, I exhale, grateful they only know each other in passing.

"Please join us," the handsome blond gentleman offers, motioning his hand to the booth.

Harlow slides into the spare space next to him, meaning I have no choice but to sit next to Isaac. The instant I slip into the booth, he leans in to take a sizable whiff of my scent.

"Fuck, you smell good."

His voice is ruggedly smooth, sending a thrill through my body from the strands of my hair to the tips of my toes. I try to conceal my smile at his compliment, but my lips curve upward, giving away my true feelings. This is the first time I've seen Isaac since the morning I left his apartment six weeks ago. *Oh, well, that's a blatant lie.* I haven't seen him in person since that day would be a more accurate response. He's still under investigation by the FBI, and I'm still required to scan all the tedious, meaningless tasks he gets photographed doing every day into the Bureau's database. I just haven't seen him personally.

I probably shouldn't say 'tedious, meaningless tasks' as I'm sure some people would see multimillion-dollar business takeovers as a riveting experience, but it doesn't match the impression of what one would expect a suspected mob boss to do every day.

I've tried relentlessly to eradicate Isaac from my thoughts the past six weeks. I've read every file the FBI has on him to taint my interest in him, but nothing has worked. As unavoidable as the plague, everywhere I go, Isaac is right there in front of me.

Dangling Isaac in front of me is like taking a kid to a candy store and telling her she must buy a piece of fruit. Even though you know the candy will give you cavities and make your hips wider, you still want the candy. Isaac isn't good for me. I should stay away from him, but when he is dangled in front of me, my inhibitions evaporate.

Isaac runs his index finger along my forearm, causing the hairs on my body to bristle. "How do you know Cormack?"

"Who?" My one word is wheezy from his close proximity.

He points to the blond gentleman seated across from us. "Cormack."

"I don't know him. He just offered for us to be seated with him when we couldn't get a table."

Scooting across the bench, I try to increase the space between our bodies since we're sitting intimately close to each other. My body's awareness of Isaac's proximity is wreaking havoc with my shrewdness.

His lips crimp at my action before shifting closer to me, leaving less room between us than there was previously. Rolling my shoulders, I firm my stance. I try to keep my focus planted on Cormack and Harlow gabbing across from us, but my eyes incessantly sneak glances at Isaac, whose eyes remain planted on me.

"How do you know Cormack?" I ask, endeavoring to keep our conversation in friendly territory.

"We met in college. He was my roommate slash manager."

"Manager?" My curiosity is piqued as to why someone like Isaac would require a manager.

He smirks vainly. "Not that type of manager. No one is the boss of me, baby."

I try not to sway toward him, but this is the first time he has referred to me by a nickname. Call me crazy. Call me a freak, but I liked hearing it.

"I fought my way through college. Literally."

"You didn't fight, you just showed up," Cormack interrupts, his tone cheeky.

"Don't believe anything this guy tells you," Cormack banters, gesturing his head to Isaac. "He acts all innocent, then bam, you'll be on your ass before you know it."

"Who are you to talk? You're the one who created the ruse," Isaac jests, his lips tugged into a broad grin.

"It worked, though, didn't it?" Cormack arches his brow into his blond hairline.

Isaac doesn't respond. He merely laughs a thick, vociferous chuckle that makes my pussy pulsate with desire.

"Come on, out with it," Harlow requests a short time later, her eyes bouncing between Cormack and Isaac. "This is more suspenseful than the *Game of Thrones* cliffhanger. You can't share tidbits of information, then leave us hanging. We need details. Very informative details."

"All right." Cormack leans over the table to build the suspense. "Imagine Isaac all decked out in corduroy trousers, a pair of leather-strapped sandals, a button-up, short-sleeve shirt two sizes too small, and a pair of suspenders."

"I didn't wear fucking suspenders," Isaac interrupts. Although his voice sounds stern, his eyes glimmer with mischief.

"It was a few years ago. Maybe my memory isn't as good as it was, but I swear at least once I got you into a pair of suspenders."

Both Harlow's and my chuckles break the silence surrounding us.

My gleeful eyes turn to Isaac. Even decked out in the most hideous, unsightly clothes you could find, he would still be the most strikingly handsome man I've ever seen. It is, after all, what's under the clothing that's the most appealing.

When he notices my eyes wandering over his body, Isaac runs his index finger down my arm.

"Anyway, we have him all decked out like a choirboy about to go to church on Sunday. Isaac arrives on the scene of an underground fight ring acting all innocent like it's the first time he's been to an event like that. Only once an impressive purse was negotiated for a fight, did Isaac reveal his true self. By then, it was too late for his opponent to back out. An easy five G's for ten minutes of work," Cormack informs.

Cormack leans back into the booth and takes a sizable gulp of the brown liquid from the crystal glass in his hand.

"Wow."

Now part of Isaac's FBI file makes sense, like where he got the money he invested in stocks while he was still in college. His file leads us to believe it was from him illegally distributing and manufacturing drugs. And although underground fighting is illegal, it doesn't hold the same repercussions as drug manufacturing and dealing does.

"How many years did you fight?"

My interrogation is exclusively based on personal motives. I find Isaac intriguing. The more time I spend with him, the more personal information I want to unearth about him.

"Just under two years," he replies, his brows lowering.

"Why did you stop fighting?"

His jaw muscle tremors before his eyes flick to Cormack. When he shakes his head, Cormack's brows furrow before he nods. My eyes shoot to Harlow. She shrugs, feeling the tension as well. The longer the silence continues, the more the air surrounding our group permeates with the thick stench of awkwardness.

The uncomfortable silence is only interrupted when the restaurant hostess saunters her way to the booth and notifies our group our table is ready. Cormack gestures for Harlow to follow the hostess.

My anxious eyes dart to Isaac, wordlessly questioning if he still wants us to join his table. His eyes roam my face while he contemplates a response. When he motions for me to follow the hostess, I hesitantly slide out of the booth.

Cormack and Isaac follow closely behind us. I can hear them talking, but with the hum of activity inside the restaurant, I'm unable to understand any of their words.

The instant we're seated, Isaac signals for the waiter to bring him a glass of whiskey. "Bring back the whole bottle." His tone is surly and rough.

For the next hour, Isaac spends the majority of our meal silently brooding and consuming whiskey as if it's coffee. Although I try to keep my focus on Cormack and Harlow, my eyes persistently shift to Isaac. Cormack has been a faultless gentleman the entire meal, and Harlow hangs off his every word, but my attention remains on what caused the sudden shift in Isaac's personality. Why did such a simple question spark such an adverse reaction? He went from flirty, friendly banter to cold and distant in a matter of seconds.

When the waiter removes Isaac's untouched plate of food, I place my hand on his thigh and give it a gentle squeeze. His eyes lift from his glass of whiskey to me. He assesses all the features of my face in silence. His gaze still causes a shiver to run through my body, but this time, it's more from his icy glare than excitement.

"Don't take his lack of interest personally, Isabelle." I stray my concerned eyes to Cormack. "For as long as I've known Isaac, he has never been interested in dating brunettes."

"Oh." My eyes turn back to Isaac as my throat works hard to swallow. "Is there any particular reason?"

I stare into Isaac's despondent eyes, begging for him to deny Cormack's statement, to acknowledge the confusing, flirtatious connection we have. Even though Isaac appears to be staring straight at me, he isn't seeing me—he's looking straight through me.

"It's a personal preference," he replies coldly. "No brunette I've ever *fucked* has maintained my interests once we leave the bedroom."

My heart plunges into my stomach. I try to mask my hurt with a smile, but my deception is revealed when my hand rattles as I reach for my wine glass.

Isaac stands from the table, looking prepared to excuse himself for the night. His hasty getaway is foiled when a group of waiters moves toward our table singing a rendition of 'Happy Birthday.'

My cheeks enflame as my embarrassed eyes flick up to Harlow. She's smiling radiantly and waggling her eyebrows. When a giant chocolate cake covered in candles is placed down in front of me, Isaac curses under his breath and flops back into his chair.

Ignoring the obvious tension plaguing our group, Harlow excitedly instructs, "Make a wish."

My focus flashes between the three sets of eyes complacently staring at me. My gaze loiters on Isaac's a touch longer than the other two. His beautiful eyes quell my anxiety. I close my eyes before blowing out the candles in one swift motion.

Clapping and laughter dispel when I brush my lips against Isaac's soft, plump lips.

CHAPTER 14

*T*he brush of my tongue against Isaac's lips is met with a mouth that's hard and stern. My heart pounds so profusely, it's nearly deafening. Tears burn my eyes as my nose runs. I've always been an ugly crier. Tonight will be no different.

I kissed him with the hope of proving him wrong. I kissed him wanting to force him to recount the lie he just told. I kissed him because I couldn't wait any longer to feel his lips on mine. Now, I feel like a fool. I can't even coerce the guy who has gotten under my skin to give me a pitiful birthday kiss. *I am pathetic.*

Slowly pulling away from his snapped-shut mouth, I pray his desire for me overwhelms him so much, he refuses to relinquish my mouth from his.

With every millimeter I gain between our lips, my heart sinks further into my stomach. The wrath of rejection has never hit so hard.

After sucking in a big breath, I open my eyes. Isaac's gray eyes are staring into mine, but they don't give any indication to his feelings about my failed attempt at seducing him.

Biting my bottom lip, I turn my tear-filled eyes to Harlow and

Cormack. Cormack's brows are knitted together, and he looks utterly confused. Harlow's mouth is ajar, and tears are in her eyes.

"Thank you for a lovely evening," I inform them.

Leaping from my chair, I snatch my black silk clutch from the tabletop. I need to leave before my foolishness becomes more exposed.

When I attempt to dash away from the table, Isaac's hand jerks out and seizes my wrist, causing the cutlery on the table to clang together. *Never show your fear, Isabelle.* Raising my shoulders, I gather my composure before turning my gaze down to him, endeavoring to show him I'm not affected by his rejection.

"I'll drive you home," he offers, his voice rough.

I shake my head. His eyes narrow, forcing me to swallow a lump formed in my throat. Not releasing my hand, he stands from his seat and aggressively throws his unused napkin down onto the table. When he digs into his back pocket, Cormack gestures his hands in front of his body, indicating he will pay the bill.

"Can you take Harlow home?" Isaac's voice is deeper than I've ever heard it.

"Yeah," Cormack replies, nodding. "If Harlow is okay with that?" His gaze seeks Harlow's.

Harlow's anxious eyes lift to mine, seeking permission. I nod. Just one look into Isaac's stern eyes is all I need to know he's going to drive me home whether I agree or not.

Harlow leans over the table to give me a brief, friendly hug. "I'll call you later."

Nodding, I return her hug the best I can with the one arm I have free since Isaac is still clutching my other hand.

Cormack and Isaac must say a silent goodbye as neither utter a sound before Isaac walks toward the exit of the restaurant. I have to jog in my heels to keep up with his quick strides.

Halfway there, he yanks his phone out of his pocket, lifts it to his ear, and commands Hugo to bring his car around. By the time we make it outside, my arm feels like it's been tugged out of its socket from his harsh pulls. I attempt to remove my arm from his rough grip, but instead of releasing me, his grip tightens, and my wrist spasms with pain.

"Let go of my arm." I pull away from his grasp.

He releases me from his tight grip before dragging his hand through his hair. I've never seen someone so furious over a little kiss before. I wouldn't have kissed him if I knew it would get this reaction.

He's acting like, like, *oh my God.*

"I'm sorry if I embarrassed you." Irritation is heard in my voice. "It was just a harmless kiss. It didn't mean anything."

"Then why did you do it?" His stern eyes turn from the blackened night to me. "If it didn't mean anything, why did you kiss me?"

"Because I wanted to," I reply honestly. "And I wanted you to admit you lied."

"I didn't lie," he snaps, his tone unwavering. "I said no brunette I have *fucked* has maintained my interest outside of the bedroom."

So, he's admitting I have gained his interest? He takes a step closer to me, forcing me to take a step back. His eyes are unnerving. They're the darkest I've ever seen them.

"If you want to prove your point, Isabelle..." even though his voice is gruff, my name still rolls off his tongue seductively, "... I'll have to fuck you first."

I should be offended by his crudeness, by his lack of respect, but I'm not. For months I've been torturing myself over this man. He's in my thoughts day and night. He is under my skin. He even invades my dreams. The intriguing Isaac Holt I read about every day on paper has nothing on the suspense and intrigue I feel when I'm with him in person. His aura makes it seem as if he's two different people.

He steps closer to me. He's so close there isn't enough space between our bodies for my lungs to fully expand. His tormented eyes filter over my face before he cradles my cheek. His thumb glides over my dry top lip. It's dry from my inability to produce saliva—my mouth is parched from his intense gaze.

"Is that what you want, Isabelle?"

At first, I'm confused by his question. I've become so immersed in staring into his entrancing eyes, I've completely forgotten about his earlier comment.

"Because your body is saying one thing, and your eyes relay another."

His intense eyes convey his absolute confusion. He isn't the only one confused. My brain knows our bizarre kinship is unethical. It may even be illegal, but my heart and body don't want to hear the logical thoughts of my mind. All they want is Isaac. They have craved him ever since the day I collided with him at the airport, but can I do this? Can I sacrifice everything for a man I hardly know?

Before any words can seep from my lips, a dark, sleek sports car pulls in next to us. Isaac removes his hand from my cheek and shoves it into his trouser pocket.

"Get in the car, Isabelle."

Shocked and frozen in place, I watch Isaac stride toward the driver's side door Hugo is stepping out of. Isaac and Hugo talk in hushed whispers. Hugo nods before his blue eyes lift to mine. He offers me a wary smile before moving around the vehicle and opening the passenger side door.

Isaac's eyes lift to mine. He gestures for me to enter the car before he slides into the driver's seat, not bothering to wait for my response. Although this is a prime opportunity for me to make a calculated getaway, I can't force myself to walk away from him. Reluctantly, I head to the sleek black car.

"Are you okay?" Hugo's concerned eyes roam my face.

I nod, before accepting his assistance into the car.

"Thank you," I whisper graciously.

Because of how low the car sits, I have to slide into the leather seat. My black pencil skirt glides up high on my thigh, exposing a significant portion of my bare skin. I pull down on the hem, hoping to stretch it to a respectful length, but there's no give in the sturdy material.

The instant Hugo closes the passenger door, Isaac pulls his car away from the curb. His engine roars to life with the heavy compression of the accelerator, his tires squealing as we whiz away from the restaurant.

He weaves his car in and out of the heavy commuter traffic, the veins in his arms flexing when he changes gears. Although his attention never veers from the road, I catch his gaze occasionally peering at me from the corner of his eye.

If he's trying to scare me, he's failing miserably. With his assertiveness and astute business mind, he'd never take an uncalculated risk. He just wants to flaunt his superiority because I embarrassed him.

His next shift of the gears is so rough, I'm surprised the gearshift didn't snap off. His hand curls around the steering wheel so tight, his knuckles are white.

All this anger over a simple kiss.

"I'm sorry I kissed you," I apologize. "I shouldn't have done it."

His eyes snap to mine. Even in his angry mood, his sultry gaze still wanders over my body, lingering on my bare thighs longer than what could be classed as an acceptable glance.

He glowers into my eyes as he sneers, "I won't be strong-armed, Isabelle."

I nod, accepting that a man as dominant as Isaac would never willingly relinquish his power. His jaw muscle slackens when he notices my agreeing gesture.

He returns his gaze to the road. "That has only happened once. It won't happen again."

I study his profile in silence, striving to work out what he meant by his statement. I don't believe a sane man would strongarm a man with a reputation like Isaac's. They would have to be a certified lunatic if they did. So, I'm going to assume his statement isn't about a man. It has to be a woman he's referring too.

Ignoring the pang of jealousy hitting my chest, my gaze shifts to the blackened sky to ponder in silence. I've been over Isaac's entire FBI file with a fine-toothed comb. There's nothing in there indicating any romantic interests, past or present, so it must be something that happened before he attracted the attention of the law enforcement office—something that can only be discovered by unearthing the real

Isaac Holt. Something that will remain buried as I don't believe anyone will ever fully unravel the mystery of Mr. Holt.

When Isaac pulls into the driveway of Regina's house, I return my gaze to his, which is focused straight ahead.

"Thanks for everything," I whisper. "It was the most *interesting* birthday I've had in years."

I unbuckle my seat belt before leaning over to press a peck on his cheek. When he abruptly turns his head, my kiss lands on his stern mouth instead. I freeze, panicked at what his reaction will be from me kissing him a second time without permission.

He growls a low and menacing snarl that forces me to exhale a shaky breath. Before any apologies can spill from my lips, he seals his mouth over mine.

My insecurities vanish the instant his tongue plunges into my shocked mouth. A throaty groan erupts from my lips when he fists my hair and yanks it back to deepen our kiss. My excited moan urges him on. Our kiss is intense, desperate, and needy. He kisses me as I've never been kissed before, a stimulating blur of nibbles, sucks, and licks. It's a kiss so potent my thighs shudder. A kiss every girl fantasizes about.

I respond with the same amount of intensity as if it might be the last time I'll experience his awe-inspiring kisses because it most likely will be.

I'm aroused and emotionally moved by his kiss at the same time. I don't know whether to burst into tears or combust into ecstasy.

By the time he pulls back from our embrace, my mind is a blurred mess of confusion. "Happy birthd—"

He stops talking mid-sentence, his eyes darting between mine. His thumb dabs my right eye, gathering the dampness I didn't realize had pooled there. When he observes the moisture on his thumb, he expels a ragged breath. Although he doesn't utter a sound, his eyes relay the words he wants to say. *I'm sorry.*

"Thank you," I reply, acknowledging both his silent apology and his birthday wishes.

I stammer a quick goodbye before yanking open the passenger

door and rushing into Regina's house, not once risking a glance back. When I close the front door, I glide down to sit on the floor and cradle my knees in my arms.

When did my life become so complicated?

When I'm immersed in Isaac's world, I completely forget he's under investigation. When I'm with him, I only see him, a man who makes my hairs bristle to attention with a single touch. Then I turn up to work, and my head clutters with confusion. It's like he's two different people because that incredibly appealing man I can't force myself to forget can't be the same Isaac Holt his FBI file leads me to believe he is.

He can't be.

CHAPTER 15

"*Y*ou have to cancel the cake orders before my ass explodes."

Isaac's gorgeous face is puzzled until he realizes who is accosting him in the street. When I saw his sleek black town car in front of the restaurant I'd initially spotted him at several months ago, I decided to approach him regarding his extravagant but heartfelt gift.

The day after my birthday when I arrived at Harlow's bakery to place my morning coffee order, Harlow presented me with a giant decorative cupcake. It was red velvet, and it was the most scrumptious cake I'd ever eaten.

The second day, I was presented with another cupcake. That time, the enticing flavor was chocolate mint. By the third day, my curiosity intensified.

After wrangling Harlow for nearly thirty minutes, she finally enlightened me. Because Isaac and I had left the restaurant before I sampled my birthday cake, Isaac requested for Harlow to supply me with one originally flavored cupcake per day for an entire year. *A YEAR!*

"It was very sweet of you, but after only five days, the struggle to squeeze into my jeans is already real."

Isaac's lips curve into an authentic smile, making my heart palpitate faster. When his eyes dart down to my jeans, I stand straighter and suck in my bottom. I may not yet have a Kim Kardashian butt, but if I keep eating the cupcakes Harlow is supplying me with, I don't think it will be too far off.

"That just means there will be more Isabelle to explore."

He can say that, I've seen him naked. I swear there isn't an ounce of fat on his entire body. Well, except for that one area where thickness is a necessary and wanted requirement. However, someone with my lagging metabolism will have to run a minimum of three miles a day just to ensure those cupcakes don't make it onto my already curvy backside and squidgy belly.

Before I can derive a witty comeback to his remark, a lady joins our conversation. She looks to be a similar age to me, but her aura of grace and dignity makes her appear more mature.

"Isaac, honey, are you going to introduce me to your friend?"

Her tone is friendly, and her interest in me appears genuine, but my irritation still irks from her calling Isaac 'honey.'

"Isabelle, this is Clara. Clara, this is Isabelle Brahn."

My brows meet my hairline, surprised Isaac knows my last name, but considering I've slept in his bed half-naked, kissed him on the lips without permission, and am spying on him every day as a career, I brush off any concerns over the fact he knows my last name.

Clara inhales as her blue eyes drift between Isaac and me. After a beat, she extends her manicured hand to accept the greeting I'm offering.

"It's a pleasure to meet you, Isabelle."

After the awkward introduction, our gathering plummets toward uncomfortable. Isaac, as always, is impeccably dressed in a tailored black suit. Clara is wearing a gorgeous pale blue slip dress, so I stand out like a sore thumb in a pair of jeans I squeezed into, a short-sleeve blouse, and a pair of black ballet flats. I couldn't feel any more out of place if I tried.

"Well, I better get going." My eyes nervously shift to Isaac. "I just wanted to thank you for the gift, although it was completely unnecessary."

His lips tug high as he dips his chin.

"It was a pleasure meeting you, Clara," I inform her before spinning on my heels and head toward the bakery.

"Oh, don't go. Can't you join us?" Clara requests.

I hesitate, then turn back around. Isaac's eyes are staring into mine, but they don't give me any indication if he objects to Clara's invitation.

"Umm, thank you for the offer, but I'm slightly underdressed." I motion to my jeans.

The last time I attempted to enter this restaurant dressed as I am, I was advised there's a public restroom located one block over.

Isaac's eyes wander over my body before returning to my face. "You look perfectly fine."

I try to hide my smile, but my lips furl at his compliment, especially considering the fact it was the exact words he said to me months ago outside of the business class lounge.

"Thank you," I whisper. "But I have to return to work."

After all, I was only walking down this street to get the team's early morning coffee.

Isaac curtly nods but remains quiet. Clara clasps her hands together as if she's considering a plea. I awkwardly wave, spin on my heels, and cringe at my lack of elegance.

I don't turn around, but I can feel Isaac's heated gaze tracking me until I enter the bakery. Upon entering, I spot Harlow standing near a noticeboard in her bakery. Her head turns toward the door when she hears the bell chime.

"Are you still looking for an apartment?" She yanks down a flyer from the noticeboard.

Nodding, I bridge the gap between us. I've been seeking an apartment since I arrived in Ravenshoe. I just haven't secured one yet. Most apartments in the area are either out of my price range or the moderately-priced ones have hundreds of applications, and mine is always denied.

"This place sounds ideal." She thrusts a piece of paper into my hand—two bedrooms, two bathrooms, an underground garage, and a balcony all for twelve hundred dollars a month.

"What's the catch?"

I've always believed if something is too good to be true, it is. This apartment seems too good to be true.

"Is it located in Ravenshoe's equivalent of the Bronx?"

Harlow laughs boisterously and slaps my forearm. "There's no Bronx area of Ravenshoe. Call and make an appointment," she suggests. "Then crumple up the advertisement and throw it in the bin. That will stop anyone else applying."

The advertisement does look newly printed, and none of the slips at the bottom have been torn off yet. Maybe if I'm quick enough, I could beat the other applicants.

I yank my cell phone out of my pocket and dial the number displayed.

"Because this apartment has just become available, the owner wishes to keep it on a month-to-month periodic lease," the real estate agent advises, moving toward the glass double door that opens onto a beautiful balcony.

"Okay, that's fine."

A month-to-month basis suits my requirements perfectly. In my line of work, I can't commit to anything permanently, not even a relationship. *Well, that's a somber thought.*

"All appliances are supplied with the apartment, and you'll have access to a laundry downstairs."

I nod, acknowledging I've heard her as I wander around the apartment. The living area is large and would comfortably fit two double sofas. The kitchen is compact but is adeptly equipped with a range of high-end stainless-steel appliances.

All the rooms have ample natural light, and the master suite has a walk-in closet, but the one thing that stops me in my tracks and makes my heart flutter is the clawfoot bathtub in the main bathroom. I could imagine spending hours soaking in there after a long day at work or dancing.

"Will you require an application package?" the real estate agent queries.

"And that's the very last box." Harlow plops onto my red suede sofa while blowing her hair out of her eyes.

We've spent the majority of our morning moving into my new apartment. Because I was miraculously the sole applicant, my application was approved the next day. After paying a deposit and one month rent in advance, I picked up the keys the following morning, but with Alex's stringent work regime, I've only moved in now, three weeks later.

"Can you smell that?" Harlow eyes me curiously while taking in a large whiff through her nose. "That's the smell of freedom!"

I giggle at her comment, even though she's accurate. I love Regina. She's like the mother I never had, but no self-respecting twenty-five-year-old likes living with their mother. Although I rarely have the opportunity to go out on dates, it's nice to know I can invite private companions to my residence if I want to. *Why was Isaac's face the first one to pop into my head during that thought?*

Harlow returns my head from the clouds. "Speaking of freedom, did you get your hard-ass boss to give you the long weekend off?"

"Yes."

It was as painful as pulling teeth, but after groveling, begging, and pleading, Alex let me have the long weekend off on the condition I work the next four weekends in a row.

"Where are we going again?"

Harlow has nagged me the past three weeks to get the weekend off, but whenever I ask her where we're going, she only responds with, "It's a secret."

Harlow's eyes dart to mine. If looks could kill, I'd be dead right now. When I stick my tongue out, her face morphs into her adorable smile. Harlow rises from the sofa and saunters to a box of mismatched kitchen accessories.

"What are you looking for?" I question, just as she pulls two coffee mugs out of the box.

"We need something to wash down this overpriced bottle of champagne with." She raises the bottle of champagne that was sitting on my doorstep this morning.

When I saw the bottle, my heart leaped. Although it still raced when I read the card, it wasn't as fast as when I discovered the bottle. It was lovely of Cormack to send me a housewarming gift, but when I spotted the bottle sitting on my doorstep, I presumed it was from Isaac.

"Do you think we should drink it?"

I don't know much about champagne, but considering this one has Dom Perignon written on the label, I'd say it's expensive.

Harlow doesn't grace me with a reply. She merely pops open the bottle of champagne and pours us both a generous helping into a pair of dirty old mugs.

"To freedom and expensive bottles of champagne," she says showily, handing me a chipped mug.

"To freedom." I take a mouthful of the delicious aromatic champagne.

And to finally being able to entertain special guests.

CHAPTER 16

Four weeks later...

"*B*randon." My greeting is drenched with sugary, sappy sweetness.

Prancing my way over to Brandon, I prop myself onto his wooden desk covered with files and blacked-out documents. When his apprehensive hazel eyes lift to mine, I flutter my lashes and purse my lips. To add even more allure to my intricate ruse, I undo the top button of my blouse, daringly exposing a portion of my cleavage scarcely contained in my white lace bra.

I fan my flushed cheeks. "It's so hot today," I sigh, fighting the urge to cringe.

I've never been good at flirting, and this is by far my worst attempt at seducing somebody.

Brandon gulps as his gleaming eyes rake my body, stopping at my undone button for an appreciative glance before reaching my eyes. His mischievous eyes glimmer with skepticism.

"What do you want, Izzy?" His mouth curves into a vast grin.

I huff. "What gave it away?"

"The greeting was okay. It gained my attention, but you lost me on unbuttoning your shirt and saying it was hot today," he critiques me. His eyes lower to my undone button before they return to my face. "You do realize summer is over, don't you, Isabelle?"

"Ha ha."

Brandon light-heartedly growls when I button my blouse back to a more respectable level, soothing the sting my ego took from my botched attempt at seducing him.

"So, what brought you strutting over to my desk?"

Air whizzes between my teeth. "I wasn't strutting."

"You were strutting. The hips were swinging, and you had an extra spring in your step. Total strut," he teases me.

My lips tug higher on my face. Obviously, my ruse wasn't that ineffective.

"I'm glad you took such detailed notes of my performance."

When I close my fist and punch Brandon in the bicep, he chuckles before rubbing his arm. Brandon isn't as built as some of the other male agents, but I have no doubt he can hold his own. People are less suspicious of the smaller guy, unaware they're usually the ones who pack the hardest punch.

My anxious eyes dart around the room before returning to Brandon's. "I need a favor."

"Anything," he replies without a moment of reluctance.

"I need access to a sealed file from the DA's office in New York."

His eyes meet mine. His brows are furrowed, and his gaze is troubled.

"I can't, Izzy."

"Please, Brandon, you know I wouldn't have asked you if it weren't important."

From the personal stories Brandon has shared with me about his life, I can comprehend his hesitation, but I need access to this file for my ongoing private investigation on Hugo. Because the Bureau is focusing their investigation solely on Isaac, they're missing several essential elements that warrant Hugo receiving his own investigation.

The only shred of evidence I've gathered on any Hugo Marshall in the country is a sealed court file for his sister, Marjorie. It's sealed so tightly shut, not even an FBI agent can access it.

"I haven't had any contact with her in years, Izzy. She'll probably hang up the instant she hears my voice."

My eyes plead with Brandon's. Without this file, I'll have nothing on Hugo, and my investigation will become stagnant. I can't let this go as my intuition is telling me I need to follow this lead.

Brandon scrubs his hand down his face. When his eyes return to mine, they're no longer brimming with mischievous. They're tentative and apprehensive.

"I'll try, but I can't guarantee I'll be able to get the file for you."

Childishly squealing, I sling my arms around his shoulders. "Thank you, Brandon, thank you."

"You're welcome."

When I pull away from our embrace, which has gained us the attention of our fellow officers, I notice Brandon's cheeks have turned pink.

"It will cost you, though."

I eagerly nod. I'll accept any meaningless task to get my hot little hands on that file.

"I need you to do a search on this lady." I snatch the record he's holding out for me while nodding. "And you have to go on a date with me."

My wide eyes shoot to his. Confusion clusters in my mind on why guilt is the first thing clouding my judgment. In the past four months, I've only seen Isaac a handful of times, but he's always in the forefront of my mind. I'm also shocked. Brandon hasn't asked me out on a date in months. I assumed he either got the hint or another lady caught his eye.

"One date, Izzy, that's all I'm asking."

Ignoring the ridiculous notion there's any type of relationship between Isaac Holt and me, I murmur, "Okay, but it will have to be after I return. I'm going away with Harlow this weekend."

He nods as a grin stretches across his handsome face, easing my uncertainty. He's a wonderful guy, and he's been nothing but kind to me since I arrived, so I ought to be thankful someone like him is interested in me, not apprehensive.

"Why don't you come to my apartment, and I'll cook dinner?"

Brandon smiles a full-toothed grin. "Sounds great."

Returning his smile, I open the manila folder he supplied me with. There are numerous surveillance photos of a lady with shoulder-length brown hair. She's of medium build, and I'd guess her age to be mid-twenties. She's attractive, but there's something about her that makes me want to cringe.

"Who's this lady?"

Brandon shrugs. "We don't know. We've noticed her a few times hanging around the nightclub the past several weeks. We believe she may be a companion of Isaac's."

My stomach recoils from the way he says 'companion.' No wonder I got a peculiar feeling when I glanced at her photos.

"I haven't seen Isaac with a girlfriend the entire time he has been under surveillance, but this lady has been in the picture a lot more regularly than his standard dates, so she may be someone significant in his life."

"All right, I'll see what I can find out about her," I reply, ignoring the harsh bitterness rising to my throat.

It wasn't difficult to track down Isaac's mysterious companion. She was photographed several times sitting in a yellow vehicle in the parking lot of his club. Just entering her license plate into the FBI database gave me access to her driver's license details.

Megan Patricia Shroud is twenty-six years old and lives in a country town four hundred miles from Ravenshoe. She's unmarried and has no next of kin reported on her driver's license.

I expand my search on Megan, more out of curiosity than necessity. When my eyes glance down at my cell phone vibrating on my desk, a grin furls my lips when I discover a text from Harlow.

Harlow: *Champagne is chilled, wine glasses are ready, and my bag is packed. I just seem to be missing one essential element???*

After jumping up from my seat, I snare my jacket from the back of the chair. I snatch the print-out of Megan's license, then make a beeline to Alex's office, passing by Brandon's desk on the way to hand him Megan's details.

"Thanks, and have fun," he shouts as I bolt by.

Alex's eyes lift from the documents he's scrutinizing when I tap on his office door.

"I just wanted to let you know I'm heading out for the weekend." I apprehensively step into his office. "I also wanted to say thanks for letting me have this time off."

Even though I had to grovel, he did have a legitimate reason to refuse my request. I've only been a part of his team for a little under five months, and I've already put in a request for vacation, so I'm grateful he accepted my pleas.

"It's fine, Isabelle." The sternness of his tone doesn't match his words.

"Bye," I murmur when his eyes resume perusing the documents in his hand.

Just as I'm about to exit his office, Alex calls my name. Cautiously, I pivot back around to face him.

"Make sure you keep your phone on you. If we need you, you'll have to return from your trip early."

Smiling, I nod and walk out of his office. "Like filing and scanning can't wait until I return."

I pull my cell phone out of my pocket to return Harlow's message.

Me: *Pop that cork. I'm on my way!*

CHAPTER 17

"I'm not taking it."

I remove my microscopic bikini from my suitcase for the third time in the past thirty minutes. Every time I turn my back, Harlow places the minuscule scraps of material back in against my wishes.

"Trust me, you'll want that bikini." She over accentuates the words 'trust me.'

She cocks her sculptured brow as she holds my tiny black string bikini out in front of her, pleading for me to take it. I've already packed a swimsuit, but it covers a lot more skin than my scant bikini does. Harlow extends her arm, placing the bikini to within an inch of my hands, and executes her best puppy-dog eyes.

She smiles and murmurs, "Yes," under her breath when I confiscate the thin scraps of material from her hand and shove it into the side pocket of my suitcase.

I enter my walk-in closet in pursuit of a slip I can wear over my bikini. Harlow rolls her eyes when she notices me packing a Hawaiian print cover-up into my overstuffed suitcase.

Once I've finished packing my bag, I wheel it into the entryway in preparation for our departure.

A short time later, my intercom screeches through my apartment.

"Hi, come on up," I greet into the intercom.

Leaning over, I push the button to unlock the security door in the lobby. A massive buzz shrieks through my eardrums when the door latch is released. Dropping down to my knees, I refasten the zipper that just busted. My head clusters with giddiness from my sudden movements. I probably shouldn't have mixed Xanax with champagne, but when Harlow said we were flying, I knew I needed something to take the edge off my fear.

"I'll get the door, shall I?" Harlow suggests when she notices me wrangling with the stubborn zipper on my bag.

I nearly choke on my spit when she swings the door open, revealing the awe-inspiring visual of Isaac Holt.

Oh God. Please tell me he's just popping in for a random visit. I can barely survive being in the same room with him for ten minutes, so I stand no chance in hell of being in his vicinity an entire long weekend.

My eyes rocket to Harlow, who's greeting Cormack more intimately than a regular friend would.

So that's where she has been vanishing to the past several weekends?

Isaac gazes down at me before smirking. If the lust in his eyes is anything to go by, he appreciates the visual of me kneeling in front of him. The yearning to crawl toward him overwhelms me. I'm a strong and independent woman, but the idea of kneeling for a man as powerful and authoritative as Isaac makes my core clench.

"Isabelle."

The way it rolls off his tongue makes me wonder how it would sound in ecstasy. Would it be as deep as it sounds now or more breathless and ragged?

When he stops in front of me, I raise my eyes to his, admiring his muscular physique on the way. Although he's no longer smirking, the expression on his face makes my heart race.

He pinches the material covering his thighs before crouching down next to me. Air sucks from my lungs when his deliriously handsome face comes to rest in front of me. "If we were alone, you wouldn't be moving from that position."

I throw my dignity out the window by pleading for him to make true on his threat with nothing but my eyes. His eyes dance between mine before he stands and extends his hand, offering to assist me off the ground.

After whining, I accept his gesture. Electricity shoots up my arm when he curls his masculine hand around mine. The rush of dizziness I was experiencing earlier returns full pelt, but it's not the Xanax causing my light-headed wooziness. It's the incredibly attractive Mr. Isaac Holt.

"Are you ready?"

Cormack's eyes dart down to Isaac's hand clasped around mine. Upon noticing the direction of Cormack's gaze, Isaac drops my hand quicker than a cake would disappear at a Weight Watcher's convention. When he gathers my suitcase off the ground and strides into the corridor, I stray my eyes to Harlow, who's gawking at me with waggling brows.

"You have no idea what you've done," I whisper, wanting to ensure Isaac doesn't overhear my statement.

"You're welcome." She curls her arm around my waist to drag me into the corridor.

I squirm in my seat the entire drive to the airport. Not just because Isaac's intense gaze hasn't stopped since I sat across from him or the fact I'm petrified of flying, but because I'm terrified of spending the entire long weekend with the man seated across from me. Terrified is a strong word, but the way my body reacts to Isaac and how all rational thinking ceases to exist when he's in the same room as me is genuinely terrifying.

No one should have that type of control over another, let alone a man I barely know. He doesn't need to touch me, and my body teeters close to ecstasy. My heart skips a beat every time his eyes assess my body, and just hearing the profound rasp of his voice makes my sex throb. *Imagine how much harder the battle will be once he gets close to me?*

I take a calming breath before stepping out of the stretch limousine. The instant my feet hit the blacktop and my head rises, my first thought is to run.

My hasty getaway is foiled when I crash into a rock-hard chest. "The plane is that way." Isaac points behind me.

I swivel my head, gulp, then resume my quick exit. Isaac chuckles at my reaction. Even though it's a chuckle I've only heard escape his mouth a handful of times, it doesn't warrant enough interest to stop me from fleeing. That plane he's pointing at is *NOT* a plane, it's a sardine can. I barely survive getting on a commercial-size aircraft, so there's no chance I'll board a plane that looks like it came from a child's toy box.

I already have one foot back in the limo when Isaac seizes my wrist, halting my quick exit. Inhaling a lung-filling gulp of air, I raise my fretful eyes to his.

"I can't get in that plane," I contest.

My eyes convey to him this isn't a ploy to gain his attention. I'm seriously terrified.

The longer I gaze into his eyes, the more my irrational panic pacifies. He runs his spare hand down my heated cheek. When his thumb brushes across my parched, gaped lips, a shallow moan escapes my mouth.

When he takes a step backward, I take a step forward, not wanting the intangible string between us to be snapped. He runs his thumb over my hand, gripping his so tightly, my nails dig into his flawless skin, then he takes another step backward. Before I know it, we're standing at the bottom of the stairs leading up to the galley of the toy plane.

Isaac stands behind me. He's so close, his impressive manhood braces my curvy backside.

"Are you coming, Isabelle?" he whispers in my ear, his words laced with a sexual undertone.

I gulp even louder than I did when I saw the plane. Clenching my hands at my side, I climb the stairs into the private jet. My knees knock together with every step I take, but it isn't from fear—it's to calm the rampant tingling sensation coursing through my body.

I plop into the first plush white leather two-seater sofa I stumble upon in the galley. Ignoring the elegantly decorated surroundings, I search in vain for my seat belt. My panic surges when my hands come up empty. *Oh my God, where's the belt?*

Isaac stoops down in front of me and lurches his hands into the back of the leather chair. My pulse quickens when his hands brush past portions of the bare skin on my thighs. He produces the belt and fastens it around my waist. Flashbacks of him doing the same thing months ago rush into my brain, along with the forbidden scenes of our hot and explicit kiss in his car weeks ago. My cheeks flame as undeniable lust overwhelms me.

Raising my lust-filled eyes, I'm confronted with Isaac's pussy-clenching gaze. His mouth curves into a sensuous smirk, and he winks before turning his attention to Cormack. They utter something to each other before Isaac takes the seat next to me. I raggedly pant when the plane jerks forward.

"If you need me to carry you into the bedroom, just let me know."

My eyes snap to Isaac's. "There's a bedroom?"

Smiling, he gestures his head to a polished door located at the back of the plane.

"I'll give you a private inspection later." He winks seductively.

Gulping, I swallow the lump sitting in my throat.

When Isaac places his palm on my thigh, I nearly vault out of my chair. Smiling at my skittish response, his index finger traces a figure-eight design on my bare skin. His meekest touch keeps my mind absent of any thoughts not associated with him.

Although my body is screaming for him to shift his finger a few inches higher, never once does his touch switch to being disrespectful.

He doesn't need to move his fingers, though. My imagination is wondrous. Images of his fingers running along my naked body, gripping, probing, and exploring me makes my daydream vividly graphic.

It also proves without a doubt that sexual endorphins can overrule fear-inducing chemicals.

"You're getting better with flying. You didn't require nearly as much stimulation this time around," Isaac says once the plane is no longer ascending.

Biting my bottom lip, I try to hide my smile. Forever diligent, Isaac notices the curve of my lips. His captivating eyes don't falter from mine as he releases my bottom lip from my menacing teeth.

Tilting his head, he leans in intimately close to my neck. "Everything you just imagined, I'm going to do to your body tonight."

My core tightens when he licks my earlobe.

Holy crap!

I need to reel back in my shrewdness. I can't sleep with Isaac Holt. It's not just my reputation I'm putting on the line by conversing with him, it's also the impeccable reputation of my uncle, an impressive reputation that took him years to earn. My name is associated with his, and I can't shroud it in controversy.

"I have a boyfriend," I lie.

Isaac's eyes missile to mine. His lips are thin, his gaze furious and unyielding. He scrapes his hand across his unshaven jaw as his eyes scan my face, studying me in silence.

"I can tell by your eyes you're hiding something, Isabelle," he snaps, his tone stern and clipped. "But it isn't a boyfriend."

I should have known he'd see through my deceit. Isaac has eyes that can see straight through to my soul.

That, in itself, is a terrifying notion.

CHAPTER 18

*L*urching, I sit up, causing a rush of giddiness to cluster in my stomach. My disoriented eyes dart around the lavishly decorated room I've awoken in. *I really need to stop waking up in strange bedrooms.*

When my eyes shoot down, I sigh when I discover I'm wearing not only a short-sleeve shirt but also my bra and panties. My panicked gaze rockets to the side of the room when I hear a toilet flushing.

My heart stops beating as I freeze in fear. The hinges on the white panel door creak while opening. Groaning, I slump back onto the soft down pillow when Harlow prances into the room.

"Sleeping beauty finally wakes."

I grunt and throw my arm over my eyes to shelter them from the bright sunlight streaming through the thick, pleated curtains.

The king-size bed dips when Harlow sits on the edge. "Here, take these. They will help with your head," she suggests.

Her voice makes me wince when it screeches through my eardrums before clustering in my thumping head. Peering out of my left eye only, I spot her holding a full bottle of pain medication in one hand and a bottle of water in the other. A broad grin is stretched across her adorable face.

I scoot up the bed until I'm leaning on the plush black leather button-pressed headboard. Unscrewing the cap of the water, I swig down half the bottle with three headache tablets.

"Are you sure it was champagne in that bottle? My head is telling me a different story."

I feel more hungover now than I did when I downed cocktails like soda water three months ago.

"Yes, it was only champagne." She giggles. "But if you had mentioned you took Xanax, I'd have limited the number of glasses I allowed you to consume."

"Oh." *Now my pounding headache makes sense.*

"Yeah, oh. That's the best blackout concoction I know of." She grins and shakes her head.

"But oh... my... God, girl, you should've seen Isaac. He was all frantic and possessive when you wouldn't wake up. He wouldn't let anyone go near you, let alone touch you. It was h-o-t HOT. He only settled down when Cormack discovered the bottle of Xanax in your purse, and I explained we were drinking champagne before we left."

"Cormack went through my purse?" My mind frantically strives to remember if I placed my FBI identification in there.

"Yeah." Her mischievous eyes stare into mine.

"Harlow?" My tone is low, demanding further explanation.

"They also found your strip of condoms."

"I don't have condoms in my. . ."

Oh shit. Yes, I do.

"They're an old stash. I haven't used them in months. I packed them when I went on vacation. They were an emergency stash. Everyone has an emergency stash. Just in case... in case—"

"You need to have sex in a bathroom thirty thousand feet in the air?" Harlow waggles her brows.

I slap her arm. Her giggles erupt into a fit of boisterous muscle-clenching, cheek-tightening laughter. Her legs and arms fling out as she flops onto the bed dramatically.

Once her infectious laughter calms down, her eyes, glistening with tears, lift to mine.

"What was Isaac's reaction to the condoms?" Curiosity echoes in my tone.

Harlow leans over and clenches my hand in hers. Her eyes bore into mine. It's the most serious I've ever seen her.

"He growled. Not a dainty pussycat roar. He full-on growled a sexy-as-sin growl. Then he scooped you into his arms, and that's where you stayed until he laid you on this bed." Her eyes gloss over with excitement.

Upset I missed hearing Isaac's sexy-as-sin growl, a ping of disappointment twists in my chest.

"He only left thirty minutes ago because he had some business calls to attend to. He made me promise I wouldn't leave your side until he returned."

"What time is it?"

Harlow rises from the bed and paces toward the floor-to-ceiling windows on each side of the headboard. Grasping the burgundy and gold pleated curtains, she dramatically opens them to reveal a blinding stream of sunlight that makes my eyes wince in pain from the brightness.

"I slept all afternoon and night?" I ask, my mind a jumbled mess of confusion.

The plane was scheduled to land at three o'clock in the afternoon, but there's no doubt it's morning sunlight streaming through the window.

"Yep." The 'p' pops from her mouth.

She moves back to the bed, her face morphing from playful to taut with concern.

"Please don't leave me alone with them for that long again."

I initially giggle at her comment until I realize she's serious. Tilting my head, I arch my brow, requesting further information.

"Cormack and I have been on a couple of dates."

"I figured that part out when you rammed your tongue down his throat yesterday," I interrupt, my tone cheeky.

Harlow grins before continuing. "He's great, I like him, but I didn't realize he was... *this*."

Her hand gestures around our elegant surroundings. The room I've awoken in is massive, easily the size of a studio apartment. It's elegantly decorated with antique furniture and abstract paintings, giving it the distinct aura of wealth and superiority.

"First a stretch limousine, then a private jet, and now..." She stops mid-sentence, her brows scrunching. "I don't think calling this residence a mansion would be a justified response. I've already gotten lost three times this morning."

This time when I chuckle, she joins me.

"You won't be laughing when you get lost, and no one finds you for days."

"I don't understand the problem, Harlow. If you like him, and he likes you, why does it matter if he's rich?"

"He isn't just rich, Izzy. He's filthy rich, never-needs-to-work-a-day-in-his-life rich, and I own a bakery with books that spend more in the red than in the black," she responds forlornly. "I don't belong here."

"Harlow." I seek her gaze. "I saw you with Cormack yesterday before the limo and the private jet. You like him, so don't judge him on his wealth. Judge him on the man he is, the same man you greeted with jubilation yesterday."

"I do like him."

"Then that's all that matters. Ignore everything else because it doesn't matter. It's just static noise in the background," I encourage her. "If you like someone, throw everything else aside and worry about it later."

She nods as her lips tug high. I return her smile, happy I eased her uncertainty. She thrusts her hand in front of my body, startling me. I eye her curiously before accepting her offer of a handshake.

"Hi, Pot, I'm Kettle. It's a pleasure to meet you," she introduces herself, her tone cheeky.

Her loud, boisterous laugh booms around the room when I dive at her and knock her onto the bed to relentlessly tickle her ribs until she begs for me to stop. Our immature banter halts when the main entrance door opens with a creak. The pulse in my neck thrums when

Isaac strolls into the room looking ravishing in two parts of a three-piece suit.

His eyes rigorously study my face before wandering over my exposed body since my shirt has risen while I was tackling Harlow. Pulling my shirt down to a more respectable level, I scoot up the bed to lean against the headboard. I'm so entranced by Isaac, I don't notice Harlow sneaking out of the room until Isaac takes her place on the bed.

"How are you feeling?"

I smile. "I'm good."

"Did you take the tablets I left on the bedside table?"

He smirks when I nod. We sit across from each other in silence for several minutes. It's not awkward, it just feels right. He runs his hand over his head before his concerned eyes lock with mine.

"Do I need to be concerned that you have a problem with drinking?"

I smile, pleased he cares enough about me to be worried about my well-being.

"No, I don't have a problem with drinking. That champagne was the first drink I've had since the last time you took me home," I reply. "I knew we were flying, and I accidentally mixed medication with alcohol. My thumping head alone will ensure it will never happen again."

Trying to lessen the concerned scowl marring his handsome face, I ask, "Do I need to be concerned that you have a problem with taking inebriated women into your room and undressing them?"

He chuckles a scrumptious laugh that rumbles through to my core. I smile, loving that I can witness a side of him his FBI file fails to show.

"At least this time you let me keep my panties," I quip.

His chuckles stop as his eyes lift to mine. My pulse races when his tongue darts out to moisten his lips. Our kiss was weeks ago, but I can still recall how delectably sinful he tasted.

"I didn't take your panties last time, Isabelle," he corrects me.

Just my name rolling off his tongue has me chasing climax.

"You gave them to me."

That secures my fall into orgasmic bliss and places it safely back onto the ledge.

My confused eyes dart between his. "No, I didn't."

"Yes, you did," he interrupts. "When you found my... *trophies* other women had left behind, you removed your panties before shoving them into the drawer with the explicit remark it would be the only way I'd add your panties to my collection."

"Oh."

That does sound like something I'd do in a moment of drunken angriness. *So, my panties were in that drawer all along? Yuck!*

"No, Isabelle, your panties aren't in that drawer."

I really need to stop mumbling out loud.

Brazenly, I question, "Where are they then?"

Mortified by my bold question, my eyes seek anything that isn't Isaac's amused face. Sheets ruffling fills the awkward silence when he adjusts his position. The fine hairs on my body prickle when his warm breath flutters against my neck.

"They're in my *very exclusive* private collection."

A grin tugs my lips higher, pleased my panties are valuable enough to be added to Isaac's private collection.

"And unless you want to add another set of your panties to my collection, I suggest you have a shower, get dressed, then join the rest of us for breakfast."

Harshly gulping, my eyes flick to his. I stare at him in silence, contemplating his request. My eyes absorb every attractive feature of his striking face before I climb out of bed and walk toward the bathroom Harlow exited earlier. Isaac groans in frustration. That groan alone will warrant an icy cold shower.

CHAPTER 19

J just broke the world record for the quickest shower. Not just because I failed to put any heat into the water to lessen the excitement coursing through my body, but because I'm interested in finding out what had Harlow so rattled earlier. Once I throw on a pair of denim shorts and a short-sleeve shirt, I exit the elegant guest bedroom.

Holy crap!

If the hallway is this elegant, what's the rest of the house like? Leisurely strolling down the hall, I stop to appraise a range of beautiful oil paintings adorning the corridor. One painting captures my attention for a little longer than the rest. It's a beautiful self-portrait of Frida Kahlo. If it's an original—and I have no doubt it is—its estimated worth would be in the millions.

"She isn't my type," says a raspy voice in the distance. "The whole one eyebrow thing just doesn't cut it."

Turning my gaze to the voice, I'm met with a pair of light blue eyes brimming with mischief. His eyes offset a very handsome, preppy face. His blond hair is long enough the tips curl upward. He's wearing long, black board-shorts and a light blue tee that matches his eyes perfectly. A smile stretches across my face when I notice he's also barefoot.

Once his eyes finish studying me as eagerly as I pursued him, he winks.

"You, on the other hand, are very much my type." He struts toward me. "Colby McGregor." He offers me his hand to shake. "If I'd known you were out in the hall waiting for me, I would've awakened earlier."

A broad grin creeps onto my face from his playful banter. "Isabelle Brahn." I accept his handshake. "Is it an original?" I nudge my head to the painting.

"Uh-huh," he answers, not the slightest bit impressed he has a painting worth millions of dollars hanging on the wall in his corridor. "When my mom found out Madonna brought some of Frida's self-portraits, she had to get one, too." He shrugs. "If you think this one is impressive, wait until you see my favorite painting."

Placing his arm around my shoulders, he directs me down the impressively long hallway. When we reach the very end, he swivels me to face an oil painting displayed in an ebony frame.

A giggle erupts from my mouth when my eyes roam over the hideous painting in front of me. Seeing an unimpressed frown forming on Colby's face, I quiet my laughter and appraise the picture with more diligence. When I squint my eyes and tilt my head to the left, I can see the outline of a face.

"Is that you?" I try my hardest not to laugh.

"Yep. I figured if Freda could make millions selling self-portraits, I may as well give it a go."

"I hope you didn't quit your day job." I bite hard on my bottom lip to stop inappropriate chuckles escaping my lips.

The portrait is beyond revolting. It looks like someone painted a picture then threw a glass of water over it, but it's endearing his family framed his painting and displayed it just as proudly as the masterpieces worth millions of dollars.

"Maybe self-portraits aren't my thing. Maybe I need something more inspirational to paint," he remarks. His gaze turns from the painting to me, so he can run his glistening eyes over my body. "Maybe nudes are more my thing?" He gives me a cheeky wink.

"Jeez, Colby, could you lay it on any thicker?" interrupts a perky female voice. "Did you check if she was here with someone, or are you going to whip it out and pee on her leg before any other guy sniffs her?"

"I'm going to whip it—"

Before Colby can get his entire sentence out, his chest is slapped so hard it winds him, which stops his playful taunt mid-sentence.

"Hello, I'm Cate McGregor. Cate with a C. This douchebag's little sister," introduces a cute, petite blonde.

Cate is so short she'd be lucky to be five-feet tall. She appears several years younger than me. If I had to guess her age, I'd say late teens. She has platinum blonde hair cut in a daringly bold pixie design. Her small-framed body is dressed in a pair of tiny, fringed denim shorts and a pink bikini top. Cate has the aura that makes me want to befriend her.

"Hi, I'm Isabelle," I give her a friendly reply.

"Oh shit." Cate's inquisitive eyes dart between Colby and me. "Don't go there, Colby," she warns, staring into Colby's mischief-filled eyes.

Colby doesn't grace Cate with a reply, he merely chuckles a bois-terous laugh that bellows down the hall. Hearing his laughter, Cate narrows her eyes before securing my hand in hers. She guides me through various hallways, doors, and impressively large rooms. Harlow wasn't joking. This place is massive. I'm pretty sure I'll get lost trying to find my way back to my room.

The smell of freshly-baked bread and bacon becomes more prom-inent the farther we walk. When we enter a massive kitchen that looks like it belongs in a fancy restaurant, Cate relinquishes my hand and approaches an elderly Spanish-looking lady placing muffins into a woven basket sitting on the island bench.

The muffins aren't the only scrumptious-looking treats on display. Croissants, Danish pastries, donuts, bacon, eggs, fresh-cut fruit, and every possible thing you could think of is laid out. My stomach is rumbling, my hunger more rampant since I failed to eat dinner last night.

"Help yourself to anything you want," offers Cate, handing me a porcelain plate. "Once you're done, come join us outside."

She gives me a nudge with her hip before sauntering her way out a set of French doors at the side of the kitchen. I cram my plate with a range of scrumptious goodies before walking out to the patio.

I feel Isaac's smoldering gaze before I see him. He's seated at a table alongside an impressive grotto pool. He glances my way, and our eyes lock before his wander over my body. Once he has finished his robust inspection, he gestures for me to join him.

Smiling, I walk toward him, my body trembling with every step I take. My pulse strums faster when my eyes connect with his. His gaze is powerful and solely focused on me. My smile enlarges to a full grin when he pulls a chair out for me to sit.

"Thank you," I whisper graciously.

He eyes my plate with a roguish sparkle in his eyes. "Hungry?"

"Starving." My cheeks heat with embarrassment at my lack of dignity.

When he raises his coffee mug to his mouth, his Adam's apple bobs up and down in a sensual way. My hunger is no longer associated with food. I can't stop staring at the handsome features of his face.

When my stomach grumbles, Isaac commands, "Eat, Isabelle."

Turning my gaze away from him, so I can focus on something other than his captivating eyes, I'm surprised to notice Clara sauntering toward us. *What's she doing here? Is she here with Isaac?* She's wearing a black pleated pencil skirt and a ruffled, red silk sleeveless blouse. She looks extremely elegant compared to the way I've seen everyone else casually dressed this morning, everyone but Isaac.

"Isabelle, what a pleasure to see you again," Clara greets me in a friendly manner before leaning down to press a kiss to Isaac's cheek.

"Hi, Clara." I pull off a chunk of the chocolate croissant and pop it into my mouth.

Even though the croissant is delicious and my mouth salivated when graced with its presence, trying to swallow it is like eating cardboard. Clara has all but crawled onto Isaac's lap. Her arm is draped around his shoulders and she has perched herself on his suit-covered thigh.

Clara sneers as she lifts Isaac's coffee mug to her mouth. Her red-painted lips press against the rim where Isaac's lips were mere moments ago. It's the smallest gesture, but it has the most significant impact on my already faltering ego. *If they're this intimate in public, what are they like behind closed doors?*

Clara is beautiful, and with her aura of grace, she'd be an ideal partner for Isaac. I can't stop the wave of jealousy crashing through me, even though I have no right to be jealous. I have no reason to be jealous over a man I have no claim to, but I can't help the uncontrollable connection I feel when he's near.

No longer hungry, I leap from my chair. "Excuse me."

Isaac's hand shoots out to seize my wrist, then forcefully pulls me back into the wrought iron chair with a thud.

His darkened eyes lift to mine. "Eat."

His narrowed eyes don't leave mine until I take a large bite out of a bagel slathered with cream cheese. Clara tumbles to the ground when Isaac stands from his seat. She graciously regains her footing and runs her hand down her black skirt to smooth it back into place before moving in close to Isaac's side. Her glare is furious and solely focused on me.

"I'll be back in a minute."

When I nod, Isaac grasps Clara's hand and strolls to the French doors. I try to keep my focus on anything but Isaac and Clara, but like you can't tear your eyes away from a train wreck, my eyes continue to shift to them.

Isaac's arms cross in front of his well-defined chest, but his composure remains calm. Clara waves her arms frantically in front of her body, and she motions to me several times. Her face constricts with tautness, and her eyes well with tears.

I don't know how I missed it before, but now it's as evident as the sun shining in the sky. Clara has the same blonde hair, light blue eyes, and flawless beige skin, just like the rest of the McGregors I've met so far this weekend. Mr. and Mrs. McGregor must have a fascination with the letter 'C,' considering all their children were given names beginning with 'C.'

Clara's loud, exasperated huff echoes in the silence of the morning before she disappears through the French doors. I turn my attention back to my overflowing plate, pretending I wasn't spying on their private discussion.

When Isaac returns to our table, his sultry gaze locks with me, but he remains quiet. I try to ignore the massive elephant sitting in the room, but my quintessential need to know everything gnaws at my insides until I blurt out, "Have you slept with Clara?"

Isaac freezes with his coffee mug halfway between the table and his lips, his eyes drifting to me. His gaze is unyielding, and it would make most people quake in fear, but my thighs tremor in excitement.

His lips curve into a sly smirk. "Are you jealous, Isabelle?"

"No," I reply in exasperation.

His smirk turns into a genuine smile as his eyes study my face. "You have absolutely nothing to be jealous about."

"Stop skirting and answer the question," I retort, ignoring my inward scream that's delighted by his compliment.

He shakes his head. "No, Isabelle, I have not slept with Clara."

I try to hide my smile, but my inner vixen is hollering too loud to conceal it.

"So, what was that about then?" I pop a piece of bagel into my mouth since my hunger has returned full force. "Because she was acting very much like she was your girlfriend."

"Do I need to call a lawyer?" Isaac's brow arches high. "Because this sounds a bit like an interrogation."

"Only people who have something to hide need to call a lawyer."

"I have nothing to hide." He cockily shrugs. "Because I always ensure my hands are thoroughly clean."

"Just because your hands are clean now doesn't mean they weren't stained previously."

"Just because your hands are clean now doesn't mean they won't become stained," he interrupts. "You don't know what the future holds, Isabelle. Nobody does. So, until the day your body is laid into its final resting place, you can't guarantee your hands will remain clean."

"Yes, I can. Morally and ethically—"

"What about for someone you love? You wouldn't get your hands a little bit dirty for someone you love?" he interrupts, his tone clipped and stern.

My brows scrunch as my eyes dart between his. Just being here this weekend abundantly proves what he's saying is true. I've only associated with Isaac a handful of times, and I'm already willing to risk my career just to be near him. So, imagine what I'd be prepared to do for someone I love.

"Not everything is black and white. There's a whole heap of gray no one pays any attention to," he utters before standing from his chair and striding back into the house, not once glancing back at me.

CHAPTER 20

I sense Isaac's presence before I see him. An aura like his permeates the air, and you can't help but be drawn to him. My eyes lift to his when he sits on the smidgen of the daybed that doesn't have my body sprawled on it. I've been lazing in the midmorning sun reading.

After dropping my Kindle on my face numerous times, I flipped onto my stomach and have been kicking my legs wildly into the air. I've been reading nonstop for the past two hours. Harlow and Cormack did invite me to go out to lunch with them, but I've never enjoyed being the third wheel on dates.

Isaac places his hand on my lower back and leans over my shoulder to peruse the book I'm reading. His touch could be classified as friendly, but my body reacts as if it's a sexual one. I haven't seen him since breakfast. I assumed he must have been agitated from our conversation this morning and was avoiding me, but the fact he's sitting so close to me, I'd say my assumption was wrong.

"Phew, I was getting worried it was another Mills and Boons book."

Smiling at his huff, I roll over to face him. Because he doesn't move his hand splayed on my lower back, it brushes past my hip bone and lands on the bottom half of my stomach when I roll.

The veins in my neck thrum as my pulse surges just from the sheer closeness of his god-gifted body. He's more casually dressed than he was previously, his muscular physique well-displayed in a tight-fitting white shirt and a pair of black running shorts.

When I spot a trail of sweat running down his cheek and detect the slight aroma of his delicious manly scent, I assume he must have just returned from a run.

"What are you reading?" His tempting purr makes my insides warm.

"*Thoughtless* by S. C. Stephens." I'm breathless from his close proximity. "It's about two people who shouldn't be together but are destined to be together. I've read the entire series three times already."

His brow arches high as his mouth etches into a firm line.

"You just don't understand the wondrous entrapment you feel when you read about a character like Kellan Kyle," I reply cheekily. "He's my number one book boyfriend."

His lips twist. "It's guys like him who make it hopeless for a man to date these days. All girls are expecting a guy like Kell—"

"Kellan Kyle."

"Yeah, and instead, they get a guy who comes home stinking of B.O. after working ten-hour-plus days. He drinks beer that smells like it was fermented in old college socks, and snores louder than the freight trains running through Philly."

My cheekbones lift as the grin spreads across my face. Even a rowdy giggle manages to escape my lips. I can't help but laugh. A man like Isaac Holt would never have to worry about being compared to a book boyfriend. A real-life man would have a hard enough time competing against him, let alone a fictional character.

Air snares in my throat from the intense look radiating from his exquisite eyes. My giggles halt as my body stiffens. When he remains quiet, I tilt my head and cock my brow in silent questioning.

His eyes appraise my face before he says, "That's the first time I've heard you laugh."

My cheeks inflame, and another grin furls my lips high. Our intimate gathering plummets into silence, but it isn't uncomfortable or awkward. It's electrifying. The intimacy bouncing between us is so sharp it feels as if we're being invisibly bound.

I sigh when he stands from the chair. I'm disappointed by his hasty retreat. My disappointment doesn't linger for long when Isaac thrusts his hand out in offering.

He pulls me up from the daybed. We stand across from each other with only the merest portion of air between us.

His enthralling eyes study my face before skimming my body. Once they return to my face, he smirks. "Did you pack a swimsuit?"

Unable to form a reply through my dry, gaped mouth, I nod.

"Go and get changed."

"Okay."

I reluctantly walk away from him.

I clench my fists at my side before begrudgingly turning around to face the full-length mirror in my room. I've spent the last ten minutes debating on whether I should wear the semi-indecent string bikini or the full one-piece suit I packed. Stupidly, I listened to my lust-fueled heart and put on the tiny bikini.

"Okay, it's not too bad."

No nipples are showing, and most of my breasts are covered. Turning around, I frown. There's more of my backside exposed than I'd have liked. My apprehensive eyes dart over to my hideous Hawaiian print cover-up and my more conservative suit.

Before my rational thinking head overrules my naughty inner vixen, a knock sounds at my door. Panicked, I yank my denim shorts up my legs before advising my caller they can enter. Time slows to a snail pace when Isaac walks into the room wearing nothing but a pair of swim trunks.

Holy shit!

His body is just as good, if not better than I'd remembered. I gulp harshly, aiming to soothe my dry, scorched throat as my eyes absorb every spectacular muscle, dip, and plane of his perfect body. His eyes assess my body just as thoroughly, and my insides cheer when a broad smile etches on his face.

No words escape either of our lips as he encases my hand within his and walks us toward the expansive beach that stretches each way for miles. Although it's Fall, the weather is beautiful, and my shoulders happily absorb the warm sun.

Once we reach a wooden shed attached to a jetty, Isaac releases my hand to gather a short-sleeved wetsuit and a life jacket from inside.

When he returns, he clutches my hand in his and guides us down to the end of the wooden jetty. Excitement rushes through my body when I notice two Wave Runners tied to the end of the pier. I've always wanted to ride a jet ski.

He dumps the life jacket on a wooden bench before demanding, "Strip."

I eye him curiously, unsure of what he means. I'm barely clothed as it is. His brazen gaze darts down to my denim shorts. Cringing, I slide my shorts down my quivering thighs, which are shuddering from Isaac's intense gaze as he watches me. Once my shorts are removed, he crouches down in front of me to assist me into the wetsuit. Images of me kneeling in front of him yesterday morning come flashing back into my mind. Even though it was less than twenty-four hours, it seems like it was a lifetime ago. I shake my head to clear my thoughts before placing my feet into the tight openings of the wetsuit.

It takes several pulls and yanks to get the rigid material of the wetsuit up my thighs and over my stomach. During the process, his hands brush across my inner thighs and stomach. Every fine hair on my body bristles as my sex pulsates with desire. Isaac inhales loudly before his eyes lift to mine. My breathing shallows from his commanding gaze. He winks before continuing to pull the wetsuit up and over my shoulders. By the time he has the wetsuit zipped, my rampant horniness is teetering on the edge, threatening to fall at any moment.

"Do you want to wear a lifejacket?"

Unable to form words, I shake my head.

When Isaac straddles the Wave Runner, the muscles in his arms flex, and an unexpected, bold moan spills from my lips. Hearing my shameless response, his lips tug high before he offers me his hand. The muscles in his stomach clench when I band my arms around his waist. I let out an excited squeal when our Wave Runner darts away from the jetty.

The past forty-five minutes have been pure torture. Every jolt the Wave Runner does makes my sex convulse. My barely-covered chest is squashed against Isaac's naked back, and my erect nipples scrape his smooth skin as they bounce along with the movements of the Wave Runner. My bikini is so thin it feels like I'm naked under my wetsuit, so my vivid imagination is getting carried away.

A sense of reprieve washes over me when the visual of the jetty comes over the foreshore. Having Isaac so close and fighting not to touch him is the worse form of cruelty. I adjust my position to lessen the immense tingling sensation running rampant through my body. My thighs tighten around his hips when he yanks me back in close to him until my chest is once again plastered to his back, and my pussy is rubbing his backside. We're so close, not an ounce of space remains between our bodies. Not even air exists between us.

Excitement sparks through my body when every feeble movement I make causes his muscles to contract. Something in the air shifts when I stop fighting the Wave Runner's actions to allow my hands to slither the ripples of his stomach. My pulse thrums in my fingertips when I run them along his six-pack. My lengthened breaths indicate I'm treading into dangerous territory, but I can't stop myself. My body's needs, desires, and cravings are outweighing my shrewdness.

A raspy groan escapes Isaac's lips when my index finger glides over the fine hairs on his perfect V muscle. His gruff moan spurs on my pursuit as my impending climax overrules rational thinking. My breaths rebound off his shoulder before the lash of my tongue cools his salty, sun-scorched skin.

His grip on the handlebars tightens when my hand glides into the rim of his shorts. My thighs quake when my fingertips graze his swollen cock that's struggling to be contained in his black shorts.

The Wave Runner stops surging forward when I curl my hand around his shaft. Although I'm being spurred on by a massive surge of brazenness, I freeze, hesitant from my boldness. I want to touch him more than my lungs crave air, but should I be doing this?

Sensing my hesitation, Isaac curls his hand over mine to guide it up and down his impressively large shaft. His rhythm is fast enough to be pleasurable but slow enough, he won't come anytime soon.

"Just like that, baby," he breathes out, his words thick and raspy.

When he releases my hand from his grasp, I slide it up and down his veined cock in the rhythm he demonstrated. He groans when my thumb runs over his knob to gather a bead of pre-cum formed there. I use it as lubrication to quicken my strokes. My seamless pumps have his body coiling tight, racing toward release at a record-setting pace.

Slithering my spare hand into his shorts, I cup his balls, squeezing and kneading them. When his breath catches in his throat a short time later, I know he's close to climax.

"Fuck, Isabelle."

The sexy roughness of his voice has my climax hovering toward the edge. It usually takes a lot more stimulation to make me come, but hearing his gruff moans have my orgasm teetering on the brink. Once he topples into ecstasy, I'll be right alongside him.

My eyes pop open when Isaac's hand suddenly stills mine. I groan as my insides scream, demanding their release.

Lifting my gaze, I discover what caused his swift reaction. Colby is on a Wave Runner heading toward us, his speed unchecked. When I attempt to pull my hands out of Isaac's shorts, he seizes my wrist and holds it in place. I squeeze his cock hard, trying to force him to relinquish my hand. My sex gets wetter when his cock twitches in response to my painful squeeze.

Colby pulls his Wave Runner close to ours. "Are you guys okay? Are you out of fuel?"

"We're a little busy." Isaac's tone is arrogant.

Cocking a brow, Colby assesses my face. I'm sure my flushed expression and wide eyes will clue him in on why we're busy, but instead of being angry at what he's just stumbled upon, he grins and winks.

My brows scrunch as a mask of confusion slips over my face. *How is he not as embarrassed as me?*

Colby throws a rope to Isaac. "Here, let me tow you back."

"We don't need a fucking tow." Isaac clutches the rope and throws it back to Colby.

Since Isaac has relinquished my wrist from his hold, I remove my hand from his shorts.

"Come on, Isaac, everyone needs a hand every now and again," Colby remarks with sarcasm.

Overcome with embarrassment, my gaze drifts to anything but Colby's cheeky face. He chuckles at my response, his laughter echoing in the uncomfortable silence now plaguing our group.

"I'm just joshing with you, Isaac. Don't be so riled up all the time," Colby quips.

Instead of replying, Isaac tightens his jaw.

"I just came out to tell you Henry Gottle is here to see you," Colby informs him.

Isaac curses under his breath. "I forgot about an important meeting with him."

Assuming he's talking to himself, I don't bother replying.

"Thanks, Colby, tell him I'll be there in a few minutes."

With a final flirty wink, Colby's Wave Runner whizzes back to the jetty. Once he's out of eyesight, Isaac pivots around to face me. My cheeks flush with heat when he places a kiss on my palm.

"We'll finish this later."

Since it's more a statement than a question, I don't grace him with a reply.

The ride back to the jetty is made in complete silence. My orgasm that was racing toward the brink has been secured and locked away. My excitement vanished the instant Colby mentioned Henry Gottle was here to see Isaac. I was tempted to ask Colby if he meant Henry Gottle, the third, or his father, the suspected mob boss of New York City. Luckily, my levelheadedness resurfaced before that question seeped from my lips.

Even knowing he has a guest waiting for his arrival, Isaac assists me out of my wetsuit. Once it's dumped on the wooden jetty, he clasps my hand in his before striding toward the main house. When we round the corner of the vast verandah, we're greeted by a gentleman in his early thirties with inky black hair. I'm somewhat surprised at how attractive he is. Anytime I think of the mob, my thoughts stray to wrinkled, overweight men with moles on their faces.

"Henry, sorry I forgot about our meeting." Isaac's tone exudes authority and reveals he's the alpha male in the room.

"That's fine, Isaac." Henry's eyes turn to face me. "I can understand your forgetfulness."

Isaac's gaze narrows when he notices Henry's eager judgment of my body. When Henry spots Isaac's stern glare, he diverts his amused gaze back to Isaac.

"Isabelle, this is Henry Gottle, a business associate of mine," Isaac introduces.

"I would have said long-time friend, but I guess business associate will have to do," Henry replies coolly.

Accepting the handshake Henry offers, my eyes bounce between Isaac and Henry. It's hard to tell if they're friends or business associates. Isaac is more reserved around Henry than he is with Cormack, but he seems more laid back than he appeared in surveillance photos with his real business associates.

"I may have said friend if I weren't left handling the repercussions of your wretched wife," Isaac interjects. Although his tone is serious, it still has an edge of wittiness to it.

"Try living with her," Henry grumbles. "Three years I had to put up with that."

Isaac and Henry shudder at the same time before they chuckle full-heartedly.

I take it neither of them are fans of Henry's ex-wife, Delilah Winterbottom?

"Well, I got her out of your hair, and now I'm calling in those chips," Isaac advises.

Henry's eyes shoot to mine. His uneasy gaze reveals his concern about me being present during their private conversation.

"I'll go and grab some lunch."

I smile when Isaac says, "If you want to stay, Isabelle, you can stay."

"It's fine, I'm famished anyway."

I also don't want to run the risk of unearthing anything I may be forced to disclose to the FBI. I'd never intentionally spy on Isaac in private, but I did swear an oath to uphold the law, and if I stumbled upon something significantly illegal, it would be my moral obligation to inform the authorities. *Wouldn't it?*

My worry settles when I overhear a portion of Isaac's statement as I'm exiting the room.

"I need you to find a loophole in the UFC, so my fighter, Jacob, can fight a current UFC contender."

CHAPTER 21

For the past half an hour, Cormack, Harlow, and I have been seated at an elegant Italian steak restaurant. The restaurant is a hive of bustling activity, but with the hum of conversations, laughing, and cutlery scraping against plates, it's difficult for me to participate in any discussions being held across the table. The conversation between Harlow and Cormack is engaging, but it doesn't seem appropriate for three unless you're into that type of thing.

"Thank you," I say in appreciation when the waiter hands me a black and gold embossed menu, grateful for the distraction. *I should have listened to my intuition. I've always known being the third wheel on dates isn't fun.*

When I scan the prices on the elegant menu, I nearly fall off my chair. Every entrée listed costs more than I make in an entire day. Gnawing on my bottom lip, I ignore the pang of hunger rumbling in my stomach and order the most inexpensive item I can find on the menu—a side serving of salad.

"*E per il vostro corso principale?*" the waitress questions.

"I'm sorry, I don't speak Italian," I reply, praying she can understand English.

SHANDI BOYES

"She's asking what you would like to order for your main course," advises a ruggedly sexy voice.

Isaac's scrumptious aroma engulfs my senses the instant he slides into the seat next to me. My breath hitches when he leans over and places a brief peck on my cheek.

"Sorry I'm late," he whispers into my ear. "I had some business I had to take care of."

This is the first time I've seen Isaac since our ride on the Wave Runner earlier today. I'm not sure if his meeting with Henry was for the entire afternoon or if he had other business matters to attend to. I tried to keep myself immersed in the world of Kellan Kyle, but my mind kept drifting to Isaac. My views on him have significantly swayed the past twenty-four hours. More so since I've yet to stumble on a shred of evidence that matches Isaac to the person his FBI file shows him to be.

"Do you know what you want?" he queries, interrupting me from my thoughts.

My hairs bristle when he runs his index finger down my arm.

"Umm... a side salad is fine." My voice trembles from his close proximity.

"She will have the 16-ounce steak with a baked potato and a side salad." Isaac hands her back my menu. "I'll have the same."

"I'm still full from lunch. That's why I ordered a salad."

He arches his perfect brow. "The half a club sandwich and few slices of pear you ate at lunch weren't adequate enough to skip dinner."

My heart rate doubles. *I may not have seen him all day, but he's clearly been watching me.*

"I can't afford two hundred dollars for a piece of steak." My cheeks heat in embarrassment.

His lips form into his panty-clenching smirk before he leans in intimately close to my neck. My thighs shake when his breath flutters along my neckline.

"How fast can you run in those heels?"

When my confused eyes dart to his, he winks before continuing,

"We either run before the bill arrives or wash dishes with Roberto for the next week."

He gestures his head to a gentleman sauntering his way back into the restaurant from a side alley. Roberto's white waiter's apron barely covers his vast waistline and is covered with food and red wine stains.

"I'll be sure to kick off these bad boys before our dessert arrives." I click my black pump heels together. "Hold on, how do you know his name is Roberto?"

He drapes his arm behind the back of my chair. "This is pretty. Did you do something different?" He tugs on the strands of hair cascading down my back, completely ignoring my question.

I smile while nodding. "Harlow curled the ends."

My grin enlarges over the fact he noticed the humblest change in my hairstyle. Isaac's eyes rake over my fitted, white wrap dress before lifting to my face. His gaze is hungry. It isn't a hunger for food.

"You look beautiful."

His voice causes a shiver to run through my body.

"Thank you," I reply breathlessly.

For the next two hours, I enjoy splendid food, wine, and even better company. Isaac has been the frankest I've ever seen him. From the stories he shared, I can easily perceive his fondness for his younger brother, Nick, and his excitement about becoming an uncle for the first time is also paramount. I feel privileged I've experienced a side of him not many people witness, and I've quickly become trapped in his incredible allure.

Isaac chuckles when I lean down and unbuckle the latch on my shoes when the waiter hands us the dessert menu. My heart leaps when he orders both of our dessert selections in fluent Italian. I'm impressed with his impeccable pronunciation and how effortlessly the words roll off his tongue.

"My nonna was Italian. She taught me to speak Italian fluently by the time I was eight," he responds to my curious glance.

"Are you close to your nonna?" I reach for my freshly filled wine glass.

"No, she passed away five years ago." He removes the wine glass from my hand and places it back on the table.

"I'm sorry," I sympathize as my gaze darts back to my full glass of red wine.

"You've already had three glasses."

"Yes, and I told you I don't have a problem with my drinking."

"You don't have a problem, but I do."

I cock my brow, requesting further information.

"I don't converse with drunk women."

He swivels his body, leaning in more intimately. I remain quiet, baffled by his statement.

"I don't converse *sexually* with drunk women," he clarifies, his unyielding eyes relaying his intentions.

Oh. My. God.

My pupils widen as a strong urge of desire runs through my body. The sexual charge between us is so strong, it crackles in the air.

My hand trembles when I accept the plate of tiramisu from the waitress, shamelessly exposing my arousal to Isaac's statement. Sensing my excitement, Isaac places his open palm on my bare thigh. His touch sends a jolt of pleasure to my throbbing sex. Now tiramisu is the last thing on my mind.

"Are you not hungry?" Isaac questions a short time later, eyeing my untouched dessert.

Brazenly, I reply, "I'm hungry, just not for food."

In a two-minute lusty haze, I've gone from being seated in the restaurant to sitting in the passenger seat of Isaac's car. I think I murmured a goodbye to Cormack and Harlow, but my body is coiled so tight, I've lost the ability to focus on anything but the incredibly alluring man seated next to me.

It has been over a year since I've had sexual contact with a man. It's been so long because my last bed partner squelched most of my desire. His ruggedly handsome face didn't quite match the rest of his body—his body hair was vast, thick, and stunk like a wet dog. Our two-minute tumble in his bed didn't create half of the spark I get from one glance of Isaac's entrancing eyes.

I'd only just finished unlatching my bra when the whole event was over. He murmured it was the greatest sex he'd ever had, rolled onto his side, then spent the five minutes it took for me to gather my clothing off the floor and dart out of his house snoring. From that day, I've been apprehensive about dating until I met Isaac.

Isaac curses under his breath when a cell phone shrills through the silence of his car. The monitor on his dashboard announces he has an incoming call from Hugo.

"What?" Isaac greets, his annoyance for the interruption heard in his tone.

"Sorry for the intrusion, boss, but we have a problem with 57." Hugo's tone conveys his genuine regret for the interruption.

"Send Patrick," Isaac snaps.

"I can't. He's away with his kids this weekend."

Isaac's eyes turn from the road to me. "What kind of problem?"

"The manager was vague, but he said he has some issues with a staff member issuing free drinks to his friends."

"Why the fuck can't the manager handle this type of situation?" Isaac interrupts, his tone stern.

His grip on the steering wheel tightens as the conversation continues. Hugo remains quiet. His ragged breaths shrilling down the line is the only reason I know he hasn't hung up.

"It's okay," I assure when I see the indecisiveness in Isaac's gaze.

"Oh, hey, Isabelle," Hugo greets, his tone cheeky.

My lips curve into a smile over the fact Hugo can recognize my voice from only hearing me speak two simple words.

"Hi." I bite my bottom lip.

"I'll take care of it," Isaac informs him before disconnecting the call without giving Hugo a chance to reply.

He leans over and frees my lip from my teeth. "Five minutes tops, and I'll be biting that lip."

Unable to speak through my parched mouth, I nod.

I've been waiting over five months, so what's another five minutes?

CHAPTER 22

$\mathcal{I}$saac's nightclub is located a few blocks over from the Italian restaurant where we were having dinner. It's a stylish looking club that screams sex and sensuality. That saying really does work—sex does sell, and Isaac is using it to his full advantage in his nightclubs. The club is packed with patrons, and the line to get in goes all the way down the block and around the corner. Upon entering the manager's office of his nightclub named 57, Isaac's eyes assess the room.

There are four people seated in the impressively large manager's office. Two male faces appear petrified, one male is smirking broadly, while the only other female in the room is glaring at Isaac's hand wrapped around mine.

"You're both fired," Isaac informs them, pointing to the gentleman with shoulder-length blond hair whose nametag says 'manager,' and to a twenty-something-year-old male staff member.

The manager attempts a remark, but the instant Isaac's livid eyes land on his, his mouth etches into a thin, straight line.

"If you can't handle a situation like this in-house, then you're not management material for my clubs," Isaac snaps.

"You." Isaac glares into the eyes of the employee caught stealing from him, "Will pay for any drinks you gave to your friends before you leave here tonight."

The employee's throat works hard to swallow as he nods.

"And if you ever step foot in any of my clubs again—"

"I won't," interrupts the employee, his short reply incapable of hiding his fear.

Isaac turns to face a brute of a man with a shaved head who is standing at the side of the room. He is massive. His bicep alone would be bigger than my head.

"Make sure he pays his bill before he leaves and be sure to add a *very* generous tip on his account for the bar staff."

The bouncer smiles while nodding. He heads for the employee, yanking him out of the chair he's sitting in by the scruff of his collar before dragging him out the door. Isaac relinquishes my hand and heads for the mahogany desk. His strides are effortless, yet commanding, making my pussy pulse with every step he takes. Watching Isaac in his element is a riveting experience. He's bossy, demanding, and sexy as sin.

When he reaches the desk, he yanks open the top drawer and removes a checkbook from inside.

"This will cover your severance." Isaac thrusts a torn-out check toward the manager.

Just as the manager is about to take the check, Isaac yanks it out of his grasp.

"Or perhaps the fact you're leaving here unscathed should be reward enough," he growls viciously.

Isaac crumples the check in his clenched fist before dropping it onto the desk.

His head shakes like a bobblehead toy. "Y-y-yes, thank you, boss."

He scampers out of the office, leaving the crumpled check untouched. The veins in my neck throb when Isaac's eyes run over my body before lifting to my face. Although most people would mistake his gaze as infuriating, I only see unbridled lust reflecting back at me.

"Come here, Isabelle," he commands.

His lips thin into a harsh line when I shake my head, denying his request. My eyes shift to the corner of the room where the female staff member remains, watching our exchange with her mouth ajar.

"Get out." My excitement intensifies when Isaac's gaze never once leaves mine as he orders her out of the room.

"Boss, while you're here, I wanted to ask…"

"Get out!" Isaac growls.

She nods before scurrying out of the room even faster than the manager did.

"Come here, Isabelle," Isaac demands again.

His tone is clipped, but it doesn't stop the tremor coursing through my body from my name rolling off his tongue. Although the sheer sight of him instigates wetness to pool between my legs, his gaze is unnerving. It has me pinned, unable to move.

Isaac mutters something under his breath before he moves away from the desk. He glides instead of walking as a mere man would. That's not surprising. Nothing about him could ever be seen as mere.

His strides don't slacken until I'm pinned between him and the heavy wooden door of the manager's office. The lash of his tongue on my gaped mouth causes my knees to weaken. His kisses convey his personality perfectly—powerful, alluring, sexy, and knee-buckling hot.

He cups my thigh with one hand to steady my swaying movements, while his other hand slithers over my dress until stopping at my neck to pull my mouth closer to his. His kiss is sumptuous and toe-curling good. It once again goes above and beyond my highest expectations.

I snake my fingers over the ridges of his muscular back before raking them through his hair. He groans a rattled moan. The sound alone almost causes me to combust.

His talented tongue soothes the sting of his bite before it glides along mine, stroking and absorbing my taste.

When he pulls away from our embrace, a whim escapes my mouth. I draw in a long and shaky breath when I open my eyes. His eyes are reflecting his torment, his internal battle.

I throw my dignity out the window. "Please."

Just the sensation of his fingertips probing the pressure points on the back of my neck and the skillfulness of his tongue and gifted mouth has me close to orgasmic bliss.

No longer capable of restraining myself, I thrust my pelvis upward. A rough moan erupts from my throat when my oversensitive pussy connects with Isaac's thick and lengthened cock. One expert roll of his hips has me throwing my head back and my eyes snapping shut.

He bites, nibbles, and caresses my exposed neck. His slow, purposeful movements lead him toward the region of my erratically panting chest. He jerks on the material holding my dress together, rendering it open, exposing my barely covered breasts. His eyes rocket to mine. They no longer show his torment and indecisiveness —they show his unbridled desire.

A smirk tugs on his lips when his index finger glides along the thin, white lace material of my bra. His finger feels rough and smooth at the same time. My mouth becomes parched when he releases my breast from its restrictive restraints and traps my erect nipple in his warm, inviting mouth.

After lavishing my breasts with his skilled tongue, he diverts his attention to underneath my breasts and across my stomach. He bites, sucks, and nibbles on my skin, making every hair bristle with attention.

His name rumbles from my throat in a ragged groan when the tip of his nose grazes my panty-covered clit. He chuckles a pussy-clenching laugh at the wail escaping my lips from him veering away from the one part of my body screaming for his attention.

Raking my fingers through his hair that's damp at the tips from the stifling heat in the office, I guide his head back to my weeping sex, which is begging for his attention.

"Patience, Isabelle." Isaac's gaze lifts to mine to wordlessly command my focus.

Unable to tear my gaze away, I watch him bite and suck on my right inner thigh. The sting of his teeth and the roughness of his five o'clock shadow brings a rush of excitement to my sex.

Usually, it takes dedicated attention to bring me to climax, but I'm so close to the brink right now, just the slight brush of his fingertip on my clit will have me free-falling.

Crouching down in front of me, Isaac guides my left leg onto his shoulder. My body is so lax, my movements are sluggish and slow. My toes curl when his nose runs along the seam of my panties. He inhales a vast, undignified whiff, not the slightest bit ashamed.

"You smell so fucking good."

I scream as an orgasm rips through my body so hard and fast, stars form in front of my eyes when he sucks my clit into his mouth through my lace panties. Although we're in public—and there's a possibility we could be exposed at any moment—I can't stop the moans erupting from my throat when Isaac slips my panties to the side to devour my drenching sex. The ability to control my body has been relinquished to the man who just caused it to implode with one heart-stopping suck.

Isaac's name spills from my mouth on repeat as the lashes of his tongue slowly guide me down from the most intense orgasm I've ever experienced. He consumes my pussy with dedicated sweeps and playful bites, not the least bit confronted I combusted within seconds of our exchange commencing.

Just as I rein in the uncontrollable shudders racking through my body, Isaac clenches my panties in his hand and shreds them off my body—their feeble material no match to his strength. He devours me without pause, his eagerness adding to the giddiness hazing my mind. The throaty moans he releases vibrate on my clit, intensifying the wetness between my legs.

"*Oh...*" I moan, stunned at how rapidly my second orgasm is building.

I lose the ability to hold up my weight when another toe-curling climax rockets through my body. The only reason I don't tumble to the floor is that Isaac has my thighs pinned to the door, stopping my concern. The ease of his hold makes it appear as if I'm as light as a feather.

After every shudder in my body has been exhausted, Isaac stands from his crouched position. My arousal glistens on his face as he narrows in to kiss me hard on my mouth. I can taste myself on his mouth when his tongue slides along my lips. He groans a sexy-as-sin growl that has my knees buckling when my tongue laps up my climax from his sinful mouth. He kisses me until I'm close to combusting a third time in under ten minutes.

When Isaac drags his mouth from my neck to my breasts, I throw my head back and call out. Spotting a blinking red contraption in the corner of the room, I snap my eyes shut, trying in vain to ignore that our every move is being monitored and possibly recorded.

It's an impossible task.

Forever diligent, Isaac senses my hesitance. After pulling away from our embrace, his confused, lust-filled eyes dart between mine.

"I want this," I assure without hesitation when I notice the forlorn look on his face. "I just don't want it recorded," I nudge my head to the camera.

Isaac curses, but the concerned expression on his face relaxes when he notices the camera in the room. *Did he seriously think I was rejecting him?* He's the most riveting man I've ever met. I'd never reject him. My body isn't capable of saying no to him.

If it isn't bad enough I just participated in raunchy foreplay in a manager's office of a bustling nightclub, having it recorded makes my embarrassment ten times worse. My stomach swirls just from the thought someone may be watching us right now.

"Can you get Hugo to turn the camera off?" My voice is husky from the erotic screams torn from my throat but also pleading.

My body is thrumming from the two toe-curling orgasms that just shredded through me, but I don't want our night to end just yet.

Isaac's mouth carves into a yummy smirk. "I could." His tongue darts out to lick his lips.

When his eyes darken, I know he can taste me on his mouth.

"But I want to fuck you in bed."

His rough tone vibrates through my soaked sex, impelling a throaty moan to spill from my lips.

"Because once I'm done with you, you'll no longer have the ability to walk straight."

I gulp, knowing without a doubt what he says is fact, not fiction. He barely touched me, and my orgasm was teetering on the brink, dying to break free.

Winking at the lust creeping across my cheeks, Isaac yanks his cell phone out of his pocket. "Hugo, I need you to wipe the images off the camera in the manager's office at 57 for the last hour."

His mouth seductively crimps. "Thanks, Hugo."

Disconnecting his call, he places his cell phone into his pocket along with my shredded white lace panties.

Not speaking, he disappears into the bathroom, only to return five seconds later with a washcloth. My clit throbs when he places the washcloth between my legs to clean me in a nurturing manner. The rough and abrupt Isaac from when we first arrived at the club is no longer in existence, replaced with an attentive and gentle lover.

With an impish grin on his face, he ties my dress back into place. I eye him curiously, studying him in silence for further information.

"Hugo turned the cameras off the instant he knew you were coming to the club with me," Isaac tells me, his smirk enlarging to a full-toothed grin. "At times, it's like he knows me better than I know myself."

My lips curve into a grateful smile. *The elusive Mr. Hugo is growing on me.*

Once I'm respectably dressed, sans underwear, Isaac clasps my hand within his and walks us out of the manager's office. Blaring music booms into my eardrums the instant we step out the door. The smell of sweat and sex lingers in my nostrils from the mass of bodies dancing under the warm, strobing lights.

Ignoring the shocked stares of the patrons in his club, Isaac weaves us through the densely populated dance floor. When the crowd sees Isaac coming, they part, giving us an unobstructed path to the front door of the club.

The cold night air is refreshing to my sweat-slicked face and neck when we merge onto the sidewalk. My thighs are still quivering, and

I'm exhausted, but my excitement on what's about to come enhances my eagerness.

Isaac's grip on my hand tightens so much I wince in pain when a heavy, profound voice says, "The prodigal son returns."

"Get in the car, Isabelle." Isaac releases my hand, spinning on his heels.

Ignoring his demand, I pivot around and come face to face with the non-stoic face of Col Petretti, suspected mob boss and the number twelve man on the FBI wish list.

Shit!

To Col's right is the man FBI believes to be his top henchman. He has been with Col for longer than I've been born, yet he still remains nameless. The FBI simply calls him Col's right-hand man. To Col's left is his youngest son, Dimitri. He does not yet have an FBI file, but they believe he's being groomed by Col to take over the family business.

Isaac glares at Col furiously, the twitching of his jaw so profound I can almost hear it ticking.

"What has it been... six years? And I don't even get a greeting from you." Col's words drip with sarcasm.

Isaac remains quiet with his fists clenched. The veins in his neck are protruding so far, they look like they're about to burst. When Col's depraved gaze assesses my body, my skin crawls.

Noticing the direction of Col's gaze, Isaac pulls me in close to his side. When Col sees Isaac's protecting gesture, he inhales a large, undignified whiff through his nostrils, mocking Isaac, pretending he can smell his fear.

Isaac's angry eyes glare at Dimitri. When Dimitri's gaze drops to his polished black shoes, Isaac sniffs back. Col follows Isaac's gaze to Dimitri, his jaw ticking and nostrils flaring when he notices Dimitri's passive stance.

"Go!" Col's loud voice rumbles through the bustling side street.

Dimitri's eyes lift from the ground and shoot to his father. He appears to be considering a response. I wait with bated breath. From what I've read in Col's file if Dimitri denies his father's command, his punishment will be severe, favorite son or not. I expel the breath caught in my throat when Dimitri does as commanded and walks away from our group.

The sting of Isaac's fingers on my hip firms when Col steps toward us, stopping in front of me. His eyes scan my flustered, post-orgasmic face.

"You're exquisite." Col's evil eyes stare into mine. "You have the face of an angel," he whispers. *"E voi diventerete uno."*

When Col raises his hand to my face, Isaac snatches his wrist. His grip is so firm, even the massive set of wrinkles in Col's face can't hide his grimace.

"Don't fucking touch her," Isaac snarls, his tone clipped and unnerving.

My heart skips a beat when Col's right-hand man moves closer to our gathering. He adjusts his suit jacket to expose he's carrying two semi-automatic Glocks on his waist.

"Isaac, let's go."

I scramble backward, pulling Isaac with me, but his stance is so strong, he doesn't budge an inch. His infuriated gaze remains focused on Col. His jaw is ticking so furiously, his back molars grind together.

"Please, Isaac, he has a gun," I beg, motioning my head to Col's henchman.

If Isaac doesn't agree to come with me, I'll blow my cover and announce I'm an FBI agent. Col Petretti has always been paranoid about being under surveillance or infiltrated by an undercover agent, so my confession may be enough to force him to leave our group immediately.

Isaac's eyes flick to Col's henchman. He sniffs, goading him. "A real man doesn't need a gun. His body is his weapon."

"It'll be in your best interest to remember that," he threatens before he relinquishes his grip on Col's wrist.

I sigh when Isaac grasps my wrist and spins on his heels, not once glancing back on Col or his henchman left standing on the sidewalk.

CHAPTER 23

"Get out."

I shake my head and re-latch my seat belt Isaac just unlatched.

"For once, do as you're told and get out," he screams, making me jump in fright.

Gritting my teeth, I shake my head once more. "No."

Isaac growls. This time, it isn't a sexy-as-sin growl, it's a growl that shows his unrelenting anger.

He throws open the driver's side door so hard I'm surprised he didn't break the hinges. He stomps toward the passenger side door and pulls it open so violently, I have no chance of holding it closed.

Leaning in, he unclasps my seat belt and lifts me out of the car. His angry strides don't stop until he dumps me onto a wicker chair on the front veranda of Cormack's mansion.

His icy gaze turns to mine the instant I spring out of the chair. "Stay here."

I freeze, truly scared by his infuriating gaze.

I'm not stupid. I know where he's going and what he's planning on doing. That's why I'm trying to stop him from leaving. You can't insult a man with a reputation like Isaac's and not create a devastating ripple.

Isaac didn't speak a word the entire drive home. His fists clenched the steering wheel tightly, and his gaze remained planted on the road. I tried to soothe his anger, but nothing I said altered the furious mask marring his handsome face. He was physically in the car with me, but his mind was occupied elsewhere.

Tires screech as his car whizzes out of the driveway, gaining the attention of Harlow and Cormack, who are sitting in the den.

Cormack rushes onto the front patio. "What's going on?"

"We ran into Col Petretti on the way home," I stutter, my mind blurred with confusion.

"What happened?" Panic echoes in Cormack's tone. "Did he say anything, do anything... Izzy?"

He grasps my biceps and shakes me, lifting my fogged haze.

"He didn't say anything. He... umm... said I have the face of an angel." I'm utterly confused as to why it would cause such a negative response from Isaac.

"Fuck." Cormack scrubs his hand over his head. "Where did you see Col?"

"At 57." My panicked eyes lock with his. "Can you stop him?"

"No one can stop Isaac, but that doesn't mean I won't try."

He places a peck on Harlow's shocked mouth and darts toward a garage housing his extensive collection of cars.

By the time Isaac and Cormack return, two hours have ticked by on the clock. Harlow encouraged me to have a shower and change out of my dress, then I spent the last hour and a half wearing a hole in the expensive Persian rug in the den with my ponderous pacing.

Isaac's eyes stray to mine the instant he walks into the room. His anger is still visible in his slitted gaze. I scan his body and sigh noisily when I notice he doesn't have any physical damage to his body.

My steps toward him halt when he roughly shakes his head and exits the room as quickly as he arrived. When I dash after him, Cormack grasps my elbow, stopping me.

"You won't get anything out of him, Izzy," Cormack warns, his tone as low as my heart rate. "He locks up his emotions tighter than Fort Knox."

"Then, you either tell me what's going on, or I'll force him to tell me." My tone tells him I'm not kidding. I want answers, and I want them now.

"Then, you'll lose him forever." Cormack's tone is as bitter as the bile sitting in my throat.

Tears well in my eyes so fast they burn from the sudden rush of moisture.

Spotting my dour expression, Cormack says, "I haven't seen him look at anyone the way he looks at you in years. Not since Ophelia, but if you force his hand, you'll lose him, Izzy."

My eyes dance between Cormack's, silently pleading for more information. *Who's Ophelia? What does it mean that he looks at me differently? Was it Ophelia who forced Isaac's hand previously? Is Isaac as captivated with me as I am with him?*

"If he wants you to know, he will tell you himself," Cormack responds to my wordless interrogation.

I've been tossing and turning in bed nonstop the past several hours. My body is still relishing my previous orgasms, but it's the gnawing pit twisting my chest that's keeping me awake. There was palpable tension between Col and Isaac, but it seemed to be so much more than just rivalry. Their hate for each other is personal and goes much deeper than some stupid mob turf war.

I stiffen when the hinges on the old wooden door in my room creak. My pupils widen when Isaac strides into the room. He's still wearing the same three-piece suit he was wearing at dinner. I remain quiet as he removes his shoes and jacket. My pulse quickens when he continues undressing until he's wearing nothing but a pair of black boxers.

I squeal when he slides in between the sheets and flips me over. His hand splays across my stomach, pulling me back toward him. My curvy backside snuggles in close to his erect crotch, and his bare chest heats my barely covered back.

"No questions, just sleep, Isabelle."

I don't know how he expects me to sleep. Not only are there hundreds of questions running through my head, I feel his monstrous manhood grinding my backside. Sensing my reluctance, Isaac glides his hand up and down my arm in a soothing motion. Over time, my blinking lengthens, and my breathing slows until I fall blissfully asleep.

I don't need to open my eyes to know Isaac isn't in the room with me. The aura of a man like him permeates the air. His power, his stature, his importance—it's all something you feel, not visualize. That's how I know he left the room hours ago.

Sluggishly opening my eyes, I stretch my arms out in front of my body, which is still adoring the two toe-curling orgasms I had last night. Although Isaac's confrontation with Col filtered through my mind all night long, I had the most restful sleep I've ever had. Two consecutive mind-blowing climaxes shattered me, rendering me physically exhausted. Then being snuggled into Isaac had me sleeping like a baby.

I climb out of bed and head into the expansive guest bathroom attached to my impressive suite. My toes grip the plush, luxurious carpet pile as I increase my strides, the shower beckoning me to it. I take my time shampooing my hair with the deliciously fragrant toiletries supplied.

Spurts of warm water slide down my face before stopping and clinging to my top lip. All the forbidden images of Isaac nipping, lashing, and tasting my mouth come rushing back to the forefront. When my tongue darts out to lick my top lip, I can still taste him on my skin.

My leisurely shower becomes hurried, my urge to see Isaac outweighing my love of long, heavenly showers. I dry myself with a plush towel before running my fingers through my shampooed hair and securing it into a messy bun. Because of my late awakening, the temperature has already heated up enough to know I'll be either spending the majority of my day in the coolness of the sea breeze or by the grotto pool.

Turning my eyes to my suitcase, I catch a glimpse of my minuscule bikini hanging on the railing in the bathroom. *Maybe it will aid in releasing Isaac's tension from last night?*

Once I'm dressed in a pair of tiny cotton shorts, a bikini top, and a crushed natural linen blouse I've left open at the front, I exit my suite. Compared to the constant bustle of the main house yesterday, today it's eerily quiet. I move through the vast rooms of the palatial McGregor residence, seeking any other signs of life.

A hive of activity sounds through a pair of French doors attached to the rec room. Upon exiting, I notice a substantial buffet has been set up on the paved patio next to the pool. I spot Harlow, Cormack, Cate, and Colby gathered around a wrought iron table enjoying the splendor of croissants, fresh fruit, pastries, and coffee.

Harlow smiles and motions for me to join them at the table. Returning her smile, I signal that I'll join them once I have my required morning caffeine fix in my hot little hands.

I nearly drop my mug of freshly brewed coffee when 'Isabelle' rolls off a tongue that had me quivering last night.

Isaac is standing so close, I'm trapped between his firm body and the buffet table. His elongated cock is felt through my thin cotton shorts, and his delicious scent lingers in my nostrils.

Air catches in my throat when he snags a croissant off the table, his forearm skimming the side of my boob on the way past.

Raising my eyes, I catch him smirking down at me. He winks before striding away, his cockiness uncontained. I'm unable to move from my spot, frozen in place with desire. When he enters the French doors without a backward glance, I sigh, disturbed by my lack of self-control when he's in my presence.

Once the shred of dignity I barely hold is collected, I mosey to the table where everyone is gathered.

"Holy fuck," Colby murmurs under his breath.

I'm pretty sure his comment is directed at me, considering the fact he's staring at me with his mouth opened wide, his eyes roaming over my body. Colby stumbles out of his chair, tripping over his own feet. Once he regains his footing, he gestures for me to sit in the chair he was sitting in.

"T-take a seat."

I try to hide my smile at his clumsiness, but I find it so endearing that the sight of me has him falling over himself, my lips tug higher. When Colby notices my smile, he shakes his head and chuckles.

"You have me stumbling around like a teenage boy." He doesn't stutter this time around. "But seriously, Izzy, you need to issue a warning before you bring out that ammunition." His gaze locks onto my chest. "Where the hell were you hiding them yesterday?"

I don't know if he wants me to answer him or not, so I remain quiet.

When he cocks his eyebrow at me, waiting for a response, I answer, "Under my shirt."

Colby chuckles. "Well, you need to bring those puppies out to play more often."

Our banter is interrupted when a stern cough bellows across the table.

Cormack shoots daggers at Colby. "You were warned yesterday."

Colby doesn't seem phased by his older brother's stern glare or statement. He just smiles at him and winks before removing his shirt.

Holy cupcakes! Did I die in my sleep and wake up in a 'Bachelor of the Year' contest?

I'm not the only one hiding desirable *assets* under my shirt. Colby's pecs are impressive, his stomach is ridged, and his guns are—*Oh. My. God!* But even with his drool-worthy body on display, Colby still can't compete with Isaac. Isaac's body isn't just perfect, it's pussy-clenching delicious. I don't think any man will ever steal my attention away from Isaac.

My bare feet pad along the beautiful ebony hardwood floor as I make my way back to the room Cormack assigned to me this weekend. I'm in desperate need of a shower to rid my body of the sand and salt embedded on my skin. I'm still wearing my bikini, but I've placed a light, flowing, blue cotton dress over the damp material.

Tonight's setting for dinner was casual, but I still don't think it's suitable to wear only swimwear to a dinner table, although it appears no one informed Colby of that. He sat barefoot and in just a pair of board shorts. His long blond hair was tousled loosely on the top of his head, and his skin had color from spending hours at the beach.

Colby is a real lady charmer. There's no doubt in my mind he could woo the panties off any girl he sets his sights on. He has just chosen the wrong lady to pursue. My attention remains focused on Isaac, even though he wants to be left alone.

I felt Isaac's eyes on me throughout the day, but he hasn't uttered a word to me. His dark, gloomy mood makes me hesitate to interact with him. Not that his appalling attitude should be rewarded with attention, but I can't help but feel I'm missing out on a prime opportunity to unearth the real Isaac Holt.

My mind is still a jumbled mess of confusion. I'm beginning to wonder if the explicit sex scene in the nightclub office actually happened, or if my overactive imagination is more phenomenal than I comprehended.

One might assume most of my thoughts would be consumed with unearthing everything about Col and Isaac, considering unraveling that secret would be critical for the FBI's investigation, but it isn't. I can't stop thinking about what Cormack said.

Who is Ophelia, and what does she mean to Isaac? Why would I lose Isaac if I tried to force him to share information with me? And why did a dark pit form in my chest the instant I thought I might lose him? These are the questions I want answered, but no one seems willing to talk about them.

Upon entering the long, dark hallway, the sudden flash of a smirk halts my long strides. Mere feet from me is Isaac, leaning in the door-jamb of my room a few doors down from where I've stopped. His arms are crossed in front of his well-formed chest, and the danger in his eyes would have most men shuddering in their boots, but instead of feeling fear, my body quivers with anticipation, and stupid butterflies form in my stomach.

I strengthen my posture before finalizing the last strides down the hall. Offering him a quick smile, I skirt past him to enter my room. He seizes my wrist, halting my reluctant retreat. My pulse quickens from his simplest touch.

Air traps in my throat when he leans in close to my neck. His hot breaths flutter my earlobe when he hisses, "Stay away from Colby."

Gritting my teeth, I yank open my bedroom door so hard it slams into Isaac's trouser-covered hip.

"You shouldn't have a problem with my request unless you're interested in sleeping with him," Isaac snarls, following me into my room. "Are you interested in him, Isabelle?"

His pathetic question doesn't warrant a reply, so instead, I glare at him. He isn't the slightest bit intimidated by my angry stance. If anything, he seems to find it amusing. His eyes are shimmering with mischief, and his lips are curved high.

"I'll answer your question if you answer one of mine."

"Ain't going to happen," he replies, not considering my suggestion.

"Then get out of my room." I march into the bathroom and slam the door.

I have the longest shower I've ever had. Taking my time, I pamper my tired and exhausted body. The past forty-eight hours feel like the longest days of my life. I'm not just exhausted, I am also emotionally drained.

Isaac's emotions are worse than whiplash. He goes from lavishing me with his attention to cold and distant in an instant, but no matter how hard I try to put him to the back of my mind, he always pushes into the forefront. Although I barely know him, my heart yearns for him when he isn't around.

I freeze. Even with my body covered in a thick coating of body wash, I step out of the shower, dazed and confused. *Holy shit.* I catch my wide-eyed expression in the vanity mirror. No, I can't be. *Oh God.* I'm falling in love with Isaac Holt.

No, no, no, no, no! I can't let this happen. I can't fall in love with a man I'm investigating. I hardly know him. He is a stranger. So what if he can make every hair on my body bristle to attention by the simplest touch of his fingertip, that doesn't mean anything. *Does it?*

Stunned and muddled, I remove the bubbles from my body with a luxuriously thick towel and throw on a pair of panties and a short-sleeve cotton shirt I found discarded on the floor. Exiting the room, I freeze for the second time.

"Get out of my bed." My voice croaks with emotion.

Isaac's shirtless torso is leaning against the leather headboard of my bed.

"This is my bed," he responds, "and that's my shirt." He points to the shirt I've just put on.

"What?" Negative thoughts clusters in my head so fast I feel giddy. "This is the room Cormack assigned to me."

Isaac shakes his head. "This is my room. I brought you in here the first night when you blacked out on the plane and last night—"

"Oh my God, you didn't sleep with me last night because you wanted to. You slept with me because I was sleeping in your bed," I interrupt. *I'm going to be sick.*

"I'm sorry." I shove my clothing into my suitcase. "I didn't realize."

Isaac clambers out of bed to yank my suitcase out of my grasp. In silence, he places it back onto the luggage stand.

"Get in bed, Isabelle."

I shake my head. There would be at least a dozen spare rooms in this mansion. I'm sure I'll have no trouble finding a warm bed for the night.

"Now!" Isaac barks, startling me.

He moves back to the left-hand side of the bed. As he glides back in between the sheets, his stern eyes never once leave mine. I suck in numerous breaths to settle my rattled nerves. *Is this what you want, Isabelle?* My head is screaming no, but my heart pleads louder than my brain.

The sternness in his eyes lessens as I step toward the bed.

"Good choice," he murmurs when I slide into the bed next to him.

By the time two hours have passed, I've counted every rose petal adorning the ceiling medallion. It took longer than usual as I had to wait for the moon to adjust its position to finish the lower half. I shift to lie on my hip and catch the profile of Isaac. Even in the shadows of the night, my heart still skips a beat when I appraise his tempting features.

"Stop staring at me."

My lips curve into a smile. "Are you awake?"

Isaac rolls onto his hip, mimicking my position. "Yep. You need to learn to count in your head."

"I'm so sorry," I respond, mortified. "I have a terrible habit of mumbling out loud."

"I've realized that," he jibes, his tone playful.

We lay across from each other in silence for several minutes, each appraising the other's moonlit face in great detail. I have so many questions I want to ask him. Not one of them has anything to do with the investigation the FBI is running on him.

Isaac runs his hand over his head. "One question, Isabelle."

After drawing in a shaky breath, I ask the one question I've wanted to ask since last night. "Did you love Ophelia?"

"Yes," he replies without a smidge of hesitation.

Tears well in my eyes, and a stabbing pain hits my chest.

"Do you still love her?" I whisper.

"I said one question," he replies bluntly before rolling onto his opposite hip.

CHAPTER 24

I stumble into the plane, and my knees knock with every step I take. When I raise my wide gaze, I spot Isaac sitting in the only single reclining chair. This is the first time I've seen him today. By the time I woke up this morning, he had already vacated the room.

He jerks up his chin in greeting before devoting his attention to the plane's window, revealing his dreary mood from yesterday has returned full force. I plop into the closest chair before fumbling with my belt. I'm all thumbs, meaning I can't get the buckle to latch together. Seeing my struggle, Isaac curses under his breath before he releases the mechanism of his belt to aid in securing mine.

Once my belt is tightened around my waist, he heads back to the reclining chair. With everyone seated, the plane taxis toward the runway. While biting on my lower lip, I grip the armrest. I want to wipe away the annoying tear sitting high on my cheek, but I'm too terrified to loosen my grip.

The closer we get to the end of the runway, the more my panicked pants fill the silence of the cab.

"Breathe," Isaac demands upon hearing my loud wheezes.

My body snaps to his command, but my panic is too intense. I can't get enough oxygen, and my lungs are burning in protest. I truly feel like I'm suffocating.

When I shake my head, wordlessly relaying I can't fill my lungs, Isaac magically kneels in front of me. I want to scream at him to return to his seat, but my fear is rendering me speechless.

He clasps my hands in his. "Breathe, Isabelle."

This time, my body obeys. The crippling pain in my chest lessens when I inhale a sharp, quick breath.

"Good girl."

He brushes away the tears marking my white cheeks, his touch gentle almost loving. Once he has taken care of the moisture on my face, he traces the cupid's bow on my top lip. The saltiness of my tears can't stop tingles dancing across my face.

Fat, salty tears are streaming down my face. It isn't just my fear that has me sobbing, though. It's glancing into the eyes of the man I'm falling in love with knowing I can't have both him and my illustrious career.

"What are you doing?" I blubber out when he unlatches my seat belt without warning.

He doesn't grace me with a reply, he just scoops me into his arms, then walks toward the back of the plane. When we enter the luxurious bedroom at the end, he secures the latch, then places me on the bed. My insides tighten when he stoops down to unclasp my shoes. Once they're removed, he dumps them next to the bed before removing his polished dress shoes.

I watch him with zeal when he undoes his cufflinks to remove his jacket. My mouth dries when his eyes lower to mine. They're as teasing as his impromptu strip.

Electricity bolts up my arm when he clutches my hand to yank me up from the bed. My breasts press against his chest, budding my nipples.

He gazes into my eyes. "Do you want this?"

I nod.

His lips crimp, apparently unimpressed by my non-verbal reply. "No, Isabelle. Say it."

My thighs quake as I reply, "I want this."

The most mouth-watering smirk sneaks onto Isaac's face as he steps away from me. Upon hearing my shameless groan at the loss of his contact, his grin enlarges, making my thighs shudder more.

His eyes rake my body before they return to my face. "Strip."

My cheeks inflame, but the desire in his eyes has me feeling more daring than usual, so I strip as instructed. He stares at me in admiration like I am his salvation.

My heavy pants push my breasts up and down as I undo each button of my shirt. His eyes remain fixated on my face until the last button on my blouse is undone. I shimmy my shoulder, sending my shirt plummeting to the floor.

He draws in a sharp breath when his eyes land on the steel-gray Dream Angel Victoria Secret padded lace bra I'd purchased. When I saw its dark gray coloring matched his eyes, I had to buy it.

When his eyes return to mine, the primal, hungry look in them has me squirming on the spot. I stop slithering my arms around my back to unlatch my bra when he shakes his head. "Leave the bra."

His devilishly wicked smile makes me wet. While chewing on my bottom lip, I undo the button of my jeans then lower the fly. As I tug them down my thighs, Isaac loosens the knot on his tie, his eyes never leaving me. His smile grows when he notices my matching steel-gray lace panties.

"Please don't shred these. They cost way more than you think."

Isaac doesn't grace me with a reply. He merely smirks while skimming his eyes over my body. As he twists his tie around his right hand, he pads closer to me. "Are you a screamer, Isabelle?"

"No." *But that may be because no guy has made my body ignite the way Isaac can.*

"You're about to become one."

I roll my eyes at his pigheadedness, but the lash of his tongue on my gaped mouth has them freezing halfway.

Our kiss is furiously violent as the pent-up sexual frustration the past two days is unleashed. I yank his white business shirt out of his trousers before fumbling with the pearl buttons. When the buttons refuse to cooperate with my trembling hands, I clasp his shirt and rip it open.

Isaac groans into my mouth when buttons sprawling onto the polished wooden floor tinkle around us.

"That shirt cost way more than you think!"

I tug on his black leather belt. "I'm sure you can afford another."

My blood thickens when his chuckle rumbles through my pussy. Through a stimulating blur of bites, sucks, and kisses, I find myself trapped between the wall and him. Gripping my thighs, he curls my legs around his waist. I grind my sensitive clit along the ridges of his erect cock, my patience to feel him inside me stretching thin.

"Do you have a condom?" I ask, praying to the Lord he has some form of protection. I'll never forgive myself if I have to stop this now.

He smirks before slipping his hand into his pocket. My lips tug into a victorious grin when he produces a Trojan condom. The tingles wreaking havoc with my core grow when he rolls the condom down his gorgeously thick cock.

Once it's in place, he raises his eyes to mine. Air leaves my lungs in a rush when he shreds my panties off my body in one rapid movement, their frail material no match to his brutal force.

"You're buying me another pair." I pull his lips to mine by his sweat-drenched head.

"It will be my pleasure," Isaac talks over my mouth.

Cupping my ass cheeks in his hands, he guides my body backward until my torso is leaning on the wood-paneled wall. My breasts thrust forward when my arms band around his shoulders. When the head of his cock brushes the entrance of my wet sex, my eyes drift to the bed.

Noticing my gaze, Isaac mutters, "Next time."

A smile stretches across my face, pleased there will be a next time.

"Hold on, baby, this is going to hurt."

My nails dig into Isaac's shoulders when he impales me in one ardent thrust. Tears spring to my eyes as I struggle to acclimate to taking a man of his size without adequate preparation.

Sensing my hesitation, Isaac remains motionless, giving me time to adjust to the sheer girth of him. Although my body is stinging with pain, it's also aching in pleasure at being the fullest it's ever been.

My cheeks heat when Isaac murmurs, "Fuck, you're tight."

Suddenly, he stiffens before his eyes rocket to mine. No words need to escape his lips. His freaked expression is questioning enough.

"Thank fuck," he mutters when I shake my head at his unspoken question.

It's been a while since I've participated in sexual activities, but I'm definitely not a virgin.

He adjusts my position to a better angle before asking, "You ready?"

Instead of gracing him with a reply, I squeeze his cock with the walls of my pussy. The raspy moan roaring from his throat nearly makes me combust on the spot, much less his cock slowly inching out of me.

The first few pumps of his thick shaft are painful, but the pleasure far outweighs the discomfort. My orgasm builds with every relentless pound, and I'm soon quivering without restraint.

My body coils tight, striving for release as my moans turn husky. When Isaac pulls down my bra and traps my nipple in his warm mouth, I throw my head against the wall. Maintaining his tempo that's driving me into a quivering, blubbering mess, his skillful tongue teases my nipples into hardened peaks.

I'm moments away from falling into orgasmic bliss, my body heightened beyond belief.

"Eyes on me, Isabelle," Isaac demands when the power of our exchange overwhelms me so much my eyelids flutter shut.

Snapping my eyes back open, I tighten my grip around his shoulders, afraid I may topple to the ground during ecstasy.

"I've got you," Isaac advises, sensing my concern.

Oh God, he has got me, and it feels so good. He is so deep, and I'm stretched so wide.

His name thunders from my lips when I implode into the most body-shattering orgasm I've ever had. I moan on repeat, relishing the spark adoring every inch of my body.

Overwhelmed by the sensation heating my veins, my eyes snap shut.

"Eyes, Isabelle," Isaac commands, never once easing his unrelenting pummeling that has reduced me to a tremoring mess.

When my eyes pop back open, my climax intensifies from peering into his primal, alpha gaze. He stares at me in adoration, enhancing the electricity crackling in the air.

Once every pleasurable shudder has been exhausted, Isaac moves us to the bed. A disappointed moan spills from my lips when his throbbing cock slides out of my drenched pussy.

"Bend over the bed, open palms flat on the sheets." Isaac's voice is hoarse with lust. "Legs open wide."

Blinded by excitement, I do as requested without protest. When I hear shuffling behind me, I tilt my head to the side. My mouth salivates when my eyes lock in on Isaac's magnificent naked body. Just watching a bead of sweat roll down the bumps in his stomach before being absorbed by the dark patch of hairs above his mouthwatering cock nearly has me toppling into ecstasy all over again.

My heart rate kicks into overdrive when Isaac places his dark blue tie over my eyes, then secures it behind my head.

"It will heighten your senses."

Swallowing harshly, I nod instead of telling him I don't need any assistance in enlightening my senses when he's in my vicinity.

Placing his hand on the lower half of my belly, he adjusts my position, so my ass is thrust high into the air. My knees scrape across the crisp sheets when his index finger glides past my sensitive clit not even two seconds later.

"Open wider, Isabelle. I want to see all of you."

Oh God.

When ruffling sounds behind me, I prick my ears, straining to hear every move he makes. Thankfully, I'm not left waiting for long.

Time stands still when the head of Isaac's cock braces the entrance of my weeping sex. "This will be hard and fast." The rasp of his voice sends a revitalizing shiver through my body.

He waits for me to nod before slamming back into me in one quick thrust. I purr a grunted moan of satisfaction, relishing being filled by him again.

My moans lengthen when one of his hands grips my hip while the other fists my hair. His hold is dominant and strong, and it has my second orgasm rapidly gaining in intensity.

The coils in my womb tighten when Isaac tilts my head back so he can cover his mouth over mine. His tongue invades my mouth as roughly as his cock assaults my pussy. It's a stimulating kiss that hits every one of my hot buttons, and it thrusts my climax to within an inch of the finish line.

Gripping the satin sheets in a white-knuckled hold, a second orgasm rockets through my body like fireworks exploding in a dark sky. When I muffle my grunted screams into a pillow, Isaac's raspy groans become more prominent. I never thought I was a screamer, but Isaac has proved me wrong. My throat is as raw as my heart.

I knew Isaac would be fantastic in bed, but I'm still astounded by his impressive stamina.

"One more," Isaac suggest once I've returned from climax oblivion.

I shake my head. My body is slack, unresponsive, and covered head to toe in slick sweat. The only reason I'm still upright is because of the tight grip Isaac has on my hip. The sting of his fingers cakes my skin with more excitement.

An unexpected squeal rips from my dry mouth when Isaac flips me onto my back. My eyes blink in quick succession to adjust to the bright light illuminating the room when he removes my blindfold. Any protest on further contact is disregarded when I catch his intense gaze scanning my face as he slides back inside me. His eyes look as content as my body does.

A husky moan rolls up my throat when his mouth seals over mine. This time, his kiss is passionate and slow, expanding my heart with every caress, nibble, and lick he does. Even the relentless rhythm of his pounding eases.

Placing his open palm on my back, Isaac tilts my hips higher, giving him unrestricted access to my throbbing pussy.

I'm surprised a short time later when a familiar tightening in my lower stomach gains intensity again so quickly.

"Eyes," Isaac demands.

My orgasm rushes to the surface, excited he can already intuit my body so well he knows I'm moments away from climaxing.

Isaac's hoarse groan booms through my sex when I hook my leg higher on his waist, so our hips can grind in sync. He pumps into me on repeat, stealing the air from my lungs with every perfect stroke.

"Oh God..." I pant, overcome by the tingling in my core.

The desire to snap my eyes shut is overwhelming when a third orgasm roars through my spent body, but I keep them open, fighting through the sensation eating me whole.

When my nails dig into Isaac's back with force, spurts of cum brutally erupt from his throbbing knob.

"Fuck, Isabelle," he groans before leaning over and entrapping my bottom lip between his teeth. The sting of his bite is painful, but his tongue soon soothes the pain.

Once every drop of his spawn has been released, he frees my lip from his menacing teeth before rolling off me. His eyes remain locked on mine as he removes the condom from his still throbbing cock. Disposing the condom into a trash can, he rejoins me in bed. Even exhausted beyond comprehension, my lips tug high when he spoons his body in close to mine.

With three earth-shattering orgasms rendering me immobile, I soon fall into a blissful post-orgasmic sleep.

"Isabelle..."

My hand shoos away something brushing my lips. When a profound chuckle booms through my eardrums, I jolt upright and crash into a hard surface.

"Shit." I rub the brutal sting on my head.

Peering out of my eye, I catch the incredibly attractive and fully dressed Mr. Isaac Holt, pinching the bridge of his nose.

Oh shit!

I scamper my naked body across the bed and yank his hand away from his nose to inspect it. "Is it bleeding?"

"It's fine, Isabelle," Isaac remarks.

I continue with my perusal of his nose while his eyes appraise my naked body. I'm too mortified that I've managed to headbutt him twice in less than six months to form a response to his overly eager assessment.

"Isabelle, I'm fine," Isaac growls when I continue to fuss over him.

He must have been sitting very close to me when I struck him as his nose already has a red bump forming. When I lick my dry lips, I can taste him on my skin.

"Were you kissing—"

"We're back in Ravenshoe."

"What?" I'm utterly confused.

My eyes dart to the window. I gasp when I notice the plane is in an airport hangar instead of the sky.

"Why didn't you wake me?" I dart out of bed.

"You look tired. I wanted you to sleep."

My lips curve into a broad grin as I yank on my shirt and jeans, sans underwear. *Hold on!*

"So, we did the whole landing without a seat belt? Are you crazy?"

"Do you truly believe a scrap of material will save you when a plane is plummeting to the ground?"

My quick movements freeze as my brows furrow. *I'm never flying again.*

Isaac chuckles at my reaction before clasping his hand around mine. My brows scrunch more when I walk out of the bedroom and discover the plane is deserted. My bewilderment intensifies when I spot Hugo leaning on Isaac's town car when we exit the galley of the aircraft.

"We landed over two hours ago."

My eyes bulge. "You let me sleep that long?"

"You looked tired."

My lips tug into a broad smile that remains planted on my face while Hugo stows our luggage in the back of Isaac's car and during the entire trip back to my apartment. It only falters when I catch the quickest glimpse of remorse in Isaac's eyes when he follows me into the elevator of my apartment building.

"Did you want to come inside?" I ask once I reach the front door of my apartment.

My heart plummets into my stomach when Isaac shakes his head. "I have some business to take care of."

He's lying. Isaac always maintains eye contact, but his eyes strayed to the floor the instant I asked if he wanted to come in.

"Okay." Ignoring the gnawing pit in my chest, I thrust my hand toward him. "Thank you for a lovely weekend."

He smirks at my gesture, but he doesn't shake my hand. He raises it to his mouth and places a kiss on my palm. My heart leaps.

"The pleasure was all mine, Isabelle," he croons before spinning on his heels and striding down the hall.

I stand mute in my hall, utterly confused. I also have the worst case of whiplash I've ever experienced in my life.

CHAPTER 25

"*I*f you sign a contract, you're required to fulfill your contract for the set amount of time on the said contract."

"But…"

"No buts, Isabelle. You're not getting out of your contract. I don't care if your cat gets run over by a truck or your grandma dies. You signed a contract. You'll fulfill your obligation," Alex snarls. "Now go and do the job you're paid to do." His angry roar reverberates through the office building.

After gathering the scraps of dignity I have left, I scamper out of his office. I've just experienced the worst shredding of my life. He literally tore me apart.

After tossing and turning all night long, I concluded my relationship with Isaac, no matter how confusing it may be, is highly unethical. Not wanting to shroud Alex's team and my uncle's name in controversy, I decided it would be best to have my position relocated to another unit.

There are hundreds, no scrap that, there are thousands of people the FBI targets every week, so it wouldn't be difficult to be transferred to another unit, but the instant I suggested a transfer to Alex, he shot it down. He refused my request, wadded up my transfer application into a ball, and then threw it into the trash. He then went on a half-hour long rambling tirade about my integrity and due diligence to his team, and how I'd be letting everyone down by transferring to another unit.

Who would have thought a coffee girl was such an integral part of a team?

Brandon's eyes lift to mine as I scurry past his desk. "What crawled up his ass and died?" I ask.

Brandon grins a full grin while shaking his head. Dumping my satchel into the bottom drawer of my desk, I plop into my chair and fire up my computer. The first thing that pops up onto my monitor is the extended search I'd started for Megan Shroud before I went away. I'd completely forgotten about her the entire weekend.

I'm so immersed in reading Megan's extensive medical history, I don't notice Brandon sitting on my desk until he waves a blue manila folder in my face.

"Hey," I greet, my mind hazy. "Did you look any further into Megan Shroud over the weekend?"

"No. I showed Alex her license details you gave me. He said to drop it. It looks like she's just a random acquaintance who has formed an attachment after a one-night stand. Every guy's worst nightmare." Brandon chuckles over his comment.

Gritting my teeth, I snub the pain burrowing my chest from his comment.

"Why, what did you find?"

"Your worst nightmare." I swivel my monitor to face him.

The more Brandon's eyes glance at the screen, the more his brows furrow.

"Jeez, that's what you call a certified lunatic."

"When was she last photographed at the nightclub?"

"Umm..." Brandon flicks through a selection of photos in the blue manila folder he's holding. "She was at the club this weekend." He hands me two pictures of Megan standing in the queue to enter Isaac's nightclub, The Dungeon.

"Shit. According to her medical records, she's supposed to be admitted as an inpatient at a psychiatric hospital in Hopeton."

Brandon eyes me apprehensively, but he doesn't utter a sound as I print out the extensive collection of medical records on Megan and bolt toward Alex's office.

"Come in," Alex instructs, his mood still surly.

When he notices me approaching his desk, he rolls his eyes. Snubbing his imprudent response, I hand him Megan's medical information. His eyes lift to mine and narrow before he snatches the documents out of my firm grasp.

"Who's Megan Shroud?"

My brows tack as my gaze turns to seek Brandon, who is sitting on my desk, eyeballing the exchange between Alex and me. He just informed me he advised Alex of Megan this weekend, didn't he? Shrugging, I turn my gaze back to Alex.

"She has been photographed at Isaac's club on numerous occasions the past several months."

Alex's stern blue eyes meet mine. "Hundreds of women are photographed at his clubs every day."

"But she was there day and night, every day for the past several weeks." I try not to let my genuine concern for Isaac be heard in my voice. "She has also been in and out of psychiatric hospitals her entire life."

"Then he should've been more cautious about who he takes to bed."

"Who said he slept with her?" I ask through gritted teeth.

Alex glares at me. The expression on his face reveals he thinks I'm an imbecile.

When I remain quiet, he continues, "Would you like me to supply you with the extensive list of women Isaac Holt has slept with?"

"No." My swirling stomach amplifies so much I feel queasy. *They have a list?*

"Then drop it," Alex instructs. "We're here to investigate Isaac, not every floozy he's slept with."

Grimacing, I nod, although my gut is telling me not to drop this.

With reluctance, I head for my desk. Brandon doesn't need to ask how it went. The distressed look on my face tells the whole story.

"Maybe try again in a few days when his brooding mood improves," Brandon suggests.

"He's never in a good mood." I flop into my chair.

Brandon chuckles at my statement before his eyes lift to mine. "How was your weekend away?"

A smile tugs my lips higher. "It was good." Even with the whole Col Petretti and whiplash issues that plagued my weekend, I still thoroughly enjoyed my time away.

"How was your weekend?" I ask.

"Quiet."

I arch my brow. Even though my day is full of the most boring, tedious tasks you could imagine, Alex's team is always a bustling hive of activity, so I find it surprising Brandon had a quiet weekend.

"The surveillance team lost track of Isaac for three days. No one knew where he was," he tells me.

My eyes snap to his.

"That's why Alex is in such a pissy mood. Isaac only resurfaced again last night."

Brandon hands me the blue manila folder he has been grasping the past twenty minutes. A lump lodges in my throat when I scan through the surveillance photos. Isaac, as always, looks impeccable in a black three-piece tailored suit, and his vibrant red tie matches the dress of the slender blonde intimately attached to his side.

"I don't know how the surveillance team keeps losing him, but..."

He knows we're tailing him.

I realize I said my last statement out loud when Brandon asks, "How do you know that?"

Air snags in my throat as my eyes roam over the photos, trying to think of a legitimate reason I'd know that.

"Look." I lift a picture of Isaac helping his companion out of the back seat of his car at the back entrance of his nightclub. "He's looking at the camera and smiling. He knows we're watching him."

Brandon removes the photo from my grasp to appraise it. "He is, too. Good call, Izzy," he comments, his tone proud.

I smile at his praise, but can't tear my gaze away from the final surveillance photo sitting in the manila folder. It's time-stamped three hours after the picture Brandon is holding. It shows Isaac and his female companion standing next to the open back door of his Mercedes-Benz.

They are kissing.

CHAPTER 26

Two weeks later...

"Wow, Isabelle, swanky residence." An impressive whistle sounds from Brandon's lips.

Smiling, I lean over and press a chaste kiss to his cheek before gesturing for him to enter. A grin curls my lips when he hands me a floral bouquet of irises and baby's breath.

"Thank you." I offer to take his coat.

Once I have his black woolen jacket on a hanger in the coatroom, I enter my compact but well-designed kitchen to search for a vase for the flowers. Brandon shadows closely behind me with his eager eyes darting around my apartment. I've lived here the past nine weeks, but this is the first time I've invited him inside. I like my privacy in general, but I appreciate it more since I've started working with the FBI. Privacy is a very undervalued commodity in the world of the Federal Bureau of Investigation.

I giggle when Brandon walks into my kitchen and inhales a vast, impressive whiff through his nostrils.

"It smells delicious in here." His hand rubs circles on his t-shirt-covered stomach. "It smells just like my grandma's kitchen used to smell."

He sucks in another gulp of air.

"Mariana meatballs?"

Grinning, I nod.

"Hold on." He holds his index finger into the air, requesting a minute before taking another unbashful sniff. His moan is one that should only come out of a man's mouth when he's in ecstasy. "Oh, for the love of God, please tell me that's homemade peanut butter and chocolate chip cookies?"

My lips curve into a full-toothed grin.

"They're due out of the oven any minute," I answer just as the oven dings.

Brandon doesn't respond, he merely growls, and his mouth salivates. After removing two trays of cookies from the oven, I spend the next five minutes slapping Brandon's hands away.

"They need to cool and harden," I reprimand. "And you'll spoil your dinner if you eat them now."

Rolling my eyes at his pleading gaze, I submit and hand him the still-warm tray of cookies. I swear he demolishes the first cookie so fast, his taste buds didn't get a chance to sample their scrumptious flavors.

"Would you like a glass of milk with your cookies?" I question since he's acting like a boy who's never eaten homemade cookies before.

"Yes, please." He sprays crumbs over my countertop.

I smile, glad he's enjoying the treats Harlow made for him. I lack any real domestic skills. I can cook a mean batch of Mariana meatballs and spaghetti bolognese, but that's about the limit of my culinary skills.

Harlow remembered Brandon telling her months ago how much he loved his grandma's peanut butter and chocolate chip cookies, so she made me a double batch and brought them over this afternoon. All I had to do was place them on a tray and bake them in the oven for twelve minutes, and presto, fresh-baked cookies.

For the first week, I hesitated every time Brandon tried to schedule the date I'd agreed to before I went away for the weekend, but after a week of endless surveillance photos of Isaac surfacing from his clubs with a vast range of blonde beauties on his arm, I decided to uphold my original offer.

I can't believe I was so stupid to think I could fall in love with a man like Isaac Holt. He couldn't even go a night without a female companion warming his bed. I guess that's why he shared his bed with me. He is probably one of those guys who can't sleep unless they're next to a warm body.

"Brandon, can I ask you something?" I move to the fridge to get the glass of milk I offered.

"Anything," he replies without hesitation.

"Do you think Isaac Holt is a criminal?"

Even irately angry at Isaac, he's still in the forefront of my mind. *Why can't I just forget about him?*

Brandon stops gorging on the cookies like it's his final meal as his hazel eyes lift to mine. His brows furrow before he begins to answer, "His file—"

"Don't tell me what his file says, tell me what *you* think."

His eyes dart down to the countertop. He takes several moments to seriously contemplate my question. "I don't know what to think."

He isn't the only one.

"But I'll say one thing. I've been part of this investigation for nearly a year, and I've not yet stumbled on one shred of information that corroborates Alex's presumptions of Isaac."

"Do you think he's hiding something?"

Brandon chuckles under his breath. "Are we still talking about Isaac, or have we switched to Alex?"

"Both."

"Everyone is hiding something, Isabelle," he replies. "Even you."

I don't refute his accusation. Even if I did, he'd see through any elaborate ruse I'd dangle in front of him. Brandon appears laid-back, but when you watch him closely, you soon realize he's a genius wrapped up in a humble boy-next-door disguise.

"Speaking of secrets." His mouth is stuffed to the brim with cookies. "That file you requested has arrived."

My shocked eyes meet his. Smiling, he nudges his head to his leather satchel resting on my dining table.

"Can I?"

When he grins and nods, I smack a sloppy kiss on his cheek. His face flushes with heat as his jaw drops. I probably shouldn't be so bold, but I've been waiting to get this file in my hot little hand for weeks.

"You have to promise Alex will never find—"

"Alex will never know," I interrupt. "I promise, Brandon."

Brandon went through an immense amount of hassle to secure this file for me. I'd never allow him to be reprimanded for it.

"Come on, I'm dying." He nudges me in the ribs with his elbow.

After releasing the butterflies in my tummy, I open the thin, cream manila folder. My eager eyes run over the police report displayed on top of the documents and photos. Brandon's concerned eyes lift to mine when he spots a tear rolling down my whitened cheek.

Marjorie Anne Hawke, a twenty-four-year-old native of Rochdale, was struck by a vehicle on May twelve, five years ago. She was thirty-four weeks pregnant at the time of the accident. Marjorie survived the initial impact, but her son was delivered stillborn by cesarean the same day. Marjorie's husband, Carey Hawke, returned from active duty in Iraq, and on his request, Marjorie's life support machine was switched off. She passed away three hours later.

"That's incredibly sad, but it doesn't warrant the shroud of secrecy," I blubber through the sheet of tears flowing down my face.

"No, but this does." Brandon hands me a heavily blacked-out court document.

One name stands out in thick black ink when I scan the document —Mr. Roberto Petretti, son of Col Petretti. *Oh God.*

"Roberto didn't do any time behind bars, even with being arrested at the scene and recording a blood-alcohol level three times over the legal limit," Brandon advises, his eyes darting up from the documents in his hand. "His name was never reported in any news or press articles. He'd have had to give the DA something substantial to get a plea that lenient."

"Or someone," I interrupt.

There's no doubt Marjorie is Hugo's sister. He's in nearly every family picture in her file. My heart breaks when I see the photo of Marjorie and her husband, Carey. It looks like it was taken not long before her accident. They're smiling at each other, and he has his hand hovering over her protruding stomach. It's a beautiful photo that shows their unbridled happiness before their lives were brutally ripped apart.

Now Isaac's reaction two weeks ago makes sense. His hatred of Col is personal. It has nothing to do with the mob.

CHAPTER 27

"Thanks for a great night, Izzy! But next time, I'll cook."

I slap Brandon's arm. "It wasn't that bad." My bottom lip drops into a pout. "It was your fault the Mariana sauce burned. You shouldn't have told me about the file until after I finished cooking."

He chuckles a hearty laugh that bellows down the corridor. Removing my arm from the crook of his elbow, I push the down button on the elevator dashboard. Although we spent the majority of our night discussing work-related matters, I enjoyed the past two hours in his company. Brandon is a great guy. He is very witty, and our conversation flowed as freely as the wine.

"I appreciate you getting me that file, Brandon."

It would have taken Brandon a lot of wheeling and dealing to get me that file, and he came through for me.

"No worries, Izzy. I was happy to help."

A thick cloud of awkwardness plagues the air when the elevator dings, announcing its arrival to my floor. Sensing Brandon's apprehension, I lean in to place a peck on his cheek. Just as my lips brush his cheek, he tilts his head, and his lips land on mine. I freeze in shock when his tongue glides across my gaped mouth. His lips are smooth, and his tongue is laced with the red wine we drank with our dessert.

Placing one hand on my neck and the other on my back, he pulls my body closer to his. Unexpectedly, a moan simpers from my throat, my body choosing its own response to Brandon's slow and tantalizingly teasing kiss.

My eyes open when he draws away from our embrace. His cheeks are pink, and his eyes are glossed with lust.

"I've wanted to do that for months."

My lips curve into an apprehensive smile. Brandon's kiss was touching, and he is a brilliant kisser, but our embrace didn't create the knee-wobbling reaction I get when I kiss Isaac.

"You don't have to say anything," Brandon says, noticing the worried look on my face. "I shouldn't have been so stupid to think someone as stunning as you would be interested in me."

My heart slithers into my stomach. Brandon is a wonderful guy. Any girl would be lucky to have him. *I'm the only stupid person standing in this corridor.*

Slinging my arms around his shoulders, I hug him fiercely. "If my heart weren't foolishly seeking an unattainable man, I'd have forgone my three-date rule and dragged you back into my apartment."

He chuckles before his hazel eyes seek mine. Although his gaze still shows his confusion, the hurt in his eyes has lessened.

"So, I was too late?"

I nod. "That's the only reason, Brandon. Any girl would be privileged to date you."

"Can you get me their numbers, then?"

I giggle at his playful comment.

"I'm not joking. Have you tried dating these days? It's a battlefield."

I don't reply to his statement. I simply shrug and grimace. 'Battlefield' is too kind of a word for dating in this new age. When the elevator dings again, Brandon and I end our night back in friendly territory. After a kiss on the cheek, we embrace each other with a brief hug.

Once he walks into the elevator, he turns around to face me. "If it doesn't work out with Mr. Unattainable, let me know."

I smile and nod. "Without a doubt."

Brandon grins as the elevator doors snap shut.

Upon entering my apartment, my long strides halt. Isaac is in my dining room. His fists are balled at his side, and his narrowed gaze is roaming over the empty dishes and wine bottles sprawled on the wooden tabletop.

"What are you doing in my apartment?"

My voice quivers, not just in fear but because of how quick my pulse is racing from seeing Isaac again. This is the first time I've laid eyes on him in person in over two weeks.

"How did you get in?" I interrogate, stepping toward him.

I'm sure I locked the door on my way out, but even if I didn't, you don't just enter someone's apartment without permission. I halt again when Isaac's icy eyes lift to mine. His gaze shows his undeniable anger.

His jaw ticks when his eyes travel over the long-sleeve jersey dress I'm wearing. I chose this dress to ensure Brandon knew our date was more a casual get-together between friends and not a romantic date. From the snarl forming on Isaac's lips, I'd say my clothing choice was a mistake on my part.

"Who was the man in your apartment?"

"How do you know it was a man?" My anger rises as the images of Isaac with a bevy of blondes rushes back to the forefront of my mind.

"Lipstick, no lipstick." He hooks his thumb to the two wine glasses.

My glass has an outline of the light pink lipstick I'm wearing while Brandon's has no lipstick smears.

"He's a *friend*." I overemphasize my last word.

Isaac growls a low, menacing groan that surges through my sex. My knees buckle as a hot slickness forms between my legs. *Stupid, traitorous body.*

Isaac's furious gaze stays planted on me as he removes his ringing cell phone from his pocket. His greeting is short and clipped. I don't know who he's talking to, but the tick in his jaw grows the longer their conversation continues. My heart stops beating when he disconnects the call and places his phone back into his pocket. His gaze is unrelenting, furious, and solely focused on me.

When he steps toward me, I back away, intimidated by his unnerving composure. He smirks at my reaction before continuing on his original endeavor. Before I can protest, Isaac has me trapped between his impressive body and the wall in my entryway.

He grips my chin, yanking it to the side. A moan tears from my mouth when he bites, sucks, and nips on my exposed neck. Gripping my ass cheeks, he pulls me into his body, so his lengthened cock braces my throbbing clit and halfway up my stomach.

I whimper when he withdraws from our embrace as quickly as he came. His eyes absorb my kiss-swollen lips and flushed cheeks before settling on my eyes.

"No more men in your apartment, Isabelle."

Since my legs are no longer capable of holding their own weight, my body slides down the wall, and I sit on the ground. Lifting my lust-hazed gaze, I watch Isaac stride toward my front door. He exits without a single glance back in my direction.

I've barely regained the ability to stand, let alone comprehend what just happened when I hear someone tapping on my front door. Begrudgingly, I scamper off the floor and pace to the door. I inhale deeply to relieve my flushed cheeks before swinging open the front door. I'm shocked and a little disappointed when I discover Brandon standing on the other side. My heart was hoping it was Isaac.

Brandon's eyes scan my face. The longer he appraises me, the more his brows scrunch.

"I... umm... forgot to get my coat." He spins on his heels. "But you look busy, so I'll come back later."

"Brandon, it's fine. I'm not busy."

I'm sure my flushed cheeks and wide eyes are awkwardly exposing my arousal, but I'm not too busy to gather his coat for him.

When he remains quiet, I grab ahold of his arm and drag him into the entryway of my apartment. His eyes bounce around the interior more eagerly than they did when he arrived hours ago. When he doesn't find what he's looking for, he returns them to me. I smile at his erratic behavior before moving to the coatroom to collect his jacket.

It's only when I catch a glimpse of my reflection in the entryway mirror do I realize what has caused his odd reaction. Right on my neck, as clear as day for all to see, is an unmistakably large and undignified love bite.

I'm going to kill him!

After ushering Brandon out of my apartment, hailing a taxi, wrangling with a colossal-looking bouncer to cut a long line, and weaving my way through a mass of sweaty bodies, I find Isaac in an impressive office at the back of his nightclub.

Two walls of his office are lined with dark mahogany bookshelves that go all the way to the ceiling. Every shelf is filled to the brim with a range of books. Isaac has his back turned and is peering out a window that faces the side street. His body is covered with an impeccably tailored three-piece suit.

Letting my anger get the better of me, I grab one of the hardcover books and send it hurtling across the room.

My anger makes me forgo rational thinking. "You son of a bitch!"

Isaac pivots around to face me, his eyes stern and unnerving. The roughness of his five o'clock shadow can't hide the tick of his jaw, and his lips have thinned.

Slanting his head, his eyes dart to the book that missed his back by mere inches before shooting back to mine. "I'll call you back."

He snaps shut the cell I didn't realize he was holding until now, then houses it in his pocket, but he doesn't remove his hand. The evil expression on his face is all the indication I need to know he did this on purpose.

"This wasn't an accident. You marked me. You branded me like some sort of... *animal*." I stop talking and grit my teeth, fighting the urge to sob.

The ticking of Isaac's jaw is more noticeable when he strides toward me. The look in his eyes is dangerous and solely focused on me. Although I should see his gaze as fearful, my body shudders in exhilaration. Not trusting myself around him, I flee toward the door I just entered and twist the handle.

Isaac's hand slaps the wooden door, holding it closed and blocking my exit. He leans in close, trapping me between him and the door. His breath flutters my ear when he hisses, "Did you enjoy his kiss, Isabelle?"

He saw me kiss Brandon?

When he lifts his spare hand to my neck, his pulse surges through his fingertips. "Did it make the veins in your neck throb faster like it does when I kiss you?"

My disloyal nipples harden when his hand glides over my breasts.

"Did your breasts become heavier and your nipples erect?"

Unable to speak, I shake my head.

Butterflies flutter in my stomach when he cups my pussy in his hand. The sting of his fingers forces a whimper of pleasure to escape my lips.

"Did you get wet?" he sneers, his tone unapologetic.

Blinded by rage, I buck against him. He has no right to be questioning me after how many women I saw entering and exiting his nightclub on his arm the past two weeks.

"He needs to learn not to touch what isn't his."

Through gritted teeth, I sneer. "I'm not yours either."

Isaac recoils at my statement as his hand holding the door shut balls into a fist. I grip the handle and yank on the door. Isaac pulls away from me so quick, air blasts my neck.

I scurry out of the door, denying him the opportunity of seeing the tears splashing down my cheeks.

CHAPTER 28

"*H*ey, Isabelle," Hugo greets when I stumble onto the sidewalk of Isaac's nightclub.

He's leaning on the back quarter-panel of Isaac's black Mercedes-Benz town car. His grin falters the instant he notices the tears dripping down my face. Ashamed at my immature tears, I brush them off my cheek with one swift sweep of my index finger.

"Get in. I'll take you home." Hugo gestures his head to the car.

"Thanks for the offer, but I'd prefer to grab a taxi."

In reality, I just want to get as far away from anything or anyone associated with Isaac Holt.

"It'll be at least a two-hour wait."

My eyes rake the street. A gasp expels from my mouth when I notice the long line at the taxi stand. Hugo smiles before opening the back door of Isaac's car. He chuckles when I walk past him and hop into the front passenger seat. I latch my belt while he jumps into the driver's seat.

Keeping my gaze planted on the star-filled black sky, I try to unravel the confusion muddling my mind. Hugo remains quiet, but I can feel his gaze occasionally shifting from the road to me.

"Did Isaac do that?" Hugo questions a short time later. His words have an edge of anxiety to them.

"Yep." I pivot to face him.

He strengthens his grip on the steering wheel and works his jaw side to side. "Don't take this the wrong way..."

I huff. Anytime someone says, "Don't take this the wrong way," it gets taken the wrong way.

Hugo's lips furl. "I know you're not happy about it, but would you rather him not care that you were kissing someone in the hallway of your apartment?"

"So, I should be happy he branded me?"

"I'm not saying that, but he cares enough about you, Isabelle, that the instant he knew you had a man in your apartment, he left a *very* important meeting to go to you."

My brows squeeze as my confused eyes scan Hugo's face. "How did Isaac know I had a man in my apartment?"

I've seen Isaac's town car parked outside of my apartment or Harlow's bakery numerous times the past two weeks. At first, I thought it was endearing. Now, I realize it's because Isaac doesn't want another man moving in on his turf.

"Are you protecting me, Hugo, or spying on me?" My tone is stern and unapologetic.

Hugo swallows raggedly before returning his attention to the road. Not a word seeps from his lips the remainder of the trip, revealing where his loyalty lies.

When Hugo pulls into the front of my apartment building, I unlatch my belt and climb out of the car while mumbling a quick thanks for the lift. When I'm halfway down the sidewalk, Hugo calls out my name. His face is marred with apprehension, his eyes full of remorse.

"Give Isaac the benefit of the doubt," he requests. "Not everything is black and white. There's a whole heap of gr—"

"Gray no one pays any attention to," I interrupt, repeating the saying Isaac quoted weeks ago.

Hugo grins so broadly, his eyes crinkle. I return his smile before pivoting on my heels and stalking away. After a few strides, the fog in my brain clears. I stiffen before spinning back around. My lips curl when I see Hugo standing by his car waiting for me to enter my building.

"I'm sorry for what happened to your sister, Marjorie."

For the quickest second, Hugo's face scrunches before a mask of composure slips in its place.

"Thank you."

I want to offer him a more heartfelt condolence, but Hugo doesn't seem like a hugging type of guy. So instead, I awkwardly wave and walk into my apartment building.

My lip crimps into a snarl. "Stop smiling, Harlow. It isn't funny," I growl through clenched teeth.

Ever since I entered the bakery, Harlow has been eyeing me curiously. When I yank the collar of my shirt up high, trying to hide the gigantic hickey, she boisterously laughs. Her chuckle is so loud, she startles the lady sitting in the window seat. Her scared yelp echoes around the nearly empty bakery.

"I'm not laughing at you, Izzy. I think it's hot." She moves to the table next to mine to gather the used dinnerware.

"You think branding is hot? What's wrong with you?"

My tone is quickly changing from angry to playful. I can never stay mad for long, let alone at someone with Harlow's personality.

"No, I don't think branding is hot, but it's sexy he wants other guys to stay away from you. That warning is a clear stay-the-hell-away message for any guy. It's more efficient than putting a ring on a girl's finger."

"A love bite doesn't discourage men, it encourages them." I grimace over all the horrid men I've crossed paths with.

Harlow's manicured brow shoots up into her hairline.

"Because they think I'll put out," I reply to her shocked expression.

She remains quiet as confusion intensifies on her adorable face.

"I once went on a date with a guy who told me he only dates single mothers. When I asked him why, he said it was because he knew she wasn't a virgin, so she'd be more likely to put out."

"That's disgusting." Harlow gags.

Her tone doesn't match her words. Her cheekbones rise as her mouth curves. The instant I spot the white of her teeth, a smile sneaks onto my face.

"At least he was honest," she says between a fit of giggles.

Rolling my eyes, I return my attention to the gossip magazine I was reading before Harlow interrupted me. My eyes bulge when they land on a gossip article in the back pages of a well-respected glossy magazine—*Three Eligible Bachelors Taken Off the Market in One Devastating Weekend.* It isn't the headline that has my heart palpitating faster. It's the photo of Isaac, Cormack, and Colby standing side by side. My eyes glance over the printed article under their picture.

Millions of women around the world are sighing in sync this weekend. Latest reports circling the gossip mill say billionaire McGregor brothers, Cormack (28) and Colby (24), are no longer on the market. The two eligible bachelors were sighted at their elaborate family beachside estate enjoying a lavish long weekend with their respective partners. It has been reported things are seriously heating up with each respective couple, and that this weekend was a way of formally introducing their new loves to their extended family.

In related matters, philanthropist, Isaac Holt, was also spotted the same weekend riding a jet ski with a brunette female companion. Later that same night, he was sighted exiting his award-winning multi-million-dollar nightclub, 57. Several patrons were surprised when he was spotted holding the hand of an attractive brunette. Sources believe it was the same brunette he was spotted with earlier that day. Isaac is well known for his playboy lifestyle, and it's the first time the public has witnessed a significant partner in his life the past six years.

Many single females are waking up to this sad news!

"Did you see this article?" I ask Harlow, who has finished gathering the crockery from the table next to mine.

"Yeah," she replies apprehensively. "Thankfully, the paparazzi didn't get any photos of the actual weekend. Cormack said that's an old photo from the Fourth of July weekend."

My heart stops beating. I didn't consider the fact Isaac and Cormack would be followed by the paparazzi. I only scanned the areas for surveillance vans. I sigh, glad no incriminating evidence was captured that weekend.

"You should be sighing in relief," she jests. "You're the brunette in both reports. Colby didn't bring a girlfriend that weekend. They're quoting from people who witnessed you guys at the beach together on Saturday morning."

Harlow smiles before sauntering toward the bakery counter. I grin back before returning my attention to the photo of the boys. It's a good photo of them all. I can mentally picture the devastated faces of millions of women around the world when they read this article. It's just a pity the report is only accurate for one of the three men photographed.

"Oh, before I forget, can I borrow your black pumps Friday night?" she asks, turning around to face me.

"Sure, no worries." I waggle my eyebrows. "Do you have a romantic date with Cormack?"

Harlow only freezes for the quickest second, but it was enough for me to notice. She smirks before dashing to the counter. Her quick movements cause the dishware in her hands to clang together.

"Harlow?"

I follow her to the counter. Noticing no customers are waiting to be served, I shadow her to the kitchen located at the back of the bakery. She is washing dishes. Her anger is so paramount, she chips two plates during the process. I've never seen Harlow pissed. I'll admit, she's as scary as hell when she is mad.

I rush for her, easing her hurried movements with my hands. Her glossed-over green eyes apprehensively lift to mine. She swallows hard before telling me, "I'm going on a double date with Cormack Friday night."

I eye her curiously. From the stories she's been telling me the past two weeks, things are going great with her and Cormack, so I don't understand her apprehension.

"We're going with Isaac. I assumed his date was you. Obviously, my assumption was wrong considering the fact you don't have any clue about Friday," Harlow enlightens me.

I grit my teeth hard, fighting the urge to sob. Isaac marked my skin as a warning for other men to stay away, then not only does he continue to date, he throws it in my face by ensuring my friend witnesses his dates firsthand.

Harlow moves to her handbag stored on a wooden shelf. "I'll cancel the date."

I bolt toward her and snatch her phone out of her grasp.

"Don't cancel," I request. "Add another two people to the reservation."

She eyes me curiously before the most mischievous grin etches on her mouth.

Returning her smile, I yank my phone out of my pocket.

"Hey, Regina, remember that hot detective you wanted to hook me up with? Can you see if he's free Friday night?"

CHAPTER 29

D amn! I underestimated Regina's hotness radar. Glacier-blue eyes, straight and prominent nose, a razor-sharp jaw hidden under day-old stubble, all combined on a face that looks like it belongs on the cover of *GQ* magazine. Although his blue suit doesn't look nearly as expensive as the suits Isaac wears, it showcases his muscular physique well.

His eyes peruse my body just as vigorously as I appraised his. His glowing gaze glides over my freshly shaven legs, lingering on the indecent length of my skirt before filtering over the curves of my breasts. My breath snags when his intriguing gaze settles on my face. When he smiles, my heart freezes. Straight pearly white teeth and small dimples in the creases of his mouth add even more allure to his already rugged appeal.

"I might need to start paying more attention to Regina's recommendations."

His voice is thick and gruff as if he smokes a pack of cigarettes per day. I know he doesn't, though, because I got his life history from Regina this morning. Ryan is twenty-eight years old. He's been working at Ravenshoe Police Station since he left the police academy at the tender age of nineteen. He was promoted to detective three years ago. He's unmarried, has no kids, and although he has no troubles attracting the ladies, Regina assures me he's not a ladies' man.

"Did you want to come in for a drink?"

Even though I originally planned to use Ryan to exact my revenge on Isaac, his incredibly gorgeous face has me reconsidering my initial approach.

Ryan smiles before glancing down at his watch. "With how dense the traffic is tonight, I don't think we'll have enough time for a drink, but I won't say no to a nightcap later." He returns his intense eyes to me.

Smiling, I grab my coat from the entryway table before closing my front door behind me. "I have a stringent three-date rule."

"I'm free all week." He gives me a sassy wink before offering me the crook of his arm.

The drive to the restaurant was pleasant. Our conversation flowed freely, and there was never any awkward silence. Although Ryan doesn't know I work for the FBI, he has heard of my Uncle Tobias. He even shared a few stories with me about my uncle that I hadn't heard before.

By the time we walk into the restaurant, I'm so immersed by Ryan, I've forgotten we're meeting other guests until the restaurant hostess walks us to the table Isaac and his date are already seated at.

Isaac's date is beautiful in a slutty type of way. Unsurprisingly, she's blonde as that seems to be Isaac's preferred choice of late. She's wearing an elegant dress that cost more than I earn in a week. It's just a pity she ordered it two sizes too small as her silicon breasts are threatening to spill out of the top of it at any moment.

Isaac glances up at me, our gazes colliding with palpable tension. He lowers his heated gaze down my body, loitering on my bare thighs longer than what could be classed as an acceptable glance. My ego awakens. I chose this dress with my four-inch-high stilettos as I knew it made my legs look like they went on for days and days. My outfit is the perfect cock-teasing ensemble.

His gaze turns icy-cold when he notices Ryan and my interlocked hands. After working his jaw side to side, he returns his eyes to mine.

His stare quickens my pulse, but I remain quiet, letting him stew, grateful the shoe is finally on the other foot.

"Isaac, I haven't seen you in months. Where have you been?" Ryan releases my hand to offer it in greeting to Isaac. "How is Nick? How many months left until we have another Holt player running around?" he continues, making me realize he knows Isaac more personally than just a casual acquaintance.

Isaac stands from his seat, his demeanor commanding the attention of everyone surrounding him. Numerous women—and even a handful of men's eyes—turn to watch him as if he's performing an act instead of doing something as simple as standing.

"I've been around. I've just been busy." Isaac's infuriated gaze shifts to me before he continues in a friendlier tone, "Jenni is due in a couple of months."

A smile curls on my lips. Even in his bad-tempered mood, he can't hide his excitement when he talks about his nephew due in a few months.

"Isabelle, this is Isaac Holt. I've not yet had the pleasure of arresting him, but I'm sure my day will come soon. Isaac, this is my date, Isabelle," Ryan introduces us, unaware that we've already met.

Isaac isn't the slightest bit fazed by Ryan's cheeky statement. His captivating gaze remains steadfast on mine as he offers me his hand to shake.

Rolling my eyes, I accept his offer. My heart thumps in an unnatural rhythm when he raises my hand to his mouth to kiss my palm. Although my heart is flipping, my outward appearance doesn't give any indication that his simplest touch has affected me.

"Are you going to introduce us to your date?" I drop my gaze to Isaac's date, who's more interested in the polish on her nails than participating in an adult conversation.

"Isabelle, Ryan, this is…" Isaac's brows draw together as confusion slides over his face.

"Tatiana," she informs us.

Her nasally whine screeches through my eardrums. If I'd only heard her speak, I would've assumed she was a twelve-year-old boy going through puberty.

"Tatiana." Isaac shakes his head before his mouth carves into a smirk.

I huff, disgusted he doesn't know his date's name. Sighing, I plunk down in a spare chair and skim my eyes around the restaurant while Isaac and Ryan continue with their chit-chat.

Thankfully, not long later, Harlow saunters toward our group. My mouth gapes, and my pupils widen. It isn't just her beautiful canary yellow dress that has my eyes bugging. It's the pair of Jimmy Choo gold and black Lana stilettos encasing her feet, capturing my attention. When we were fantasy shopping online a few weeks ago, she told me they were her dream pair of shoes, but at nearly twelve hundred dollars a pair, they were to remain a fantasy.

"Cormack's two-month anniversary present," she explains to my shocked expression before sitting down in the chair next to me. "I got him a present, but it's only suitable for him to open in private." She gives me a cheeky wink.

Her playful commentary improves my sour mood. I'm glad things are going well for Cormack and Harlow.

When Ryan takes a seat next to me, I jump when he places his hand on my bare thigh. Lifting my eyes, I meet his rugged grin. He seems pleased my body reacted to his touch. Although it did respond, it was more because I wasn't expecting his hand on my thigh than a zing of intimacy. Ryan is gorgeous, but no man can make my senses ignite as Isaac does.

"How do you know Isaac?" Ryan probes, gesturing his head to Isaac, who has sat back down next to his date.

Hearing Ryan's quiet interrogation, Isaac's unique colored eyes lift to mine. He shifts his head and cocks his brow, not attempting to conceal he's eavesdropping on our conversation.

"I don't know him. He's practically a stranger," I reply, my tone pompous.

A ravenous smile morphs onto Isaac's face before his tongue slides out to lick his top lip. When his eyes darken, I know he's recalling our time in the office of his nightclub.

Isaac's pussy-clenching chuckle sounds around our group when I dart my eyes away from his, needing to look at anything but his sinfully striking face.

For the next hour and a half, I keep my focus on Ryan. He has been a perfect gentleman with the occasional flirty line thrown in. He asked me what I'd like to eat instead of assuming, and not once did he bat an eyelid when the waiter filled my wine glass numerous times throughout the evening—unlike Isaac. Every time the server returned with a bottle, Isaac's eyes connected with mine. His lips would thin into a sharp line, and his brow would arch when I nodded at the waiter's silent question of a refill.

Although it has been awkward sitting across from Isaac, the night has gone surprisingly well. But I swear if I hear, "It feels so big," come out of Tatiana's mouth one more time, I'm going to snap.

I was always under the impression restaurants made sure each of their patrons had their own chair to sit in, but apparently, no one has informed Tatiana of that. She's been sitting in Isaac's lap since the first course was served. Isaac doesn't seem concerned about her closeness, but I've heard several other restaurant patrons' gasps of disdain when Tatiana's immature giggles bounce around the restaurant. Tatiana is beautiful, but she's a dimwit. I'm surprised someone as entrancing as Isaac would have any interest in wanting to date someone like Tatiana.

This time, when Ryan places his hand on my bare thigh, I don't jump in fright. Looking up from the extensive dessert menu, I lock eyes with his twinkling baby blues.

"What would you like for dessert?"

"Umm." My gaze returns to the menu. "There are too many choices. Why don't you pick something for me?"

His face spreads with a full-toothed grin as he waggles his eyebrows. My interest piques when he swivels his back and sneakily orders from the waitress. *What is he up to?*

"It feels so big," screeches Tatiana.

Gritting my teeth, I clench my fists around the white napkin on my lap. The urge to scream the obscenities running through my head is overwhelming. Before I can come up with a more respectable response, Harlow snarls.

"Okay, we get. It feels so big. It's so big. Isaac has a ginormous cock, but can you please shut your mouth for the next thirty minutes so I can enjoy my dessert without having to hear your nasally, whiny voice anymore? Thirty minutes of peace! That's all I ask."

My eyes snap to Cormack, wanting to gauge his reaction to Harlow's outburst. He's staring at Harlow in complete awe and admiration. Harlow gives me her I've-got-your-back look. I bestow my silent thanks with a grateful smirk before turning my annoyed gaze back to Tatiana. Her mouth is ajar, and her slitted green eyes are shooting daggers at Harlow.

"You're just jealous," Tatiana sneers.

"Oh, honey, please. I have absolutely nothing to be jealous of."

She doesn't. Harlow wins hands down in the looks department and don't even get me started on personality.

A bitter taste scorches my throat when Tatiana informs Isaac he can show her *exactly* how big it is tonight. Shifting my eyes to Isaac, I catch his gaze at me. When I grit my teeth and narrow my eyes, he winks. *Arrogant asshole.*

"Open up," Ryan croons.

My lips curve into an illustrious grin when Ryan dangles a cherry in front of my mouth. Since I was distracted by Isaac, I didn't notice the waitress serving Ryan one of the biggest banana splits I've ever seen.

Feeling playful and a little tipsy, I accept Ryan's offer. A long, salivating groan erupts from my throat when a burst of cherry goodness engulfs my taste buds. Ignoring Isaac's menacing growl vibrating across the table and Harlow's boisterous giggle, I dig my fingers into the gooey ice cream and fish out a cherry from the sticky goodness for Ryan. My cheeks heat when Ryan's teeth graze my fingertips before his moist tongue delves out to collect the cherry.

Holy shit!

Ryan winks before leaning in close to my side. He's so close, we could be perceived as an intimate couple. My eyes snap to his when he questions, "How far do you want to take this?"

My nervous eyes dance between his. "You're striving to make Isaac jealous, aren't you?"

My heart stops beating until I realize he isn't the slightest bit upset I've been using him to antagonize Isaac.

Twisting my napkin, I ask, "How did you know?"

"I'm a detective." His mouth curves into a huge grin. "And I'm not just good at my job, I'm the best they have ever fucking seen." He stills my nervous fidgeting before continuing, "That and the fact Isaac hasn't taken his eyes off you all night."

My eyes shift to Isaac, whose infuriated gaze is flicking between Ryan and me. His freshly shaven jaw is ticking profusely, and his hand resting on the white tablecloth is clenched in a tight fist.

"He will kill you." My tone is crammed with sarcasm as I turn my eyes back to Ryan.

"Please, you don't think I can handle Isaac Holt?" He smiles an evil grin. "The bigger question is, can you handle Isaac Holt?"

My pulse quickens as my core tightens. Not just at the idea of making Isaac jealous, but from having Ryan's incredibly handsome face so close to mine. "I can handle Isaac better than you think." The alcohol running through my body is making me more brazen than usual.

"All right, if you ar—"

Before all the words spill from Ryan's lips, I enclose my mouth over his. A fiery warmth ignites in my chest from his skillful kiss. Ryan is a talented kisser, and he knows how to use his skills to his advantage.

Just as a husky moan tears from my throat, an arm curls around my waist. With a growl, I'm yanked away from Ryan. At first, I'm too dazed to configure a response. My mind is a blurred mess of confusion, not just from Ryan's thrilling kiss, but from a few glasses of wine as well. It's only when Isaac's scrumptious scent fills my nostrils does realization dawn.

"Put me down," I request as my mortified eyes dart around the restaurant to see several patrons watching our exchange.

I'd hoped Isaac would react, but I would never have thought he'd drag me out of an elegant restaurant while hundreds of patrons watch in hilarity.

"Isaac, put me down," I demand more sternly.

Jerking my arms and legs out, I try to get him to release his grasp around my waist. He doesn't utter a word, but I can hear his jaw ticking relentlessly. Frigid air causes my arms to bristle with goosebumps when he walks us outside. I stop wailing, expecting him to put me back on my feet now that we're outside and no longer attracting the attention of other patrons, but he doesn't put me down. Instead, he shoves me into the backseat of his Mercedes-Benz town car.

"Stay here," he demands through gritted teeth before slamming the door.

I crawl across the plush leather seat and yank on the door handle. Growling in frustration, I flop into the dark gray seats. The door is locked, and there's no locking mechanism in sight.

I stop banging my fists on the window when a chuckle echoes in the cab. Turning my infuriated eyes, I'm greeted by the mischievous grin of Hugo, glaring at me through the rearview mirror.

"Hey, Isabelle," he greets, his tone full of amusement.

"Unlock the doors, Hugo."

He shakes his head. "No can do. I like my job."

I glare at him, unappreciative of the humor in his tone. He isn't the least bit fazed by my irate scowl. His grin enlarges the longer I stare at him.

Just as I'm about to crawl over the privacy divider to unlock the doors myself, the back passenger door opens, and Isaac peers inside.

Time stands still when I catch his angry glare. It's pulse-quickening delicious.

When he throws my coat and purse to me, a smile curves on my mouth. My inner vixen is pleased that even while angry, he's still considerate enough to collect my belongings.

My smile is wiped right off my face when Tatiana slides into the seat next to me. Her cheap floral perfume makes my wine-sloshed stomach churn.

When Isaac slips in next to her and slams the door shut, my anger returns full pelt.

"Open the door, Hugo," I demand when my rough yanks on the door latch are fruitless.

My jaw twitches so badly, my back molars grind together, and blood surges through my veins so fast, I'm afraid I may soon have a coronary.

Hugo snubs my request. "Where to, boss?"

"Isabelle's apartment," Isaac's eyes flick to mine.

He's watching me but has Tatiana snuggled in the crook of his arm. I nearly heave on the expensive leather seats when he runs his index finger along my clenched fist, and the hairs on my arms bristle from his touch.

Stupid, traitorous body.

Disgusted with my body's reaction to him, I grunt, "Move!"

When I dive over Tatiana's barely-covered stick-thin thighs, I kick my legs out wildly, ensuring my four-inch heels dig into Isaac's trouser-covered leg as I throw my body over the privacy partition.

"Close your eyes, Hugo, or you'll cop an eye full," I warn before scissoring my legs into the front seat as he speeds down the street.

My maneuver is extremely unladylike with my backside being thrust into Hugo's face, but effective when I plop into the seat beside him.

Hugo remains quiet, but his teeth glow in the moonlight when I lean over his chest to raise the blacked-out partition, blocking my view of Isaac and his date.

By the time we arrive at my apartment, my anger has gone from a slow simmer to a full boil. I thought listening to Tatiana's annoying voice was torture, but not hearing it was ten times worse. Once I raised the privacy partition, I couldn't hear or see one thing Isaac and his date were doing the entire trip. I chewed off two of my French-manicured tips just to force myself not to lower the partition.

"Thanks for the lift," I grunt when Hugo finally releases the lock mechanism.

Mumbling incoherently under my breath, I flee to my apartment building. My angry strides slow when I hear a car door opening in the distance. Turning my head, I spot Isaac gliding out of the back of his vehicle.

I huff before quickening my pace. Darting through the spinning glass doors of my building, I rush toward the elevator banks, my heart rate increasing with every step I take.

"Thank you," I praise to the gentleman holding the elevator open for me.

I race to the dashboard, pushing the close door button before Isaac can board the elevator. A triumphant grin morphs on my face when the doors slam shut just as Isaac enters the foyer.

I suck in numerous big breaths as I mosey to the back of the elevator. My overheated skin relishes the coolness of the mirrored walls when I lean my back against them.

Hearing my loud sigh, my elevator companion questions, "Exciting night?" His tone is friendly, but it still has an edge of cheekiness to it.

"You could say—"

Before the whole sentence spills from my lips, the elevator jolts before plunging into terrifying blackness. It's darker than usual as the elevator dashboard isn't illuminated. My stomach lurches, all the wine and food I've consumed tonight threatening to resurface as my panic surges from being trapped in a small, dark box. *Claustrophobia and I have never been close friends.*

"It's okay. It should only be a few minutes before it begins working again," assures my companion when he hears my ragged breaths filling the cab.

My death grip on the railing lessens when the elevator lights flicker back on as it jerks back into action.

Only once I calm the reckless beat of my heart do I realize the elevator is descending instead of ascending.

Retightening my grip on the stainless-steel rail, I watch my companion step toward the dashboard.

"Push any button." I'd rather walk the stairs than be stuck in this death trap as it plummets to the ground.

My companion swallows in dismay when he illuminates every button on the dashboard, but the elevator continues descending, not once stopping on any of the floors we have requested. It's only when the doors ding and open on the ground floor do I comprehend what's happening. There, in all his six-foot-plus glory, is the incredibly alluring Mr. Holt, smirking condescendingly.

"You're an asshole."

He grins at my comment before shifting on his feet to face a security officer who works in the lobby of my apartment building. While slipping the attendant a folded-up bill, they shake hands before Isaac steps into the elevator.

His infuriated gaze darts to my elevator companion. "Get out."

My companion doesn't argue with him. He just scurries out of the elevator as fast as his legs will take him. *Coward.*

I try to follow him, but Isaac seizes my wrist before I can get a foot out of the elevator. Even fuming with anger, my body can't deny the sexual energy zapping up my arm.

Yanking out of his grip, I head to the back of the elevator to lean on the cool, mirrored wall. Isaac's presence is so strong it suffocates the air surrounding him. My cheeks are already flushed from his closeness.

Once the elevator starts ascending, Isaac pivots to face me. His narrowed eyes study my body before lifting to my face. His gaze is unnerving and primal, and it has my pulse quickening. When he drinks in my flushed cheeks, he cockily winks.

"You're a pig." I cross my arms in front of my chest, still annoyed at spending the last two hours in the presence of him and his dim-witted date.

"And yet, you still want to fuck me."

My eyes shoot to his. His hungry, heavy-lidded gaze stares into mine, daring me to deny his statement.

"You wish," I snarl in a whisper.

He inhales an unashamed whiff through his nostrils. "Deny it all you want, Isabelle, but I can smell how aroused you are."

My knees pull together as a bashful whimper hums my lips. When he steps closer to me, I hold my hand out in front of my body, stopping him midstride. I can feel my qualm slipping, so the closer he gets to me, the more my levelheadedness will falter.

Ignoring my silent warning, Isaac nods, smiles a devilishly evil grin, then steps closer.

In a blur of bites, tongue lashes, and mini-climaxes, I somehow end up being held against the wall in my apartment. My dress is bunched around my stomach, and two of Isaac's long, gifted fingers have my orgasm teetering on the brink. Our movements are frantic, both blinded by a lust-filled frenzy. Stars form, I scream his name, and my legs buckle when an explosion of fireworks erupt through my body so hard and fast I nearly tumble to the ground.

Once my womb stops clenching, Isaac removes his talented fingers from my soaking wet pussy. He tightens his grip on my ass before sliding down the zipper of his trousers. His pants slip off his muscular legs, gathering in a heap around his ankles. I suck in a breath when his perfect cock springs free from his black boxers. Just the sight of his cock has a fiery warmth building in my lower gut.

When plastic ripping sounds through my ears, my insides tighten and not in a good way.

"Any guy who tells you he's carrying a condom in his wallet in case of an emergency is full of shit. We only put a condom in our wallet with the full intention of using it the night we put it in there."

Oh God, I'm going to be sick.

I slap my hand over my mouth as my stomach heaves. Isaac didn't know I would be at the restaurant. So, he was planning on using that condom on, on, Tatiana.

Gritting my teeth, I place my open palms on Isaac's sweat-drenched, shirt-covered chest and push with all my might. The biggest grunt of anger erupts from my lips, but Isaac doesn't budge an inch.

"Get out," I sneer, clenching my fists and digging my nails into my palms. My breathing returns, but instead of panting in ecstasy, I'm gasping in pure, unbridled anger.

Isaac's brows scrunch together as he glares at me in confusion. He shouldn't be confused. He knows the game he's been playing.

For weeks, I've watched him emerge from his nightclub with a range of women on his arm. I stupidly told myself that not everything is as it seems. I remembered what he said about there being a whole heap of gray no one pays any attention to. I gave him the benefit of the doubt as Hugo requested. *How could I have been so stupid?*

"Get out!" I shout again as tears spring down my face.

When Isaac remains standing in the entryway looking baffled and angry at the same time, I slip under his arm and bolt to the bathroom, locking the door behind me.

By the time I've scrubbed my skin red raw to remove Isaac's intoxicating scent from my body, tears are streaming out of my eyes more forcefully than the water flows from the faucet.

CHAPTER 30

Two weeks later...

"Hey, it's nearly ten o'clock, and we have the weekend off." I amble into the dimly lit conference room no one ever uses. "So, what are you still doing hiding out in here?"

My enthusiasm about having the weekend off gets sucked right out of me when my eyes roam over the various moldy boxes surrounding Brandon. For the past two weeks, I've thrown myself into work. The only time I've been cooped up in my apartment is when I need to shower and sleep, but no matter how occupied I keep my brain, my thoughts always drift to Isaac.

"I no longer have the weekend off." Brandon's tone relays his disappointment.

Brandon's eyes lift from the document in his hand. He grimaces and gags. Smiling at his playful response, I walk into the room and lift the lid on the first storage box. It's filled to the brim with documents and reports.

My lips twist as I spin around to face him. "What are all these

194

files?"

"They're your Uncle Tobias' records Alex had shipped here," he explains, his tone reserved.

I remain quiet as Brandon heads for a larger section of boxes on the right-hand side of the room. "These are your uncle's files from when he worked undercover in the Petretti Family. And these are his records on the Gottle family." He points to the smaller pile of boxes I'm standing beside.

My brows scrunch. I didn't know my uncle worked undercover in either of those families.

An overwhelming sense of deceit plagues me when I blurt out, "Isaac Holt doesn't have any business connection with either the Petretti or the Gottle family."

My statement isn't a total lie. From what I've perceived in private, Isaac's connection with both families is personal, not business-related.

"We already know Isaac is acquainted with Henry Gottle from the surveillance photo you got of Delilah Winterbottom months ago, but I agree, there has been no known association between Col Petretti and Isaac that would warrant me investigating them. Other than being rivals, I can't find any connection between them, but Alex is adamant I have to spend my weekend rifling through these documents until I unearth Isaac's dark secrets."

"Do you believe Isaac's secrets are held within these boxes?"

Brandon stays quiet as his curious hazel eyes filter over my face. He curses under his breath and runs his hand through his hair before his eyes collide with mine.

"Maybe ask me again next month?"

My lips curve into a smile. "Where do you want me to start?"

"It's fine, Izzy. Go and enjoy your weekend off." His eyes relay his appreciation of my offer to help.

I don't grace him with a reply. I just remove my coat and hang it over the back of Brandon's jacket flung over a spare chair. Brandon grins at my silent response. Once he finishes rolling up the sleeves of his crisp, blue business shirt, he pulls out a handful of manila folders from the closest box and gestures for me to take a seat opposite him.

His grin enlarges to a full smile when I murmur, "You're paying for the pizza."

Brandon's eyes lift to mine as he snags the last slice of pizza out of the grease-lined box. "So, we have worked out Delilah is a cradle snatcher, dating a man six years her junior. Her husband, Henry Gottle the third, Isaac Holt, and Cormack McGregor went to the same university," he says through a mouthful of cheese pizza.

"Yep. Cormack and Isaac were roommates, and Henry was their RA."

"Henry now works as a promoter for the UFC in New York City, and he hasn't had any known contact with his father in over five years."

"Nearly six," I interrupt, checking the information my Uncle Tobias noted in his file on Henry Gottle, the third. "Isaac's fighter, Jacob Walters, was a UFC fighter before he was issued a two-year probation for assault on a gentleman named Callum Parker. Jacob retaliated when Callum brutalized his on-and-off-again girlfriend, Lola. Isaac paid Jacob's extensive legal bills."

"But why would Isaac be interested in organizing a fight for Jacob in the UFC? Wouldn't he make more money by keeping him in his private fighting circle? The rumors are those fights can range from five thousand to over one hundred thousand a fight."

"This is why." I hand him an arrest warrant for domestic abuse filed three years ago for a Curtis Parker. "That's Callum's brother, Curtis. Curtis is a contracted UFC fighter. His contract is locked up so tight, he can't fight anyone not in the UFC for at least the next three years. Jacob and Curtis fought early in Jacob's UFC career. That's the only match Jacob was defeated in so far in his illustrious career. After that match, the referee was cited for biases. Maybe if Isaac can organize this fight for Jacob, Jacob will continue to fight in Isaac's fighting ring?"

"So, Jacob is the one forcing Isaac's association with Henry. It has nothing to do with the mob. Jacob just wants a chance at a fair rematch?"

Smiling, I nod. "Henry's ex-wife, Delilah Winterbottom, started working at Destiny Records one month before her husband filed for divorce. Destiny Records is owned by Isaac's best friend, Cormack. Some may say it's a coincidence, but I think Isaac did Henry a favor by getting Delilah out of his hair in the hopes Henry would help him find a way for Jacob to fight Curtis."

Brandon's brow arches as his lips curl into a grin. "It's plausible." He seems genuinely surprised. "I'll put it in a report and see what Alex has to say in the morning."

I smile, glad that Brandon's views on Isaac are swaying toward the positive. Even being hurt by Isaac, I'll continue to defend his integrity until I find a credible reason to believe he's the man his FBI file portrays him to be. My Uncle Tobias may not have taught me to cook or clean, but he did teach me to make my own informed opinions. *Oh, and how to shoot a pistol like a real gunslinger, but that's a story for another day.*

"So that's one mystery solved. Now, onto the much bigger one." Brandon's eyes lower to the stack of boxes.

Following his gaze, I catch a glimpse of the time on my watch. My eyes bug when I realize it's almost two in the morning. "Holy crap, it's close to 2:00 a.m.!"

"I'm so sorry, Izzy. I didn't know it was that late," he apologizes. "I hope I'm not keeping you from anything."

I expel a puff of air. "Watching re-runs of *Sex and the City* or unearthing the secrets of an enigma. I'll take what's behind curtain B, please, Roger."

Deliriously fatigued, I giggle louder than usual at my pathetic joke. My immature laughter halts when I catch Brandon's admiring gaze watching me in awe.

"What?"

I pull up the sleeves on my shirt since the room has become stiflingly muggy.

"You have a beautiful laugh, Izzy."

Through heated cheeks, I respond, "Thank you."

After the severe beating my ego took two weeks ago with Isaac and Tatiana, I'll accept any compliment I can get. Not giving us the chance to slip into uncomfortable territory, I grab a handful of the manila folders in the vast Col Petretti section. When I sit back at the desk, Brandon smiles before holding out his hand for his share of the pile.

Mumbling, I shift my head away from the sharp pointy object digging into my cheek. A groan rolls up my throat before I reluctantly open my eyes. The morning sun is barely contained by the white vertical blinds on the window in the conference room. My head is thumping from the minimal amount of sleep I got, and my mouth is parched from being left hanging open.

Peering down, I soon discover what was piercing my face the past few hours—my open red ballpoint pen. I run my hand down my face to check that there are no red smear marks on my cheek.

A ghost of a smile forms on my face when I catch the figure of Brandon slumped on a hard chair across from me. My smile enlarges to a full-toothed grin when I discover Brandon's blazer jacket draped around my shoulders. He must have placed it there after I'd fallen asleep. Brandon is a real sweetheart, but for some reason, I'm drawn to an alpha male who infuriates me more than he nurtures me.

My bones creak when I stand to stretch my weary body. After spending three hours reading Col Petretti's file, we're no closer to finding any connection between him and Isaac. Other than me personally knowing they've met, there's not one shred of information in Col's file that alludes to them knowing one another privately or in business.

"Shit," I croak when my cell phone beeps in my pocket.

Fumbling, I yank my cell phone out and silence it before it wakes Brandon. I sneak out of the conference room while glancing down at my phone screen. Confusion smashes into me when I read Harlow's message.

Harlow: *Get your coffee at Starbucks this morning.*

My heart thrashes my ribcage as I dial the number for Harlow's bakery and press my phone to my ear.

"Harlow's Scrumptious Haven, how can I help you?"

"Hey, Harlow, it's Izzy. Is everything okay?"

"Oh, hi, Mom, how are you?" she replies quickly.

I remain quiet, completely dumbfounded.

"I heard you and the ladies from the bowling alley got into a little mischief last night. *Dad* isn't happy with you this morning. How many times have you been told if you're going to spend all night out with your *friends,* you should inform someone?"

"What the hell are you talking about, Harlow—"

"Hey, give the phone back. I'm talking to my mom."

I can barely control my breaths when the deliriously seductive voice of Isaac Holt sounds down the line two seconds later. "Where are you, Isabelle? And don't you dare say your apartment as I know you haven't been back there all night."

One, how the hell does he know that? And two, he has no right to be questioning me. His *dates* haven't stopped since we returned from our weekend away. The long line of women didn't even falter after I kicked him out of my apartment two weeks ago.

Before I can form a response, Alex walks through the glass door of our office. When he notices my wide-eyed expression, he closes the distance between us. He appears surprised to see me in the office so early.

"Good morning, Isabelle."

"Morning," I babble, trying my hardest to ignore the angry growl of Isaac grumbling down the line.

"If he touched you, I'll break every fucking bone in his body," Isaac snarls viciously.

Although I can't see him, I can imagine how fast his jaw is ticking right now.

Unleashing my inner bitch, I reply, "I'm sorry, I'm indisposed right now, but be sure to say hello to Tatiana for me," before disconnecting the call.

There must be something wrong with me because not only is my blood rushing through my body so fast my veins are bulging, but my sex is soaking wet. An angry Isaac is sexy as hell, so imagine what an angry *and* jealous Isaac would look like?

Raising my hand to fan my flaming cheeks, I catch Alex's confused gaze raking over my face.

"Are you okay?" he questions, noticing my flushed expression.

Unable to form words through my lust-filled haze, I smile and nod. I may be treading in shark-infested waters, but I'm fine nevertheless.

I freeze as part of Isaac's statement runs through my mind. *"I'll break every fucking bone in his body."*

My heart rate quickens as I skedaddle back to the conference room to rustle through the folders my eyes skimmed early this morning. My quick movements wake Brandon from his restless sleep. He rubs his eyes before moving to stand next to me.

"How many years ago was Col Petretti's son admitted to the hospital?" My words come out in a hurry.

Brandon takes his time considering a response to my question. His brain is obviously still jumbled from only two hours of sleep. "Umm, around six, seven years ago," he eventually replies.

After I find Col Junior's (CJ's) hospitalization record, I move to the stack of Isaac's bank records, which date back to when he was a freshman in college. My eyes dart between the date on the hospital files and Isaac's bank statements. *Bingo. I've found a connection between Col Petretti and Isaac.*

"Look." I thrust the papers toward Brandon. "Isaac's hefty Monday morning cash deposits during his first two years at college ceased the weekend Col's son was admitted to the hospital. CJ's medical report indicates he was extensively covered in bruises, and he sustained multiple broken bones and fractures."

Brandon examines the extensive medical report.

"Isaac was a fighter in the underground fight ring, just like his fighter, Jacob, is now. I'd put money on it that Isaac and CJ fought that weekend..." I suddenly stop talking, realizing I just spilled private information on Isaac I gained in confidence.

Alex enters the room. "How do you know Isaac was a fighter?"

Shit!

"Umm... I'm just assuming." My heart rate increases. "It doesn't seem like an industry you would get into unless you had some prior knowledge about it."

"Your investigating skills are starting to flourish, Isabelle. I'm very pleased with your dedication of late," Alex commends me.

I remain quiet, riddled with guilt that I just snitched on Isaac. Even angry at him, I didn't intentionally mean to break his trust.

"We recently discovered Isaac was indeed a fighter in an underground fighting ring during his years at college. That fighting ring's organizer was Col Petretti," Alex informs us.

"Ah, hold on," Brandon interrupts, his eyes meeting mine. "CJ's injuries weren't from a fight. That weekend he was involved in a car accident with his sister, Ophelia."

My eyes burn from a sudden rush of moisture in them. "What?"

"CJ and his younger sister, Ophelia, were involved in a fatal car accident six years ago." Brandon hands me back the medical record along with a police record on the crash.

My hand trembles when I remove the documents from Brandon's hand. As I scan the reports, my mind flicks back to the night Isaac ran into Col.

"The prodigal son returns. What has it been... six years, and I don't even get a hello."

"He hasn't looked at anyone the way he looks at you in years. Not since Ophelia."

Oh God!

"Was anyone else in the car with them?"

Brandon shakes his head

"Did Ophelia survive the accident?"

My vision blurs with tears when Brandon once again shakes his head.

CHAPTER 31

"*Where* is he?"

Hugo's tormented eyes lift to mine. He smiles before releasing the lock mechanism of Isaac's town car. When I slide into the passenger seat, he pulls the car into the midday traffic and heads outside the city. He remains quiet, but he occasionally glances my way.

As soon as I could, without drawing attention to myself, I left the office and went straight to Harlow's bakery. I knew either Isaac or Hugo would be there waiting for me. I've noticed the past few weeks whenever I exit the bakery, Isaac's town car would be parked somewhere along that street.

I used to think it was because Isaac is a dominant alpha male, and he couldn't stand the idea of another man moving in on his turf. Although part of his stalker behavior is because of that exact reason, I now believe I have a better understanding of why his behavior can be so erratic. After experiencing a loss, most people are reluctant to form an attachment again. They fear if they do, they may also lose that attachment. Although finding out Isaac has suffered a significant loss doesn't excuse his poor behavior of late, my heart still yearns to comfort him.

My anxious eyes dart to Hugo when he pulls into a rundown building located an hour from Ravenshoe. He remains quiet, not answering my silent questions as he parks next to Isaac's sleek black sports car. Once he turns off the ignition, he nudges his head to a roller door slightly ajar at the side of the warehouse.

I unlatch my belt and open the door. My steps freeze when Hugo starts the car and backs away from the rundown warehouse.

"Isaac will give you a lift home," he says to my panicked expression before skidding out of the driveway, leaving nothing but a cloud of dust in his wake.

Clenching my fists at my side, I stride toward the metal and glass warehouse. Air traps in my throat when I walk into the desolate, rundown building. Isaac is wearing nothing but a pair of black gym shorts and dark running shoes. He's covered head to toe in sweat and is undertaking a grueling routine on a cracked boxing bag hanging from the ceiling by a sizable rusted chain.

Sensing my presence, Isaac's punishing onslaught on the bag stops. When his livid eyes turn, I'm rendered motionless, pinned in place. His heavy-lidded gaze rakes my body before returning to my face. He works his jaw side to side before turning his attention back to the bag. This time, his fury is unleashed with so much force, sand trickles from it like blood seeping from an open wound.

My panties moisten watching him work the bag so expertly. The way his muscles contract as he moves around the bag is an incredibly arousing visual, but even with it being a sexually inspiring sight, his anger projects off him in invisible waves. *That anger is only there because of me.*

Knowing there's only one sentence a dominant male like Isaac wants to hear flowing from my mouth, I shout, "I didn't sleep with anyone last night."

My voice barely projects over his loud, angry grunts. "I haven't had sexual contact with anyone but you in over a year."

Isaac's unbridled onslaught against the worn bag halts. He remains facing the bag, allowing my eyes the chance to absorb every muscle, dip, and curve of his sculptured back. He's breathing so hard, his heavy pants echo through the deserted warehouse.

When he turns to face me, my pupils enlarge. His gaze is unnerving, but even with his eyes showing his anger, I see a small amount of reprieve forming in them.

"Say it again," he requests, his voice hoarse from the harshness of his panting.

"I haven't had sexual—"

"Not that statement. The one about last night," he interrupts, his tone clipped.

Swallowing hard, I repeat, "I didn't sleep with anyone last night."

"Where were you?"

"I was working."

His eyes stare into mine. He can see through to my soul, so he knows I'm telling the truth. Furthermore, he'd detect my deceit, so it would be fruitless for me to lie to him.

"Why didn't you say that this morning when I asked you the same question?"

"Because I was angry with you." Honesty echoes in my tone. "I wanted you to feel what I felt when I saw you with Tatiana."

"I already felt it, Isabelle," he retaliates with a snarl. "When you had your lips on not one, but two men in a week."

"That isn't even close to the hurt I felt watching you fuck your way through half the female population in Ravenshoe."

My anger boils when he smugly smirks. Shaking my head, I spin on my heels and pace toward the roller door. "I don't know why I bothered coming here."

"Stop, Isabelle."

Ignoring his request, I increase my long strides. My tears are threatening to spill, and I don't want to give him the satisfaction of seeing he has upset me.

Without warning, Isaac bands his muscular arm around my waist, halting my rapid steps. "I said stop!" he hisses into my ear.

My anger over everything I've witnessed in his surveillance photos and in person the past five weeks is unleashed when I vehemently throw my legs and arms out. Angry grunts emit from my lips as I struggle to breathe through the tears streaming down my face.

No matter how hard I fight, Isaac doesn't release or loosen his tight grip.

My ferocious battle lessens when he whispers, "I haven't slept with anyone since you."

"You're a liar!" I fire back. "You had a condom in your wallet. You were planning on sleeping with Tatiana."

Isaac's clutch on my waist constricts. "Let's get one thing straight, Isabelle. I don't fucking lie, ever!" he rebuts. "And two, I got that condom out of *your* purse. That night, I gave you the benefit of the doubt that you put it in there for me, not Ryan, but you didn't consider giving me the same courtesy?"

My struggle halts. I did put a condom in my purse that night. I went into that date wanting to spark a reaction out of Isaac, so I went in fully prepared. I knew my desire for him always outweighs my levelheadedness. I didn't think to ask him where he got the condom. I just assumed he had brought it with him.

"Not everything is as it seems, Isabelle, but I haven't been with anyone sexually except you since our weekend away. Whether you choose to believe me or not is your choice."

Once he places me down onto my feet, I brush my unnecessary tears off my cheeks and pivot around to face him. His handsome face is taut and constricted, and his beautiful eyes are shifting between mine. He's still panting heavily, making his well-toned chest rise and fall with every breath he takes. His black UFC open-fingered, glove-covered fists are clenched at his side. This is the rawest I've ever seen him, and it's an equally stimulating and emotional sight at the same time.

Although I have deep-seated trust issues from my childhood, I trust what Isaac is saying. You can't fall in love with someone and not trust them. *Without trust, there would be nothing.* So as much as my brain is telling me to wait and evaluate the situation once I have a clear and conscious head, my heart has already formed its own decision.

"I believe you." I take a hesitant step toward him.

The agitation marring his beautiful face softens the instant the words filter from my mouth. Lifting my hand, I cradle his sweat-drenched cheek in my palm. The muscle in his cheek tremors from my touch. A smile curves on my lips pleased his body reacts to my meekest touch just as robustly as my body does to his. Brazenly, I propel onto my tippy-toes and seal my mouth over his. His mouth is warm and inviting and tastes salty from the sweat running over his lips. I Inwardly cheer when Isaac allows me to control the pace of our kiss.

When Isaac caresses my ass cheeks in his hands and squeezes them, my legs lift and curl around his waist. A husky moan rumbles up my throat when my pussy connects with his stiffened shaft. His dominant nature is unleashed when he increases the tempo of our kiss.

Unashamed, I grind my aching sex along his cock in a rhythm matching the lashings of his tongue. Because he's only wearing thin running shorts, the massive ridges of his cock are felt through my damp panties. A familiar coil twists in my drenched sex as my anger morphs into desperate need. Isaac plays my body like a gifted musician plays guitar, and it doesn't take him many strums to have it prepared to topple into ecstasy.

Sensing my impending climax, Isaac withdraws from my embrace.

"No," I gasp breathlessly, my voice whiny.

"Not here," Isaac replies to my shameless protest.

Placing me on my feet, Isaac yanks my skirt to a modest level before clasping my hand in his. I struggle to maintain his frantic pace to his car parked outside. Acknowledging my fight, he scoops me into his arms before continuing with his long strides.

Remaining quiet, he places me in the passenger seat before latching my seat belt. The air sucks out of my lungs from the sheer closeness of his striking face. My God, he's a handsome man. Beautiful, yet enigmatic.

Suddenly stopping, Isaac inhales a vast whiff through his nostrils. The growl he releases when he exhales causes a pleasurable zap to my sex. I squeeze my thighs together when his sultry gaze locks with mine. It's hot and heavy, and they have me wiggling in my seat.

"Stop looking at me like that, Isabelle, or I'll take you on the hood of my car."

My sex aches. "Please," I whimper, unashamed.

Isaac smiles an evil grin. "As tempting as that offer is, you've been a bad girl, Isabelle, so your punishment is only suitable for behind closed doors."

My cheeks flame as unbridled desire heats my veins. Winking at my enthusiastic response, Isaac jogs around the car and slides into the driver's seat. In the process, he slips on a cotton shirt and removes his gloves. When he cranks the ignition of his flashy car, I barely hold back a soft moan. The purr of his engine sends a thrill of excitement to my already oversensitive pussy, adding to my eagerness.

I still my breathing when Isaac revs the engine several times before shifting the gears. After fishtailing in the loose gravel, his car whizzes toward the road.

Once we're on the highway, Isaac places his hand on my bare thigh. His is high enough his pinkie finger can teasingly graze my panties, but not high enough to subdue my eagerness. Although his touch is as soft as a feather, it commands my body's full attention.

I shift my position, craving more. My core is twisted up so tight, I'm confident one touch of his talented fingers will have me toppling into orgasmic bliss.

"Not yet," Isaac teases, lowering his hand to its original position.

Groaning, I shift my focus to the derelict buildings whizzing by my window, hoping the bland scenery will quell my excitement.

It doesn't.

I thought the forty-five minutes on the Wave Runner was torture, but this is ten times worse. Isaac's seductive scent is invading every surface of his car, and his index finger tracing a figure-eight pattern on my inner thigh has my sex dripping wet. Furthermore, just being aware of his sexual prowess has my anticipation of what's about to come overwhelming all rationalism. I'm so worked up, I could cry.

After thirty torturous minutes, Isaac pulls his car into the underground garage of his apartment building. Our elevator ride is intense with the heady lust energizing the air between us.

Isaac calms my fidgeting hand, twisting my skirt by holding it in his. His simple touch surges my horniness to an even higher level. When an elegantly dressed elderly lady enters the elevator at the lobby, her narrowed eyes bounce between Isaac and me. Seemingly unimpressed with my flamed cheeks and wide eyes, her top lip forms into a snarl.

"Cute dog," I praise, nudging my head to her toy poodle she's cradling in her arms.

Huffing, she turns her indignant face to the elevator doors. A giggle spills from my lips when she covers her dog's eyes. Anyone would swear she caught us in a lewd act from the way she's acting, where all she saw is a couple holding hands.

Hearing my immature giggles, Isaac's grip on my hand tenses. Before I can comprehend what's happening, I'm spread against the elevator wall, and Isaac's skillful lips and tongue are exploring my mouth.

The elderly lady's loud gasp of disdain mimics the throaty moan rolling up my chest. While she frantically stabs the 'Open Door' button, my hands eagerly explore the firm ridges in Isaac's torso and back. His body is as scrumptious as his mouth.

When the elevator lurches to a stop on the next floor, the old bitty flees like her backside is on fire. Her disgruntled mumblings and the yap of her dog barking is the last thing I hear before my sole devotion returns to Isaac and his sinful mouth.

I unashamedly whimper when he pulls away from our embrace, but my disappointment doesn't linger for long. He looks as torn as me.

He runs his finger along my kiss-swollen lips. "If you're going to be accused of something, you may as well do it."

A disgruntled growl emits from my lips as I clench black sheets in a white-knuckled hold. Isaac's chuckle booms through my pussy before his God-crafted body glides along mine. Although his mouth is glistening with evidence of my arousal, I'm annoyed beyond comprehension. *I'd thought the car ride was agony, but this is ten times worse.*

Isaac is so well in tune with my body, he's using it as punishment for kissing Brandon and Ryan. Until I beg for forgiveness, he refuses to let me come. Over the past hour, his tongue, fingers, and mouth have teased my core so tightly it has nearly snapped more times than I can count, but seconds before my climax topples into oblivion, he withdraws contact.

It's been hell—absolute agony. I'd rather be spanked with a paddle than go through this for another hour.

"Not yet," Isaac mutters before sealing his mouth over mine.

Bombarded with sexual frustration, I snap my mouth shut and crank my head to the side, denying his kiss. I'm so annoyed. If his knee weren't in between my legs, I'd snap them shut too.

Isaac chuckles against my mouth, seemingly pleased he has me rattled. Sliding his hand up my sweat-slicked body, he cups my engorged breast in his hand. His talented fingers soon tease my nipple into an erect bud, encouraging a raspy moan to spill from my lips.

The instant my lips part for a needy breath, Isaac's tongue slides inside my mouth. I fight with all my might to deny his kiss, but I can't. It's too scrumptious to ignore.

Weaving my fingers through his hair that's damp at the tips, I pull him onto my overheated body. A throaty moan rolls up my chest when his rigid cock brushes my throbbing clit.

Tilting my hips higher, I seek direct contact. I nearly cry in frustration when Isaac pulls back from my embrace.

"Not yet," he teases, nipping at my lips with his teeth.

While kneeling between my milky white thighs, his smoldering eyes rake my naked form. I study him with just as much eagerness. His body is nearly enough to make me come just by looking at it.

Air hitches in my throat when he leans over to snag a condom out of his bedside table. Peering at me with lust-crammed eyes, he rests his backside on the balls of his feet before ripping open the foil packet with his teeth.

I watch in awe when he rolls the condom down his erect cock. Once it's in place, he bands his hands around my back to tilt my hips high into the air. A long, purring moan topples from my mouth when his cock sinks into my pussy at a painstakingly slow pace.

Once every delicious inch of his manhood has invaded me, his movements cease. I wiggle my hips, wordlessly begging for him to increase his tempo. He grips my hips, snubbing my plea without words.

Growling, my eyes pop open and lock with his. "Please," I shamefully beg, my high tone leaving no doubt to my excited state.

Isaac's lips curl into a heart-fluttering smile as he withdraws his cock all the way to the tip. Pleasure rockets to my womb when he slams back into me in one ardent thrust. I moan, adoring being filled by him once more.

When Isaac stills his movements again, I barely hold back a sob. The veins in his neck are bulging profusely, showcasing his arousal, but there's a gleam in his eyes that reveals he can maintain this pace for hours if required.

"I'm not going to beg," I snarl through gritted teeth.

"Yeah, you are." Isaac's tone is as cocky as his facial expression.

Rolling my eyes, I shake my head. Isaac executes an expert roll of his hips, faltering my firm stance. Pleas for forgiveness come spitting out of my mouth so hard and fast, my lips can't keep up with the words they're trying to form.

"Now, that wasn't so hard, was it?"

My shameful begs turn into a shallow moan when Isaac increases the tempo of his thrusts. His speed is perfect, and it has me racing toward release at a record-setting pace.

I dig my nails into his back as an orgasm waves in my stomach before cresting in my aching core. My body heats up as his magnificent thrusts dominate my pussy. This is brilliant, the best sex I've ever had.

He drives me to the brink, screwing my body as well as he fucked my mind the past hour. He claims every inch of me, making me feel thoroughly whole. I'm moaning on repeat, incapable of intellectual thoughts, much less words.

"This is mine," Isaac grunts between big pants.

His possessive eyes scan my naked body, activating every one of my hot buttons. "All of this is mine. Say it, Isabelle. Say it, and I'll let you come."

"It's yours, all of it is yours. I'm yours," I purr without hesitation, not only encouraged by my rampant horniness but because I've wanted to be his since I crashed into him at the airport.

Isaac thrusts into me deeper, rolling his hips at the exact spot that drives me crazy. Shudders wreak havoc with my frame as my climax wavers on the edge. My body is heightened and primed for release, knowing it's moments away from pure bliss. I'm purring like a pussy-cat, loving the sensation bristling the fine hairs on my body.

"Oh. Oh. Oh." My veins thicken when a fiery warmth spreads across my skin, coating it with a thin layer of sweat.

"Eyes on me, Isabelle." Isaac's voice reveals I'm not the only one caught off guard by the brilliance of our exchange.

My eyes pop open when his thumb circles my pulsating clit. His name roars from my throat in a grunted moan when I freefall over the edge. My nails bend harshly into his back as an orgasm scorches my body like an out-of-control wildfire.

My violent orgasm inspires Isaac's release. He fills me to the hilt seconds before spurts of hot cum explode from his throbbing cock.

My pussy clenches around him, milking his veined manhood. Once every drop of his spawn has been released, his hooded eyes collide with mine.

"You are mine," he says before sealing his mouth over mine.

He kisses me so passionately, and my sex clenches around his still convulsing cock. "Every inch of you is mine, Isabelle."

CHAPTER 32

Groaning a long and tedious grunt, my eyes flutter open. My muscles are weary, and my temples are throbbing from the lack of sleep I've gotten the past two days. Scanning the room, I realize it's just as bland and uninviting as it was months ago. The walls are void of any paintings or pictures, and no knick-knacks adorn the bedside tables. When I roll over and snatch my satchel from the bedside table, my face winces. It isn't a bad pain, but more of a reminder of what Isaac and I did numerous times earlier this evening.

What Isaac said the last time I was in his room is undoubtedly accurate. You don't have any doubts when you've been bedded by Isaac Holt. If every muscle in your body aching in pain isn't an adequate sign, the surge of adrenaline running through your veins hours after the event is a sure-fire indication.

My nose screws up when I fire up my phone and see it's ten o'clock at night. As much as I'd like to sleep until next week, I can't go back to bed now, or I'll be awake in the middle of the night.

Reluctantly, I scamper out of bed. My lips curve into a broad grin when I snag Isaac's shirt he was wearing this afternoon off the floor. I shift my eyes around the room to ensure it's empty before raising his shirt to my nose and inhaling a huge whiff. A shiver runs through my body when his delicious scent invades my senses.

My eyes skim the room, seeking any article of clothing that was discarded when we barely made it from the entryway to the bedroom. Since my impromptu gaze has come up empty, I pull Isaac's shirt over my head. After removing my unruly hair from the collar, my bare feet pad along the floor as I exit the room.

My long strides halt when, "Oh, hey, Isabelle," sounds through my ears.

I freeze as my hands shoot down to the hem of Isaac's shirt. Yanking on the hem, I pray my private parts aren't visible. Hugo chuckles boisterously at my panicked reaction. *I'm glad he can see the humor in the situation.* I stiffen even more when Isaac strolls out of the kitchen with a crystal glass in his hand. His smoldering eyes run down my body before lifting to my face.

Swallowing harshly, I scramble back, intimidated by his darkened glare.

"Stop, Isabelle."

I halt, rendered motionless by his pinning gaze. Smirking at my passiveness, he glides toward me, his steps as striking and bold as his handsome face.

He stands so close to me, his whiskey-scented breath fans my lips. "As ravishing as you look right now, I don't like other men eyeing what's mine." His words are only for my ears.

Although his warning could be mistaken as intimidating, his tone doesn't reflect that.

"There are clothes in the closet for you. Go and get dressed, then I'll take you home." He runs his thumb under my eyes to remove the mascara caked there.

Ignoring the disappointment clawing my chest that he already wants to take me home, I pivot on my heels and stalk back to his bedroom. I'm barely two feet away from Isaac when he calls my name. My heart beats at an irregular rhythm when I crank my neck back to peer at him. It grows wilder when I spot the dominant gleam brightening his dark eyes.

"From now on, anytime you leave my room, you're only to wear my shirts," he commands as his eyes scan my body.

My brows squeeze together as I hesitantly nod. *Didn't I just get reprimanded for wearing his shirt out of his bedroom?*

Shrugging off my confusion, I head for the hidden walk-in closet. My bewilderment intensifies when I enter the expensive space. The vast collection of suits that were housed here months ago have been removed, replaced with a handful of dry-cleaning bags.

My toes dig into the plush carpet as I saunter further inside. My breathing labors when I spot over a dozen Jimmy Choo shoe boxes lined underneath a handful of designer dresses and ball gowns. Allowing my love of Jimmy Choo to overrule logical thinking, I stoop down and pry open the lid on the first box.

An excited squeal emits from my lips when I spot a pair of Kia 110 boots. My eyes absorb every perfect stitch and exquisite design when I lift them from their box. My excitement is squashed when I see they're a petite size six. Even on a non-humid day, my size eight feet will never squeeze into them. After giving them one final hug, I place the shoes back into their box.

Once I've changed into a fresh set of clothes, I saunter back to the living room. My pulse quickens when Isaac's eyes lift and lock with mine. The dominant gleam I spotted in his eyes earlier triples when he absorbs the white-wash jeans and light pink cashmere sweater I chose from the women's clothing in his closet that was my size. All the designer dresses were two sizes too small for my generous breasts.

As I glide past a grinning Hugo, I mouth a silent apology for the awkward predicament I placed him in.

"It's all good, Isabelle. I saw more the night you climbed over the privacy partition," Hugo replies to my wordless apology, a sassy wink adding to the playfulness in his tone.

My eyes snap to Isaac when he growls at Hugo's taunt. His jaw is quivering, and his hands are balled at his sides.

"I'm joking," Hugo assures as his confused eyes flick between Isaac and me. "You know me, boss, I never water another man's turf."

Remaining quiet, Isaac lifts a crystal glass to his mouth. He downs the generous nip of brown liquid inside in one swift motion. After running the back of his hand across his stern lips, he sets the glass on the coffee table, then rises from the white leather sofa he's sitting on. Although Hugo's eyes show his apprehension, he's the first man I've met who doesn't cower from Isaac's infuriating glare.

Pretending he can't feel the tension in the air, Hugo rubs his hands together. "So, where are we off to?" His inquisitiveness conceals his unease.

"Your services won't be required again until Monday morning." Isaac's words are for Hugo, but his eyes are for me.

An unexpected giggle erupts from my mouth when Hugo vaults off the sofa. His excitement at having the weekend off is displayed all over his ruggedly handsome face. "Hell, you don't have to tell me twice." He wiggles his brows. "You've got my number if you need me."

He bolts for the door so fast, air glides over my forearms.

Once the vault-like door slams shut, I drift my eyes to Isaac. "You need to give him more days off," I jest, my tone lighthearted.

Isaac doesn't grace me with a reply, but a smirk tugs his full lips higher. "You ready?"

Smiling, I nod.

My brows join together in a scrunch when Isaac turns left at Remington Avenue T-intersection, instead of right.

"My apartment is that way?"

Isaac has been to my apartment on three occasions, so I'm somewhat surprised he has forgotten the directions. *I never expected a man with an astute business mind like Isaac to be forgetful.*

"We're not going to your apartment." His grip on his steering wheel tightens.

I arch a brow. "You said you were taking me home."

Isaac shakes his head. "No, I said I'll take you home. I didn't say whose home we were going to," he corrects as his gaze drifts from the road to me. Excitement slicks my skin when he clarifies, "I'm taking you to my private residence."

In a nanosecond, my eagerness dampens, and anger takes its place. "Where did we just leave if that isn't your home?" I ask, my tone indicating to my growing aggravation.

Isaac's lips twitch, but not a word is spat from his mouth. He returns his eyes to the road, ignoring my question with the skill of a narc. Every second he delays answering me has my anger intensifying. It brews in my gut until I can't hold it back for a second longer.

Struggling to keep down the contents of my stomach, I clench my teeth together. "Was that your fuck pad?"

Isaac's eyes snap to mine. Although his livid glare could cut through ice, I don't back down from my angry stance.

"Was that your fuck pad?" I ask again, my tone sterner this time around.

He works his jaw side to side. "I don't call it that, but I guess most people would see it that way."

"How many other women have you slept with in that bed?" I ask before I can stop my words. "Actually, don't answer that. I don't want to know. I already feel sick enough."

My reply isn't a lie. My stomach is rolling, threatening to spill at any moment. I also have an overwhelming desire to take a shower. I've never felt as dirty as I do right now.

"Take me home," I request, fighting my hardest to ignore the moisture welling in my eyes.

"I'm taking you home."

"No, take me back to my apartment."

Isaac's grip on the steering wheel tightens so much, his knuckles go pasty white. His jaw muscle quivers as he inhales a large breath through his nostrils.

"No, Isabelle. You're mine. Which means my home, my bed, my rules." His tone is as dangerous as my heart rate.

I glower at him, too stunned to form a response. I fought Alex tooth and nail not to become a commodity, but Isaac is making me precisely that. I'm not a possession. Nobody owns me.

"Don't look at me like that, Isabelle." Isaac's tone lowers in warning.

Rolling my eyes, I turn my infuriated gaze to the star-filled night, thankfully blocking him from seeing the tears splashing my cheeks. Anger is burning through my body, but it isn't potent enough to dry my tears—*unfortunately.*

Not even a heartbeat later, my hands shoot out to brace the dashboard when Isaac slams his foot onto the brake and yanks his car to the side of the road. After unclasping my seat belt, he drags me across the center console to sit side-straddled on his lap. His nostrils flare with every breath he takes as his remorseful eyes dance between my tear-filled ones.

The pain scorching my veins fades when he cups my face with his hands, so his thumbs can rub away my tears. Not a word spills from his lips, but his eyes beg for forgiveness. His beautiful gray irises are my biggest weakness. They're the gateway to his soul and the key to unlocking the real Isaac Holt. Although Isaac has a reputation for being cold-hearted and ruthless, his eyes relay an entirely different story. They're my greatest ally in unearthing the man behind the enigma.

Once my tears have settled, Isaac presses his lips to mine. Even upset, my body melts into his embrace, incapable of denying his affection. His kiss is scrumptious and sweet, and it clears the turmoil swirling in my stomach.

Our heated exchange doesn't lessen until the windows of his sports car are covered with fog, and the air in the cabin is stifling.

While rubbing my plump lips with his thumb, Isaac's eyes filter over my face. "I shouldn't have taken you there, but I needed to be sure you were mine before I fully let you in."

Tears form in my eyes so fast they sting, but this time, they're from happiness, not hurt. Isaac is a highly private man, so for him to accept me into his life has my heart enlarging so much it's close to exploding.

Shocked by my uncommon response, Isaac eyes me curiously. I'm certain I look ridiculous with tears flooding my cheeks while a huge grin spreads across my face, but my response can't be helped. I'm too happy to hold back my excitement.

Slapping my hands on each side of his cheeks, I place a dramatically sloppy kiss on his stern mouth. I feel him smirk against my lips before he takes our kiss from playful to teasing.

Isaac's talented mouth soon has me wishing we weren't in the tight confines of his car. I meet the lashing of his tongue stroke for stroke as my hands slither over the contours of his chest and abdomen.

I'm seconds away from tackling the impressive bump extending in the crotch of his trousers when a brief tap hits his driver's side window.

"Move along," A male police officer in a fluorescent yellow vest waves us along.

When Isaac lowers the window of his car, the officer's stern glare lessens. "Oh, good evening, Mr. Holt. I'm sorry, I didn't realize this was your vehicle," the handsome African American officer apologizes.

"That's okay, Jimmy, it's new. I've only taken her out a handful of times." Isaac's eyes scan my face.

I return his stare, confused by the gleam in his eyes. *Is he talking about the car or me?* When his cock twitches under my backside, my eyes open wide. *He's talking about me.*

"How are Marisha and the kids?"

I'm shocked Isaac can engage in conversation without alluding to his sexual arousal, which is struggling to be contained in his trousers.

The officer smiles. "They're good. Bobbi just made the varsity team."

When his eyes drift to a car approaching on the other side of the road, I swivel my hips, vying to alter Isaac's flawless composure.

Although his cock stiffens to a mouthwatering thickness, Isaac's conversation doesn't falter in the slightest. His tone remains neutral, not responding to the raging boner sending my thoughts into a tizzy.

After Isaac bids the police officer farewell, I flop into the passenger seat. Once my seat belt is latched, Isaac pulls his car back onto the road, waving to the police officer on the way by.

A shiver of excitement, and if I'm being totally honest, a slight tremor of fear runs through my body when Isaac mutters, "You'll pay for that tease later."

CHAPTER 33

oly moly! My breathing stills when my eyes absorb the impressive private residence in front of me. Isaac opens his window and leans over to enter a security code into the black box at the edge of the driveway. The black wrought iron gate in front of us creaks as it opens, exposing a curved path that weaves up to a beautiful brick house sitting at the top of a hill. The manicured gardens are well maintained but have a classic bachelor design with manly-trimmed hedges and a collection of potted plants.

Isaac drives up the pebbled driveway, stopping in front of his remarkable mansion. Stepping out of the car, the first thing my eyes zoom in on is the beautiful arched window on the third floor. Each window in the mansion is either a circular or curved design, but the only window on the third floor is a perfect half-circle.

Noticing my gaze, Isaac says, "That's my bedroom."

The purr of his voice roars through to my sexual core, igniting my senses.

"At night, you can see the whole of Ravenshoe from my bed."

"It's beautiful, a fitting castle for a prince."

He chuckles at my comment. "There's nothing princely about me." His brow arches into his dark, luxurious hair.

I shrug. He may not be a prince charming, but not every girl wants a prince. Some want a brainy geek, some want a rock star, and others want an alpha male who makes them scream his name at the top of their lungs while the most earth-shattering climax rips through their body so hard they see nothing but fireworks exploding before their eyes.

Feeling my composure waving, I question, "How long have you lived here?"

I occasionally need to rein in my desires and participate in other activities with Isaac that don't involve sex. He places my hand within his and walks us toward the curved glass French doors at the front of the mansion.

"I've owned this house for nearly three years." He stops his long strides when he reaches the front door and pivots around to face me. "This is my private residence."

My heart warms, loving that he's inviting me into his private sanctuary.

"I don't think you fully understand what I'm saying. This is my *private* residence. I don't let anyone come here. Hugo has only been here a handful of times."

Oh.

"Anything you hear or see behind these doors has to stay behind these doors." He motions his head to the front door. "I share enough of my private life with the public. I'm not willing to give them any more of myself than I already do."

"I understand." A broad smile spreads across my face making my cheeks ache.

He shifts his head to the side, and his brow bows high into his hairline as if to ask why I'm grinning like the cat who ate the canary.

"You *like* me." I overemphasize the word 'like.'

He shakes his head at my bold comment, but the smallest curve of his lips reveals his true reply. My heart skips a beat when he walks us through the front door, not attempting to refute my claim. *Yes!*

The inside of Isaac's house is just as spectacular as the outside with beautiful antique furniture, rich and luxurious material draped over arched French doors, and even priceless paintings and sculptures adorning the walls of each room. My impromptu private tour of his private oasis ends in his impressively large black and cherry oak kitchen. Releasing my hand, he strides toward the refrigerator.

"What do you feel like eating for supper?"

Snubbing my grumbling stomach, I reply, "You."

Isaac's head pops out of the fridge. Tremors shake through me when his sultry eyes absorb my body. "You'll be dessert, but first, I need to feed you so you can keep up with my stamina."

I chew my bottom lip, lessening the intense fire building in my womb. Isaac winks before returning his attention to the refrigerator.

"Being Saturday, our options are limited, so it's either Catherine's lasagna or chicken parmigiana."

My lips purse as I struggle to work out which meal sounds more enticing. My brain is in such a lust-filled fog, I can't decide which I'd rather eat.

Sensing my reluctance, Isaac decides on my behalf. "Lasagna it is."

My eyes track him as he places two containers of lasagna inside a convection oven. After hitting the reheat button, he walks to an over-head cupboard located above a wine fridge and pulls down two china plates. He places them on the island countertop on my left before proceeding toward a stack of drawers next to the double sink to remove two sets of cutlery. Even watching him do something as simple as setting the table is an exhilarating experience.

Once he has the countertop set for an intimate dinner for two, he motions for me to join him. A girlie squeal spills from my lips when he lifts me to sit on a high-backed barstool. Flashbacks of him doing the same thing six months ago in the business class lounge come rushing to the forefront of my mind.

"Can I ask you something?" I ask, my tone apprehensive.

Isaac freezes for the quickest second before replying, "Can we have dinner before the interrogation begins?"

I remain quiet while watching him remove his jacket and sling it on the beautiful wooden bench. Once he has his cufflinks undone, his eyes lift to mine. Our gazes lock and hold for several electrifying minutes. There's no doubting the sexual connection between us, but there's also something much greater drawing us to each other.

I grin when he asks, "What do you want to know?"

"What did you think when I tumbled at your feet at the airport?"

Relief washes over his face before he smirks. "You continue to surprise me every day, Isabelle."

"Why, what type of question were you expecting?"

He smirks again before moving to the convection oven that's signaling our meals are ready. "To be honest, I thought your fall was a ruse to gain my attention. I've become accustomed to the tactics women use to secure my devotion these past few years."

He removes the lasagna from the oven before placing a generous serving on my plate. "But the instant your big, beautiful eyes looked up at me, I knew it wasn't a ploy. You were truly embarrassed and seemingly unaware of who I was."

"I didn't have a clue who you were until after I arrived at Ravenshoe..." I stop talking, wondering if I've revealed too much.

Slowly raising my gaze from the plate of lasagna, I catch Isaac staring at me cautiously. Seconds feel like minutes as we undertake an intense, chemistry-riddled stare-down. A smile curves on my lips when he breaks the connection first by nodding and striding toward the fridge.

"I guess I allowed my stellar reputation in Ravenshoe to get the better of me." He pulls a bottle of red wine from the wine fridge. "I'm certain everyone in Ravenshoe knows who I am, but you've humbly reminded me there's a whole world outside of Ravenshoe that doesn't have a clue about some arrogant businessman named Isaac Holt."

Hoping to ease the tension in the air, I reply, "Their loss."

His chuckle has my mind wandering away from the food in front of me.

Forever diligent, Isaac says, "Eat, Isabelle. You'll need your energy."

He wasn't joking. Once we finished our dinner and two glasses of wine, Isaac had his dessert on the very countertop we were eating on. Then in the shower. Then in his monstrous four-poster bed.

By the time we're preparing to go to sleep, the sun is already rising over the horizon. Isaac emerges from the bathroom. He has disposed of his used condom and has a washcloth in his hands. Even sexually sated and deliriously tired, the pulse in my neck thrums when he places the washcloth between my legs and cleans me. Once all the residue of my climax is removed, he slips back in between the sheets and pulls me in close to his body.

An appreciative moan tears from my throat when the soft curves of my body mold into the hard firmness of Isaac. "Stop moaning, or neither of us will get any sleep." He sounds as exhausted as I feel.

"Is that even possible?" My words are muffled by a yawn.

My heavy-lidded eyes flutter open when his stiffening cock digs into my backside. "Does that answer your question?"

Biting my bottom lip, I roll over to face him. My glowing eyes bounce between his as he saves my bottom lip from my menacing teeth.

"You're going to be the death of me," he says before sealing his mouth over mine.

CHAPTER 34

"I didn't know there was a muscle there," I grumble to myself.

Every muscle in my body is throbbing. Now, don't get me wrong, it's a good pain, one I'd happily choose to feel every day, but I'm suffering soreness in areas I didn't know housed muscles.

After working my neck side to side to relieve the kink formed there from sleeping on Isaac's drool-worthy pectoral muscle the past several hours, I climb out of bed. Unsurprisingly, I'm once again waking up in an empty bedroom. I feel like a zombie, so I have no clue how Isaac can live off such little sleep.

This room is much more adeptly decorated than the room in Isaac's fuck pad. The color theme is a luxurious burgundy and charming dark steel gray. His bedside tables have pictures and knick-knacks on them, and the ceiling isn't mirrored. I guess the mirrored ceiling in his apartment should have been my first clue that it wasn't his primary residence.

"Wow."

The view from his bedroom window is remarkable. My attention was so focused on Isaac last night, I didn't pay any attention to the spectacular view out his window. You can see nearly the entire downtown area of Ravenshoe from this vantage point. A smile curls my lips high as I slide my arms into the sleeves of Isaac's blue business shirt he was wearing last night. Once I have the top three buttons done up, I pull my unruly hair from the collar and exit his room.

It takes wandering around his imposing mansion for nearly twenty minutes before I locate him sitting behind a mahogany desk in a vast office.

He's seated in a black leather chair, swiveled around to face an arched window behind his desk. He's talking to someone on his phone. From his tone and demeanor, I'd say it's a business associate or a staff member.

I prop my shoulder on the doorjamb, intending watch him in silence. Forever vigilant, Isaac senses my presence. My breath hitches when he pivots the chair around to face me. He's wearing a pair of dark washed jeans and a fitted white shirt. To add even more allure to his sexiness, he's also barefoot.

As my eyes absorb the sexually satisfying visual of a casual and laid-back Isaac, his eyes study my body with just as much eagerness. He smirks a panty-clenching smile when he notices I'm wearing nothing but his blue shirt from last night.

"Yes, I'm here," he snaps down the phone when his perusal of my body interrupts the flow of his conversation.

My pulse quickens when he gestures for me to join him. Fiddling with my shirt, I pad into his office. When I accept the hand he extends, he pulls me down until I'm sitting on his lap. A strong surge of yearning ripples through me when his erect cock digs into my backside. I'm surprised when he continues with his call, his authoritative tone not once faltering, not even when his hand slips under my shirt to tweak my nipples into stiff peaks.

"Henry, enough stalling. I don't care what it costs, just get it done."

He disconnects his call, not giving Henry the chance of a reply.

"Was that the Henry I met when we went away for the long weekend?"

"Yes," he answers as his gaze becomes more hooded.

A moan seeps from my lips when he massages my aching shoulders. "Are you sore?"

"Uh-huh." I moan, loving his fingers kneading the painful kinks in my neck and shoulders.

A groan rips from my throat when he withdraws his talented fingers from my neck. He stands from the chair, scooping me into his arms at the same time. His long strides down the hallway are quick and efficient. A grin curves on my lips when he places my naked backside down onto an expansive marble vanity in the main bathroom.

My grin turns into a full-toothed smile when he draws a bath. After squirting delicious smelling bath products into the fast-running water, Isaac turns to face me. Although his gaze is hungry and lust-ridden, there's also a sparkle of something else shining in his eyes.

My breathing slows when he pulls his shirt over his head in one fluid movement. Then my pulse quickens when he undoes the button on his jeans. Once his jeans and boxers are removed, he undoes the top button of my shirt. My mouth is ajar as my eyes drink in his magnificent body.

"See something you like?" His words are drenched with cockiness.

Unable to speak through my gaped mouth, I nod. Winking, he slips his shirt off my shoulders. A triumphant grin stretches across my face when he inhales a sharp breath, my inner vixen pleased he finds my body as tempting as I find his.

My voice drips with sarcasm when I quote, "See something you like?"

He doesn't grace me with a reply, but from the stiffening of his cock, I can make my own assumption.

After assisting me off the vanity, he walks us to the nearly overflowing bathtub. He slides into the bubble-filled tub before offering me his hand. A moan seeps from my lips when I join him. The warm water is heavenly to my overworked muscles.

When I lean against Isaac's torso, a gush of water splashes over the rim of the tub.

"You're dealing with Catherine tomorrow," he informs me, his tone hindered with laughter.

I moan, adoring his happy mood. "Who's this Catherine I keep hearing about?"

My body melts when he rubs my shoulders. "She's my..." He stops talking mid-sentence.

My closed eyes snap open since my curiosity is piqued.

"Trying to give Catherine a title is like trying to give Hugo one. They're both all-rounders. I'd say Catherine is a housekeeper, personal assistant, shopper, grandma."

My heart warms when he says, "grandma."

"So, she isn't someone I should be worried about?"

Isaac chuckles. "Ah, no. She and her husband celebrated their fortieth wedding anniversary last month."

He shifts my position until I have a clear view of his handsome face. "You don't have *anyone* to be worried about, Isabelle."

Unsure of a reply, I nod. I rest my cheek on his pec muscle so my eyes can absorb all the striking features of his face. The longer I stare at him, the more his jaw muscle ticks.

"What?" I question when the tension in the room reaches a breaking point.

"Do I have anyone to be worried about? Because I'm already acutely aware of the stellar impression you made on Ryan, so I was wondering if there might be anyone else I should be informed of."

My breasts flatten on his glistening chest when I roll over. When I lift my eyes, I'm met with the infuriated gaze of the incredibly attractive Mr. Isaac Holt. My heart skips a beat. *I knew a jealous Isaac would be just as sexy as an angry Isaac.*

"As handsome as Ryan is..."

Water splashes over the rim of the bath when Isaac clenches his fist so fast it creates a ripple.

"Let me finish my sentence before you get all tense."

His eyes darken with every second that ticks by, but it isn't scary enough to stop me from saying, "As handsome as Ryan is, no one makes my body ignite the way you do. No one ever has, and no one ever will. You've ruined me for any other man."

I slide my body along his until we meet eye to eye. "And no man could ever compete with a man as incredibly gorgeous as you. Not even Kellan Kyle."

Stealing his ability to reply, I seal my mouth over his. His lips curve into a smile before he returns my kiss with the same amount of intensity I'm giving.

Our kiss starts slow but soon builds in urgency. I drink him in, tasting, licking, and absorbing every delicious portion of his mouth.

Spurred on by his raspy moans, I slither my hand down the ridges of his six-pack before grasping his erect cock. Isaac's rugged pants overtake spilling water when I drag my hand down his lengthened rod. My seamless—and somewhat frantic—pumps soon have him chasing his release.

A husky gasp expels from my mouth when the tip of his cock grazes the entrance of my pussy. Blinded by lust, I adjust my position so his shaft can dip into my weeping sex with each stroke of my hand.

Overcome with desire, each stroke has him inching into me more and more.

Sensing my qualm slipping, Isaac's heavy-lidded gaze pops open as he calms my frantic movements. "As much as I want to plunge into your pretty pink pussy right now, we need a condom."

The throaty deepness of his voice spikes my relentless pursuit. "I'm on the pill."

Isaac stiffens for the quickest second before pinching my chin to raise my downcast head. When I stare into his beautiful eyes, his reluctance reflects back at me.

"Are you sure, Isabelle? Because once I make you entirely mine, there's no turning back. There will be *nothing* between us again."

Deciding to give my reply by using actions instead of words, I remove my hand from his throbbing cock and slam down. Water splashing onto the marble tile echoes around the room along with our gruff moans.

"Fuck, Isabelle."

The sting of Isaac's fingers when he grips my hips add to my excitement. After adjusting my position, I increase the tempo of my thrusts, encouraged by Isaac's provocative groans.

"You feel so good. So tight. So fucking wet."

He releases me from his grasp to clutch the bathtub. A rumbling moan tears from my throat when he adjusts the tilt of his hips. Our new position allows every inch of his cock to fill my clenching pussy.

I purr his name when his hand slithers between our connected bodies. He rubs my clit in a circular motion, forcing me to call out.

"Oh..." I want to say more, but I can't, lust has stolen my words.

My nails dig into Isaac's shoulders as I scream in orgasmic bliss. My pleasurable moans reverberate through the bathroom as an orgasm cascades through my body. It's so strong, even I'm surprised by its intensity.

My orgasm deepens when hot cum rages out of Isaac's cock, coating the walls of my pussy. I clench my sex, greedily milking his throbbing member, craving every drop of his spawn.

Several body-shuddering minutes later, I collapse onto his sweat-glistening torso. I'm exhausted and gasping for air.

After sinking back into the tub, Isaac runs his hand down my frazzled hair. Even with the temperature of the water beyond chilled, the heat of our bodies is enough to keep us warm.

My heart flips when Isaac presses a kiss to my temple. "That was a first."

Once my heart rate settles, I peer into his sparkling eyes. "That was a first for me, too. I've never had sex in a bathtub."

Isaac stiffens, and his cock still caressed inside me softens. "I meant it was my first time without a condom."

Although I should be mad he just mentioned previous sexual encounters in front of me, a smile curls my lips.

I slip off his semi-erect cock. "I'm glad I was your first."

Isaac's jaw ticks so profusely, it's heard over the sloshing of the bathwater when I step out of the tub.

"Isabelle..." His angry roar would usually have me freezing in fear, but not this time. I wrap a plush towel around my quaking body, pretending I'm not the least bit concerned.

My trembles from the cold water turn into shudders of excitement when Isaac stands from the tub. His domineering stature already demands my attention, but it's his relentless gaze securing my utmost devotion. It's infuriatingly angry and solely focused on me. He glares at me, demanding I answer the silent questions pumping out of him.

Without a doubt, I can testify that a jealous Isaac is by far the sexiest Isaac I've ever seen.

His stern gaze lessens when I admit, "It was also my first bareback ride."

CHAPTER 35

$\mathcal{A}$fter my tease in the bathroom, I spent the next two hours paying for the repercussions of my frisky taunt. Isaac's stamina astounds me. I've never met a man with so much self-control in the bedroom. I lost count of the number of orgasms that ripped through my body this afternoon. I was left sated, delirious, and unable to move. I had so much adrenaline running through my body, I felt drunk even though I haven't had a drop of alcohol the past week.

Thankfully, Isaac let me rest the majority of the afternoon, only waking me when it was time for dinner.

We've spent the last hour in his living room, eating homemade tacos and talking. I've loved every moment I've spent with him, whether we're in the bedroom or just hanging out. Only thirty-six hours have passed since we left the abandoned warehouse, but it feels like a lifetime.

"I'll be back in a minute." Isaac collects our empty plates from the coffee table before heading to the kitchen.

After placing my phone on the coffee table, I glance at an extensive collection of pictures proudly displayed on the mantel above the fire-place. There are over two dozen photos of various people in different poses. Their ages and gender range between each picture, but I notice one gentleman appears in the photos more than any other individual.

When Isaac walks back into the room, I ask, "Who is this man?"

He stands next to me, his lips arching when he peers at the photo I'm clutching. "That's my brother, Nick."

When he removes the picture from my hand, the grin on his face enlarges to a full-toothed smile. My brows lower down my face as my lips purse. Although the gentleman in the photo is handsome, he has no similar features to Isaac at all. Isaac has brown hair, gray eyes, and a light olive complexion. This gentleman has blond hair, dark blue eyes, and his skin is pasty white. Let alone the fact Isaac's persona demands respect and authority, while his brother seems a little roguish and cheeky.

Noticing my odd expression, Isaac chuckles. "He's my brother. There's no doubt in my mind."

He places the photo back onto the mantel before turning to face me. Air snags in my throat just from the sheer closeness of his ruggedly handsome face. I don't think I'll ever get sick of seeing his tempting features.

"Do you have any siblings?"

Grimacing, I shrug. Isaac eyes me curiously but remains quiet, patiently waiting for me to decide if I want to respond any further. Sensing my reluctance, he sits down on the sofa and gestures for me to join him. A smile sneaks onto my face when he interlocks our hands and lowers me to straddle his lap.

I settle my nerves with some big breaths. "I have siblings, but half of them probably don't remember me, and the other half don't know I exist."

When our gazes collide, I suck in a sharp breath. Although his eyes reveal his comfort, he remains quiet, giving me the chance to gather my composure. I'm grateful for his patience as tears are already welling in my eyes.

"You don't have to say any more," Isaac assures a short time later, his voice deep. "But I'm ready to listen once you feel comfortable."

A smile curves on my lips, grateful he isn't going to push me. Just knowing he won't force me makes me want to share information I've never shared before.

"My mom fell in love with the wrong man." My voice is barely a whisper. "My father was already married and had a handful of kids with his wife and mistresses by the time they met. He promised my mom a lavish life if she'd give up her current lifestyle and become his mistress. Because my mom grew up in a family living well below the poverty line, and she was only seventeen, she readily agreed. Instead of a life of luxury, my mom got a long list of false promises."

I stop talking when a tear splashes my cheek. My heart leaps when Isaac beats me to wiping it away.

"She got pregnant with me not long after they got together, and that's when her life spiraled out of control." My words croak with each one I speak. "My father preferred to have sons, and since I was born a girl, he despised me on sight."

I swallow hard before continuing with my story before I lose my nerve. "My mom died of a drug overdose when I was six years old."

Isaac's thighs stiffen, but his face doesn't alter from his usual expression.

"My father didn't want me, and his wife didn't know I existed, so I was... umm..."

I stop talking to wipe under my nose to ensure the contents inside doesn't spill. *This is harder than I ever imagined.*

When an unexpected sob tears from my mouth, Isaac says, "That's enough for tonight, Isabelle."

His thumbs wipe away the tears now cascading from my eyes before he leans over to place a kiss on each of my eyelids. His loving gesture causes a sudden shift in the air. Sexual tension builds as we assess each other's faces.

When the tension grows too great to ignore, I tilt my hips forward, seeking his cock I feel thickening beneath me. My movements are slower than the pace we've been going the past two days, but fire-sparking at the same time.

Goosebumps break across my stomach when Isaac slips his hand under my shirt. Although his touch is as light as a feather, it's robust enough to gain my body's full attention. His slow but sensual pace heightens my senses, making sure they pay careful attention to his every move.

A shallow moan vibrates my lips when he kneads my breasts. He rolls my nipples, sending a roaring sensation through my body, only stopping when they cluster in my needy pussy.

Standing from the leather sofa, Isaac places me onto a white fur rug in the living room. He guides me backward until my back molds into its soft fibers.

Moving his hands to my shirt, he glides it over my head. Once it's removed, his lust-ridden gaze lowers to mine.

"Stretch your arms above your head and clasp your hands together." His soft rumble has my insides purring.

When I do as instructed, he uses my shirt to secure my hands at the wrists. "Keep them above your head."

Biting my bottom lip, I nod. My pulse quickens when he tugs off his shirt. My pulse thrums when he stands before me barefoot, wearing nothing but a pair of jeans undone at the button. My eyes greedily absorb his magnificent body, drinking in every spectacular ridge as if it's the first time they've sampled it.

Once he removes his jeans, he crouches next to my trembling thighs to unbutton the three-button fly on my jeans. My core clenches when he slides them down my legs, his hand brushing my sensitive pussy on the way by.

His fluid movements continue until I'm lying before him as naked as the day I was born. After his eyes appreciatively study my body, he stands and moves out of my vision.

Confusion slips over my face, confused by his sudden departure.

A short time later, he returns with a pillow in his hand. My lips furl high when he places it under my head. "Your eyes are never to leave mine, Isabelle."

Unable to speak, I nod.

After gracing my skin with gentle nips and caresses, Isaac's attention shifts to lavishing the throbbing areas of my body.

Any time my gaze falters during his tantalizing teases, he

commands my eyes back to his. Watching him worship my body is an exhilarating experience that has me freefalling into ecstasy more times than I can count.

Once my body is lax from sexual exhaustion, Isaac adjusts my position. A familiar tingle builds in my stomach when his swollen knob braces the entrance of my sex. Even exhausted beyond comprehension, my body can't help but react to his.

My back arches with a throaty moan when he inches his cock into my drenched pussy.

"Eyes, Isabelle."

My eyes snap to his as a long, salivating moan rumbles from my throat. Our bodies are joined in the most intimate way, heightening my senses even more.

Isaac's muscles flex with every thrust his body makes. Each grind fills me to the brink before his rolling hips send a jolt of pleasure to my tightening core.

Sometime later, I wriggle my hands, fighting against the restraints binding them together. The urge to run my hands over Isaac's sweat-slicked body is so overwhelming, I can't hold back my desire for a moment longer.

Noticing my struggle, Isaac releases my hands from their restraints. My hands dart to his body to eagerly run them along his bulging biceps before raking them down his sweat-drenched back.

With every pump of his hips, pleasure rockets through my body. I moan his name when a long and intense orgasm lights up my body. I shudder in ecstasy, growling his name on repeat.

"One more," he requests through panted breaths.

He adjusts his position, so he's kneeling before moving his hands to my back. Scooping me in his arms, I end up straddled on his lap. My breasts squish against his smooth chest when my arms band around his neck.

I inwardly squeal when Isaac mutters, "Choose your pace, baby."

Barely able to move since my legs are Jell-O, he shifts his hips upward, gliding his throbbing cock in and out of my saturated pussy.

"Like that?"

I don't grace him with a reply. I just groan a long, purring moan as warmth flames my skin. A bead of sweat runs down Isaac's cheek as his precise rhythm has me chasing my next climax.

If I weren't already close to the brink, his dirty mouth soon has my orgasm teetering on the edge. All his comments about how much he loves fucking me, how good my pussy feels wrapped around his cock, and that he could fuck me for years and never get enough, has my climax building at a rapid pace.

His cock thickens as his sprint for release grows. Spurred on by his impending climax, I increase the tempo of our thrusts. Our pace turns wild that only skin slapping skin echoes around the living room.

"Fuck, Isabelle, you get tighter when you're about to come."

"Oh, God," I pant before fireworks explode in front of my eyes.

Isaac's name tears from my throat in a rumbling scream as I quiver through a blinding orgasm. My climax lengthens when the sting of his teeth is felt on my shoulder blade, closely followed by the hot spurts of his seed erupting inside my convulsing pussy.

CHAPTER 36

My eyes flutter open when Isaac scoops me into his arms and strides through his impressive mansion. I snuggle into his sweat-slicked chest, loving that he can carry me with such ease.

Once we reach his bedroom, he continues with his fast pace until we're standing at the entrance of the double shower located in his ensuite bathroom. Adjusting my position, he turns on the faucet, not once relinquishing me from his grasp or making me concerned he might drop me.

When the water is warm, he steps us into the shower. The heavy spurts of the hot water flowing from the showerhead massage and revive my overtired muscles. Once the ache in my body lessens, Isaac places me down onto my feet.

In silence, he squeezes body wash onto a shower puff and lathers it over my entire body. Once he washes away the suds, his pampering shifts to my hair. My heart swells from witnessing a side of Isaac I don't think many people have ever had the pleasure of experiencing. The powerful and ruthless businessman has succumbed to a mere man, lovingly nurturing a person he cares for.

"You really *really* like me," I mumble through a heavy-lidded gaze.

His dedication to my hair halts as his darkening eyes lower to mine. "Why do you think I forced myself to stay away from you."

He returns his attention to massaging the shampoo in my hair. His thick, powerful fingers have goosebumps breaking out over my skin.

Since his remark was more of a statement than a question, I don't bother compiling a response. Instead, I nervously chew on my bottom lip. I know the reason why I had to stay away from Isaac, but I was unaware he was fighting the same internal battle. How many months have we wasted fighting an urge greater than us both?

Sensing a change in my composure, Isaac expels a sharp breath. "I'm not a good man, Isabelle. I tried to stay away from you so I could protect you."

My brows draw together as my eyes shoot up to his. Before a reply can form in my mind, he silences any response from seeping from my lips with his index finger.

"It would have been safer for you if we'd never met, but now that I've claimed you as mine, I can't give you up, but I promise I'll protect you, and no one will ever hurt you." His beautiful eyes relay the truth in his declaration.

His statement adds more suspicion to a theory that's been running through my brain the past several weeks. Realizing this may be my only opportunity to ask a question that's been haunting me for weeks, I blurt out, "What did Col Petretti say to me in Italian the night we left your club?"

Isaac stiffens as his gaze shifts to the side. Although he could be perceived as looking at my face, he isn't. He's glancing straight past me. How do I know this? His gaze is so hot, when it leaves you, you experience the loss of its warmth.

Before any lies can spill from his lips, I demand, "Don't lie to me, Isaac. You said you never lie."

His gaze snaps back to mine. The loving man who was mere minutes ago shampooing my hair has been replaced with a man whose gaze alone would have the toughest men shivering in their boots.

Clenching his fists open and closed, he answers, "And you will soon become one."

My brows pull together as confusion bombards me. *Why did such a simple statement create such an adverse reaction from Isaac that night?*

It's only when the first part of Col's sentence filters through my mind do I understand Isaac's reaction.

"You're exquisite. You have the face of an angel... And you will soon become one."

My heart constricts as tears form in my eyes. Grimacing, I snap my eyes shut to stop my tears from falling. "Is that why you went out on all those dates? So Col would think I wasn't any more significant than the woman keeping your bed warm that night? You were protecting me?"

He coughs to clear his throat, which forces my eyes back open. "That was my original plan, but even Col could see..." He stops midsentence to swallow hard. "Whatever this crazy thing is between us. He knew the instant I retaliated to his threat that you were more than some random one-night stand."

I try to hide my smile, but the smallest one creeps across my lips. Isaac stares at me, seemingly dumbfounded by my odd response. I shouldn't be grinning, but having him admit there's some 'crazy thing' between us makes my heart palpitate.

My smile is slapped right off my face when he informs me, "Col Petretti has been spotted several times the past four weeks in Ravenshoe."

Now it makes sense why I've noticed Hugo outside my apartment several times the past few weeks.

"You have Hugo watching me?"

The tick in his jaw becomes prominent. "I won't let Col hurt you, Isabelle."

"I know that." My tone is confident. "To begin with, I'm more worried about why Col wants to hurt you. Why does he have a vendetta against you?"

Isaac's throat works hard to swallow as the room plunges into an awkward silence.

Just when I think he won't answer me, he says, "He blames me for his daughter's death."

Before I can reply, his guarded barrier mentally rises in front of my eyes. His face is marred with remorse, his beautiful eyes dark and stormy. No words are uttered from his lips as he washes the shampoo out of my hair and steps out of the shower. Although his face is full of confusion, he still dries my body with a lush towel before carrying me in his arms into his bedroom. Once he places me down, he moves toward a cabinet of tall drawers.

My heart cracks when he pivots back around to face me. His eyes are riddled with remorse. Not only does Col blame Isaac for Ophelia's death, so does Isaac. I can't comprehend why he'd think a traffic accident was his fault?

"Thank you," I whisper when he places his t-shirt over my head.

Once he has removed my hair from the collar, his gorgeous eyes run over my face. A smile tugs my lips higher when he cradles my cheek. When I lean into his embrace, wanting to offer him quiet comfort, he pulls away.

I stalk him as he moves around the room. Even though my urge to know everything is gnawing away my insides, hounding me to probe him for answers to the questions muddling my mind, my heart knows now isn't the time to drill him. He needs comfort, not an interrogation.

Once he dons a pair of black cotton sleeping pants hanging down low enough I can tell he's commando underneath, he slips into his side of the bed. I scoot across the mattress to rest my cheek over his heart. Blood surges through my veins more rapidly when he doesn't repel from my loving gesture.

His mouthwatering scent invades my senses and spurs on my pursuit to offer him comfort in the only way I know how. *Sexually.*

My hand slithers over the ridges of his abdomen. My heart flutters when his muscles spasm with each movement I make.

"Isabelle," he groans in warning when my hand skims the rim of his pants, his tone indicating I'm treading into unchartered waters.

Ignoring his gruff growl, I place a kiss on his unshaven jaw before shifting my focus to his chest. When I nip and tug on his erect nipple, he releases a throaty moan.

His pleasurable growl turns menacing when I shoo his hand out from underneath my shirt.

"It's my turn to play," I advise him as my sparkling gaze lifts in anticipation of participating in an intense stare-down.

His brow shoots into his hairline.

"Please," I shamelessly beg, wanting him to relinquish his dominance for just one night.

Shockwaves shiver through my sex when he smirks a ravenous, wicked smile before adjusting his pillow. Once he has scooted up the bed, positioning his back on the headboard, he glides his hand down his body, granting me access to his smorgasbord to do with as I please.

My inner vixen cheers before my pursuit commences with more eagerness. My desire to taste him for the first time spurs on my eagerness. Wetness slicks between my legs as I glide my way down his magnificent body. When I place a kiss on each muscle of his six-pack, he groans. My heavy breasts brush against his stiffened cock, which his pants are struggling to contain.

I connect my eyes with his intense gaze as I yank his pants down his thighs. My jaw gapes open when his cock springs free from its restraints. It's beyond perfect.

Not being able to wait any longer, my tongue darts out to moisten my lips before they cover the wide crest of his cock. My cheeks hollow from the pressure I apply when I suck him into my mouth.

"Yes, Isabelle," he moans. "Suck me hard and fast, baby. Make me come in your pretty little mouth."

While groaning at his sinful mouth, I run my tongue along the seam of his hot flesh, absorbing his delicious taste.

By paying careful attention, I soon work out which method of sucking produces the most intense reaction. Once I get the perfect combination of suction and speed, his hands grip the bed sheets tighter, and his eyes snap shut.

"Eyes," I babble through a mouth full of cock.

His eyes darken with amusement from my playful taunt. They

watch me eagerly sucking, licking, and stroking his cock. His gaze is hot, heavy, and solely focused on me. My excitement at knowing I'm the one causing his lack of composure is thrilling. It sends a shiver scuttling through my veins, making every fine hair bristle.

Over and over again, I draw his wide-girthed cock into my mouth, only occasionally triggering my gag reflex.

The longer my seamless pumps progress, the more Isaac's moans spur on my own climax. His hips buck off the bed when I increase the strength of my sucks.

Over time, my jaw aches, but my rampant horniness overrules that zing of pain. Having him unravel before my eyes is a thrilling experience that will always outweigh any discomfort.

His grip on the sheets tightens as the thrusts of his hips become more urgent. He's so close to orgasming.

A short time later, when the veins on his cock throb more urgently, I draw him in until the crest of his cock hits the back of my throat.

"Fuck, Isabelle," Isaac roars as spurts of salty cum pump onto my tongue.

I drink it all in, swallowing eagerly, loving the taste of him in my mouth. Greedily, I milk his cock with my hand, relentlessly pumping his stiffened shaft until every last drop of his seed is expelled into my mouth.

After licking my lips to gather any spilled cum, I crawl up his body to rest my head on his glistening torso. His heart is thrashing wildly as he comes down from his brutal climax. My lips curve into a triumphant grin, glad I'm capable of rendering him mindless while also lessening his agitation.

After some time, his heart rate returns to a safe level. He runs his hand down my hair, smoothing the damp, frazzled pieces back into place. Feeling the safest I've ever felt snuggled on his chest, my mouth starts spilling secrets I've never shared with anyone before.

"My uncle who raised me isn't really my uncle." He stiffens at my comment but remains quiet. "I was sold to him when I was six years old."

His grip on my hip tightens so much, it sends pain shooting through my hipbone.

"My father hated me so much he didn't care who bought me. He just had one stringent requirement. Whoever was the highest bidder had to pay for me in cash."

Isaac's teeth grinding together shrills through my eardrums. Lifting my head off his chest, I prop myself on my elbow so I can look into his beautiful eyes.

"My uncle was a good man, Isaac. He saved me from a life of misery. If it weren't for him, who knows where I'd have ended up."

His Adam's apple bobs up and down. "Did he…" He doesn't need to finish his question, the terrified look in his eyes is questioning enough.

"No, Isaac. God, no. He wasn't that type of man. He never touched me like that, I promise."

Isaac expels a quick exhalation of air.

"He treated me as if I were his daughter. I'll be forever grateful for the day he came into my life." Before I can chicken out, I blurt, "My father is Vladimir Popov."

When Isaac's breathing ceases to exist, I realize he's heard of my father before.

CHAPTER 37

Gripping the marble vanity bowl, I lift my eyes to the large mirror in front of me. My face is white and gaunt, and my pupils have sunken. The dark circles plaguing my eyes make it look like I haven't slept in over a year, but it isn't a physical illness afflicting my appearance, but the muddled mess of confusion in my mind making me feel physically ill.

Being immersed in Isaac's world the past forty-eight hours made me forget the FBI is investigating him. When I'm with Isaac, I only see him. Everything else is just a blur of white noise, but now that the dreaded Monday morning has arrived, reality has come to painfully bite me on the ass.

After my confession last night, Isaac remained quiet. Even with not seeing his eyes, I knew he was awake. He ran his hand along my arm for nearly an hour before he slipped out of bed and left the room. I considered following after him, but remembering Cormack's advice from weeks ago, I left him alone to contemplate.

Isaac is a very guarded man, so I wanted to give him time to process my confession in privacy. It isn't every day the woman you're sleeping with acknowledges being the daughter of a well-known mob boss. That type of revelation would rattle even the strongest man.

I'll be frank, Isaac's apprehension of my confession last night did make me wary of advising him that I'm an FBI field agent. Although legally I cannot disclose I am a field agent to anyone, morally, it's the right thing to do. My heart wants to be truthful and tell Isaac everything, but my head is telling my heart it's not the rational thing to do.

My heart-and-head fight continued well into the early hours of this morning. After many hours of silent debating, my head eventually overruled my heart. The reason my head won isn't what you might think. It's because I truly don't believe Isaac is the man his FBI file portrays him to be. So, I've made it my mission to ensure Isaac's investigation is handled fairly. Once Isaac's investigation is closed, and he's acquitted, I'll make sure his file reflects the true Isaac Holt. I'm confident once he realizes I defended his integrity, he will forgive me for deceiving him.

At times, government departments can be unjust. My own childhood story reflects that. My Uncle Tobias was undercover in the Popov family for nearly five years before I was put up for auction. Once I was old enough to understand, Tobias explained that he initially tried to have the sale canceled legally, but since the FBI didn't believe I was a valuable enough asset for him to break years of cover for, the auction went ahead as originally planned.

My memories of Tobias at the time are vague as I was so young, but the image of his huge smile and roguish face when he'd bring me and my brother groceries will always have a special place in my heart.

My mom was unfortunately addicted to meth. The urge for her next fix was greater than her desire to feed and look after her children. Since my mother graced my father with a son a year after I was born, he arranged for a family member to assist her in raising his children.

Although my Uncle Tobias isn't related by blood, he was still addressed with the title of uncle. Any male with a close connection to the *family* was classed as uncle, even if he weren't blood-related. Uncle Tobias was the man my dad tasked with looking after me and my little brother, Enrique. Tobias said I was just shy of my first birthday when he came into my life. He gave me the nickname 'Rabbit' because I was nothing but skin and bones. That nickname stuck until the day he passed away.

Since the FBI refused to help, my Uncle Tobias went against their strict protocols. He mortgaged his family home in Tiburon and over-drew every credit card he owned to ensure he had enough cash on hand to buy me. When his bid was successful, Tobias and I left Las Vegas that very same day. Once news of Tobias's abandonment surfaced through the FBI, he created the ruse that he was in a rela-tionship with my mother the whole time he was undercover and that Vladimir had found out about his indiscretion, meaning he was shunned by the family. The FBI believed his story, and he was soon recruited to a new task force.

With the help of Regina, I was issued a birth certificate stating I was the daughter of Tobias's deceased brother, Abraham, who had died three years earlier. For the past nineteen years, I was raised by Tobias and his *Dedushka*—grandpa in Russian—in the house Tobias mortgaged to bid for me. To this day, the FBI is none the wiser of my connection to the Popov family.

My gloomy thoughts are interrupted when a heated gaze ignites every nerve in my body. Lifting my eyes, I discover Isaac leaning in the doorjamb of the ensuite bathroom, watching me inquisitively. His enthralling eyes are raking my body.

Happily, my eyes absorb the satisfying visual of Isaac in an impec-cably tailored dark blue three-piece suit. His primal gaze has my pulse quickening when he returns his eyes to my face.

I shake my head. "No, Isaac."

Our rigorous physical activities this morning have already stretched my time thin. I'll be late to work if I don't leave this house within the next thirty minutes.

Isaac chuckles while strolling into the bathroom. Rolling my eyes, I turn back to face the mirror to continue my fruitless attempt to hide the dark circles plaguing my eyes with the compact foundation I carry in my clutch purse. It appears to be a shade too light since my skin is blessed with the hue of ecstasy, but it's the only makeup I have avail-able, so it will have to do.

My heart flips when Isaac leans over to place a quick peck on my freshly shampooed hair before snagging his toothbrush from the ceramic holder on the countertop.

Every hair on my body bristles to attention because of his close proximity. His erect cock scorches my curvy backside when he leans over my shoulder to dampen his toothbrush under the running tap, and a tiny shudder flows through me. Even being sexually sated numerous times the past forty-eight hours, I can't stop my body from reacting to Isaac. The more I have him, the more I want him.

Swallowing hard, I stash my compact back into my purse and grab the spare toothbrush from its holder. Isaac remains quiet, but my awareness of his closeness is paramount. I don't need to look at him to know he's watching me. The heat of his eyes is an obvious sign.

Intimacy fires in the air as we brush our teeth side by side. Although there's a double sink, Isaac spits his toothpaste into the one in front of me. Every brush of his body against my arm heightens my senses, and every time my body responds to his touch, his smirk enlarges.

I nearly choke on the mouthwash I'm gargling when he tugs open the knot on the towel curled around my body two seconds later. After drawing in a sharp breath, his eyes assess my body. From the bulge his dark blue trousers are straining to contain, I'd say he appreciates the visual of me standing before him naked.

I spit my mouthwash into the sink before turning around. "You have twenty minutes," I warn him with my brow cocked in the air.

His lips crimp into a mouth-watering smile that makes my body quiver and my heart beat in my throat.

Returning his smile, I throw myself into his arms and seal my mouth over his minty lips.

Over thirty minutes late, I scamper into the office as fast as my quivering legs will take me. I should have known a man with impressive stamina like Isaac wouldn't have known the definition of a quickie. Even with Hugo driving like a maniac and taking every shortcut he could find, there was no way I could gain back the hour I lost in the bathroom earlier.

My nervous eyes shoot to Alex's office as I scramble toward my desk. I sigh in relief when I spot Alex sitting on his desk with his gaze planted out the window. Plopping into my chair, I fire up my computer before throwing my purse into the top drawer of my desk.

A girlie squeal erupts from my lips when I raise my gaze. Brandon has sneakily moved to my desk, undetected.

"Holy crap, you scared me." I clutch my breathless chest.

He smiles and wiggles his eyebrows. "Sorry, Izzy. I just thought these might stop you from getting another one of Alex's famously long tirades for being late this morning." He gestures his head to the eight cups of steaming hot coffee he's holding.

My eyes bulge. "Oh my God, Brandon. I love you. I love you. I love you." Leaping out of my chair, I plant a huge, sloppy kiss on his cheek.

His face turns the brightest shade of red. "That's okay, Izzy. I'd do anything for you."

Just as he hands me the two crates of coffee, Alex pivots around. Our eyes lock and hold for several terrifying seconds. Seconds feel like hours anytime Alex's stern blue eyes reprimand me. His gaze is so troubling, a sweat mustache forms on my top lip. My breathing returns when Alex's eyes snap down to the coffees in my hand, and his lips curve into a smile.

"I owe you, big time," I whisper to him before racing around the office to dispense the coffee to each recipient, making sure I drop off Alex's black coffee first.

By the time lunch rolls around, my neck no longer feels the dull ache from Isaac's fingers when he arched over the bathtub this morning. It's from scanning hundreds of documents into the geriatric copy machine in the dingy, cramped supply closet. Alex wants a digital copy of my uncle's hand-scribbled notes and files, which means thousands of documents need to be manually scanned into the FBI database. In a much larger office, this task may take a couple of days, but using an ancient copier that only scans one page at a time, it will take weeks, if not months to complete this meaningless task.

I'm still rubbing the kink in my neck when the supply closet door creaks open. My breathing levels when Alex strolls into the room. The air in the minute-size closet turns stifling when a thick stench of awkwardness suffocates us.

After offering Alex a quick, unassured smile, I return my focus to scanning the documents. Clearing his throat, Alex makes his way to the corner of the room to gather some camera equipment. Because of the lack of space, his hand accidentally connects with my backside as he passes by me.

After gathering a digital camera with a long zoom lens, he makes his way back out of the room. I draw myself in as close to the copier as possible to ensure he can glide by without bumping into me.

Upon exiting the door, he spins around to face me. "You can make up your late arrival by either skipping your lunch break or staying back later tonight," he advises, his tone stern.

Swallowing harshly, I nod. Obviously, Brandon's clever ruse has been unhatched.

CHAPTER 38

Two hours later, Brandon discovers me sitting on the floor in the supply closet. He offers me a reassuring smile before making his way into the room. An appreciative grin forms on my mouth when he sits down next to me and hands me a club sandwich and a bottle of OJ from Harlow's bakery.

"I heard you had to work through your lunch break." He leans his back against the shelving I'm resting on.

"Yeah. I think Alex is more watchful than either of us perceived." I run the cuff of my blouse under my eyes to ensure I don't have raccoon eyes from my mascara running down my face.

Once the smears of mascara are on the sleeve of my white blouse, Brandon asks, "Why are you crying?" His genuine concern shows on his adorable face.

I hand him the photo I'm clutching in my shaking right hand. "Ophelia Whitney Petretti was only nineteen years old when the car she was driving was struck by a B-double truck that veered onto the wrong side of the road. She was killed on impact," I answer.

Brandon's eyes snap down to the photo I found of Ophelia in Col Petretti's file. Ophelia was beautiful. In the picture Brandon is holding, she has light brown, wavy shoulder-length hair with some caramel highlights. Her dazzling brown eyes are so light in color, they're nearly transparent. She's smiling, even with the tip of her pointed-up nose red from a sprinkling of snow landing on it.

A smile curls my lips when Brandon places his arm around my shoulders and pulls me in close to his side, offering quiet comfort. "I read the police report on her accident over the weekend. It's always sad when you hear of any life being taken too soon." Even with him offering me comfort, he sounds hesitant. I guess it's hard for him to understand the reason for my tears.

I'm genuinely upset that Ophelia's life was cut short at such a young age. Just from her photo, I can tell she was a wonderful person, but my tears aren't for her—they're for Isaac. Once I dove into more of Col's file, I discovered several handwritten notes my uncle had scribbled on napkins from a diner called Buck's. Ophelia was a waitress at Buck's Diner for a little over a year before she was involved in the accident.

All the handwritten notes were about Ophelia and a young man he'd spotted her with numerous occasions over a three-month period. From the timeline of the napkins and some more detailed reports, it appears Isaac and Ophelia were an official couple for nearly six months before she passed away.

I hesitantly hand Brandon the second photo I'm clutching. It's a picture of Isaac and Ophelia together. It's time-stamped a few hours before she was killed in the traffic incident. Isaac is wrapping a scarf around her neck. He's grinning a smile I've never seen on his face before, and his beautiful, entrancing eyes are staring into hers. You can see nothing but love and admiration all over his face.

Brandon's eyes drop to absorb the photo before lifting to mine. "Isaac and Ophelia were a couple?"

His eyes sparkle with excitement when I nod. "Izzy, you have to tell Alex you've unearthed the connection between Isaac and Col Petretti." His voice is laced with euphoria. "This will get you off coffee and filing duties in an instant."

Brandon jumps up off the worn carpet, excitement beaming from him in invisible waves. I accept the hand he thrusts out in front of me.

His sharp yank on my arm pulls me off the ground and has me crashing into his firm chest. My breasts squash up against his well-defined pectoral muscles. *Brandon is a lot harder under his clothes than I'd initially perceived.*

Grimacing, I step backward and run my hand down my blouse to ensure it didn't rise to an absurd level during Brandon's eager lift. When I raise my gaze, I'm confronted with Brandon's flushed face. *Obviously, I'm not the only one who noticed our inappropriate closeness.* With a hesitant smile, I turn my attention back to scanning the documents into the old copier.

"I don't have time to type up a whole report on their relationship." My eyes roll at my dim excuse. "This scanning will take me months as it is."

I turn back around to face Brandon, who is eyeing me curiously. "You spent your whole weekend going through Col's file. Eventually, you would have discovered these photos yourself." I return Brandon's confused stare. "If you're willing to type up the report, I'll let Alex believe you discovered the photos."

"I don't want to take your credit, Izzy."

"You're not taking my credit, Brandon," I interrupt. "You're helping me out. I'm snowed under here." I gesture to the mountain of papers I still have left to scan. "This isn't even a small dent in the boxes left in the conference room."

Brandon remains quiet as his concerned eyes shift between mine. After what feels like a lifetime, but is more like minutes, Brandon agrees to compile the report to present to Alex. "But you'll get the credit for finding the connection between Isaac and Col," he says before walking out of the supply closet.

I drag my palm over my sweat-drenched neck. This leading a double-life business is a lot harder than I originally anticipated. My heart is pounding just from sharing one snippet of Isaac's personal life. Although I feel guilty, either way, this secret would have been unearthed eventually. If it weren't by me, Brandon would have found it.

Once my erratic heart rate is back under control, I scarf down the sandwich and OJ Brandon brought me before recommencing with the scanning. I'm famished since my breakfast was burned off during my impromptu romp in the bathroom with Isaac this morning.

A short time later, Brandon's head pops back into the room. "Your phone has been vibrating nonstop on your desk the past thirty minutes," he tells me apprehensively.

My lip drops into a frown. I don't know who would be contacting me with such urgency. I mumble a quick thanks to Brandon before scooting past him to make my way to my desk. The muscles in my body creak with each step I take. I've spent the last nearly five hours crammed in that small office, and my body is screaming in protest.

"Holy crap." There are over a dozen missed calls and text messages from an unknown number and a handful of messages from Harlow.

My brows tack closer with every message I read.

Unknown number: *Isabelle, I'll meet you at Harlow's bakery at 1 p.m. sharp.*

Unknown number: *Isabelle, where are you?*

Harlow: *Did you know Isaac was meeting you here for lunch today?*

Harlow: *Jesus Izzy, the veins in Isaac's neck are about to burst.*

Unknown number: *I've been waiting for nearly an hour.*

Harlow: *Will you hurry up? Isaac is scaring my customers away ;)*

Unknown number: *You will be lucky if I let you come for a week after standing me up. Call me as soon as you get my messages.*

Harlow: *He's gone, but you have some explaining to do young lady... p.s. an angry Isaac is as sexy as fuck.*

A chuckle escapes my lips when I read Harlow's last message. If she thinks an upset Isaac is sexy as hell, wait until she sees a jealous Isaac.

My uneasy gaze bounces around the room. Other than catching the eye of Brandon, the rest of the team's focus remains on other tasks. I send a message to Harlow telling her I'll pop into the bakery later this afternoon and explain everything. Once I have the crumpled business card Isaac scribbled his cell phone number on months ago in my hot little hands, I scamper back to the supply closet.

I nearly lose the grip of my phone while dialing Isaac's private cell phone number since my palms are slick with sweat. I'm nervous Isaac will uphold his threat of not letting me orgasm for a week. *I really hope it's an idle threat.*

Isaac connects our call before one full ring sounds through my ear. "Isabelle."

Although his tone is clipped, my name rolling off his tongue sends an excited thrill through my body.

"I just got your messages now," I blurt out.

A length of silence crosses between us.

"Because I was late this morning, my boss made me work through lunch," I explain, my tone getting edgier.

It is technically Isaac's fault I arrived late, so if anyone should be punished for my tardiness, it should be him.

"A simple message advising me you were unable to attend lunch would have been appreciated. Then I wouldn't have been spending the last two hours panicked something horrible happened to you."

My heart clutches in my chest. "I'm sorry." Tears dampen my eyes. "I left my phone in my desk drawer, but I promise I'll carry it with me at all times from now on." I'll say anything to relieve his worry. I don't want to be responsible for any more concern in Isaac's life.

Another stretch of silence fills the void. "Hugo will pick you up outside of your office building at six o'clock."

Before I can reply, Isaac disconnects the call.

Pulling my phone down from my ear, I return a message to the unknown number.

Me: *I'll make up for our missed date tonight. Dessert is on me. ;)*

A short time later, my phone dings, indicating I've received a text message.

Isaac: *Dessert IS you, Isabelle.*

Warm slickness pools between my legs... until my phone dings again.

Isaac: *But that doesn't mean I'll let you come.*

Pouting, I shove my phone into my pocket and spend the next two hours miserably scanning documents before going to Harlow's bakery for the afternoon coffee run.

While Harlow prepares the coffees, I give her a rundown on everything that happened over the weekend, skimming over the parts of the story I uncovered immorally. She fans her cheeks during some of the more heated parts of our conversation. Once I've finished spilling every sordid detail of my weekend with Isaac, my jaw muscle is burning in exhaustion from how much talking I've done.

"I'm so glad you guys have finally gotten your shit together." Harlow hands me the two crates of coffee she just finished preparing. "I'll text Cormack later and see if we can organize a double date sometime next week."

I freeze. I can't risk being seen with Isaac in public. Well, not until his investigation is finalized.

"Why don't we have a more intimate gathering. I could cook dinner at my place?"

Harlow glares at me like I've grown a second head.

"I could *try* and cook us dinner," I add on.

Harlow's boisterous chuckle echoes around the nearly empty bakery. "We'll work something out."

Rolling my eyes, I wave goodbye as well as I can while carrying two full crates of coffee before exiting the bakery.

CHAPTER 39

$\mathcal{A}$t precisely six o'clock, Isaac's town car pulls up to the curve in front of the building my office is housed in. I scan the surrounding area, ensuring no one is watching before opening the passenger side door and slipping into the front seat.

"Hey, Isabelle," Hugo greets me in his usual friendly tone before pulling the car into the dense commuter traffic.

After securing my seat belt, I reply, "Hey, Hugo," trying to mimic the long drawl of his rugged voice.

He chuckles at my taunt. My smile freezes halfway when I hear my name roll off a tongue that has made me quiver more times the past seventy-two hours than I have in the entire span of my sexually active life.

I twist my head to the back of the car so quick, I nearly give myself whiplash. My mouth waters when I spot Isaac sitting in the backseat. He has removed his jacket and tie, and the sleeves of his shirt are rolled up near his elbows. Even with his handsome face marred by an angry scowl, he looks scrumptious enough to eat.

Unlatching my belt, I throw myself over the partition with more eagerness than I did weeks ago. Hugo slaps my backside when it's thrust in his face during my unladylike maneuver.

Isaac's face remains stern during our playfulness, but I see the slightest curve on his lips that gives away his true feelings. He's happy.

"Hi," I greet, plopping into the space next to him.

My teeth menace my bottom lip as my eyes absorb his handsome face. He appraises me with just as much eagerness while pushing a button on the console of the back passenger door.

I swallow to relieve my dry throat as my eyes flick between Isaac and the rising privacy partition.

Once the barrier is in place, Isaac lifts his eyes to me. "Remove your clothes, but leave your panties on."

A rush of heat blemishes my cheeks as my eyes stray to the partition. "Hugo can't hear or see anything," Isaac assures me.

Licking my parched lips, I do as instructed. If our time together has taught me anything, it's that submissiveness is well rewarded by Isaac.

Once my clothing is removed, Isaac slides down the zipper on his trousers. My eyes widen when he releases his stiff cock from its tight restraints before fisting it in his hand. Warm slickness builds between my legs when he slides his manly hand up and down his thickened shaft. His seamless pumps have a fire raging out of control in my sex.

"Tonight, you're not allowed to touch me, Isabelle." His husky voice adds more excitement to the sexually satisfying visual playing out in front of me.

Hell, if watching Isaac pleasing himself is my punishment, I'll happily accept it. I'm confident watching him crumble into ecstasy will have me toppling into orgasmic bliss.

My breaths increase with every stroke to his magnificent cock. He glides his thumb over his engorged knob, gathering a sticky bead of goodness pooling at the top from raking his eyes down my naked body. I groan when he slides it down his shaft, using it as lubricant to increase the quickness of his grinds.

Over time, the urge to touch him overwhelms me. I thought the visual alone would be enough to quell my need to touch him. It isn't.

Although Isaac's stern gaze hides his inner battle, his beautiful eyes relay he's also fighting the same struggle. He wants to touch me as bad as I'm dying to touch him.

"Are you wet?"

Unable to speak, I nod. I'm beyond wet—I'm drenched. Every spring in my body is coiled, prepared to snap at any moment, but my desire to touch him is more rampant than my wish to climax.

The heat in the interior of the car turns stifling when Isaac continues his pursuit of his climax. Although the visual of him stroking himself is one I'll forever cherish, not touching him is nearly killing me. One touch. That's all I want. I need to feel my skin on his.

My bottom lip drops into a pout when Isaac slaps away my hand.

"Please let me touch you," I shamelessly beg, no longer capable of fighting my desire.

I need to feel him, touch him, taste him. I need it more than I require my next breath.

"I wanted to touch you today." A bead of sweat glides down his cheek as his strokes quicken. "Even just your lips on mine, but I was denied. Now, I'm denying you the same opportunity."

"That isn't fair." My voice is nearly a sob. "I got reprimanded for being late to work because *I* gave in to *your* pleas this morning."

My anger boils when he shrugs.

Fuming with rage, I scoot across the cold leather seat.

Isaac's hand that isn't pounding his cock seizes my ankle to drag me back next to him. Ignoring the pleasing zap jolting through my body from his touch, I stab my stiletto into his thigh. I'm so angry, tears well in my eyes.

"You're being cruel," I yell. "You're taking your anger out on the wrong person..." I stop talking when a blob of moisture splashes my cheek.

My tears are more from the emotionally draining day I had going through Ophelia and Isaac's private life than Isaac teasing me, but once my tears start flowing, I have no chance of reeling them back in.

The instant Isaac sees my glistening cheeks, his frantic pumps halt. In a matter of seconds, I go from being seated on the dark leather seat to being cradled in his firm chest.

His cock braces my damp panties as his thumbs rub away my tears. "Please don't cry," he mutters so softly I can barely hear him.

My faint sobs turn into a moan when he slips my panties to the side and enters me in a slow, mouthwatering thrust. His apologetic eyes never once leave mine as he undoes the buttons on his dress shirt and flattens my palms on his sweat-slicked torso. His eyes permit me to access his body as his cock demands the attention of my pussy.

The fire in my belly gains in intensity with every kiss, caress, and pump he does.

My anger is soon forgotten when a quivering orgasm sweeps through my body, igniting my senses like fireworks in a pitch-black sky. Although I'm barely coherent, Isaac continues with his slow, soul-stealing pace. He guides his cock in and out of my pussy as his eyes remain locked on mine.

After a while, my name tears from his throat in a seductive purr as the hot spurts of his cum line the walls of my pussy.

Exhausted—both mentally and physically—I rest my head on his sweat-misted chest. He stays quiet but maintains physical closeness by keeping his semi-erect cock surrounded by my heat.

After a small amount of time, my blinking lengthens until my eyes no longer have the ability to stay open, and they flutter shut.

By the time Isaac wakes me, the night sky is pitch black. Not even the moon illuminates the sky tonight, it being hidden behind a scattering of dark clouds from a storm brewing on the horizon. My dazed eyes glance at my watch in confusion. The standard thirty-minute drive to Isaac's private residence has taken over two hours to complete.

"I asked Hugo to take the long route home."

A soft sigh seeps from my mouth when he withdraws his still-firm cock from me. The sigh is my body's way of expressing its sadness about the loss of his contact. Isaac smirks at my reaction before reaching over and snagging his suit jacket from the floor. I must have kicked it off the seat during my tantrum earlier tonight.

My heart flutters when he wraps the jacket around my shoulders and secures the buttons, so my private parts are covered.

Cranking open the passenger door, he exits the vehicle. My lips tug higher when he leans in and offers me his hand to help me out. My eyes dart around the area surrounding the car. I expel the breath I'm holding in when I don't see Hugo anywhere. Although I'm fully covered, I don't want him to see me like this.

Not one word spills from Isaac's lips the next forty-five minutes. Instead of the rough and abrupt Isaac I experienced earlier this evening, he has turned into the caring, nurturing man I encountered during the weekend.

He remains quiet as he heats us a generous serving of chicken noodle soup. My heart swells when we eat our meal by using the same spoon.

Once our dinner is consumed, he carries me into the shower and pampers my body and hair before placing me on my side of his bed. I say 'my side' as he always puts me on the same side every time I sleep in his bed.

A smile spreads across my face when he joins me in bed and spoons me until my back is splayed against his torso. Interlocking our hands, he wraps them around my waist.

My hips swivel when I feel his impressive erection straining against my backside.

He scoots back. "Not tonight. You need your sleep."

His rumbling laughter vibrates through my bursting-at-the-seams heart when I murmur, "You really really *really* like me."

My heart bursts open when he replies, "Maybe."

CHAPTER 40

Four weeks later...

"How many?" Harlow's brows etch high into her hairline. Playfully biting my bottom lip, I raise three fingers into the air.

Harlow gasps so loud, air blows onto my face. "In a row, or did he take a break in between?"

"Isaac doesn't break between orgasms." My cheeks heat as my eyes dash around the half-full bakery to make sure no one is paying attention to our private conversation.

"I thought guys need time for... you know... down there to pump back up," Harlow half-queries, half-informs.

I cock my brow before tilting closer to her to ensure the elderly lady seated next to me doesn't have a coronary from my question. "So, Cormack has never fucked you so hard once he came, he kept going until he climaxed another two times?"

Harlow's pupils dilate into saucers. "Honestly, no, he hasn't, but that's because I have a hard- enough time keeping up with his sexual prowess as it is. By the time he does come, I'm so exhausted, I can't keep my legs in the air."

Our immature giggles are interrupted when the elderly lady next to me touches my arm. "Make sure you hold onto those two fine gentlemen." Her twinkling blue eyes flick between Harlow and me. "It's rare to find a guy who can pop a cork on a champagne bottle these days, let alone find your G-spot."

Mine and Harlow's mouths gape in sync. We watch the elderly lady in awe as she stands from her seat and puts on her light teal trench coat. She'd easily be in her eighties if not older. Every hair on her head is a beautiful strand of silver, and even a full face of makeup can't hide her heavy set of wrinkles that come with her age.

"Suck them dry for every orgasm they're willing to give," she advises before strolling out of the bakery with an extra spring in her step than when she entered.

My shocked gaze remains planted on the door she exited for the next several minutes. I've been stunned into silence. It's pretty obtuse of me to think only young couples can enjoy vigorous bedroom activities. I don't believe it would matter if I were twenty or seventy, I'll never stop enjoying the bedroom antics of Isaac Holt, so why would I expect it to be any different for her?

"I think I'm in love," Harlow mumbles a short time later.

A full smile cracks onto my mouth. "She was pretty cool. I can only hope to be as rocking as her when I'm her age." I return my gaze to Harlow.

When I see the quickest second of panic smearing Harlow's face, I realize she isn't talking about the elderly lady. She's referencing Cormack.

My face scrunches. "Then why do you look so worried? Love isn't supposed to make you stressed."

The grim expression on my face grows. No matter how much my head tries to deny it, my heart has already fallen in love with Isaac. I've loved him from the moment I laid my eyes on him. I'm just too terrified to tell him.

The past four weeks have been a crazy lust-filled blur. I've spent every waking moment I'm not at work with Isaac—sleeping in his bed, eating his food, or snuggled on his lap while he makes business calls.

Because of his crazy schedule, our sleep patterns are at opposite ends of the spectrum. Before I was in the picture, Isaac never came home until after three in the morning, but because he knows I'm there waiting for him, he generally makes sure he's home no later than ten o'clock.

His business is most likely suffering because of me, but I love that he's willing to make sacrifices to ensure he has the time to see me. It's another reason why I fell in love with him so quickly.

For the past four weeks, I haven't had any struggles hiding my relationship with Isaac. Other than Harlow and Cormack, no one is none the wiser that we're a couple. Isaac wants to ensure Col Petretti never finds out who I am. I agreed with his plan, knowing I couldn't run the risk of Alex or the surveillance team finding out about our relationship.

Although the secrecy adds intrigue to our relationship, I look forward to the day I can declare we're in a relationship. I can't wait to go on double dates with Cormack and Harlow and not need to look over my shoulder every time I slip into his town car each evening.

Shrugging off my confusion about my relationship status, I return my focus to Harlow's statement. "Does Cormack feel the same way?"

Her glossed-over eyes dart down to the tabletop. "I don't know." She exhales a nerve-cleansing breath before returning her beautiful green eyes to me. "I may have accidentally declared my love during an intense orgasmic experience."

Smiling, I wiggle my brows.

"Shut up." She slaps my arm. "It was more the fact he didn't say anything back. I know he heard me as he stopped thrusting, but not a word seeped from his lips. Not even a thanks."

I giggle at the last part of her comment. "One, you would have been mortified if he said thanks."

She grins while nodding.

"And two, maybe he thought you said it in the heat of the moment. Have you said it to him outside of the bedroom?"

She shakes her head. "I'm too petrified he won't say it back."

My heart squeezes from her panicked tone. "If he didn't say it back, would it change how you feel about him?"

Harlow's lips quirk as she contemplates my question. "No. I'd still love him."

My brow arches high. "Well, there you go. That's the answer to your question. You have to tell him."

Not giving her the chance to reprimand me on my double standards, I thrust my hand toward her. "Hi, Kettle, my name is Pot."

Harlow and I spend the remainder of my lunch break discussing our plans for Thanksgiving. Isaac has invited his dad, his brother, Nick, and his fiancée, Jenni, over for dinner. Thankfully, he also arranged for a catering company to prepare the feast. He did initially ask if I'd like to make the meal, but I had to regretfully decline. I'm not going to lie, my ego took a big beating when I had to admit I struggle to make mashed potatoes, let alone a full meal.

While I am being honest, I'll admit I'm both nervous and excited about meeting Isaac's family. Worried, because I want them to like me. Excited because it's a step forward in our relationship. Although we've only been officially together a little over a month, it's been a crazy whirlwind affair that makes it seem so much longer. One I'd happily experience again and again.

Walking back into my office, a commotion of laughter gains my attention. After placing my satchel in the bottom drawer of my desk, I saunter to the window that has captured the other agents' attention.

"What's going on?"

Brandon's eyes stray to me. Unlike the other agents, his gaze is reflecting concern, not amusement. "Megan Shroud."

He continues speaking, but I don't hear a word he's uttering. All I heard was Megan Shroud, then my hearing blurred. *Why are people laughing about Isaac's mysterious, deranged stalker?*

Beyond panicked something horrid has happened to Isaac, I rush to the window. Overwhelmed, I barge agents out of the way so I can get a clear view of Isaac's nightclub. Fear clutches my heart when I spot the gigantic bouncer who usually mans the front door of the nightclub holding Megan captive in his arms. Her legs and arms thrash as she fights to free herself from his firm hold.

Ignoring her screaming pleas to be put down, the bouncer continues his long strides, only stopping to dump her next to a yellow car she's been photographed in numerous times.

As soon as the bouncer releases his hold, Megan charges toward the entrance of the nightclub. The bouncer wraps his massive arms around her waist again, thwarting her endeavors to enter the premises.

"Why isn't someone calling the police?" My words quiver with fear. "She's clearly unstable and not just a threat to the public. She's a threat to herself."

Michelle's eyes rocket to mine. The amusement brightening her gaze changes to remorse from my statement. The other agents watch the spectacle unfold without any concern for anyone's safety.

"Alex, you need to call the police."

I place my hand on his forearm to empathize he knows it's the right thing to do in a situation like this. His stern gaze shoots down to my hand resting on his arm.

His brows stitch before he returns his confused gaze to my face. "Isaac made his bed, now he has to sleep in it." His words aren't as determined as usual.

After shooing the agents away from the window, he lowers the blinds, blocking their live drama sitcom for the afternoon.

My eyes lock with Brandon. His face is marred with just as much concern as mine. He's also at a loss on what to do in this situation. He offers me a smile before apprehensively shrugging his shoulders.

Urged on by panic, I scamper to my desk and remove my FBI-assigned pistol from my second drawer. My eyes shift around the room as I secure my revolver to my ankle. Because the other agents are too busy laughing at the scene they just witnessed, no one pays me any attention—except Brandon.

Gesturing his head to the corridor, Brandon requests for me to join him outside. I nod while lifting my finger in the air, requesting a minute. I need to make a phone call before I do anything.

Unsurprisingly, my call goes straight to Isaac's voicemail. My lips quiver as I begin to speak. "I know it's early in our relationship, but I wanted you to know I love you, Isaac," I whisper into my cell.

Silencing my phone, I place it into the pocket of my trousers. After ensuring no one is watching me, I make a beeline for the corridor.

When Brandon notices I've entered the hall, he stops his panicked pacing and moves to stand in front of me. "I'll follow her."

I scan our surroundings, making sure we're alone before I reply, "They'll know you're gone, Brandon. They won't notice me as I've spent the last four weeks in the supply room scanning documents."

His brows pull together as panic clouds his gaze.

"Nobody ever comes in there looking for me but you. Cover for me, and I'll owe you big time."

Brandon runs his hand over his head. He's quiet, but I still catch part of the curse words he murmurs under his breath. After a few big breaths, his hazel eyes lift to mine.

A smile curves across my face when he places a set of keys into my palm. "It's a blue BMW coupe half a block down."

I rush toward the exit of the building before gratitude washes over me. Pivoting around, I dart back to Brandon. He balks when I sling my arms around his neck and whisper my thanks for his support into his ear.

Brandon returns my hug with so much force, he squeezes the bejeebus out of me. "Be careful, Izzy," he pleads, his eyes relaying his genuine concern.

Nodding, I rush out of the building.

CHAPTER 41

*M*egan fights the bouncer for nearly twenty minutes before she gives in and walks back to her compact yellow car. Her steps are slow, and her shoulders are slumped in defeat.

I stab the key into the ignition. Brandon's car roars to life, startling me. Its engine is a lot bigger than I'm used to driving, plus it's a stick shift. I was taught to drive an automatic, but this is the only car I have access to, and I will not lose the opportunity to follow Megan because I can't drive a stick shift.

The instant Megan pulls her car onto the road, I merge Brandon's car into the heavy traffic. Several motorists honk their horns, annoyed I pulled out without signaling.

Metal grinding together roars through my ears when I forgot to push in the clutch before shifting the gearshift.

I crunch through my first gear change. "Shit. Sorry, Brandon."

My knuckles go white from my determined hold of the steering wheel. My heart palpitates so fast, I feel like I'm about to have a heart attack, and the gnawing pit in my chest is nearly crippling me. Even being riddled with fear, my urge to protect Isaac outweighs my panic.

Other than hearing my madly beating heart, my drive across town is made in silence. I follow Megan close enough I won't lose her in the dense traffic but not close enough for her to become suspicious.

When she pulls into an old rundown motel on the outskirts of town, I park Brandon's car along the curb at the front of a McDonald's restaurant.

A large droplet of water splats on the windshield, followed by another and then another. In no time at all, my view of the hotel is clouded by a sheet of water. Pulling my jacket over my head to shelter myself from the heavy pelts of rain, I peel out of Brandon's car. Once the street is clear of traffic, I run across the road and seek cover under the rusted hotel awning.

My fear surges when Megan emerges from a room two doors down from where I'm standing. She's mumbling under her breath. Because she's so focused on her tirade, she doesn't notice me hiding under the awning. She jumps into her car and reverses dangerously. Her vehicle whizzes out of the hotel parking lot so fast, she'll be long gone by the time I scamper back to Brandon's car.

My eyes survey the area. Because of the pelting rain, most hotel guests have congregated inside. I walk toward the room Megan just exited. My steps are so nerve-wracking, my legs shake uncontrollably. Once I'm sure no one is watching me, I crouch down onto the ground and try to jimmy the lock.

"Come on."

After two long, panicked minutes, I still haven't picked the lock. This latch is, of course, more technical than the locks I trained on.

Gritting my teeth, I ram the door as hard as possible with my right shoulder. Pain shoots up my arm so fast, and tears sting my eyes. Even grimacing in pain, a grin curves on my mouth. My harsh hit on the door was successful, and it swings open with the tiniest creak.

After darting my eyes around the area, I walk into Megan's hotel room, closing the door behind me. The room is spotlessly clean with a pungent aroma of disinfectant and bleach. From the two stars on the sign hanging at the front of the hotel, I'd say it's Megan who keeps this room so sparkly and hygienic.

The bed has been perfectly made to where you could bounce a

nickel off it. She has replaced the standard hotel bedding with a more elaborate love heart quilt. My heart plummets into my stomach when I notice a crib set up in the room.

Is Megan pregnant? Oh God, please don't let it be Isaac's baby.

Snubbing the queasiness swirling in my stomach, I head for the only desk in the room. My fear that Megan is indeed pregnant surges when I spot several textbooks on pregnancy and medical procedures stacked on a crumbling shelf above the desk.

Grabbing a wad of tissues out of a box to cover my fingerprints, I yank down the first lot of books. My eyes filter down to a picture that slipped out of a pregnancy pamphlet from an obstetrician's office in Ravenshoe. My breathing halts when I flip the photo over. It's an ultrasound picture of a distinguishable fetus. With the baby's face so prominent, Megan must be over six months pregnant, which is surprising, considering she didn't have a bump on her medium frame.

Swallowing to eliminate the lump lodged in my throat, I slip the photo back into the pamphlet, then place it in its rightful spot on the shelf.

Ignoring my hammering heart, my eyes appraise the spotless room. Other than a bed, desk, chair, and a baby crib, the room is empty. I make my way to the only other door in the room other than the entrance door.

"Holy shit."

Every surface of the bathroom is covered with a range of different size photos. Most are of a heavily pregnant female with strawberry blonde hair. In multiple images, she has her eyes gouged out and trails of blood streaming down her legs. Moving deeper into the room, I spot a handful of photos of a blond gentleman who appears to be in his early twenties.

Adjusting my eyes to the flicking fluorescent light, air traps in my throat. The gentleman in the photo is Isaac's brother, Nick. Although I've never met him, I can recognize him from the numerous photos Isaac has of him on his living room mantel.

Megan isn't after Isaac. She wants Nick?

Yanking my phone out of my pocket, I collect digital evidence in case these documents get destroyed before the investigation team arrives. Some photos have 'I hate her' and 'She must die' scribbled over the female's face and torso.

Once I've taken numerous pictures of the incriminating evidence, I walk back into the main room. My heart stops beating, closely followed by my steps. Megan is walking into the main entryway, her gaze focused on a magazine in her hand. Her grin makes the contents of my stomach lurch into my throat. I pace backward, praying she can't hear my ragged breaths.

My nostrils flare as my lungs struggle to fill with air. The burn of their fight warms my chest. Darting my eyes around the room, I realize the only safe place to hide is behind the shower curtain. As noiseless as possible, I move into the bathtub and plaster my back on the sparkling white tiles.

Closing my eyes, I try to calm my nervous breaths. The hiss of my panicked pants echo around the outdated, but spotlessly clean bathroom. Not long later, Megan walks into the room. The smell of bleach intensifies, plunging the room into a muggy, uncomfortable heat.

"I'm waiting for you, my love. We'll be together soon. You just have to be patient. Wait for me."

I adjust my position so I can get a better view of Megan. She has a torn-out magazine page in one hand and a roll of duct tape in another. She rips off a large section of duct tape and sticks a paparazzi photo of Nick and his bandmates onto the wall solely dedicated to pictures of Nick and cardboard hearts.

Megan's fidgety movements halt as her manic eyes dart around the bathroom. I plaster my back on the tiles and keep my body void of any movements. I don't even breathe as I'm afraid she may hear my inhalations of air.

After several terrifying seconds, Megan darts out of the bathroom as quickly as she arrived. I wheeze in a shaky breath, and my burning lungs relish the fresh air even being riddled with toxic bleach.

Another twenty minutes pass before Megan leaves again. I rush out of the hotel room as fast as my quivering legs can take me. My eyes widen when I cross paths with Megan in the corridor of the hotel. She's carrying a full ice bucket in her hand. A sigh spills from my lips when I realize how close I came to having my escape foiled. Dangling on the front of the ice machine located next to Megan's room is an out-of-order sign with the instruction to use the ice machine one floor above. If that ice machine were working, Megan would have busted me exiting her room.

By the time I park Brandon's car outside of my office, my erratic heart is still pounding out of control. Although I'm relieved Megan isn't targeting Isaac, I'm beyond panicked at what Isaac's reaction will be when he finds out Megan is threatening his brother. The whole drive back to the office, my mind replayed Isaac's statement from months ago. *"What about for someone you love? You wouldn't get your hands a little dirty for someone you love?"*

Isaac undoubtedly loves his brother, and deep down in my heart, I know he'd do anything in his power to protect him. Anything at all.

Brandon's eyes lift to mine the instant I walk back into the office. He gulps before he rushes toward me.

"I should have never let you go alone." He pulls me into his arms and squeezes me tight.

It's lucky I went alone as there was no way Brandon and I would have both fit in that shower!

"Did anyone notice I was gone?"

My eyes dash around the office. Surprisingly, the usually bustling space is relatively quiet for the late hour.

"No, they've been too busy with the local cops versus FBI turf saga that happens in every town we go to." Brandon's voice gains a hint of arrogance. "A local detective arrived on the scene not long after you left. Alex is worried he's going to quote 'piss all over his investigation' unquote."

My heart swells, pleased Isaac sought legal help to deal with Megan.

Over the next three hours, Brandon helps me compile the longest and most tedious report I've ever filed. We both want to ensure we have dotted every 'i' and crossed every 't,' so the report doesn't have any chance of being dismissed. Once the report is perfect, we head to Alex's office to share our findings.

"Are you ready?"

After a quick breath to calm my nerves, I briskly nod.

Alex's head lifts from some reports when he hears Brandon's curt taps on the glass door. Brandon gestures for me to go first when Alex permits us to enter his office. Once we gain Alex's full attention, Brandon hands him the extensively-noted documents along with several printouts of the photos I took in Megan's bathroom. The more Alex's eyes wander over the report, the closer his eyebrows become.

"How did you get these photos and information?" Alex's tone is surprised.

"I followed Megan to a Motel Six on the outskirts of town."

I wait to be reprimanded for going out in the field unassigned. Astonishingly, no negative remarks leave Alex's mouth.

"I'm very impressed with the caliber of this report." Alex's shocked eyes dart between Brandon and me. "First thing in the morning, I'll have two special agents assigned to Megan."

"Really?" I interrupt in surprise.

As a grin stretches across Alex's face, Brandon squeezes me tightly. "Good job, Izzy."

My smile falters when I slide into the back of Isaac's town car at six o'clock, and Hugo tells me, "Unfortunately, Isaac is indisposed tonight, and he has asked me to take you back to your apartment."

CHAPTER 42

I probably shouldn't have told Isaac that I loved him over the phone. If I waited and did it in person, I'd have been able to gauge his reaction by reading his face or staring into his enthralling eyes. Now, I have the misery of wondering if my message was the cause of his sudden change in routine the past four weeks, or if he really is indisposed for the night.

What does 'indisposed' mean, anyway?

"Are you sure you don't want to come inside? It's getting a little chilly out there."

Half of me is being genuinely friendly, whereas the other half wants to probe Hugo until he spills the beans on where Isaac is tonight.

"For the fourth time, I'm okay out here," Hugo replies from his station outside of my door.

He's sitting on a wooden chair that's part of my dining table set. After the first hour ticked by on the clock, I gave him one of the cushions from my sofa as his bottom would have to be getting sore sitting on the firm seat.

A smile tugs my lips high when Hugo drones under his breath, "I prefer my nuts attached to my body."

"And here I thought you were the first guy I met who isn't scared of Isaac Holt," I reply in sarcasm. "I guess tonight I'm being proven wrong."

Hugo works his jaw side to side before rising to his feet. I try to hide my smile when he looks at me, but just from the gleam in his eyes, I can tell he knows I'm goading him.

"You do remember what happened the last time you had a man in your apartment, don't you, Izzy?" he replies, wiping my smile right off my face.

"So, since it isn't me who will cop the punishment for denying Isaac's request, I guess I can come inside."

A shiver of excitement and a tremor of fear runs through my body at the same time.

Trying to pry information from Hugo is like drawing blood out of a stone—impossible! After two hours, I give up and toddle off to bed. After tossing and turning for nearly an hour, I give up my endeavor of sleep and pull my phone off the bedside table. My nose screws up when I see it's a little after two in the morning. I haven't received any messages or calls from Isaac all day today. Even though it has only been a month, my bed feels cold without him.

Deciding I can't dig my hole any deeper than it already is, I send a message to Isaac's private cell.

Me: *I miss you. I'm lonely and cold without you.*

I lie in silence, staring at the phone's screen, willing for it to ding saying it has received a message.

After twenty minutes, my eyes grow weary.

I don't know how long I've been sleeping when I'm awakened by someone slipping into my bed. My tense body relaxes when Isaac whispers, "Don't scream, it's me."

275

SHANDI BOYES

"What time is it?"

"It's nearly dawn." My heart rate quickens when his lips brush my ear. "I only just got your message."

I want to ask which one. The one that said I missed him and I'm cold or the one where I declared my love for him?

Before any words can spill from my lips, Isaac silences me with his perfectly etched mouth. His kiss is lush, deep, and passionate. Every lash of his tongue and nip of his teeth has my heart enlarging.

While raking my hand through his luxuriously thick hair, I pull him closer to deepen our kiss. My relationship with Isaac could be construed as only being based on lust, but it's the affection we display during sexual contact that proves even if the fiery passion dampens, something greater will still tie us together.

He tweaks my nipple until it's a stiff peak, every roll increasing the tingle in my aching sex.

"Could you come just from me playing with your nipples?" Isaac asks when my pants of ecstasy purr throughout the room.

"Uh-huh." I'm not the slightest bit embarrassed. "I could come just by looking at you."

Isaac emits a sexy-as-sin growl that has my thighs trembling. My sex grows wetter when he adjusts the position of my leg, so his rapidly hardening rod can rub the seam of my panties.

Not long after the first orgasm rockets through my body, my alarm clock on my bedside table starts hollering. Not adjusting the speed of his seamless pumps, Isaac grips my alarm clock, yanks its cord out of the wall, and throws it across the room. The alarm clock shatters into pieces when it hits the wall with a thud.

Surprised, my eyes missile to Isaac.

"I don't care if I have to fuck you for twelve hours straight, you're not leaving this bed until I hear those words come out of your mouth in person."

Oh God.

Without warning, an intense, core-clenching climax rushes through my body. My back arches off the bed as my nails drag down Isaac's back so harshly, I'm certain I've drawn blood.

Isaac lessens my purrs of ecstasy by sealing his mouth over mine, stealing every breathless moan with lashes of his tongue. My skin is coated in a fine mist of sweat, and my hair on my body bristles to attention.

Once my trembles lessen, he rolls over, keeping his big cock hilted in me during the process. The change of position means he can plunge into me deeper with every thrust he does.

When I lean back, my nails dig into his muscular thighs. I ride him hard and fast, overcome with chasing my next release. My speed is relentless and unforgiving. Although my pussy is swollen from our hours of sexual contact, my body is still hungry, craving, and needing more.

It wouldn't matter how many orgasms ravished my body, the chase never ends when I'm with Isaac. I want to unravel him, to have him exposed and as open to me as I am to him. I want him raw.

"Eyes on me, Isabelle," Isaac demands when the shiver of orgasm shudders my body.

Releasing my grip on his thighs, I lean toward him and entrap his mouth with mine. My kiss is selfish and starved like I haven't tasted his mouth in months when it has only been mere minutes.

"Oh God," I purr in a grunted moan along with, "I love you, Isaac."

Upon hearing my declaration of love, Isaac's eyes darken before the hotness of his seed coats the walls of my clenching sex. Even though he doesn't return my words, his actions make my heart swell, and a violent climax shreds through me so hard and fast, my vision blurs.

A leisurely hot shower, more orgasms than I can count, and access to my endless supply of cosmetics have me walking out of my room with an extra spring in my step.

My mouth curves into a grin when I spot Isaac sitting in my living area. When I rented this apartment, I thought the living room was an adequate size, but having a man like Isaac sitting in it depreciates its size dramatically. It isn't the room's fault a man with an aura like Isaac's suffocates the room, making it appear smaller than it truly is.

Seeing Isaac is on a call, I enter the kitchen and pour myself a freshly brewed cup from the coffee pot Isaac brewed earlier.

Isaac's eyes lift to mine when I enter the living room. His gaze is stern, but it still causes a shiver of excitement to run through my body.

Not waiting for permission, I dump my phone and mug onto the coffee table, then straddle his lap. His conversation never falters, but his cock does stiffen. I feel sorry for whoever he's talking to. His tone is clipped and furious, his surly mood bouncing off him in invisible waves.

Snubbing his dreary mood, I press kisses on his unshaven jawline. His skin smells fresh as if he's recently showered, but his hair is dry, so I'm going to assume he's been awake for a while longer than me.

"Good morning." I tug his earlobe with my teeth.

His smirk makes me purr like a kitten. He glides his hand down my back until he cups my backside to give it a gentle squeeze. I return his flirty move by grinding my pussy against his thickened cock.

A thrill of anticipation rockets through my body when he hisses at my playful tease. Usually, his calm composure never falters, so I love that I can spark reactions from him, little flaws no one else has the privilege of seeing.

"I'll call you back."

Isaac disconnects his call, stealing his caller's chance of a reply. Remaining quiet, his tired, withdrawn gaze studies my face.

"Are you okay?"

He considers my question before nodding. Although he nods, I can hear his brain ticking over, no doubt overrun with all the information he has jammed in there.

"Is there anything I can do to help?"

He smirks a deliciously wicked smile that has my core clenching.

"Oh, no. I remember what happened the last time I arrived late to work. That's *not* happening again."

When I attempt to remove myself from his lap, Isaac seizes my wrist before I get two steps away from him. His hot, heated gaze absorbs my body before his eyes return to my face. His desire, his needs, his every want is projected from his beautiful eyes. A smile curves my mouth when I realize his every wish is me.

"You'll get me fired."

He chuckles a laugh so thick, it rattles through my body before stopping to swell my heart even more.

Actually, getting fired could be the best thing for our relationship.

"Good afternoon, Izzy," Hugo greets me, rolling down the window of Isaac's town car.

"Harlow threw a couple of extra treats in the bag for you."

I hand him a cup of coffee and a white bag stuffed with freshly baked goodies. His eyes bulge when he spots the scrumptious treats Harlow has supplied him with. Ever since I found out Isaac has Hugo shadowing me, I added Hugo into my morning and afternoon coffee orders. I've tried numerous times the past several weeks to tell Isaac I don't require Hugo's services during working hours, but Isaac is adamant that if I'm not with him, Hugo will be with me.

Hugo must be bored out of his mind sitting in a car for a minimum of eight hours a day. I figure if there's anything I can do to ease his boredom, I'll do it. Coffee and cakes might not be much, but it's better than nothing.

"If this storm ends up brewing, wait under the awning of your building, and I'll pull up at the front." Hugo gestures his head to clouds in the sky.

"All right." I smile. "I'll see you in a couple of hours."

The hairs on my arms bristle when a cold breeze shivers through my body. Goosebumps form and my body shudders, the air is riddled with gloomy darkness.

When I step into the foyer of my office building, my heart stops beating. A hive of frantic activity flurries around me. Agents run in all directions gathering bulletproof vests and holstering pistols onto their waists. My heart thrashes my ribs as panic scorches my veins.

Brandon rushes toward me. He yanks the coffees out of my grasp, dumping them into a waste bin in the foyer.

"You need to get your vest on." He places a bulletproof vest over my head.

"What's going on?"

Brandon doesn't grace me with a response. He just continues putting my bulletproof vest on me before handing me my FBI-issued revolver I usually store in my desk drawer.

"We have a five-minute window. Move in quickly, secure the target, and move out. This needs to be done fast and with minimal fuss," Alex yells over the buzz of activity.

"Who are we arresting?" I ask anyone who might be listening.

"Let's go. Move, move, move!" Alex screams, ushering the agents out the double-glass doors.

Brandon and I shadow the other agents hustling out of the office building at a frantic pace. My heart plummets into my stomach when they race across the street and storm into Isaac's nightclub.

"Get on the ground!" is yelled over and over again by numerous agents. Their screeching roars through my ears so loud, it overtakes my frenetic pulse.

Riddled with fear, I adjust my position to improve my view. With every shaky step I take, I pray we aren't here to arrest Isaac. A sharp ache stabs my chest when the image of Isaac standing in front of a handful of agents with their guns drawn comes into my peripheral vision. Isaac's livid eyes glare at Alex. His nostrils are flaring, and the tick of his jaw is noticeable even with me being halfway across the room.

"Get on the ground," Alex sneers, directing his gun at Isaac's head instead of his chest.

My heart constricts as time stands still. "Please, get on the ground, Isaac," I silently chant.

Isaac's infuriated gaze shifts sideways. I can't breathe when our eyes lock and hold for several terrifying seconds. I wordlessly plead for him to get on the ground before Alex or one of the other agents shoot him.

Even with numerous guns pointed at him, Isaac's dignified stature beams out of him. His eyes never relay his fear, they merely convey his anger and disgust.

"Please get on the ground." My appeal is more a plea than a demand.

The agents surrounding Isaac grow panicked when he storms away from them. His long, powerful strides as he rushes my way quickens my pulse, but this time, it's fear, not euphoria responsible for its spike.

After holstering his gun, Alex grips Isaac's shoulder. He attempts to tackle Isaac to the ground, but Isaac's pursuit to reach me is too strong for Alex to overcome. Isaac's determination is unnerving and solely focused on me.

My legs quiver when I raise my gun to Isaac's erratically panting torso. Tears well in my eyes so fast, they burn from the sudden rush of moisture.

"Please get on the ground," I beg, my nerves so rattled, my gun shakes in my hand.

Isaac's delicious scent engulfs me when he stops to stand in front of me. The barrel of my gun digs into his suit-covered chest as his eyes furiously glare at me. They're the darkest I've ever seen—desolate and broken. My heart cracks from the utter hurt reflecting from his beautiful gaze.

A frightened squeal omits from my lips when gunfire ricochets around the room.

"The next one won't be a warning." Alex's tone is as vicious as the tautness of his face.

After inhaling a shaky breath, my eyes pop back open. I stare at Isaac, wordlessly begging for him to surrender before Alex makes true on his threat.

"Please," I beg, staring at him as a tear runs down my cheek.

For the quickest second, remorse flashes through his squinted gaze. He seems torn, unsure if he's coming or going. *He's not the only one.*

A shudder runs through my body when he drops to his knees. Although I didn't hear a gunshot, my panicked eyes scan his body.

I sigh upon discovering he's uninjured.

Remaining quiet, Isaac places his hands behind his head as Alex instructs from across the room.

When I raise my eyes, I'm met with the confused gazes of several agents watching the exchange between Isaac and me. The only face not showing confusion is Alex's.

He instructs me to arrest Isaac.

In a blur of tears, I holster my gun and place my hand on Isaac's tense shoulder. "I'm sorry."

I lower him onto the ground until his torso hits the mahogany dance floor in his nightclub. The loud thump his defeated body makes when it hits the ground adds more nicks to my already crumbling heart.

In an instant, several male agents scurry toward us. My heart shatters more with every brutal knee and harsh elbow they inflict on Isaac's still body, but he remains completely motionless.

Not a noise seeps from his lips as he's cuffed and read his rights. His gaze only leaves the ground when I stop to stand in front of him.

His eyes are livid and broken—they appear almost soulless.

"If you're going to be accused of something, you may as well do it," he mutters through gritted teeth.

To be continued in Unraveling an Enigma
Out now! **We also get inside Isaac's head from here on out!**

Facebook: facebook.com/authorshandi

Instagram: instagram.com/authorshandi

Email: authorshandi@gmail.com

Reader's Group: bit.ly/ShandiBookBabes

Website: authorshandi.com

Newsletter: https://www.subscribepage.com/AuthorShandi

Hunter's, Hugo's, Cormack's, Hawke's, Ryan's, Rico's and Brax's stories have already been released. Brandon, Regan, and all the other great characters of Ravenshoe will be getting their own stories at some point during 2019.

If you enjoyed this book, please leave a review.

ALSO BY SHANDI BOYES

Perception Series

Saving Noah (Noah & Emily)

Fighting Jacob (Jacob & Lola)

Taming Nick (Nick & Jenni)

Redeeming Slater (Slater and Kylie)

Saving Emily (Noah & Emily - Novella)

Wrapped Up with Rise Up (Perception Novella - should be read after the Bound Series)

Enigma

Enigma (Isaac & Isabelle #1)

Unraveling an Enigma (Isaac & Isabelle #2)

Enigma The Mystery Unmasked (Isaac & Isabelle #3)

Enigma: The Final Chapter (Isaac & Isabelle #4)

Beneath The Secrets (Hugo & Ava #1)

Beneath The Sheets (Hugo & Ava #2)

Spy Thy Neighbor (Hunter & Paige)

The Opposite Effect (Brax & Clara)

I Married a Mob Boss (Rico & Blaire)

Second Shot (Hawke & Gemma)

The Way We Are (Ryan & Savannah #1)

The Way We Were (Ryan & Savannah #2)

Sugar and Spice (Cormack & Harlow)

Lady In Waiting (Regan & Alex #1)

Man in Queue (Regan & Alex #2)

Couple on Hold(Regan & Alex #3)

Enigma: The Wedding (Isaac and Isabelle)

Silent Vigilante (Brandon and Melody #1)

Hushed Guardian (Brandon & Melody #2)

Quiet Protector (Brandon & Melody #3)

Bound Series

Chains (Marcus & Cleo #1)

Links(Marcus & Cleo #2)

Bound(Marcus & Cleo #3)

Restrain(Marcus & Cleo #4)

Psycho (Dexter & ??)

Russian Mob Chronicles

Nikolai: A Mafia Prince Romance (Nikolai & Justine #1)

Nikolai: Taking Back What's Mine (Nikolai & Justine #2)

Nikolai: What's Left of Me(Nikolai & Justine #3)

Nikolai: Mine to Protect(Nikolai & Justine #4)

Asher: My Russian Revenge (Asher & Zariah)

Nikolai: Through the Devil's Eyes(Nikolai & Justine #5)

Trey (Trey & K)

K: A Trey Sequel

The Italian Cartel

Dimitri

Roxanne

Reign

Mafia Ties (Novella)

Maddox

Demi

Rocco

Clover

Smith

RomCom Standalones

Just Playin' (Elvis & Willow)

Ain't Happenin' (Lorenzo & Skylar)

The Drop Zone (Colby & Jamie)

Very Unlikely (Brand New Couple)

Short Stories

Christmas Trio (Wesley, Andrew & Mallory -- short story)

Falling For A Stranger (Short Story)

Coming Soon

Skitzo